ALAN BAXTER'S
SERVED
COLD

PRAISE FOR SERVED COLD

"Step into the ring with Alan Baxter, I dare you. He writes with the grace, precision, and swift brutality of a prizefighter. *Served Cold* is a stellar showcase for his talents. If you haven't had the pleasure of reading him yet, start here!"

— **Christopher Golden, *New York Times* bestselling author of**
Ararat* and *The Pandora Room

"In *Served Cold* Alan Baxter shows off his impressive versatility and range with a host of stories that mix old school terrors with very now concerns. At turns creepy and visceral, Baxter delivers the horror goods."

— **Paul Tremblay, Bram Stoker Award-winning author of**
A Head Full of Ghosts* and *The Cabin at the End of the World

---

"*Served Cold* is a powerful collection of Alan Baxter's writing at its best. These stories never shy from the darkness or the weird and yet are, at their core, deeply human. As readers, we identify with his characters even—or maybe especially—when we would rather not. Be it twisted desires or impossible choices, the harshest of consequences or the depths of despair, in these stories Baxter shines a light into the darker corners of what it means to be human."

— **Joanne Anderton, award-winning author of**
The Bone Chime Song & Other Stories

"Alan Baxter's *Served Cold* is a feast for readers, who will push back from the table wanting more!"

— **John F.D. Taff, Bram Stoker Award-nominated author of**
The Fearing* and *The End in All Beginnings

PRAISE FOR ALAN BAXTER

"Alan Baxter's fiction is dark, disturbing, hard-hitting and heart-breakingly honest. He reflects on worlds known and unknown with compassion, and demonstrates an almost second-sight into human behaviour."

— **Kaaron Warren, Shirley Jackson Award-winner and author of *The Grief Hole***

"Alan Baxter is an accomplished storyteller who ably evokes magic and menace."

— **Laird Barron, author of *Swift to Chase***

"Alan's work is reminiscent of that of Clive Barker and Jim C. Hines, but with a unique flavour all of its own."

— **Angela Slatter, World Fantasy, British Fantasy and Aurealis Award winner**

"Alan Baxter has joined the ranks of talented authors who seek to push the boundaries of fantasy fiction."

— *The Manly Daily*

"Alan Baxter delivers a heady mix of magic, monsters and bloody fights to the death. Nobody does kick-ass brutality like Baxter."

— **Greig Beck, International bestselling author of *Beneath the Dark Ice* and *Primordia***

"If Stephen King and Jim Butcher ever had a love child then it would be Alan Baxter."

– *Smash Dragons*

"Baxter draws you along a knife's edge of tension from the first page to the last, leaving your heart thumping and sweat on your brow."

– *Midwest Book Review*

This collection remains
the copyright of the author.

SERVED COLD
ISBN-13: 978-1-950569-04-5
ISBN-10: 1-950569-04-7
Grey Matter Press First Trade Paperback Edition - September 2019

Copyright © 2019 Alan Baxter
Book Design Copyright © 2019 Grey Matter Press
Edited by Anthony Rivera

GREY MATTER
P R E S S

CHICAGO

Grey Matter Press
greymatterpress.com

Grey Matter Press on Facebook
facebook.com/greymatterpress

For Penry.
He was the best boy.

TABLE OF
CONTENTS

INTRODUCTION
BY JOHN F.D. TAFF

LET'S NOT MINCE WORDS HERE.

Alan Baxter can write a great goddamn short story.

I was introduced to Alan through his brilliant collection *Crow Shine*. I'd never heard of Alan at that point, and was particularly gratified to read expertly crafted stories from a previously unknown (to me) author. The stories were genuinely well written, chilling and quite memorable.

Let me divert from this praise-filled Intro to relate a story about actually meeting Alan in person. Spoiler Alert: You'll learn two things here. How much Alan's stories stayed with me, and how old age has deprived me of the ability to remember names.

Anyway, I attended the Horror Writers Association's annual StokerCon in Providence, RI, in 2018. Before leaving for the con, my good friend and publisher Tony Rivera told me he'd just signed an author who would be there, too. Would I find him and say hello?

Sure. I'm a reasonably nice introvert. I can do that, I told Tony.

Cut to the con, where I'm sitting inside the Starbucks attached to the hotel, having coffee and making some notes. A man approaches and introduces himself as Alan Baxter, says that Tony at Grey Matter wanted us to meet. I invite him to sit, we chat for a few minutes, then go our separate ways.

Nice guy, I thought. From Australia, seemingly. Glad I met him.

Later that night, I go up to my room to process the remains of the day, if you get what I'm saying. And I start to think about meeting Alan and why his name seemed so damn familiar to me.

So, I haul out my tablet, go to Amazon and type: ALAN BAXTER. Oh! Duh. *Crow Shine*. I loved that collection.

I felt idiotic. A common state with me, I assure you. The next day when I saw Alan again, I had to apologize for not putting two and two together at our first meeting, and then we both had a good laugh at my stupidity.

"No worries, mate," he told me in his native accent.

I've gone on to read quite a bit more of Baxter's fiction. *Manifest Recall* is a fantastic, propulsive novella that merges two things most writers have a problem handling separately, much less together—noirish crime fiction and supernatural horror. There's enough bad versions of this out there that I had soured on the entire idea of blending these two until I read *Manifest Recall*. Yowza!

His novel *Devouring Dark* is fantastic, too. Paranormal hitman? Count me in!

But I'm not here to praise those works, as wonderful as they are. I'm here to tell you that the book you now hold in your hands, *Served Cold*, is a fantastic collection of some of the best short stories you're likely to read.

Handling yourself well in novel format or even the novella is a far different beast than handling yourself well in a short story. Longer works are like tanks—huge lumbering things that get the job done, but not terribly efficiently. Not to say that novels aren't hard to write (they are) or that many authors don't write fantastic novels (like Baxter, they do!). No, it's just my strong belief that the measure of any author is how they write short fiction.

Short fiction demands certain things of writers; things some writers find difficult to deliver. The very shortness of a short story demands clarity and focus of a writer. Streamlining story, character development and atmosphere nearly to the point of shorthand.

Succinctly put, long fiction writing is constructing a skyscraper, while short fiction writing is cutting the facets of a diamond.

Alan Baxter is an expert gem cutter.

In a collection like this, readers can experience a handful of his gems together in one setting, giving them the opportunity to see his mark. You know, that indefinable aura an author impresses onto the page identifying him or her. In writing, it's sometimes referred to as an author's voice. Come on, tell me you can't recognize the writing voice of Stephen King or Clive Barker simply by reading a few lines of unidentified text. Of course you can.

Inside the pages of *Served Cold* are some great, readily identifiable stories. Readily identifiable as the voice of Alan Baxter.

His stories often deal with the outsider and the bad place, two important definers of horror fiction. I mean the picked-on kid, the stressed-out, not-quite-making-sense guy. I mean the deep, dark forest and the odd house on the street, the one that's been abandoned, derelict for years. Because Alan understands that horror, like the predator it is, seeks out the weak and unwary, the shadowy and lonely places.

That's the who and the where both horror and predators sink their teeth into.

Stories like "Dream Shadow" and the eponymous "Served Cold"—a delicious little tale of supernaturally aided revenge—both more than successfully sink their teeth into outsiders caught in very bad places.

"Yellowheart" is a delightfully savage, almost supernatural *Deliverance*, where the forest is a bad place and the main characters—effectively you and I—are the outsiders.

The military platoon Alan Baxter introduces us to in his piece "In Vaulted Halls Entombed" is another kind of outsider—soldiers entering the unknown land of a different culture, with all the personal conflict that includes. But even then, are they the outsiders? Is that bad place really the worst? Or are there other worse creatures, other worse places even in a bad place? Alan's answer is an emphatic, frightening: Yes!

In the harrowing "The Ocean Hushed the Stones," the who and where are internalized, and so much the worse for it, because our internal geographies are the same, no matter what continent we live on.

This book, appropriately titled *Served Cold*, is just that. Sixteen immersive, very cold tales that identify Alan Baxter for what he is. A fantastic author of great horror fiction, short or long.

I can't quite believe that in the brief span of time since I first read Baxter's work, I've gone from a fan, to a forgetful fan, to an unabashed fan, to a guy who's been asked by him to introduce this collection to what will hopefully be a huge audience of unabashed fans, if they aren't already.

Get ready to open this veritable treasure chest of gems, and see if you agree (if you don't already) that Alan Baxter can write a great goddamn short story.

John F.D. Taff
Southern Illinois, U.S.A.
July 2019

SERVED
COLD

Jonathan swallowed, but the lump in his throat remained. *You're twelve*, he told himself. *Not some snivelling child*. That's what his stepdad called him, on a good day. He tried to ignore the sensation of snakes swimming in his stomach and glanced back along the path barely visible through overgrown dry grass. The three older boys in the street gestured for him to *go on*. One flapped his arms like a chicken.

Jonathan turned back to the peeling front door. A council order, yellowed with age and covered in a patina of fine, orange outback sand, exhorted the owner to tidy the yard. The house had been abandoned for years, on the farthest edge of habitation next to the empty desert, far from the industry of the town's mines. He reached out and pushed.

The door rattled, paint flaked away. But it was locked.

He looked at the boys on the road.

"Go through a window!" Chicken Wings called. "You wanna be in the gang?"

Jonathan didn't even know their names, but he wanted to be part of something. It was lonely since Brendan moved away, his only friend. Jonathan wanted to be associated with more than a drunk stepfather who meted out beatings for enjoyment and a mother who worked so hard she didn't notice. Because she wouldn't let it continue if she did. He had to believe that.

Chicken Wings pointed to a sash window with the lower half already up about six inches. It shuddered against its frame as Jonathan heaved, shifted another six or eight inches before it jammed. He could fit through the gap he'd made. Shadows in the room beyond threatened to suck him in. Smells of dryness and something less pleasant drifted out into the summer air. He touched fingertips to his upper inside thigh, felt the soft ridges of tender skin through the light cotton of his school pants. It calmed him.

He'd show them who was chicken. With a grunt, he was up and over the sill, sliding forward, hands braced for impact on the dirty floorboards below. Orange dust lay across the room, as it did everywhere in this middle-of-nowhere town where even the rain refused to come.

He gained his feet, adrenaline driving race cars through his veins. The air inside was cooler and tasted of dark and slow decay. A heavy silence cut off the world outside the window. It looked hyper-real through the narrow gap. Green and orange stains made the view through the glass oceanic, dreamlike. It wasn't as dark as it had appeared from the brightness of the day. Floral paper peeled from the walls like sunburnt skin.

Now what?

A grin spread across Jonathan's face. He would go through, let himself out the back and walk around to the front. He imagined their faces as he emerged through the tall grass and weeds. His mother had warned against playing here, but not because it was something to be scared of, she said, just because it was dangerous. Falling down and full of vermin.

Floorboards creaked as he stepped tentatively forward. They felt spongy beneath his sneakers. The desiccated, fungus-spore smell of the place increased as he moved towards the hallway, deep in shadow.

A closet door stood half-open. He glanced towards it and froze. The snakes in his stomach burst into ice water, his heart hammered in his throat. In the darkness of the closet, a grin glowed gently. Two rows of yellowed teeth, bright enough to see in the gloom, spread in a wide grimace. Shaking shuddered up through Jonathan. A scream rose and lodged in his neck with his heartbeat as he gasped fast, shallow breaths.

His eyes couldn't help but adjust to the dimness. A face emerged around the rictus grin, skin sucked close to the skull, dark like old wood. The head was tilted to one side, quizzical. The nose a narrow blade, eyes two endless tunnels of night that threatened to suck Jonathan's sanity out. The thing was standing tall, too tall, taller than a normal man and thin as a fencepost, staring at him through the gap in the closet door, absolutely motionless.

The scream burst through the constriction in Jonathan's throat. High and echoing it tore the silence and unstuck his feet. He hauled himself out the window, barking his hips against the wood in his frantic scrambling, landing heavily on his hands and wrenching a wrist—

ghostsdidit

—slamming his cheek to the dry, hard earth as that arm gave out.

He tore through the yard and burst out the gate, vomit rising along with his terror. His right wrist throbbed where he'd landed on it. Had he heard a voice? Tears blurred his vision.

Through the haze he saw the older boys hightailing it around the corner. He didn't care any more about them or their gang. Gripping his agonised wrist tightly, he ran until he fell into his house, his room, and curled tightly on the bed.

* * *

When Jonathan woke it was dark outside and his wrist was a swollen ball of agony. He knew ice was necessary for this kind of injury, but was it late enough to venture from his room? The clock said 9:18. Terry might have drunk himself unconscious already. Jonathan's mum wouldn't be home for at least another hour.

He crept to his door and listened. The television burbled in the front room, but he couldn't hear snores. On nervous feet, he approached the living room like it was a bear cave. Terry hunched in his armchair, all wiry muscles and anger and hate. Thankfully, the chair faced the TV. Jonathan watched his stepfather lift a can to his mouth, drink deeply. Several empties already littered the floor. Jonathan's mother would collect them in silence come the morning.

He was committed now and pain drove him on. He snuck past into the kitchen, searched the freezer for something to use as an icepack. Frozen corn. He slipped it free inch by careful inch and gently closed the freezer door.

"The fuck are you doing?"

Jonathan whimpered at Terry's voice, rough and heavy with the promise of violence.

"Hurt myself," Jonathan said, almost a whisper. "Was gonna ice it."

"You think you're worth wasting good food? We can afford that?" Terry strode across the torn linoleum and ripped the bag from Jonathan's hand. He grabbed the injured wrist, wrenched it up to see.

Jonathan howled, stomach turning at the sickening wave of pain—

nojustice

—that flooded his hand and arm.

"Stop crying, you snivelling idiot!" Terry let go of Jonathan and backhanded his face. Jonathan landed heavily on his shoulder to avoid putting his injury through more torture. "Go to bed before I beat you unconscious where you lie."

It had happened before. Jonathan scurried, sobbing, to his room, shut the door and sat down against it, cradling his wrist. Terry shouted about wasting money as if he ever brought a single dollar into the home, leeching off Jonathan's mother like a parasite. He spent his benefits on booze, then yelled about how awful his life was. He hadn't always been so angry, but he had always been a dick, his true nature rising to the surface like pond scum once he had his claws into Jonathan's mother. *She's my Summer all year round*, he used to say, riffing on her name. These days Terry was bleak winter for all of them. Had been for more than seven years now. Jonathan had tried to get along with him, not even knowing his real father's name. But he had grown to hate Terry so deeply it burned in his gut. He would see the prick dead if he could.

* * *

Jonathan woke with weak light leaking around his curtains. He stretched, muscles cramped from the hard floor, still using his body to ensure his door couldn't be opened. He'd lost count of the nights he had spent sleeping as a doorstop, but it didn't always prevent the beatings. Sometimes it made them worse.

He lifted his wrist. It seemed to have gone down, purple bruising emerging through the angry red. He shuddered at the memory of the injury, bolting from that too tall thing in the closet. Surely he had imagined it, some trick of light and shadow, a manifestation of his fears. But what about the voice as he'd run? He'd heard it again in the kitchen last night. It all seemed so real, the thing in the cupboard so total in its rakish presence, its cadaverous visage, its utterly still observation of him.

Trembling began again, fear and the ever-present loneliness. He'd wanted to be part of something but had only increased his isolation. He wished Brendan was still in town, then none of this would have happened. Who else could he possibly tell about that monster? Maybe he could call his friend later, but that thought brought fear of Terry berating him for running up the phone bill with interstate calls.

He stared at his wrist, raised the index finger of his other hand. Would it be the right kind of pain? He held his breath and pressed into the deepest part of the bruise. He muffled a cry as the hurt blossomed through his arm, a sick, bone deep shard of agony.

helpmehelpme

He gasped, dizzy from the intensity. The voice again. Was he going mad? Serial killers claimed they heard voices. It didn't matter, the pain was wrong. Too wide and muffled, too deep and uncontrolled. Like when Terry hit him or when he'd tried the lighter against his skin, it lacked precision. Lacked the diamond-sharp control of the razor blade. The slice that was his alone, unaffected by anyone's agenda, that he felt on his own terms.

He flexed the fingers of his hurt hand and pursed his lips. Maybe he could strap it up. If he was lucky, it was only a sprain. He took a sock from his laundry and wrapped it tightly around the swelling, tucked in the end and perused the makeshift bandage. It felt better already, supported.

He opened his door. Terry's snores rolled like distant thunder. Jonathan snuck a look into his parents' room to see the inert lump of his mother under the covers. She would be up again soon, out on her cleaning job, still exhausted from working the bar at Miller's until who knew what hour. They sometimes got to share a few words over a hurried breakfast.

Jonathan went into the bathroom. He slid the lock home and stood up on the toilet seat to reach the top of the medicine cabinet above the sink. Out of sight, tucked into the gap between cabinet and wall, his blade. He turned it over, let the light glint off it. He'd only used this one a couple of times, would be able to use it a couple more before it was spent. He didn't know why, but for whatever reason a blade was good until it wasn't. It went from pure, shining release to used and useless in an instant, and he would know when.

He dropped his trousers, sat on the closed toilet. He held the blade in his right hand, the injured one, but the sock bandage seemed to be working. In his left he scrunched up a ball of toilet paper.

His naked thighs were pale in the fluorescent light. Tiny ladders of white marched up the inside of each one. Jonathan breathed deeply, slipped into his private place. He stared until the right spot presented itself, inside the boundaries of boxer shorts. He pressed the flawless edge of the blade to his skin and drew it back. A high keening barely escaped his lips as he held the sensation in, held the pain in and—

helpmesavemehelpme

—savoured the icy, glassy perfection of the cut. All his fears and worries slipped away, nothing but Jonathan and the razor, nothing but his immaculate pain.

He watched the blood well up and bead along the fresh line in his flesh as he tried to ignore the floating words he knew he had heard. The blood swelled and overbalanced on the lip of skin to trickle in tiny rivulets towards the ground. He pressed the tissue to his leg before the blood could fall, savouring the gentle downslide of the pain, the growing sting of the wound.

nojustice

Jonathan's eyes popped open. The voice was so clear in his head. And so desperate. "Hello?" he said quietly.

The image of the creature in the closet rose in his mind and his pleasure from the cut became fear again. The crystal clarity sliced into his thoughts shattered and spun away. So unfair! A cut could keep his fears and loneliness at bay for hours, sometimes days. Had the cut triggered the voice? Every time he'd heard it he was hurting.

He dabbed at the fresh wound, made sure the blood flow was staunched. He rinsed the razor blade under cold water until it was gleaming and fresh again. Still good. He'd never cut twice in succession before.

He repeated his preparation ritual, then drew a gentle parting of the flesh below the previous one. He muffled his gasp at the delicious pain and let the sensation carry him.

pleasehelpmesounfair

That creased and woody face in his mind's eye, those staring pits where eyes should be, that rictus grin. A sob escaped Jonathan's lips.

nojustice

solonely

pleasehelp

The pure, cold sensation slipped away and Jonathan's leg stung, two burning lines in his skin. The peace was gone, but that desperate plea remained. Fear curdled his stomach and mind.

He would have to go back.

"Honey, you in there?"

His mother's voice made his heart pound. "Yes, just coming!" He rinsed the blade, stuck tissue to the lines to ensure no blood leaked into view, and pulled up his pants. The razor slipped into its hiding place and he realised it was finished.

His mother's face was concerned as he opened the door. "You were in there a long time, love."

"Probably hauling on his pencil dick like an animal." Terry's thick and slurred voice from the bedroom. He must have crawled from his armchair and into the bed. Probably why Jonathan's mother had got up.

Her eyes were so tired. "Don't be crass, Terry. You okay, sweetheart?"

"Sure."

"What's going on here?" She gently lifted his arm with its sock bandage.

"I sprained my wrist, that's all."

Terry's laughter coughed out through the bedroom door. "Told you he was whacking off!"

Jonathan's mother turned her son by his shoulder. "I'll make you eggs."

She didn't have long, as usual, but they got to share some time over breakfast. It was good, with Terry's snores marking his distance. His mother's eye regularly fell to Jonathan's strapped wrist, but she asked no more about it. He resented that, betting she wasn't asking in case he told her Terry had done it. Whenever he'd told her about Terry's beatings she always said he mustn't upset Terry, mustn't sass Terry, mustn't do this or that. Fuck Terry. And before he got angry at his mother again, he changed his train of thought. She was scared as well, and Terry beat her sometimes too.

"I went into the Horror House," he said, before he realised he was going to.

"I've told you it's not safe in there."

"I think there's a monster inside…"

"Jonny!"

"But he's sad. He needs my help."

His mother stared at him for a long moment, eventually looked away, busied herself tidying dishes. "You need to stay away from there, Jonny. It's not safe."

"But if someone needs our help…"

"Stay away from there!" She pulled her blue work vest over her T-shirt, HI, I'M SUMMER on an embroidered badge over her left breast. "I have to go to work. Don't be late for school. And don't wake Terry."

* * *

Chicken Wings and his friends avoided Jonathan at recess. In the lunch line, Jonathan caught Chicken Wings' eye and the older boy just shook his head, face sour. Maybe the screaming had scared them and now they assumed he had tricked them. At least blanking him was better than beating him up for it.

On the way home from school, he took the long route and stood staring at the Horror House. Did he really want to go in again?

He rubbed at his inside upper thigh where the morning's cuts had begun to itch. He hated the itching, but sometimes scratching the tiny line of scab would get a subtle repeat of the glassy sensation of the original incision. Subdued somehow.

Surely the monster was playing tricks to get him back within its grasp. He turned sharply, intending to go home, and clipped his injured wrist on the gate post. A burst of pain flared up his arm.

helpmehelpmehelpme

So clear, so desperate. So obviously coming from in there.

Jonathan crossed the yard, peered into the window again, willing the closet door to swing open. His telekinesis skills left a lot to be desired. Pain was his private thing, this intrusion on it was unacceptable.

His heel checked against something in the scraggly grass. A rake, long wooden handle silvered with weather, metal tines bent and rusting, missing in places. He pulled it free from the clinging undergrowth.

He held the rake in his uninjured left hand, at the end of the shaft, and fed it through the window. He leaned in as far as he could, muscles trembling with effort, but even the full length of the rake and his arm left the tines scraping air a couple of metres from the closet door. His grip gave way and the rake fell with a dull clatter.

"Right then." Jonathan steeled his nerves and climbed in. He crouched, back pressed to the tattered wall, and stared at the closet. He had time and patience.

Nothing happened.

Eventually he picked up the rake and pushed it ahead of himself. At the absolute furthest distance he could manage, he hooked the rusty tines around the edge of the door. With a shout of fear and determination, he pulled the door open.

His shout turned into a scream as he scrambled backwards until he checked up against the wall again. The tall creature was there, hairless and dark, teeth grinning in the gloom, ragged clothing hanging from it like layers of sacking.

And its feet were half a metre above the floor, toes pointing down. The quizzical tilt of its head was due to the leather belt tight around its neck, fixed to a hook in the high ceiling.

Jonathan's scream died away as he gasped for breath. It was a hanged man.

He remembered a story about an old woman who had died in her home and no one had known, her body mummified by just the right dark and dry conditions.

The hanging man's lips were shrunken back, his eyes desiccated to blackened raisins and fallen into the skull. There were scraps of curly hair clinging to the tight, darkened skin of the scalp.

Jonathan sat and gasped, dryness and decay cloying in his throat. A man. A suicide. How could he help someone who had already killed himself? What had he heard?

helpmesavemehelpme
pleasehelpmesounfair
nojustice solonely pleasehelp

Jonathan looked from the taut belt to the suspended toes. No justice. Unfair. Was this not suicide?

"How can I help?" he asked. "Do you need to be buried?" Images from B-grade horror movies drifted through his mind. Consecrated ground, restless ghosts, hungry ghouls.

No response.

The pain was the conduit. He knew that and resented it. The cut was his private, perfect, crystalline, untouchable place. But other pain worked too.

Jonathan narrowed his eyes at the corpse. It still filled him with a kind of dread, but the original terror had been replaced with bitterness. He didn't want this problem, begrudged the thing's need that corrupted the privacy of his cuts. If he helped it, maybe its voice would go away.

He laid his palm against the floorboards and levered himself up on that one arm, bending and pressing the injured joint to support his weight. Pain exploded up his arm in a hot, red wave. Not the clear ice of the incision, but a brutal, concussive fire. He cried out, vision swimming at the edge of consciousness.

make it right they killed me the ghosts I tried to help my son please find them punish them justice

Jonathan collapsed, sobbing. He gripped his agonised wrist, unable to bear a second's more pain. He curled on the floor, gasping and crying until the hurt finally dulled to a low throb.

they killed me the ghosts

What the hell did that mean?

Jonathan knew he would be missed if he was late home. Usually he came and went as he pleased, but Wednesdays were the only day his mother finished her cleaning job and didn't go directly to work a shift at Miller's. "Our time, sweetie," she constantly reminded him. Wednesday evenings and Sundays. It was better than some kids got.

He looked up at the hanging man. "Let me think." He pushed the closet door closed with the rake and clambered out of the window.

* * *

Jonathan's afternoon with his mum was strangely unsullied by the presence of Terry. The drunk had gone to a friend's and for that brief time the house actually felt safe. Jonathan and his mother hung out, she cooked a dinner and they enjoyed it at the kitchen table. They watched TV for a while.

For a couple of hours, things were like the days before Terry. Those hazy memories Jonathan was too young to truly recall, but he remembered the sensation of love and quiet. Or maybe he just thought he did. Regardless, it was precious and he made the most of it. But it was haunted by the drifting presence of the hanged man, always floating at the edges of Jonathan's consciousness. Every time his wrist throbbed, that tight, drawn face swam past his mind's eye.

He did his best to ignore it—

they killed me the ghosts

—but the mental stain was indelible.

As the clock ticked towards eight, the sound of an overworked ute burbled in the distance and grew louder. A curtain of dread fell across them both. Headlights swept the window and Jonathan said, "School tomorrow."

His mother smiled, kissed his cheek. "That's true. 'Night, sweetheart."

"⊠Night, Mum."

The unspoken remained so and Jonathan made it to his room as the front door banged open. He regretted he hadn't had a chance to call Brendan as the old loneliness swept over him again. He also regretted once more that Brendan had been his only real friend, the implications of that unconsidered until Brendan's father took a job in Queensland and they packed up and left.

Terry's slurred voice yelled something out into the night from the front door and the ute revved and wheelspun away. Terry's tone became lower, animal and cajoling. "Hey, my bright Summer…"

Jonathan's mother said something in return, her voice resigned and hesitant with a veneer of fake desire laid over it. Jonathan crawled into bed. As his mother's cries of pain-masked-as-pleasure came from the room next door, he put ear buds in and turned his MP3 player up loud.

* * *

The next morning Jonathan walked to school the long way. He stopped at the Horror House on its large block, well-removed from any neighbours. Across the street was nothing but orange dirt and scrub until the highway cut a grey scar through the landscape some two kilometres distant. A good place to be lost, on the forgotten edge of a remote town. The mines that kept the place alive were beyond the main street and shops. So were the better suburbs, even the school, all as far as they could get from this wasted brink.

Jonathan pushed through the overgrown garden to the window and leaned on the sill. "What do you mean, ghosts killed you?" he called in. "I want to help, but I don't understand." He took a deep breath and squeezed his injured wrist. Pain blossomed.

desertghosts

drugsandguns

myson

grant

Jonathan gasped and staggered back. His wrist was definitely not broken, though it hurt like hell, but it was a clumsy pain. He needed razors for clarity. Though perhaps he had enough information.

The Desert Ghosts, a biker gang. Jonathan had heard Terry talking about them, how they ran drugs and the police turned a blind eye because there were far more bikers than police officers. It had sounded like Terry respected that. "It's good to be an outlaw!" he had said with a laugh. Jonathan wished his stepfather would go and be one but the man was too much of a loser for that.

And Grant was the dead man's son. The hanged man wanted justice for his death at the hands of the Desert Ghosts because he had tried to help his son. This was a good place to kill someone and leave them to never be found. Hang them in a cupboard in a house no one cared about. Jonathan frowned. He would have to find out what happened to Grant, he supposed. If there was to be any justice and a return to peace in his mind.

He knew where the Desert Ghosts' clubhouse was. He had admired the rows of chromed and flamed Harleys parked in the yard several times when he had wandered over that way. After school he would nose around. He smiled, feeling like a detective in the cop shows he watched. He wished Brendan was here to share in the adventure. But of course, if Brendan had been with him, Jonathan would never have tried to get in with the older boys and none of this would be happening.

* * *

During lunch, Jonathan watched Cameron Hurley across the dusty schoolyard. The boy was a year older and a head taller, the kind of kid who never bothered to bully or assert his authority because it simply existed by default. No one messed with Cameron Hurley because he was tough and mean and his dad was a biker. A Desert Ghost.

Jonathan swallowed his nerves and wandered over to where Cameron sat with two other boys. "Hey."

Cameron looked up, one eyebrow raised.

"Your dad's a Desert Ghost, isn't he?" Jonathan asked, a nervous smile twitching his lips.

"So what?"

"Must be pretty cool."

Cameron laughed, rolled his eyes at his friends. "You think?"

"Isn't it?"

"How would I know? I'm not one."

Jonathan nodded, desperate to steer the conversation before he used up the boy's curiosity credit. "You get a lift to school on his bike though, eh? It's a pretty awesome Harley."

"Fast as hell too."

"I bet. Does your dad know anyone called Grant?"

Cameron's brow knitted at the non sequitur. "Grant Carter, you mean?"

"Oh, I don't know his last name."

"Grant Carter's a Ghost. Why do you care? You know Grant?"

Jonathan felt panic rising. Where could the conversation go from here? He was a clumsy idiot.

"Hey, Jonathan!"

The voice filled him with dread and relief. Chicken Wings and his friends stood behind, eyes angry. Not an ideal distraction, but a distraction nonetheless.

Jonathan tried to smile. "Yeah?"

"You think it's funny to trick us, you skinny prick?"

They'd got over their shock and come for revenge. Re-establish the pecking order.

"I saw something in there, it scared me. But it was just, you know, a shadow, I guess. I panicked, that's all."

Cameron Hurley stood, gestured with his head to his friends. "Let's leave these tools to it."

They wandered off and Chicken Wings' expression soured even more, now embarrassed in front of the big cool kid of his year. The bully wasted no time and swung a punch. Jonathan had a moment of absurd laughter as he realised he still didn't even know this kid's name, then the punch landed. He staggered—

myson

—and a shot to his stomach he didn't see coming took the wind out of him. He folded over—

stillaghost

—and fell, his eye singing with pain from the first hit.

Chicken Wings and his friends stepped in and swung kicks into his head and body, pain lanced through his ribs—

thoughttheykilledhimtoo

—and face. Sound whined away to a distant roar. Then short, harsh barks of adult voices. The assault ceased.

Jonathan's vision cleared and he gasped air into tortured lungs as two teachers dragged his attackers away. They grinned as they went, revelling in the schoolyard kudos they'd earned. It would be worth any punishment in their eyes. Cameron Hurley stood off to one side with an expression of mild respect.

One teacher led the three bullies away and Mrs. Foley came back to Jonathan. "Are you okay?"

He nodded, tears balanced on his eyelids.

Mrs. Foley touched a finger to the orbit of his eye. He winced.

"That's going to bruise," she said. "Let's get you to the nurse for some ice. What was all that about?"

Jonathan's breathing began to settle, his heart rate slowed. "Just a stupid misunderstanding."

The teacher tutted and guided him gently by the elbow. As they went, Jonathan struggled to recall what Cameron had said. And what the disembodied voice had muttered, so distant, almost too gossamer to hear as the kicks and punches landed. Grant Carter was a Desert Ghost. And he was the dead man's son. But the dead man thought the Ghosts had killed his son too. It was so confusing. It had certainly not come without cost, but Jonathan had at least gained some information this lunch break. Though he had no idea what to do with it.

* * *

The Desert Ghosts' clubhouse sat among other similar big grey metal buildings along the industrial strip, with no signage, no ostentatious display of identity. A dozen or so Harley Davidson motorcycles stood in a gleaming row inside the chain-link fence. The bikers themselves wore their colours proudly, defiantly. Jonathan asked his mother once, as they drove on some errand or other, why their headquarters wasn't equally well signposted. "A small allowance in the balance between the law and the lawless," she had said. Jonathan wondered what it was like to be an outlaw. There was appeal in the idea.

Now he had walked all the way here, he felt stupid. And sore, his face swollen and bruised from the beating, ribs throbbing. So what if he knew all this stuff? What was he supposed to do about it? What the hell could he do about anything in his stupid life?

Perhaps he should just report the body and a connection would be made, the Ghosts brought to justice for the killing. But hadn't he just been thinking how far outside the law they appeared to be?

The gate lurched, electric motors whirring as it slid back. Jonathan watched three bikers, all leather and denim, beards and patches, emerge from the building and head for their bikes. The engines fired into life with deep, machine-gun revs and peeled out, one after the other. The last through gave a little salute to Jonathan as he passed. The gate rattled and slid closed again.

There was a smaller gate inside the big one, locked with a sliding bolt and padlock. Another biker approached along the footpath, carrying a fast food bag. He looked sidelong at Jonathan as he fumbled for a key. "What are you hanging about for?" His voice was hard and rough, like Terry's.

"Just looking at the bikes," Jonathan said meekly. "They're pretty cool."

The big man nodded, beard flexing against his chest. "You want to ride a bike one day?"

"Sure, I guess." Could he get anything from this exchange? "Which one is yours?"

The man pointed to a chopper in the middle of the row, high ape-hanger bars and a low king and queen seat. The teardrop tank was flashed in blue flames and the chrome fittings reflected the hot sun in eye-watering glares. "You like it?"

Jonathan grinned, hooked his fingers in the chain-link to stare. "It's awesome." He looked up suddenly, put on his best puppy eyes. "Can I sit on it?"

The biker frowned. "Fuck, kid, really?"

"Can I?"

The padlock popped and the man pushed open the gate. "What's your name?"

"Jonathan."

"You got some bruises there, Jonny-boy. Get in a fight?"

"Some boys at school like to bully me."

The big man sniffed, nodded. "I'm Maggot. Go ahead. But don't you dare scratch it."

Jonathan ran in and dropped his school bag by the wide rear tyre. He cocked one leg over the quilted leather seat and sat, crooked as the bike leaned on its kick stand. He reached up for the bars and his fingertips only just scraped the grips.

Maggot laughed. "You got some growing to do, Jonny-boy." He pulled a burger from his paper sack and bit into it, ketchup sticking to his thick moustache.

Jonathan felt pretty cool. The idea of cruising the highways on a machine like this filled him with a deep longing. Get on a shining motorcycle and ride away. From everything. Forever. "You know Grant Carter?" he asked casually.

Maggot popped one eyebrow, chewing expansively. "Yeah. You know him?"

"Not really. I go to school with someone who does, that's all."

"That right?" Maggot took another huge bite of burger, the whole thing almost gone in three mighty mouthfuls. "Reckon you'd like to be an outlaw one day, kid?"

"Could I?"

"Sure. Get someone to vote you up as prospect, earn your colours."

"How did you earn yours?"

Maggot grinned, teeth full of burger and bread. "We don't talk about that stuff to outsiders."

Jonathan nodded, looking over the shiny dials and petrol cap in front of him. Where did he go now? He was no kind of detective. A wave of depression broke over him. "My stepdad used to know Grant's dad," he said, desperate to keep talking, to find something out.

Maggot became still and his eyes narrowed. A rill of ice tickled over Jonathan's skin despite the blistering day.

"That right?" Maggot asked.

Jonathan swallowed, mind racing. "You know how it is. Everyone knows everyone in a tin box town like this."

"Mm-hmm."

Silence hung heavy and threatening between them.

"Anyway," Jonathan said, heart pounding. "My stepdad and Mr. Carter were pals, and my friend at school knows Grant. Small world, I guess."

"Very small."

"Mr. Carter left town or something, my stepdad said. That right?"

"What do you care?" Maggot asked.

Jonathan shook his head, stared at blue flames curling across jet black paint so he didn't have to meet those cold, hard eyes above him. "Just thought it was interesting or something."

The silence descended again. Jonathan reached for the bars, feeling incredibly stupid and vulnerable. There was a rustling of paper sack as Maggot changed grip and pulled a phone from his pocket. After a moment, "Grant? Get out into the yard, willya."

Jonathan's heart threatened to crack his bruised ribs. He wondered if he should run, if his legs would even support him if he tried. "I guess I should get going. Thanks for letting me sit—"

Maggot put a hand on his shoulder. "Wait there a second."

"I'll be in trouble if I'm late."

"Just a minute, kid."

The clubhouse door squealed as it opened then banged closed. "What's up?" a voice called.

"This is Jonathan," Maggot said. "Reckons his stepdad was pals with your old man back in the day."

A tall, thin biker joined them. He wore heavy boots and jeans and a white T-shirt. His arms were mosaics of tattoos from the knuckles all the way up into the short sleeves. "That so?" He smiled. Jonathan couldn't help thinking of sharks. "And who's your stepdad?"

Jonathan had to unstick his tongue from his dry mouth. "Terry Makings."

Grant pursed his lips, looked at Maggot. "Never heard of him. You?"

Maggot shook his head.

Grant returned his predatory smile to Jonathan. "My old dad's not around any more. He, er… He went away." He flicked a wink at Maggot and the big man grinned.

He knows! Jonathan thought in horror. *He knows the Ghosts killed his dad. He's happy about it.*

"I wouldn't mind a chat with your stepdad, this Terry Makings," Grant said. "It'd be nice to catch up with someone who knew my old man."

"Sure, I guess." Jonathan's voice was little more than a wheeze.

"Where does he live?"

"I'm not supposed to give my address to strangers." Jonathan saw his hands shaking. Surely they could too.

Grant leaned forward, starting to speak, but Maggot said, "Your stepdad likes a drink as much as the next man, right?"

"More than, I'd say," Jonathan said, a slightly hysterical laugh escaping with the words.

"You're right not to tell strange men where you live," Maggot said. "Especially big scary bikers. But we'd love to catch up with Terry for a drink. What's his pub?"

"The Marlborough Hotel." Jonathan realised he'd told the truth before he could stop himself. He could have named any of a dozen pubs around town that catered to the generous appetites of the mining community.

Maggot slapped Jonathan on the back, pushed him up and away from the bike. "Run along, lad. You don't want to get in trouble. We'll look Terry up at the pub one night."

Jonathan grabbed his bag and walked as fast as he could through the chain-link gate. As soon as he was sure he was out of sight, he began to run.

* * *

As twilight darkened the streets to sepia, Jonathan stood outside the Horror House, panting and burning up, a fresh packet of razor blades gripped in one sweating palm.

Trying to play clever he had set the Desert Ghosts onto Terry. On the one hand, that filled him with a vicious joy, but surely he'd get the beating of his life for it. Maybe the last one, Terry was sure to kill him. Jonathan had to know more. Maybe he could fix things yet.

He clambered in through the window and pulled the closet door open, all fear of the corpse gone in the face of the very real threat of corporal punishment. Mr. Carter hung there, mummified and alone.

"I need answers," Jonathan said. "Do I have to hurt myself to get them?"

Nothing.

"Fuck you!" He had no idea why these were the rules, but there didn't seem to be a thing he could do about it. His leg was sore, but he had cut his upper arms before, on the inside, high up near the armpit. There was space there still, on both sides.

"Your son knows you're dead," he said to the cadaver. "He's with the Ghosts and knows they killed you. I think he was in on it. I'm sorry, but it's true. I saw his face when he talked about it." Jonathan paused, drew a calming breath. "I've fucked up. I've set the bikers onto my stepdad. He deserves it, I wish *he* was dead! But he'll beat the hell out of me because of it." A sob escaped and Jonathan felt very young and afraid and alone. "What can I do?"

He sat down cross-legged, rolled up his shirt sleeve and unwrapped a fresh, shining razor blade. He placed its perfect edge to the flesh on the inside of his left biceps and gently drew it deep. He hissed in pain.

All he heard was distant weeping.

The pain drained away. "Mr. Carter, don't make me cut myself for nothing! What am I supposed to do? This is all your fault! You have to help me."

He sat in the gathering dark and stared at the man's leather-dry skin. Eventually he lifted the blade and drew another excruciating line. The voice came more clearly than it ever had before.

stupid tried to force their hand a lot of money in Grant's room Ghost money took it hid it could have it back threw Grant out

The pain subsided again and the voice with it, but Jonathan knew there was more to be told. He closed his eyes, held his breath, cut again.

never got it never told them where they killed me thought they'd killed Grant too so sad they'd killed him such a fool

The voice faded even though Jonathan's arm still burned. "Focus!" he yelled. "Help *me!*" An idea began to form in his mind from something the dead man had said, a desperate, wild idea that filled him with terrifying possibilities. He lifted the razor, brandished it at the hanging man and cut again.

no justice for me but help you yes save you maybe some good yet there's
a list

It took three more cuts, but Jonathan left in the dark of night with a plan. An audacious, terrible plan that made him want to vomit. It could save him, and maybe give some final meaning to Carter's death, if he managed to pull it off. It was Thursday night. Terry always went to the pub on Friday and Saturday. Jonathan had one day.

* * *

Throughout the next day at school, Jonathan couldn't concentrate. Constantly nauseated, he could only wait. Even the meeting in the principal's office with the three bullies was a blur, and they all sneered at him as they were suspended until after the weekend for their actions. One day! Eventually, Jonathan was able to head home.

He wondered if Terry had gone to the pub already. He usually left sometime in the afternoon and came back late.

"The fuck are you doing here?" Terry yelled from the front room. So much for that. "Just home from school. I've got homework."

Terry hissed through his teeth. "Get on with it then. You'll have to fix your own dinner, I'm going to the Marlborough."

When did he ever not have to fix his own dinner? His mother acted like Terry fed them both, but surely she realised by now that wasn't the case. Resentment burned again, and he pushed it away.

He went to his room, half-heartedly got on with homework. He could sneak out, but if Terry caught him taking a shovel he'd be in all kinds of strife. After nearly an hour, the front door opened and slammed shut. Jonathan peeked from his window. Terry got into a beaten-up Ford sedan with one of his loser mates. They drove away and Jonathan's stomach churned.

He had to be back from his ghoulish errand before the bikers found Terry at the pub, and he had no idea how soon that might be. He grabbed his backpack, ran to the shed and found a shovel, then jumped on his rusted old bicycle. Out the west side of town, up a shallow hill, to the cemetery on the rise overlooking the sprawling community. He was thankful to see no one around.

He leaned his bicycle against a tree on the cemetery's far edge, where a thirsty forest of blue gums and scrub marched off across the rise and down out of sight. Shovel over his shoulder, he scanned the graves, nerves tickling the back of his neck. He'd covered only two rows when a voice yelled, "Oi! What are you doing?"

Jonathan cried out in surprise, the spade dropping to the ground behind him. A small maintenance shed on the far side of the cemetery had seemed deserted from a distance, but an old man stood framed in the doorway. He took long strides forward as he challenged Jonathan again.

The shovel lay forgotten as Jonathan ran and leapt on his bike. He pedalled hard away from the old man, into the cool shadows between struggling gums. Branches whipped his face and hands as he hammered along until he was sure he was well past the fellow's ability to catch up. He didn't have time for this!

He waited a few desperate minutes then walked cautiously back towards the graveyard, careful to remain in the cover of the bush. The old man was in his hut, perched like a crow on a stool in the doorway. Jonathan's shovel leaned against the doorframe.

Light faded and shadows lengthened. Dull fear began to blossom into full-blown panic as twilight passed swiftly into darkness and still the old man remained. Was Jonathan already too late?

As full dark settled, the groundskeeper finally stood. He threw the shovel inside and pulled the hut door closed, clicked a padlock into place and stalked off through the cemetery towards town.

Jonathan waited until he was well out of sight down the night-dark road. An early half-moon gave a wan light, turned everything a strangely two-dimensional silver. He stared at the groundskeeper's hut, his spade locked out of reach. Deflated, bereft, he moved to the edge of the bush and eventually found a large rock, slightly flattened on one side. He didn't have time to waste trying to find anything better.

It took another five minutes to locate the grave.

EDNA CARTER
BELOVED WIFE AND MOTHER

Mr. Carter's mother. Grant's grandmother. Jonathan dropped to his knees in the spot he had been told to and desperately began to dig. He tried not to think about what he was doing, driven by his need to fix things. Fix everything. It was hard work in the hot evening, dragging with the heavy stone. His hands became raw, sweat ran into his eyes.

But less than a foot beneath the hard, red surface, his stone hit the tin box. He clawed more dirt away and pulled it out. He refilled the hole, flattened and brushed the dirt to hide his handiwork.

The catch on the box popped open reluctantly. Wads of yellow bills sat inside, held with elastic bands. Jonathan made a quick count, estimated twenty-five thousand dollars. There was a note on top, a list of names and what looked like vehicle licence plate numbers and phone numbers. It was worth more to him than the cash. His mouth was dry, but he grinned.

The ride home was harder than the ride out, exhausted as he was, praying he still had time. As he pedalled breathlessly along the small path that connected to the end of his road, the deep rumble of V-twin motors swelled through the air. His heart hammered harder. A collection of single headlights cut through the night from the main road some two hundred metres away. His house was between Jonathan and the bikes, much closer to him, but he only had his legs compared to their mighty engines. He cried out, stood on the pedals and forced every last bit of energy he had into them.

He skidded around the back of the house, dumped his bicycle on the mostly dead grass as massed engines rolled like thunder up the street out front. He ran to the shed and tucked the metal box into a corner. It was lighter without the money. His bag was heavy with cash and his mind equally weighed down by guilt and fear as he rushed for the back door, in through the kitchen and leapt into his bed, his heart a jackhammer in his throat.

The roar of Harley Davidson engines outside was momentarily deafening, then they stilled one by one to a heavy silence. The front door banged open and Terry's protestations were high and terrified, about not knowing anyone called Carter, not having a clue what they were on about, they'd made a horrible mistake.

A gruff voice barked orders, directed people to search the house, one to go outside and check the garage.

Jonathan pulled covers over himself and curled up in a trembling ball, panting as quietly as he could as he tried to claw his breath back.

"Let's just force the information out of him," a voice barked. "He'll have spent the cash by now."

"He won't remember it all. Every name, phone number and licence plate of every competitor we know of? Could you remember all that? It took too long to compile and is way too big an advantage to give up. If that fucking list is here, we need it. Besides, it's proof he was in cahoots with Carter to steal our money."

"I don't know what you want!" That was Terry's terrified falsetto. "What list? I'd give it to you if I knew!"

Jonathan's door burst open, flooding the room with light from the hallway. He sat up in bed, eyes wide in genuine fear.

"There's a kid here," the huge silhouette in the doorway announced.

"Leave him," someone said. "Leave that room until last."

Jonathan's door closed and darkness descended again.

"You will not believe this!" a voice shouted from outside. The back door banged and there was the sound of something metal being slammed onto the kitchen table.

Laughter and shouts of surprise erupted. "Spent all the money but here's the fucking list!" someone said, disbelief evident.

"I've never seen that before in my life!" Terry screamed.

There was a short, cracking sound that Jonathan recognised all too well, fist meeting face. Terry sobbed. Jonathan swallowed a sickening combination of horror and elation.

"Saving this for your pal, Carter, huh?" a gruff voice said. "Let's go."

There were sounds of scuffling, more of Terry's sobs and denials, and slowly the place grew quiet. As Jonathan wondered if they had all left, his door opened again. He recognised Maggot in the low light. "You didn't hear a thing, did you, kid? You're a deep sleeper. That all right with you?"

Jonathan tried to swallow the dry rocks in his throat. "Yes," he croaked. "Okay."

"Thought so. See you around." Maggot shut the door. Heavy footsteps retreated through the house, then the big V-Twin engines barked and rumbled into life and slowly faded into the night. Jonathan sat in pitch black silence for a long time, mind flatlining. Eventually he jumped up and ran for the bathroom, just making it over the toilet bowl before vomit escaped.

* * *

The following days were a blur of dark and nauseous terror and Jonathan knew the cuts would do nothing to help. Terry didn't come home on Saturday. Jonathan's mother tutted and frowned between jobs, muttered about benders with his stupid friends.

Every time Jonathan heard an engine or a loud voice, panic spiralled through him. He was harrowed by guilt that chewed the edges of his heart, almost smothering the reluctant hope. Almost.

After his mother left for Miller's, Jonathan hurried across town in the gathering twilight to the one working payphone and made an anonymous call to the police. He owed Mr. Carter that much. All the way home he saw Terry lurking in shadows, about to leap furiously forth.

He was still awake when his mother came home after midnight and made phone calls of her own. *Not usually this long,* and *He's not at your place?*

Jonathan didn't sleep for hours, listening for the sounds of engines, doors slamming, shouting.

Sunday was their day together. His mother asked over breakfast if he'd seen or heard from Terry.

ALAN BAXTER |

"No, Mum." He wanted to say so much more but couldn't get the words up from his chest where they hung like lead weights. He rubbed constantly at the itching, burning tenderness of his upper arm.

They went to the park, then she bought him a burger and milkshake that tasted like cardboard and metal. They played board games all afternoon and Jonathan had to hold back tears the whole time, his stomach a churning sea. His mother looked sidelong at him now and then but said nothing.

She turned the TV on and the news stilled them with its lead story. Two bodies had been discovered in town. There was a shot of the outside of the Horror House, cordoned off by blue and white striped tape. Jonathan couldn't swallow, his mother gasped.

"The deceased were discovered in the abandoned home late last night. Police say both are suicides and there's no reason to suspect foul play."

Jonathan's mother made a small noise, almost a sob, almost a laugh. Tears broke and poured silently over Jonathan's cheeks.

His wrist was getting better but far from healed. He shifted his weight, pressed against it to send a bolt of pain up to his elbow.

at least I saved someone's son good luck

So distant and fading out.

Jonathan smiled weakly. *Rest easy*, he wished silently.

His mother looked down at him, her expression unreadable. "I wonder where Terry is."

Jonathan held her eye for a moment, finally swallowed. "He's never coming home, Mum."

She didn't say anything for a long moment. Eventually, she put one arm around his shoulders and hugged him hard, kissed his cheek. Jonathan leaned into her, wondering how the hell he was going to explain the twenty-five grand.

EXPOSURE
COMPENSATION

EACH TIME THE SHUTTER CLICKS IT BURNS THROUGH EVERY FIBRE of me, but my satisfaction helps me deal with the pain. It's working. The cunning woman told me it would hurt. That's what she called herself—a cunning woman. *Not a witch?* I'd asked, and she'd just smiled.

The shutter fires again and so do I, magic ripping through me. I force the smile to remain on my face despite the furnace wave breaking over me. I hope I have the strength to see out the shoot. The more shots he takes, the better.

You're sure about this, Kate? the cunning woman had asked me, her grey eyes hard as stone.

Yes, I'd replied. *More sure than I've ever been of anything.*

You truly understand the consequences?

I'd nodded. *I'm dying anyway.*

The shutter snaps again, like it's taking bites out of me, and I shudder with the pain.

Garth looks at me, past his old-fashioned camera. "Chin up, darlin'. What's the matter? You look like yer smelling a turd or somefing."

I shake myself, crack him the best smile I can as I look sultry and smoky for the camera.

"Tits out a bit, love. Push 'em forward."

I comply, feel a soft breeze over my naked skin just before I hear the shutter, brace for the pulse of fire.

I hadn't really believed Beverley that night so long ago, when she told me about the cunning woman. How her magic was real. "Revenge magic," Beverley had called it. "And it *always* has a *very* high price."

We'd smoked a joint, drunk expensive champagne in the VIP area of the club and laughed our arses off about revenge magic. But as the night drew on, Beverley had sobered and grown serious. "I'm going to see her. I'll make him pay." I thought I'd misheard, but she meant it.

"He's a scumbag," I'd told her. "Forget about him and all the tarts he fucked. Get on with your life."

"I loved him!"

There had been a passion in Beverley's eyes then. Next time I saw her, she was in St. Mark's, mind so damaged she didn't know me, her eyes glassy and distant. Her cheating fiancé had been found in an alley the night before, beaten nearly to death. The police said it looked like he had been attacked by a mob. He was in hospital and rehab for months, ended up blind in one eye, a permanent limp, one arm half-paralysed, a speech impediment and a colostomy bag. Never played his guitar again.

Beverley's eyes *were* glassy, but there was something in there. Deep and hard to see, it looked to me like satisfaction. Her body was unharmed, only her mind given to drive the magic. And she should come out of it, the doctors said. Eventually. Hopefully no permanent harm. That was her gamble and she obviously thought she was strong enough to make it work. *Totally worth the risk*, she'd said.

I'll never know. The magic she chose was different to what I've bought, because she wanted to survive it.

Funny how I was in St. Mark's anyway that day to get my results. That terrible news, the doctor's eyes so guarded while he told me my life was over. He started listing options and therapies and I'd shaken my head and walked out to see Beverley. I'd looked into her glassy-eyed satisfaction and ideas began to circle my grief even then. Possibilities. Revenge magic.

Given a few more months, the cunning woman said, Beverley should come around. Start her own rehab journey. The cunning woman helps all kinds of girls, in all kinds of situations. She was hot property in the seventies, she told me, but was used and abused right through her career. So she was more than happy to help me.

The shutter snaps and I burn.

"Tits forward, arse up," Garth says with a yellow-toothed grin. "Give me a side-on."

I turn and arch like Betty Boop. I even put one forefinger to my lower lip and pout.

Garth laughs, guttural and foul. "Loverly!"

Click, click, click. My skin feels like it's going to peel from my flesh. My eyes narrow, but I'm proud I don't flinch.

Garth stands up, sniffs. "That's this roll done. Call it there for a day, eh?" His eyes rove up and down my nudity, never once engaging my eyes.

"How many do you have?" I ask.

"Two rolls of thirty-six. Should be able to find some corkers among that lot. We'll make a few quid off these, you've still got it!"

"I hope so. Terrible waste of film otherwise."

"Yer never a waste of film, Kate. Yer bootiful!"

He honestly thinks that's a compliment. Like I don't remember his sweating, leering face over me when I was only fifteen, as he pumped away, promising me the stars and a career on the biggest billboards in the world. Me and all the other girls he suckered in. He can't believe I've come back to him after all these years and his ego prevents him suspecting a thing. I think I played the down-and-out, desperate bimbo pretty bloody well.

"Shall I come back tomorrow?" I ask, making my voice as little-girl as I can.

"Yeah. Come about eleven." He leers and winks as he emphasises the word 'come'.

I nod and smile and pull on my robe, tottering slightly on six-inch heels I'm not used to any more. The sheer silk is barbed wire over flesh that feels flayed and barbecued. It's all I can do not to stumble and wince as I walk away, but I stand tall and slip into the bathroom.

I expect him to come in as I dress, as I hold in tears against the agony, but he doesn't. Maybe he's planning to save that move for tomorrow. It's not like he'll have changed. He still uses film even. Which is just as well for me.

* * *

Laying in a bath of cool water eases the torture of the shoot. The pain of the cancer eating me up is never-ending, but I've almost grown used to that. So unfair to take me so young—I'm not even thirty—but what has ever been fair about life? There's nothing they can really do, so I take that as an opportunity. It was this or start chemo and lose my looks, my strength, and almost certainly my life anyway. With treatment my chances are still ridiculously slim. I saw my mother go that route and she suffered so much before she died. This way I'm in charge. And I get something.

When I close my eyes, I can see him, see what he sees, like the cunning woman said I would.

This is powerful magic, Kate. You'll be connected and when he—

I know. It's okay, really.

She nodded sagely and began the mixing and incanting, taking drops of my blood from every fingertip, every toe. Her process was fascinating. When the potion was made and the spells cast over it, she gave me the tiny vial and said, *Drink it all down in one go, right before you start. Don't miss your window. And it doesn't work with all this modern digital stuff. You need facsimiles, not pixellations or whatever they're called.*

The cunning woman's magic was so recently modern, using all kinds of film and tape, diodes and transistors to power her spells. But already the world is moving on, technology leaving her magic behind so soon after it had been conceived. Hopefully she can adapt, keep helping girls like me and Beverley. But Bev got to her musician scumbag fiancé one way, and I'll get to Garth another. It was never really going to be a problem. Old Garth, he always loved the 'grainy authenticity' of proper film.

With my eyes closed, I see row upon row of drying prints in Garth's darkroom, hanging images made monochrome by the blood-red glow. He tips chemicals into bottles and tidies away his tools, stands back, surveys his work. Seventy-two of me smile, pout and pose back at him. His hand disappears into his pants as he looks at each one and licks his lips.

My eyes pop open. He can have that all to himself, I have no need to see. To feel. I swallow bile, the pain through my flesh and skin rising up again, and run more cold water into the bath.

* * *

Eventually I find my way to my bed, lay on top of the soft covers. A few vodkas ease my mind and I'm ready to go. To witness. I'm at peace. The magic is working, reducing me. Closing my eyes, at first it's just darkness and I panic that something's wrong. Breathing deeply, I wait.

A sound comes to me, and it's from there, not here. Scraping and tapping. I feel the first sensation of separation. I see the gloomy shape of a bedroom and realise Garth has opened his eyes, awoken by the sound.

"Who's there?" he calls out, his voice weak and scared. He clears his throat, shouts again, mock bravado. "Who's bloody there?"

He rises, pads across the room into a hallway. He follows the sounds downstairs and stands before his darkroom, head cocked to one side, brow creased in confusion. I switch my vision with ease, so close to death now, sometimes viewing from above him, sometimes through his eyes. Am I already dead? His hand is slow and trembling as it reaches out. The door opens and he gasps, staggers back.

I walk out, naked and proud, wearing nothing but high heels and ferocity, grinning at him with feral hunger. But it's only part of me, my facsimile. Ghostly, the doorframe plainly visible through me, but I'm deadly for all my spectral insubstantiality. That's what I was promised.

In the darkroom I see myself peeling out of each photo, stepping down to the floor as I grow to my full height. Garth screams, stumbles backwards into a lounge room. He falls over the arm of a sofa, leaps to his feet again. More and more of me peel free, step out and grow to meet him. I surround him as he turns in circles, eyes wide and white. He gibbers and spits, trying to put his terror into words. "Who are...what...happening?"

More of me, naked and tall and oh so gorgeous, step from the darkroom into the soft light of his lounge. I gather around him, a furious legion, staring at him through so many of my eyes. "You won't hurt any more girls," all my mouths say.

Dozens of me move in on him, terrifying in my natural power. Seventy-two pairs of hands raise, fingers hooked into claws. Garth drops to the floor in a pool of his own piss and he screams and begs for mercy.

Our mouths open wide, seventy-two vengeful voices howl, and we fall on him and shred him.

We're laughing as Garth dies and it's the last thing I know.

EXQUISITE

TIM RINNEMAN HAD NEVER MET A LOCK HE COULDN'T PICK. It was his expertise, his pride. And his curse, as it had become a compulsion he could not resist. He grinned as he worked at the front door of his latest target, hidden in the night shadows of the porch. He had cased the joint for nearly a week, established it was occupied by a lonely but wealthy-looking man in his late forties or early fifties, who went drinking at the Blakeley Hotel every night from seven until around nine. Easy mark.

The lock barrel turned and Tim let out an almost silent, "Yes!" He slipped his lock picks back into the pocket of his dark grey jacket—everyone knew you didn't wear black to be camouflaged at night—and pushed the door open. His wool cap was low over his brow and a grey bandana masked the lower half of his face. Tight, rubber surgical gloves kept his fingerprints private.

He had been caught twice before, and twice avoided jail. Once, still a minor, he had been put on a good behaviour bond for two years. Then, right after he became a legal adult, he was caught again but managed to get away with community service and a three-year suspended sentence. Any further run-ins with the law and he would immediately go down for those three years, plus whatever the judge decided to hit him with for the new offence. But he simply couldn't help himself, and he wasn't going to get caught. He had been young and stupid. At twenty-two, he was still young, but not foolish any more. Worldly wise. Street smart. Savvy. That's how he knew the occupant drank red wine, like some freaking connoisseur, every night at the Blakeley. The door clicked closed behind him. He stood for a moment in the gloomy hallway, hands on his hips, enjoying the simple thrill of invasion. Then he nodded to himself. "Time to get to work!"

Usually women provided the best, most portable loot in the form of jewellery, but it wasn't the haul as much as the buzz of the crime that drove him. Anyway, these days it was easy to collect laptops and iPads and all manner of other swag both compact and valuable. Of course, that brought with it a modern problem, avoiding the internal security of such items, but Tim had contacts for that side of things.

He climbed the stairs to find three bedrooms. One a small, sparse room with a double bed, side table, and little else. The next was like an old-fashioned boudoir, all red silks and purple velvets, ivory combs and crystal perfume bottles. Tim stared. He knew the man lived alone. Did he have some kind of gender or transvestite curiosity going on? No matter, Tim wasn't the kind to judge. The room had the vibe of a museum. A well-stocked museum, for that matter. Tim sniggered and began emptying the contents of a jewellery box into the side pockets of his backpack. The stuff looked old and valuable, crusted with gems, glittering gold and silver.

The third room was clearly the homeowner's, everything about it redolent of a bachelor who was fastidiously tidy and organised. An expensive watch lay on the dresser and Tim nabbed that. His heart thrummed, adrenaline raced with the thrill of the theft. Tim Rinneman in his natural habitat, doing what he did best.

Downstairs he filled his backpack with a laptop, a Samsung tablet, several items of silver from a cabinet, an impressive carving of an entire Asian village, in delicate detail, in a single piece of elephant tusk, and nearly a grand in cash. Honestly, the stuff people left lying around or tucked into unlocked drawers never ceased to amaze him. A knitted throw rug lay over the back of a sofa, and he used it to wrap and muffle his hoard then settled the backpack comfortably into place. It felt reassuringly weighty on his shoulders, bulging almost fit to burst.

Thoroughly pleased with himself he headed for the exit. He glanced back to consider the kitchen at the back of the house, but there was rarely anything in kitchens. He paused. Sometimes a valuable item might be left on a bench... He hurried in and scanned around once. Nothing. Good.

Returning to the front of the house, he passed a door under the stairs he hadn't paid mind to before, but a new detail caught his eye. It had a Yale lock beside a small, looped metal handle. Who locked the cupboard under the stairs? He pulled on the handle, but the door didn't budge.

Curiosity burned. If it was locked it could only be because there was something of value inside. Tim pulled out his lock picks and went to work. It took less than a minute and he was in. Grinning, he pulled the door wide and saw not a cupboard, but stairs leading down into a basement. Light spilled up from below. He hadn't expected that.

He had promised himself that he would be in and out in under thirty minutes. He checked his watch. Twenty-five minutes so far. Smart thieves didn't compromise their plans. That's why plans were made, to avoid cock-ups on the job. So he had five minutes for a quick once around the basement. Or four, to allow a minute for his exit and stay within The Plan.

He crept down the stairs into the stark, fluorescent light. A long bench against one wall came into view, covered with a neatly organised array of shining silver knives and drills. And bone saws. And a dozen other implements of surgery Tim could not readily identify. The room was spotless, like a surgical theatre. As he got halfway down the stairs he noticed a couple of glass-fronted cabinets, metal gas bottles on wheeled stands with clear plastic masks hanging from them. And ten blood-stained toes. He staggered to a shocked halt.

Bile rising, heart racing, he crept a couple more steps down and the grisly display revealed itself in full. A man lay strapped to a metal table, tilted almost vertical. His arms were belted out to either side like a crucifixion, his head held against a black rubber rest with another brown leather belt. Blood transfusion bags were attached with snaking tubes. Other drips, clear and unidentifiable, stood on the opposite side. The man was naked and desecrated.

His toes were bleeding because each nail had been plucked away, as had his fingernails. In patches all over his legs and torso, small areas of skin had been flayed and folded back, neatly presenting slabs of wet, red muscle. Along one forearm, a several-inch length of bright white ulna was exposed to the air. His penis had been vertically bisected and hung open against the top of each thigh. His jaw was stretched wide with a bright, chromed device of bars and screws, and several dark, red holes dotted his gums were teeth should have been. His eyelids were gone, his eyes crimson-rimmed. And those eyes! They stared at Tim with such beseeching, such desperate pleading. The man's tongue danced in his wide gaping mouth as he expelled short, sharps breaths and gurgling grunts.

Tim cried out, his vision swimming as vomit shot into his throat and was only prevented from expulsion because his heart was already blocking the way. He staggered away, tripping and stumbling back up the stairs, wanting nothing except the outside. Fresh air, not this house, not that sight, he wanted to be far away and fast asleep and he would never, ever get that vision of atrocity out of his mind. Tears streaming his cheeks, breath in hard gasps, he spun a full three-sixty to slam the basement door, ran through the house, backpack slamming against his shoulders, and out the front. He dragged that door closed without stopping and bolted down the path, out to the street, and didn't stop running until he was a dozen blocks away and dizzy with exhaustion.

Tim found a pub and ordered a double bourbon. He downed it in one and ordered another. What the hell was he supposed to do now? His cap and bandana were stuffed into the backpack that was heavy with loot which now felt like the greatest burden a man could carry. He should just throw the lot off a bridge into the river, let it sink and never be found. His prints were not in the house, he was certain he hadn't left hair or anything else to be found by any forensics team. He could just walk away and be done with it all. Pretend it never happened, except for the image burned into his brain of that poor bastard. He shouldn't have run.

How could he walk away from that guy? But if he called it in, the police would want to know how he knew about the situation, and that would only get him busted. That meant a guaranteed three years in the can, plus a new sentence. No way was he going to do time like that if he could help it.

He could call it in anonymously, but then there was no guarantee it would be taken seriously. And he would get no closure, no knowledge the victim was saved. Then he realised that his reluctance all came back to the fact that he had fled in horror. Given all the poor man's suffering, wasn't that perhaps the cruellest cut of all? That salvation had been right there at hand, yet it had run gagging and crying from the sight? Tim needed to fix that.

A cold certainty settled over him. He would have to go back and save the man. The thought sent shudders through him once more. He was a burglar, but he wasn't a bad person. He knew right from wrong, even though he chose to do small wrongs from time to time. It wasn't his fault he'd grown up with drunk and distant parents who refused to enforce his schooling. It wasn't his fault he'd ended up uneducated and unemployable and had turned to a life of petty crime.

Well, maybe it was his fault, in part. He was smart even if he wasn't educated, and he could still turn that around. Go to night school or something, learn a trade. He could make a much safer living sweeping the bloody street if it was only about paying the rent. It wasn't. It was about that buzz, the decadence of the non-conformist. But everything had changed now. He swallowed the whiskey and ordered another, paying with the freshly stolen cash. It was well after 8:00 p.m. No way was he going back tonight and risk running into the evil prick who owned the place.

He would go back tomorrow, with his Uncle Pete's car, and rescue the poor bastard. He'd simply take him to hospital, leave him in the emergency department and scarper. Easy. Uncle Pete would lend him the car, no problem.

And if the guy doesn't go out tomorrow because he's been robbed tonight? a small voice taunted in the back of Tim's mind, but he pushed it away. Tomorrow. He'd go back and rescue the guy then.

* * *

The night was bright with moonlight when Tim parked Pete's battered old station wagon at the curb and stared along the street to the charnel house. It looked so normal from the outside, just like the dozens of others either side of it.

He sat and waited, fingers toying with the phone in his pocket. *I should just call it in anonymously. Find a public phone.* But he stayed put, watching.

He jumped as the front door opened and the large man emerged. He wore his signature three-piece suit, silk shirt and matching handkerchief in his jacket pocket. Bowtie. His shoes were shined like mirrors, reflective in the night like his slicked-back dark hair.

He headed off towards the Blakeley like it was any other night. Tim fumed at the man's nonchalance. Perhaps the fact he was leaving was evidence enough that, although he must realise he'd been robbed, perhaps he assumed the burglar hadn't found the basement hell. And given what he had down there, the bastard was surely not about to report the robbery. There was some vindication for Tim in that. Last night he stole the man's goods and chattels. Tonight he would deprive him of his sick fun. He watched the butcher all the way down two blocks until the distant figure turned left towards the Blakeley.

Tim's heart hammered as he picked the lock of the front door for the second time. He crept along the hallway, swallowing repeatedly against his nerves and the anticipation of what he might see. Would the man's torture have progressed further? There was a moment of panic at the thought the whole thing might be ended already, the body removed in the face of the previous night's incursion. Only one way to find out.

He picked the basement lock, hurried down into the brightness, and cried out in shock at the sight. The man's torture had indeed progressed. Both shins had been laid open, the flesh folded to either side like fillets of salmon, exposing stark bone. His testicles each hung down near his knees on a single thread of tissue, the scrotum gone. Glistening organs pulsed through windows carved in his abdomen. But worst of all was the poor bastard's head. The top of the skull had been removed above the eyebrows and the exposed brain bristled with filament-like acupuncture needles.

And yet somehow, the man lived. One eye rolled in its socket, the other an empty red and black cavern. His tongue was absent, and wet, slushing breaths rasped in his throat. A sob escaped Tim as he stared, dizzy and trembling. There was no way he could move this person without killing him for sure. His fucking brain was uncovered!

"Keeping them alive is the real art. Just enough new blood, antibiotics, shock treatments."

Tim cried out and spun around. The well-dressed man stood at the top of the stairs, his bulk filling the doorframe.

"That's what they pay me for, of course."

Tim shook his head, close to unconsciousness. "What?"

The man slowly descended and held out a business card. "This is me."

With shaking hands, Tim took the card and numbly read.

PATRICK MISLOVSKI
PURVEYOR OF THE EXQUISITE

"What?" Tim said again.

"I'm impressed you came back," Mislovski said, his tone calm, entirely relaxed. "You planned to save him? Very noble. But as you can see, he's deep in his experience now and it would be a travesty to interrupt it or end it early."

"Travesty...?" Tim could feel something nipping at the edges of his mind and he realised it was madness. He felt something in his head that was very ready to snap. "You're a fucking monster!"

"I am an artist."

Tim stuttered and gaped, convinced his fate was equal to that of the man strapped upright.

"I will largely ignore the outrageous liberties you took in here last night," Mislovski went on. "But I must insist you return my mother's jewellery. And then you can leave and we'll call it even, yes?"

"I… I can't leave…leave him…" Tim's mind was spinning, desperate to find purchase in some course of action, some semblance of sanity.

"There are hidden cameras throughout the house, Timothy Rinneman," Mislovski said, and Tim's bladder let go. The large man either didn't notice or chose to ignore it. "I know who you are, and I know you're hanging by a thread in regards to prison. Let me convince you that this man chose to be here, paid very handsomely for the privilege, in fact, and then you and I can go about our business as usual. We each have something over the other, no?"

The absurdity of the man's claims was finally giving Tim something to cling onto. "You can't compare a few years for burglary to this!" he said, gesturing at the brutality.

Mislovski produced a photograph from his pocket and handed it over. It showed the large man with his arm around the shoulders of another, younger man. Both were smiling. Between them they held up a piece of paper on which was written: PAIN IS THE ONLY TRUE EXPERIENCE. EXQUISITE IS THE ULTIMATE, ENDURING RELEASE. I CONSENT. Below the words was a date, from a little over a week before.

Tim looked at the man on the metal bed. Remembered him from the previous night when he was more intact. It was definitely the same person.

"I always have a photo like that," Mislovski said. "Partly as a keepsake from each client, partly as a possible defence should something go wrong. It's no real defence, of course. A person can't sign away their statutory right to life. They can't absolve me of murder. But they do consent, they do pay *very* well, and I am the best at what I do."

Tim thought back to the night before and a terrible realisation arose in his mind. Those beseeching eyes as he'd crept down the stairs. It was so obvious now in context. The man had not been pleading with Tim to rescue him. He'd been desperately willing Tim to leave. Those eyes weren't saying, "Save me!" They were begging, "Don't ruin this!"

* * *

Tim Rinneman had never met a lock he couldn't pick. But he would never be exercising those skills again. He busied himself stacking empty, flattened cardboard boxes for the huge recycling bins in the concrete yard outside and thought about his forklift driver's licence test that afternoon. A job in a big warehouse like this was perfect, keeping his body and mind busy without too many people around. Without too many people to watch, and wonder what they might have in their basements. Or wonder what they might secretly desire.

CROSSROADS
AND CAROUSELS

MARK COOPER SWEATED ATOP HIS SHEETS, wishing a breeze would blow in through the open window. Not a breath stirred the curtains and the hot night lay heavy. He sighed, rolled over. As he settled, the silence of the night covering him again, he heard blues guitar, faint as a whisper of hope in a dark cell. He held his breath, turning one ear to catch the strains. The sound of his cheek on the pillowcase drowned out the notes. As he began to think he'd imagined it, the music drifted over him again, gossamer faint but beautiful. The way he wished he could play.

He slipped from the bed, stood by the window, straining his ears to hear. The melody was distant, heart-wrenching in its perfection. Wearing only his shorts, he went out into the night. Standing on the front porch he heard it more clearly, though still it seemed a universe away. He walked to the gate, out onto the quiet country road. The night was still and close, the air heavy with summer, yet the song slipped through like cool rain. The pauses between the notes, sublimely perfect, gave him goosebumps.

Without thinking, Mark started along the road, following the sound. Who would be playing guitar at this time of night, here in the middle of nowhere? His feet stirred up dust on the still-warm bitumen. No rain had washed these quiet, broken streets for weeks. He passed his neighbour's houses, hundreds of metres apart, flaking paint and rusting tin roofs. A wet-eyed cow in the paddock opposite watched him with wary disinterest.

The music grew louder, the most soulful blues licks he'd ever heard. He imagined standing on stage with his band, turning out chops like that, and shivered despite the oppressive heat. He turned right, heading towards the coast road. He saw someone sitting on the paddock fence up ahead, bathed in moonlight. The guitar in the figure's hands reflected a deep red in the colourless whitewash of the moon.

Mark paused, notes floating to him more clearly, the guitar singing like an angel. *Where's he plugged in?*

Mark found himself walking forward again. The figure on the fence looked up, smiled. His teeth were bright in the night. He stopped playing and Mark felt as though his heart had been punched. "Hey man."

Mark smiled back. "Hey."

"I'm Nick."

Mark nodded, not sure what else to say. Nick seemed young, maybe mid-twenties, scruffy in a dashing way. He had tousled, jet black hair, bright eyes. Mark eyed the blood red guitar, smooth maple neck, scuffs from years of fingertips caressing out notes.

"You play?" asked Nick.

"Nothing like you."

Nick half-smiled. "Ah, I do okay."

"Where did you learn to play like that?" Mark asked, still admiring the beautiful guitar.

Nick ignored the question, hefted his instrument instead. "You like it? She's a beauty, eh?"

"Where's your amp?" Mark leaned over the fence, looking for a cord. He saw none.

"You could play like this if you wanted," Nick said, that bright smile again.

Mark's eyes narrowed. He looked from the guitar to Nick, and beyond to the street. Another road crossed it, heading back towards Maker's Farm and north towards town. Nick perched on the fence at the corner of the paddock. Right on the crossroads. Mark laughed, shaking his head. "I'm dreaming."

"What?"

Mark laughed again, louder this time. "I'm dreaming, right? A fantastic guitar player? At a crossroads?"

Nick grinned. "Pinch yourself."

"Yeah, sure. Wake myself up." He took an inch of forearm skin and pinched. It hurt, but nothing changed. His smile changed to a frown and he pinched again, twisting. "Ow, dammit."

"Not dreaming," Nick said, still smiling.

They stared at each other for a long time. Nick sat on the fence, relaxed. Mark grew increasingly uncomfortable. Eventually he said, "No way, man. This can't be real.'

"How badly do you want to play like me?" Nick asked.

"Not that badly, dude."

Nick picked up the guitar from across his knees and his fingers began to glide across the frets. The music pushed tears from Mark's eyes in an instant, every note and every pause touched his soul. He turned and ran, his feet whacking dryly against the bitumen.

When he slammed his front door, pouring sweat and gasping for breath, the song still carried through the night.

* * *

Mark stumbled through his day at the factory, grumbling along with everyone else about the heat and the lack of rain. They all knew moaning about it wouldn't do any good, but still they cursed gods they didn't believe in and beseeched others.

When the whistle blew he trudged out into the sunshine with his fellow wage slaves. A few raised their hands and waved in the car park, wishing each other good weekends. Mark returned the sentiments and drove for the coast and Saltspray City. The only escape from the oppressive summer was the occasional sea breeze and the air whistling around the Waltzers and rollercoasters. This was his playground, his sanctuary. He strolled the boardwalk, breathing deep of the dust and diesel. Maniacal music of carousels and flashing coloured bulbs assaulted his senses. Candy and popcorn, laughs and screams, thousands of sweat-sheened faces smiling through the hundred-year-old mechanical fun factory along the beach road. Music and funfairs, Mark's heart and soul.

He went into an arcade, drawn by the promise of giant fans working overtime and dollars to be made from the one-armed bandits. If you knew how to tease them you could switch roles and be the bandit yourself. Music blared and coins crashed and Mark let the place swallow him up.

He smiled as golden dollars cascaded into the metal tray with a rattle of riches. As he scooped them out a hand slapped on his shoulder.

"Marky Mark! What you doing tonight, man?"

He turned to see Greg and Craig standing behind him, flexing in their white singlets and board shorts, grinning under sun-bleached hair. "I dunno, guys, whatever. You?"

"Just hanging at the *carnivale*, my friend, as usual. Fuck all else to do, huh?" Greg's teeth were bright in his tanned face as coloured neon danced across his skin.

Craig leaned forward to be heard over the din. "We're gonna ride the Ghost Train. Goose the pretty girls and make 'em scream. Coming?"

Mark laughed, tipped his haul of coins into a pocket and followed them out into the dusty strip of shooting galleries and hooplas. They swaggered with the confidence of locals, standing proud among the tourists and day-trippers. *We're here all the time*, their walk said. *But you folks have fun now, you hear.*

After one ride through the cardboard and papier-mâché of the Ghost Train, Greg slipped away tailing a pretty blonde in tight denim shorts. Craig and Mark wasted a few dollars shooting dented metal targets with air rifles, threw wooden balls at coconuts they didn't want to win, chased after teenage city girls on holiday.

Mark looked at his watch. "I gotta go, man."

Craig frowned. "It's early. You sick or something?"

"No, man, I got a gig. Palisade, every Friday and Saturday for the last two years. How long have you known me?"

Craig's frown melted into a grin. "Cool! I'll come and watch. Well, I'll come and get drunk, but I like to listen to you guys knocking out twelve bars while I drink."

As they passed the switchback Mark watched the swirl of screaming faces in a blur of bright lights and blasting technopop. For a moment one pair of eyes caught his, frozen in time for a second, her scream spreading into a smile. She was the most beautiful girl he'd ever seen, deep green eyes and long, chestnut hair.

Craig dragged at his shoulder. "Come on, dude, you got me thirsting for a beer now."

Mark followed, the beauty lost in a rush of spinning lights and colour.

* * *

His band arrived at the Palisade in dribs and drabs as usual, taking the stage a bit after ten to a roomful of drunk locals and guarded holidaymakers. They pounded out their blues beats and worked up a sweat, the usual handful of hardcore fans grinding in front of the stage. Twice a week for two years they'd brought the Delta to the Palisade and Mark lived for it. But he wanted more. He wanted to play for crowds of thousands. He wanted to make music like Nick, sitting on the farm fence playing for no one. Well, no one but Mark, it seemed. He must have dreamed it, surely.

The thought of the strange young man and his perfect blues kept rising in Mark's mind, causing his bandmates to flick him concerned glances as he tripped over runs. Flustered, he dropped more notes, and their looks became annoyed. He shook the memory of the strange guitar player from his mind and rallied, but the gig was average at best.

As the night wore on and the cheap beer soaked in, he saw her again, the beauty from the fair. She watched him playing and his fingers flew as their eyes locked. He dredged up something special from the root of his being and closed out the set with a blistering cascade of sound.

His bandmates forgave him his earlier transgressions, slapping him on the back as they packed up their gear. But when he stepped off stage, the girl was nowhere to be found.

* * *

Lying on his bed that night, wishing again for a breeze through the window, Mark heard the strains of Nick's guitar flying softly through the dark. He whimpered, covered his head with his pillow, and ground his teeth until a fitful sleep took him.

* * *

The weekend arrived hot and bright like the week that birthed it, but a soft breeze carried some relief from the south. Mark rose late, made coffee, lazed on the veranda in nothing but shorts. He practiced his guitar licks, determined the entire next gig would be like the end of the night before and nothing like the start. By the time the afternoon sun cleared its zenith and began to soak the veranda in molten, golden heat, he dragged himself inside, dressed, and carried his battered guitar case out to the car.

He drove to the amusement park, WELCOME TO SALTSPRAY CITY, habit and ritual to avoid the inland afternoon swelter. Striped booths and painted clowns surrounded him as he lost himself among the sideshows, wondering about Nick and his promise. Was it possible? An offer at a crossroads in the middle of the night. Had it really happened? What would he be giving up if he agreed? What would he get?

He flicked a dollar to Sam in the glass booth at the foot of the big wheel. The wheel that had kept on turning for decades, carrying laughing people up for a view of the ocean, beach and town, spread out below them like a satellite map. He climbed into a split vinyl seat and let the wheel carry him up into the cool air a hundred feet above the carnival, the raucous sounds sliding quiet as he rose, swelling back with the descent.

At the top of the second rotation he leaned his elbows on the safety bar, letting the cool high air wash over the back of his neck, and looked down into the miniature tracks and weather-worn buildings. Cracks covered the roof of the dodgem arcade, power cables snaked through the air between fibro huts, balloons and pennons fluttered and danced in the soft, warmer breeze below.

And he saw her looking up at him. Her dark brown hair lay over her shoulders like a cape as she shaded her emerald eyes and smiled. So tiny, so far away, yet the only thing not lost in the blur. As the big wheel swept around, carrying him down, Mark stood against the bar. 'Sammy! Hey, Sammy, you gotta let me off.'

Sam leaned forward in his worn seat, dark stains under the arms of his T-shirt. He grinned and stabbed a button with one meaty finger and the wheel paused. Mark flicked him a wink of thanks and lifted the bar, hopping free of the chair. The wheel began to slide by him as he walked casually down the aluminium steps. She waited for him, still smiling.

"I thought that was you," she said. "I saw you yesterday."

Mark nodded. "Yeah, you were on the switchback. Then you came to the Palisade and watched us play, right?"

"Yeah."

"What's your name?"

She looked up at him under a dark, feathered fringe. "Let's not worry about names. I prefer strangers."

Mark raised an eyebrow. "Really? Okay. You wanna grab a drink? Something to eat?"

"Sure."

They spent the afternoon eating cotton candy and hot dogs, riding on the carousel and the switchback and the rollercoaster. They laughed and joked, played tricks on unsuspecting tourists. Mark asked if she was on holiday or if she lived nearby, but she refused to say, playing games with him as much as everyone else. He didn't mind, her company thrilled him. He showed her the tiled coolness of Tony's Tattoos, smelling of antiseptic and buzzing with needles, where he'd got his ink. "It's a kind of ritual self-torture, you know? You got any?"

She dipped her eyes, didn't answer.

The afternoon dimmed, cooled into evening and the evening wore on and Mark started checking his watch. She smiled at him after the third time. "Am I boring you?"

"No! Quite the opposite. I want to hang out with you, but I've got to go soon."

"Playing at the Palisade again, right?"

"Yeah, you gonna come down? We could have a drink or two afterwards."

She smiled. "Maybe. Hey look!"

She spun away, catching his hand as she went and dragged him up creaking wooden steps to a booth. He smiled as he read the words painted in pinks and reds, TUNNEL OF LOVE.

She pushed coins into the scratched plastic tray. "Give me two, mister."

Old Bill Denton, all grey stubble and yellow teeth, gave Mark a strange look as he took her coins, slipped two short tickets back to her. Mark grinned, still holding her hand, and let her lead him into a poor imitation of an Italian gondola. They rattled and wobbled through heavy velvet curtains into the darkness of the ride, soft reds and blues lighting romantic vistas poorly cut from cardboard and plywood. Soft music played, half drowned by the distant throb of the cacophony outside. She turned to him and slipped one leg over his knee and her arms around his neck and kissed him. Mark returned the kiss, enjoying the anonymous excitement of it.

When the shoddy gondola emerged into the noisy evening of the amusement park mere seconds and a lifetime later, Mark felt as though something had changed inside him. They stepped out of the ride, holding hands back to the strip and the lights and the noise. Mark led her between sideshows, away from the bustling crowds, determined to enjoy more of what she'd given him on the ride, this perfect angel.

"Don't you need to get going?" she asked, pulling him to a stop between a dirty white prefab wall and a rumbling diesel generator.

He looked at his watch, wincing at the time. He would be late. "Yeah. Come with me!"

She reached behind her neck, undid the clasp on a silver chain. She pulled a locket from her smooth cleavage and held it up between them. It turned gently, reflecting a hundred colours from a thousand stuttering bulbs. He tipped his head to one side, confused. As he opened his mouth to ask questions, she kissed him, silencing him with her tongue. He felt her hand slip into his pocket.

She broke off the kiss, left him feeling like she'd taken his breath away with her. He gasped air into his lungs as she walked back towards the crowded strip.

"Hey!" he called after her. "Come to the gig tonight, please? I'll buy you a drink afterwards."

She looked back over her shoulder, blew him a kiss. He could have run after her, caught up and made her promise to come along, but something made him stay.

"If you don't come to the gig, I'll see you here again tomorrow maybe?" His voice was lost in the noise of the generator as she slipped into the passing crowd like the sun swallowed by clouds.

He pulled her silver locket out, wondering if maybe her phone number was in it. When he popped it open he found nothing but a tiny dried flower tucked under the delicate folded silver edges.

* * *

The Palisade seemed both busy and empty as Mark tried to find the high point from the night before. He watched the crowd but saw no sign of her shining chestnut hair or glittering green eyes.

The music was dead and empty, disappointed like his soul, and the crowd thinned before closing time. His fingers were clumsy through the last songs and he couldn't wait for the end. If only he could find that high from the night before, the closing symphony of blues that had washed away three hours of mistakes and missed rhythms. If only he could play like Nick on the farm fence.

He ground his teeth and endured the berating of his mates after the gig. He made excuses about tiredness, too much heat, working too hard. Clive, the tall, rangy bass player, made a snide remark about needing to get laid or something, and Mark winced at the inadvertent truth of the observation.

* * *

That night, alone in the heat, frustrated and disappointed, he heard Nick's guitar again, calling out across the paddocks. With a snarl of anger he turned his stereo on, drowning out the mocking talent with strident throbs of Led Zeppelin. Eventually a troubled sleep took him.

* * *

Mark spent all day and all evening Sunday searching through the carousels and arcades, looking everywhere for a sweep of shining brown hair. He knew he wouldn't find her, but searched all the same, hoping against hope. His friends found him a couple of times and he brushed them off, ignoring their confused, hurt faces.

As the amusement park began shutting down and turning off for the night, lights going out, boards filling booth windows, Mark sat on railings in the dark, chin in his hand. The ocean shushed the sand at his back and people thinned out until nothing was left but the comatose carnival, all closed wooden eyes and shadows, waiting for the return of the people that were its lifeblood.

Mark slipped off the railing and scuffed his shoes along the seafront, staring at the concrete sliding by, feeling like a fool.

* * *

He found himself back at home in the early hours of the morning, tired and miserable. He hung the locket from the corner of the mirror in his bedroom and fell onto the bed. He would be a zombie at the factory the next day, dangerously fatigued. He didn't care. Nothing mattered but the girl without a name and he didn't know why. Would he ever get his blues back without her? Had she stolen more than his heart? He'd had flings with girls on holiday a hundred times, one of the reasons he hung out at the fair so much. But this girl had been special.

The sound of Nick's guitar drifting through the still night air didn't make him angry any more. Simply resigned. He pulled himself off the bed and walked with heavy steps through the house, across the veranda, along the dusty road.

Nick sat on the fence in the moonlight, playing his blood red guitar. Mark approached and stood there, head tipped back to the sky, tears pouring down his cheeks as Nick's magic floated up through the stars.

Eventually one last note slipped away into the night, sustained for minutes before nothing but dark silence accompanied the two men.

"I knew you'd come back," Nick said softly, his voice kind.

"What will it cost me?" Mark asked. "To play like you."

"I think you know." Nick laid his guitar across his knees, looking at Mark with soft eyes.

Mark's own eyes were still wet, his cheeks glistening. "It's too high," he said in a thin voice. "That price is too high."

"Is it? For such a gift?"

They were silent again, the zephyr breeze gently caressing their hair. "What made you change your mind?" Nick asked. "Why did you come back tonight?"

"I feel like I already lost...something. All I have is my music."

"Lost something?"

Mark sniffed, looked Nick right in the eyes. "A girl," he said, still stunned that she'd had such an effect on him. "I can live without her if I have the music. I could live without anything if I had your music. But the price is too high." He turned to leave.

"Wait." Nick's eyes were dark, almost black. He reached into the pocket of his pale denim shirt and pulled something free. "What if I gave you her as well?"

Fresh tears started from Mark's eyes as he watched the silver locket turn slowly, reflecting pure white moonlight.

SIMULACRUM OF HOPE

I HEARD THE ARGUMENT FROM MY ROOM and tried to ignore it, but thin walls mean there are no secrets in this house. Last night was a bad one. Right before the front door slammed a little after midnight, Mum spat, "I wish I'd never met you. I wasted my life on you!"

I heard Dad crying, thought maybe I should go and hug him or something. But I'm the kid here. I'm Beau's older brother, sure, he's only nine. I hug *him* when *he* cries. At twelve I'm not about to pretend I'm an adult. Dad should be the strong one. I guess he never really was.

I let him cry and he got quieter, and then it felt like I was the only one awake in the house. The only one awake in the world, except perhaps Mum driving down the dirt road to the highway, and then what? Left or right? Inland or out to the coast five hours away? I wonder if she'll come back, and can't decide if I want her to or not. I hardly slept, and Dad came in at seven, forcing a cheery smile.

"Breakfast, Adso?"

"Don't call me that."

His smile faltered and I felt bad for a moment.

"Sorry, Adam," he said. Whimpering even to me. "You want breakfast? I made scrambled eggs."

Guilt trod over me. "Yeah. You make the best eggs!"

His smile broke out again, and that was okay because I wasn't lying. His eggs are great.

"Where's Mama?" Beau asked over his plate of toast crumbs.

I was surprised it had taken him that long to question it. I guess even he knew something was up. Was he awake and listening last night too?

"Mum had to go away for a day or two," Dad said, trying to sound all casual and upbeat. I could see his throat gulping as he held back emotion.

"Where to?"

"She just needed space, Bucko. She'll be back soon."

Beau stared at his plate. Silence grew, became a thing with weight that pressed against our backs, made us hunch over the remains of the meal. A single tear dropped onto Beau's plate, and Dad shattered the stillness with a scrape of his chair as he stood up too fast.

"We need to chop wood and feed the chooks, lads. Come on, just because it's Saturday doesn't mean we can be lazy."

* * *

Mum didn't come back Saturday or Sunday. Dad kept checking his phone, going to the kitchen window and staring up the driveway to the gate, which he'd left open. He never does that. It's not like Mum doesn't know how to open the damn thing. I think he was maybe trying to draw her back in. It didn't work.

On Monday he left for work early and I helped Beau get ready for school. Normally Mum would be there with us, Dad always left before six. I knew the routine, and so did Beau. We walked out of the house, up to the end of the dirt road in silence. The day was already hot, late autumn heat where you can feel the change of season coming, but it's not quite ready yet. It takes about fifteen minutes to walk from the house to where the bus picks us up, and in all that time Beau never said a word. Then when we were standing there, kicking at the dust, swinging our bodies to make our school bags flap side to side on our shoulders, he said, "She's not coming back, is she."

It wasn't a question and something inside me cracked at the tiny voice he used. Like he was admitting it, not asking it. And I didn't want to lie to him. Among everything else, he and I had to be together. "I don't know, B-boy."

He looked up at me, eyes wet but defiant. His cheeks were smeared with dirt. We'd only walked up the drive, how the hell was he dirty already? "She's not."

I shrugged. "We'll see."

"What'll we do when she doesn't come back?"

"We'll be all right, little bro." And I meant it. He and I, we'd be all right. Somehow.

"And what about Dad?"

That was harder to answer. But I'd promised myself I wouldn't lie to him. "I don't know," was all I could think to say.

Thankfully the bus appeared over the hill then, trailing a rooster tail of red dust, old Mrs. Peabody's squinty face framed in the glass as she hunched over the wheel.

* * *

We got home from school both wondering if we'd find Mum in the kitchen, cold lemonade in a jug, asking how our day went. Neither of us said so, but the hope hung heavy and thick. As we walked through the open gate the house was still closed up like we'd left it, and our shoulders sagged.

I went in and made lemonade anyway, Mum had shown me how. We sat on the front porch, where it's shady in the afternoon because the house faces east towards the ocean so far away. And as we sipped lemonade, enjoying the freedom of no more school until the next day, a woman came walking along the dirt road.

Something stuttered in my chest when I saw her, she was so familiar and such a stranger at the same time. Maybe mid-twenties, long blonde hair in a wavy fall over her shoulders, narrow face with high cheekbones. Slim, walking confidently, her face opened up in a smile as she saw us there in the shadow of the house.

"My boys!" she said, just like Mum used to, and then I realised why she was so familiar.

Her picture was all over the house. Her and Dad in Sydney in the nineties, wearing denim and looking crazy at some grunge festival. Another of her standing beside a new car in the main street forty kilometres from here. Another of her in a big white dress, standing beside Dad, laughing as confetti fell all around them outside St Mary's Church.

"Who is it?" Beau whispered, and my heart was hammering because it was her, but it was impossible.

Mum was forty-four years old, she'd had a party in town about a month ago. Sarah from the property next door had come to babysit. Then her and Dad got home late, drunk, and there had been another of those venomous arguments. Except that time Mum slammed her bedroom door and Dad slept in the spare room. This woman walking towards us was Mum, but half a lifetime ago.

Her eyes narrowed as she got closer, the smile faltering when she saw my face. I guess I looked terrified.

"What's the matter, you two? Everything okay?"

Beau leaned right close to my ear and said, "Is it Mum?" His voice quavered with the same confusion and fear that rippled through me.

"You don't recognise me?" she said. Beau and I exchanged a glance and she laughed. "I've only been away a couple of days. Do you forgive me?"

"You look different," Beau said.

She smiled again. "I *feel* different. I feel fresh and renewed. I just needed a little break."

"Where's your car?" I asked.

She frowned at that, like she was trying to think of something. "It broke down in town. I got a lift with…Joe. He dropped me at the end of the road. What are you drinking there? It looks good."

"Lemonade."

"You made it?"

"Yep."

She beamed again. "You'll have to show me how."

Beau stood up, angry and confused. "You know how! You taught Adam!" He looked at me then back at Mum, belligerent with fear.

She paused, eyes moving rapidly like she was having a tiny seizure, then the smile broke out again. "Of course, silly me. I remember. Let's go inside and I'll make some more."

"We've had enough!" Beau turned and ran to his room.

Impossible young Mum looked at me. "You want some more?"

"I have to feed the chickens."

I walked away, not sure what else to do. I heard Beau's door slam and knew he wouldn't open it again any time soon, so I figured he was safe. I kept one eye on the kitchen window as I poured grain into plastic feeders. The young woman sat at the Formica table in there and stared straight ahead, patiently waiting for something.

After the chickens were sorted out I went down the back paddock to the dam and stood staring across the big pond of muddy water. I skipped a couple of stones, noticed the level had dropped a bit, but it was still full enough from the rain last month. Dad once said he wanted to put some fingerlings in and we could sit on the short wooden jetty and fish for them and Mum had called him an idiot. Said nothing would survive for long in there. I wish she hadn't said that even if it was true. She never even came down here. I kinda wish we were fishing off that ridiculous little jetty now, with its half-rotten planks. You had to jump over the fourth and fifth ones, they were no better than balsa wood. Dad kept saying he would fix them but never did. This dam needs some better memories.

We used to have a dog, a sandy mutt called Rex who was the friendliest creature you ever saw. One day he chased a roo across the back paddock and the roo bounced real fast into the dam. I thought it was going to drown, but Rex went right in after it and the roo turned around and grabbed hold of Rex and held him under the water until *he* drowned. I was too little then to do anything but stare in horror and scream. My dad came running, even brought the old shotgun we hardly ever used because my screams were so pitched. But it was too late, Rex already floating and still, the fur of his back rippling on the surface. The roo scrambled out the other side of the dam and I wanted Dad to shoot it anyway, but Dad said no. It's sad but just nature. I cried for a week. Apparently roos do that, my dad said. They run to water and drown things to protect themselves. Clever, ruthless bastards. I still miss Rex so much it hurts.

I couldn't think of anything else to do, and staring at the dam only made me feel worse, so I snuck past the kitchen window and went back inside, and into Beau's room.

"I don't like this," he said, understating everything. I just agreed with him and tried to distract him with games and comics.

I wanted Dad to come home, he was the grown up. He'd have to do something, he'd have an explanation.

* * *

When we heard Dad's car pull up, we hurried into the hallway. Not-mum was still sitting at the kitchen table, exactly as she had been two hours before. Silence fell as Dad turned off the engine and she looked out the window. A smile grew across her face.

We both held our breath as Dad walked into the house and into the kitchen. He stopped dead when he saw her, kind of shuddered on the spot in shock. His eyes went wide then narrow, his mouth opening and closing like those stupid fish that would never be put in the dam.

"Katy?" he managed at last.

She stood up and went to him, draped her arms around his neck. "Let's not fight any more," she said.

Dad shook his head, pushed her back away from him. I smiled, here it came. Here's where Dad demanded to know what the hell was going on.

"Katy, is it really you?"

What?

"Of course it is. You don't recognise me?"

"You look…" He shook his head again like he was trying to clear some kind of ringing in his ears. "You're young."

"Only one year younger than you."

"No, you look like you did… Like… How can this be happening?"

She stood back, tilted her head to one side like a confused puppy. "What are you saying?"

Dad stepped back into the hallway and grabbed pictures off the wall. One of the wedding with the big dress and the confetti, the other from last Christmas. In the second one Mum was fifteen kilos heavier, those high cheek bones lost under starting-to-wrinkle flesh. The long blonde hair from the wedding day had been cut short, a severe and pugnacious cut Dad had called it when he first saw it.

He waved the Christmas photo. "This is you now. But you look like this again!" And he waved the wedding photo.

She looked from one picture to the other and back, her eyes doing that juddering thing. A crease between her eyebrows came and went a couple of times, like she was trying to remember something. Then the smile spread once more, her face softening into its youthful beauty. "I guess the break did me good."

"Two days, Katy! You can't lose all that weight, grow all that hair in two days." Dad shook his head, face creased with conflicting emotions. "You're young again. How...? How can it...?" He fell silent, staring.

Beau looked up at me and I looked down at him. I shrugged. It was all too confusing, I had no idea what was happening.

"It's a miracle, I guess," she said. She moved forward and put her arms back around Dad's neck. She pressed her body hard against his and kissed him.

He was stiff for a moment, resistant, then he seemed to flop against her. I felt a kind of charge in the air.

"I don't want us to fight any more," she said. "Let's go back to what it was like before, yeah?"

There was a tear in Dad's eye and I hated that little gleam of light. How could he be so weak and useless?

"I want that more than anything, but..." he said.

She kissed him again and he was even floppier. What was she doing to him? This wasn't right, wasn't a miracle, there was something horribly wrong. Then Beau was running from my side and into the kitchen.

"Mummy, is it really you?"

"Yes, darling, it's me."

Beau looked to Dad and Dad was smiling, almost laughing. "Yes, it's your mum," he said, sounding drunk. "I don't know how, but it's your mum, as vibrant and beautiful as I remember her."

She kissed him again. His eyes were glazed over when she moved away. "I'll make dinner!" she said. "A big family feast!"

Beau stared hard at Dad for another moment, making sure it was okay for this to be all right. He was too young to understand how weak our father was. He needed stability and safety. He looked at me and I shrugged. After a moment he jumped up and down. "Yay!"

She crouched and kissed his cheek then gestured to the table. He and Dad sat down. She paused and looked down the hallway to me, one eyebrow popping up. I stared back, refusing to offer any kind of expression. She smiled then, like she'd won something, and turned away to the fridge.

* * *

It was a good dinner but tasted like dirt in my mouth nonetheless. Dad and Beau were happy and laughing, she was all smiles and gentle touches to their hands. At one point Dad turned to me, took in my sour expression.

"Can't you just be happy for me?" he asked dreamily.

For him? It was all about him. I pushed my plate away. "I'm full. I've got homework." And I went to my room, not listening to whatever he said next.

A half hour later Beau came in, looked at me with those innocent brown eyes. "It's okay, right?" he asked.

What could I say? He needed to feel safe. "Sure it is, B-boy."

"So why aren't you happy? Dad's happy, so's Mum."

"I know. I'm happy for them too."

"So it's okay?" he asked again.

It hurt, how much he trusted me. How much he needed to hear this from me. It pissed me off that he couldn't be looked after by his mum and dad. Well, by his dad at least, because I was pretty sure our mum had gone. Whoever that was in there, it wasn't her. But our dad was useless and no one was going to look after me, so I had to look after Beau. "Yeah, it's okay." I forced a grin and ruffled his hair.

He slapped my hand away with a laugh and for a moment we wrestled like everything really was okay. He turned the wrestle into a hug, which wasn't something he ever normally did. Then he was gone, out the door, and in a few minutes I heard him splashing in the bath. Her making silly noises and joking with him.

Dad looked around my door. "You okay, Ads?"

"Are you?" I asked, sarcasm heavy in my tone.

He stared at me for a moment, couldn't hold my eye. He looked down at the floorboards, then turned away, quietly shut the door. Weak fucking prick.

The noises coming from my parent's room an hour later, clear through those thin walls, made me grind my teeth. She cajoled, the bed creaked, Dad grunted and gasped, said, "Oh my god!" so many times.

The last sound I heard before everything went quiet was a soft chuckle from her. It sounded somehow accomplished.

* * *

I woke before dawn, torn with worry, the house dark and still. Then I heard movement and Dad was up and making tea, shaving, eating toast and marmalade. The same routine he followed every weekday. The same one he'd followed my whole life. But there was added soft humming this time, jaunty little tunes escaping him. They made me furious.

After I heard his car pull away, I crept along the hallway, looked into their bedroom. She lay there on the bed, head on the pillow, face towards the door. As I watched, her eyes popped open. Twice. First the eyelids, then some kind of thin nictitating membrane slid back from beneath them. In the low light her pupils seemed to be shaped like Xs before filling out to black circles. I gasped, took an involuntary step back. She smiled without moving anything but her mouth, stared at me, unblinking. Too much time passed while I waited, stupidly, willing her to blink, to move some other part of her body, but she was still as rock, eyes wide.

Biting back a sob I went to wake Beau and get us off to school.

* * *

On the bus coming home, I suggested that Beau go and play at Charlie Baker's house. They were good pals, and Charlie's mum always met him at the bus, one stop before our place. Beau was cool with it, so was Charlie. Mrs. Baker said, "I'll have Joe drop him home after dinner."

"What about a sleepover?" I suggested.

Mrs. Baker smiled. "Not on a school night. Maybe this weekend?"

"Okay."

The bus had gone and I had a two-kilometre walk home from Charlie's stop but was okay with that. It gave me time to think. Two Ks later I still had no plan. What the hell was I supposed to do? What can a twelve-year-old do about anything?

I walked down the dirt road to our house and she was in the kitchen window, staring without blinking.

"Where's Beau?" she asked.

"Hanging at Charlie's. Charlie's dad'll drop him home after dinner."

"Why did you do that, Adam?" Her voice was dangerously low.

I didn't really know why I'd done it. I just wanted Beau somewhere else, but I'd only bought him a few hours.

"Don't you want us to be a happy family?" she asked.

"You're not our family."

Her eyes darkened, a flash of what looked like pure hatred passed over her face. Suddenly nauseated, I ran to my room and closed the door.

* * *

Dad came home happy, like everything was just dandy. I stayed in my room, starving but refusing to emerge for dinner. Dad suggested to her that maybe I was becoming a surly teen a little early, like I was the one with the problem. Beau got back over-tired and went pretty much straight to bed. When Joe dropped him off I asked quietly, "Did you drop Mum home from town on Monday?" He frowned and shook his head.

The noises from their room were the same as the night before, appalling, frantic. When everything went still I crept to the kitchen and made sandwiches with leftovers in the fridge, my stomach churning.

When I turned back to the table, there she was, standing in the doorway, naked. I yelped, nearly dropped the food. My whole body began to tremble.

"You won't spoil this. I won't let you."

I stared, mouth dry, lost for words.

"I won't be here long anyway." She gave me a vicious smile and turned away, making absolutely no sound as she slid back into their bedroom.

My appetite was gone, but I forced the food down anyway because I felt like I might need the strength it would give me.

* * *

In my room, I sat in the dark, wide-eyed, unable to sleep. Through the thin walls I heard a sound I didn't recognise. At first I thought it was snoring, but it was wetter than that. Unable to ignore it, I snuck along the hallway and peeked through the small gap where my parent's door stood ajar.

She crouched over my dad as he slept on his back, her spine arched unnaturally high, lumpy ridges of oversized vertebrae showing through taut skin. Her arms were too long, her arse a pointed jutting of bone covered with stretched, grey flesh, legs stick thin. Her tits hung down like deflated inner tubes, brushing my father's chest as she sucked at his mouth. Her neck rippled and gulped.

I held in a terrified sob and hurried silently back to my room and cried into my pillow until sleep took me.

* * *

I got up when I heard Dad moving around the next morning, going through that infuriating, undeviating routine. I met him in the kitchen and he looked over at me and smiled. There were dark bags under his eyes, his cheeks a little hollow. He looked like he'd lost a couple of kilos, his eyes still glazed.

"Hey, Ads."

"You okay, Dad?"

He nodded, smiled. "I'm really tired this morning for some reason, but I'm good. Question is, are *you* okay? I need you to be okay with this."

He needs it. Doesn't *want* me to be okay, doesn't *hope* I'm okay. It's what *he* needs from me. I looked over his drawn frame, remembered her words, *I won't be here long anyway.* He had no idea of the manipulation going on.

I should let his weak ass suffer, let her have him, but then who would pay the bills? I didn't want to go into care. I didn't want Beau to lose everyone. But what the hell could I do?

"I'm fine, Dad."

He smiled again, raised his mug of tea in a toast. "Thanks, Champ."

Fucking loser. I went back to my room.

* * *

After school I tried to send Beau off to Charlie's again, but he told me Charlie had family visiting. As we trudged through the afternoon heat, kicking up dust, I said, "I need you to go to your room when we get home, okay? Stay there for a little while."

"Why?"

"I need to talk to Mum about some stuff."

"What stuff? You still don't trust her, do you? Don't spoil things, Adam, she's finally happy again."

I squeezed his thin, bony shoulder, so tiny under the pale blue school shirt. "It's okay, B-boy. I just want to ask her some stuff."

He stared up at me for a moment, then nodded, kicking stones as we carried on home. When we got there, Beau went to his room like I'd asked. He was a good boy all the way through. I stopped by the chook shed, tipped some grain into the feeders, and grabbed a roll of wire we use to repair the fencing. I stuffed the wire into the back of my pants then went inside.

She was in the kitchen, unnaturally still in that way of hers she hid from everyone except me. Without moving any other part of her body, her eyes swivelled to me as I entered. Those nictitating membranes blinked across from either side and back again, mocking me.

"What are you planning, little monkey?" she asked.

I took a deep breath, tried to ignore the vibrations in my heart. "I get it, okay. But I need to show you something."

A smile spread across her face like blood soaking through a white shirt. "That right?"

"Please? I need you to understand something about us before I let him go."

She tipped her head to one side, unblinking. Eventually she stood, sudden enough to make me dance backwards. "Okay then." She waited.

Swallowing hard I turned and walked from the house, out across the yard and down through the back paddock. Afternoon sun glittered off the brown water in the dam as we approached and I stood on the hard mud at the start of the pathetic little jetty. I gestured to it.

"After you."

"What do you think you're doing?" Her eyes were narrowed but still unblinking. "You're a *child*."

It was an insult and the truth. What the fuck was I thinking? But I had to do something.

They do that. They run to water and drown things to protect themselves.

"After you," I said again.

She shrugged, a mocking half-smile hitching up one side of her young, perfect mouth. She walked along the jetty confidently, then cried out as she went right through the fourth plank.

She thrashed, past her waist in the water, mud sucking at her feet. Her eyes flashed fury, but amusement too. I raced forward, reached down with the wire, looped it around one of her wrists. She hissed as I hauled on it, biting into that fake flesh. I wrapped another loop around her other arm as she reached up, elation starting to rise like sun over storm clouds, and I held her arms up over her head, bound her wrists together. Maybe this *would* work. I jumped up and came down on the rotten boards, went right through and crashed into her back, smashing her down into the water. She went under face first as I drove my knees into her back, pushing against the jetty above.

"Drown, you fucking beast!" I yelled, tears pouring over my cheeks, lost in the churning brown dam water.

Then her arms extended backwards, against nature, and she popped that wire apart like it was cotton thread. Her shoulders rose up out of the water and her head swivelled too far around to look at me, laughing, those pupils back to Xs, pulsing with a sickly green luminescence. I screamed as she took hold of my arms and flipped me over, then dragged us out from under the jetty towards the middle of the broad dam. Her shoulders and neck rolled and popped and she took on the semblance of normal shape again.

"You're just a *child!*" she said through incredulous laughter. She drove me down, brown water closing over my face, the sun a hazy, indistinct blur making her a silhouette that shivered with the swell and churn. My lungs began to burn, then she pulled me up again. I gasped in air, tasted dirt and silt.

She sneered, then dunked me under again. I thrashed and kicked, could only think of poor Rex and how he'd done the same, to no avail. I remembered his fur moving softly once everything else was still and Dad wading out to collect his body.

She pulled me up again, face split in a too-wide grin. "I'll make this last!" Then her head exploded in a red mist and a fraction of a second later my ears, roaring with my blood, registered the boom.

She toppled over on me and I squirmed out from underneath her suddenly lax weight, coughing up water. Beau sat on the muddy bank, crying as he held his shoulder where the shotgun had kicked back and flattened him. I rushed over as the thing's blood fanned out into the dam, her body drifting slowly towards the other side.

"I knew it was too good to be true," Beau sobbed as I gathered him in my arms.

He cried into my soaked shoulder as I held him and stroked his hair. "You saved my life, B-boy."

We sat together, shivering in the afternoon heat, and waited for Dad to get home.

HOW
FATHER BRYANT
SAW THE LIGHT

FATHER BRYANT FROWNED AS HE APPROACHED THE MAN IN RAGS beside the front gate of the church. Matted beard, sallow eyes, stench apparent even through the late afternoon rain. And sunglasses. Bryant crouched before him, did his best not to let his disgust show.

"Don't you have somewhere dry to go?"

The man jumped, looked past Bryant, and the priest realised he was blind. "Let me in the church?" the hobo asked in a voice like sandpaper over fresh wounds.

"Sorry, I have a mass starting any moment. Unless you mean to seek the absolution of God, then of course you'd be welcome."

The man laughed, low and phlegmy. "Absolution? Hardly."

"Perhaps I can give you some money for a meal?"

"Get me away from your door, eh? Make me someone else's problem."

Bryant held out a note, crackled it with his fingers so the tramp could hear. "I wish you well, that's all," he said honestly. "Somewhere dry and a meal."

The man took the money, struggled to his feet. "Thanks." He produced a foldable cane, straightened it, and tapped on the pavement ahead of him as he moved away.

"God bless you," Bryant said.

The man tipped back his head to release gales of laughter as he trudged away into the rain.

Bryant entered the church and busied himself with preparations. The poor fellow outside lingered in his mind even as the odour lingered in his nostrils. Too many people were broken by the world. He wished more would find the peace he had. At least today the man would eat.

* * *

Parishioners began filing in. Bryant smiled, wished them well as they took their seats. After six months in this new appointment, he was beginning to feel settled, comfortable in the arms of the Lord. He surveyed his small church, his first parish. A peach of a placement for a young man fresh from seminary.

He delivered more or less the sermon he had prepared, but adjusted due to his encounter with the blind man. He ad-libbed sections about caring for everyone, especially those less fortunate, easily bringing to mind memorised passages from the Bible.

Bryant smiled again as his parishioners left, their spiritual lives fulfilled for another week. A good job done. At least, he hoped so. He had yet to hear any complaints, and their thanks seemed genuine enough. Mrs. Paisley complimented him on a heartfelt sermon and old Jim Clarendon shook hands vigorously and thanked him for keeping death from the door.

"It's hard being this old," Clarendon said. "You keep me alive."

Bryant laughed. "I think it's more your own tenaciousness and God's will, Jim, but thank you."

The old man winked conspiratorially and moved away, bent and shuffling over a shiny, gnarled oak cane.

A woman approached against the flow of exiting faithful. She guided a young girl beside her. The child looked on the verge of tears.

Bryant tried to remember the woman's name, but it didn't come before she reached him. "Hello," he said simply.

"Father, excuse us for using your valuable time."

"My time is yours."

"I'm Carol Clarke." The woman nudged the girl forward. "It's my daughter, Nadia. She has been having terrible dreams. I wondered if you might talk to her? Comfort her?"

"Not dreams," Nadia muttered.

Bryant took in the face of the young parishioner, open, honest, but frightened under dark curls. The mother showed true fear in her eyes and that disquieted him. Some people were full of melodrama and the child no doubt fed off her mother's trepidations. He'd seen it before. No wonder the girl was upset.

He crouched in front of her. "How old are you, Nadia?"

"Seven."

How big could her problems be? "Tell me about your dreams."

The child's eyes held a conviction that slowed Bryant's blood in his veins. "Not dreams!" she said again, stronger. Tears rolled over rounded cheeks.

Mrs. Clarke looked beseechingly at Bryant, then walked quietly away. He watched her go for a moment before turning Nadia to sit on a pew beside him.

"Take a breath." He handed her a tissue from his pocket. "Tell me about it."

The dim interior of the church was cool, a gentle aroma of incense strangely cloying. Weak streetlight filtered through stained-glass to make a silhouette of Christ on the cross above the altar. His shadow fell across them like a benediction.

Nadia looked up, eyes suddenly dry and sharp. "You know it's the truth. In your heart, you feel it."

Mature words from a seven-year-old. "What truth?" Bryant asked.

"He's a monster, but looks like a man."

"What...?"

Nadia fixed the priest with her gaze, face firm, but her voice was soft. "You know the part of the night that seems deepest, there's nothing darker or stiller? From then, it's a slow rise back to morning? Some nights it's like that for *hours*. That's when he comes, the Gangle Man."

Bryant swallowed, though his mouth was dry. No child should speak this way. "The Gangle Man?"

"He's tall and thin, skin white as bone. He wears a tall hat. He holds his hands up like my nanna coming in for a kiss. Except he wants my eyes."

Chills tickled over Bryant's skin. "Your eyes?"

"His lips are like a cat's tongue. You know what that feels like, Father, when a cat licks you?"

Bryant nodded.

Nadia frowned. "His lips are like that, only as if they're made of cold metal. And he finds an eye and his tongue opens my eyelids and he starts to suck, and I scream and scream. I feel his nails drumming my ears and he moans and sucks and sucks."

Bryant blanched. "Nadia…"

"And as I feel my eye begin to squash, about to pop into his mouth, he's gone. Like he was never there, but my face is cold. It hurts like a headache, right behind that eye. One day he's going to keep sucking and he'll take my eye, then the other one and then I'll…" Nadia devolved into tears, wracking sobs convulsed her as she folded into herself on the pew. Tumbles of brown hair fell over her hands as she covered her face.

Bryant drew a ragged breath and moved nearer, put an arm around the child's shoulders. Whether he sought to comfort her or himself with the contact, he wasn't sure.

* * *

Bryant sat in the quiet vestry and sipped smoky single malt. The way she spoke, the words she used… It had to be abuse. So often, the most damage was caused at the hands of men, usually those very close to the victim, and it stripped childhood away. Perhaps the suppressed stress gave her icy headaches.

Hopefully he could help her, in life normal and spiritual. Bryant had looked for succour as a kid and eventually found the Bible. It was the letter of James that spoke to him, chapter four, verse seven, 'Submit yourselves therefore to God. Resist the devil, and he will flee from you.' And right there he had found a path, to God, to the priesthood, and all his fears had withered in the wake of his convictions.

He had suggested a counsellor for Nadia but Carol Clarke had been reluctant, of course. So he'd told her he would visit the house the following evening. See the family, the home. Fulfil his role. Then maybe think about more secular professionals if he could see any evidence of abuse.

* * *

Bryant's dreams were troubled. Dark and damp pervaded unclear rooms and endless corridors. He woke repeatedly and stared, shivering, into the shadows until sleep crept over him again.

A pale man stood beckoning, one finger crooked, his eyes alive with a sparkle that came from no light source nearby. The man smiled with his lips closed, a dark line like a scar in a chalk-white face. He was tall and thin, wore an old-fashioned three-piece suit and top hat, threadbare and ragged. Long, dark, greasy strands of hair lay over his shoulders. Bleached ears poked out to either side.

Bryant tried to run but the pasty stranger didn't get any further away. And still he beckoned. Still he smiled. Bryant woke with a start. Sleep didn't come again. The child's strange ability to describe her nightmares had sunk deep into his psyche, where monsters already lived.

* * *

In the morning, Bryant tried to reach the bishop, though he knew the man was uncontactable for two more days, the Synod a time of closed doors. Bryant was a young man in an old man's profession, still trying to find his way. Without immediate guidance he pored half-heartedly through psychiatric books and websites. It was a fool's errand, he had no light by which to guide himself in the morass of information.

If the child externalised some form of abuse or trauma, he was unqualified to recognise it. Yet of that he was most afraid, and thought it most likely, though doubt tickled his hindbrain. He knew nothing to help her beyond referral to social services, and that was fraught with complications.

Eventually he knelt before his altar and prayed until the weak light through the stained glass began to fade. He begged God for direction, questioned why such an innocent soul could be so distressed. When he rose, stiff and aching, he felt no closer to a solution.

Someone stood in the shadows by the door.

"Can I help you?" he called out.

A voice whispered something too quiet to hear. Or did it? Had he imagined the sound?

He caught a glimpse of a top hat and ran to the spot but no one was there. He returned to the vestry, reached for the bottle and filled the tumbler, desperate to drink the sharp edges off his nerves. Like usual. Hiding in a bottle. If he was honest, God had never been quite enough.

* * *

The twilight sky was leaden, clouds low over terraced townhouses. Bryant pulled his collar up against gusting drizzle and walked from his car to the home, a weight of expectation on his back. Families were capable of such cruelty to each other, he was thankful to only answer to Christ and the pope. And only one of those really mattered. Rome was further away than Heaven. He took a deep breath and rapped on the front door.

It opened almost immediately, Nadia's mother hollow-eyed and pale in the gap. "Thank you for coming."

"Everything okay, Mrs. Clarke?"

"Carol, please." She hung her head. "Such screams last night. The poor child is…" She lost her voice to a sob and Bryant put a hand on her shoulder.

"I'll talk with her."

The house was tidy and clean, floral carpets and comfortable furniture throughout. Carol muttered something about tea and pointed to a room on her right. Nadia sat on the floor, surrounded by colourful books.

"Hello, Father!"

Bryant smiled, sat on the edge of a sofa, elbows on his knees. The smell of fresh bread and something else, savoury and delicious, hung on the air. He scanned the room, took in the family photos on the mantelpiece, several generations in smiling groups. "Do you have brothers or sisters?" he asked the little girl.

Nadia shook her head, holding a book in each hand.

"Where's daddy?"

"Working."

"What does he do?"

"He sells...um..."

"Insurance, sweetie." Carol held a tray with cups and a teapot.

Bryant took an offered cup. "Away a lot, is he?"

"Not really. Usually home by six, always wants to see Nadia before bed."

Nothing about the home suggested discord, let alone abuse. But when was such a thing ever apparent? Bryant sipped his tea. Reluctant to confront the fear, he asked, "Nadia, how do you like school?"

She looked up, taking the question very seriously. "Great. Except I don't like Mr. Parkes."

Nerves tickled Bryant's gut. "And what's wrong with Mr. Parkes?"

"He gives us sooooo much homework!"

Bryant breathed again. "No bullying?"

Nadia shook her head vigorously. "It's not allowed."

"They have a good policy," Carol said.

Bryant nodded again. Nothing else for it. "Bad dreams again last night?"

Nadia's expression sharpened. "They are not dreams."

"Sorry, you already told me that, didn't you."

She scowled, distrusting. Her colourful books lay around her knees, forgotten.

"But again last night?" Bryant asked.

Nadia's voice took on the cool, detached tone it had in the church. "Every night, in the lonely forever, he comes."

Bryant ignored Carol's stifled sob. "Why don't you show me your room?"

"Okay. You can see my ponies."

The room was typical. Small bed, dresser covered in brushes and trinkets, posters on the walls of fairy tales and animals. One shelf held nothing but horses, plastic and china, realistic and cartoon.

"That's where he comes from."

Bryant looked to the corner where she pointed, between the dresser and a built-in wardrobe. "Comes from?" he asked.

"I feel the cold, like when you open the fridge. Then he comes from the shadows and walks towards me and I can't move and he's suddenly right over me, and his cold lips touch my face."

"Stop!" The force of Bryant's voice surprised him and Nadia jumped. She began to cry. Bryant crouched, gathered her into his arms. "I'm sorry, child." Her nightmares made him feel five years old again. Was he misremembering his own fears, from so long ago, blurring them with hers? Had he ever really stopped having bad dreams or did he simply drown them in whisky?

"One day he won't stop and he'll get my eyes!" Nadia wailed, breath hot against his neck.

He had no idea what to say, so held her, let her cry. Eventually he led her back downstairs. "I'll be back, Mrs. Clarke. I have to get something from my car."

She moved to open the front door for him. "Is she…?"

"What?"

"Possessed?" The woman's chin wrinkled.

Bryant had no idea what to say. "I'll be back in a minute, okay?"

He didn't need anything other than a moment to himself. He squinted against the rain, heavier than before, blowing down the street at a slant. He ran to his old Ford, slumped into the driver's seat, his mind tumbling with conflicting emotions.

He dialled the bishop again, knowing it was pointless. Should he leave the family alone until he could take advice? Was God testing him? Had God ever been so real as Nadia's fears? How easily a child tested the iron fortress of his faith. Surely her condition was a response to something terrible, but what? What should he do?

I've waited so patiently while you tried to hide. The whispering voice floated to him from behind.

Bryant looked up into the rear-view mirror, caught a glimpse of white face, threadbare hat pressed crooked against the roof. He cried out, scrambled around in his seat, but no one was there.

He sat gasping for breath, adrenaline making his stomach watery. "Holy God and Jesus," he said, "protect me from my madness."

Perhaps talking more to the child would help, offer her the peace he had found in God. The understanding he had never received as a child. The Bible offered him a path of light, despite his parents' lack of support. Maybe it could do the same for Nadia. And perhaps reaffirm his own convictions along the way. The street grew dark outside as he prayed for strength. Eventually he took a well-thumbed Bible from the glovebox, slipped it into his jacket pocket and returned to the house.

The door was opened by a large, smiling man with thinning hair and a beer gut. He stuck out one meaty palm. "Stephen Clarke."

Bryant hadn't noticed the father arrive home. He shook the offered hand. "Father James Bryant."

"Sorry we're wasting your time." Stephen stepped back from the door, gestured inside.

"Wasting my time?"

Stephen rolled his eyes, twisted a half-smile. "The Mrs. is easily upset. Little Nadia seems to take after her."

The living room was empty as Bryant took a seat on the sofa again. "You don't think anything serious is going on?"

Stephen raised one index finger as he sank into an armchair. "Oh, I think it's serious enough. The child is having terrible nightmares. But I'm sure my wife is over-reacting."

"Are you a religious man?" Bryant asked.

Stephen shook his head, gave an apologetic grin. "Not really my thing. Carol's the religious one, insists on taking Nadia. I don't mind," he added quickly. "I've nothing against it."

"Fair enough." Bryant ran out of small talk.

Carol appeared with her daughter, dressed for bed. "Father Bryant, Nadia has a request. I said she'd have to ask you herself."

"Will you stay tonight?" Nadia said suddenly, her voice high.

Stephen began to protest and Carol laid a quietening hand on his shoulder. She smiled, embarrassed. "She feels she'll be safer with you here."

Bryant looked to Stephen Clarke, who shrugged resignedly. Here was an opportunity to offer the child that sympathetic ear she didn't seem likely to get from her parents; just dismissal from her father and perpetuating fear from her mother. And perhaps, in the comfort of her own space, she might admit to the abuse he feared. "Well, if you think so…" Staying the night in a child's room was improper, but the girl was asking for his help.

"Run along and brush your teeth, Nadia," Carol said, and the girl bounded off.

Carol waited until tiny footsteps hammered across the landing above. "I'm sorry, Father, a terrible situation to put you in. Just talk with her, until she falls asleep? Put her mind at ease? Of course you don't have to stay the night."

"I hope I can help."

"The child is simply having night terrors!" Stephen's voice blustered in outrage. "It will pass!"

Bryant held up placatory hands. "You're probably right. I'll listen, stay until she sleeps. Maybe a little after in case she wakes. If it makes Nadia feel better."

Carol's eyes were sad but her smile genuine. "Thank you, Father."

Stephen shook his head, turned on the television.

* * *

Nadia was tucked in when Bryant entered her room. He took a chair from her dresser, sat down beside the bed.

"You know it's real, don't you?" Nadia said.

He held her open, green gaze. "I know you believe it."

Nadia stared hard at him for a long time. "You'll see," she said, and closed her eyes.

"Is there anything happening at home you want to talk about?" he asked quietly. "Your family? Anything you don't like?"

Nadia's eyes opened, her expression blank. "No, Father."

"Nobody asks you to do anything you don't want to? Tells you to keep secrets? You can tell me, I'm a priest."

"No, Father. Goodnight." She turned onto her side, the movement a full stop in the conversation.

Bryant sighed. He got up, pushed the door to and turned off the light. Wan streetlight leaked around the curtains and, as minutes passed, his vision adjusted to the gloom. He pulled out his Bible and flicked the pages.

Butterflies danced through his abdomen as he anticipated the child's dreams. Would she wake screaming? Would he sense anything beyond night terrors? He read familiar passages in the pale light. The words brought little comfort. He was out of his depth, out of his jurisdiction and his authority. He looked towards the corner she had indicated earlier. It was the darkest part of the room, the walls fading into the blackness of absolute shadow. He tore his attention away from the emptiness there.

* * *

The house grew still. Bryant wondered if Carol or Stephen would come to call him away. Nadia slept peacefully. He strained to hear the television but heard only a heavy silence.

Coolness swept the room, as though a refrigerator door had opened. Bryant jumped, gasped for breath and the air was icy against his throat. Nerves branched up from his groin, made him as cold inside as out. He tried to raise the Bible, but his arms would not respond. His feet pressed into the carpet, his back ground painfully against the chair.

The coolness increased, waves of frost over his skin. Bryant was able to move only his eyes and glanced to the darkened corner but it remained stygian, inert. He stretched his vision to the other side, tried to see Nadia in her bed.

A bone-white hand rested on the coverlet. Long fingers with dirty black nails scrabbled at the fabric. A dry cackle rose. Another hand, equally pale. As shaking wracked his body, Bryant forced his gaze up and saw hazy, stuttering impressions of a ragged top hat upon greasy hair, a sickly pale face. Black eyes and a thin, wide smile. The thing wore the ragged remains of Nadia's nightdress, and it hissed.

Bryant thrashed against the chair but couldn't move at all even as his muscles strained. He moaned, his voice emerging weak and reedy from numb lips. "Our Father, who art in Heaven, hallowed be thy name…"

The creature slipped from the bed and laughed, a papery sound. It stalked towards him, long, thin legs taking strides that hardly moved it. Though there was barely any gap between them, the creature took step after step, sliding across the space interminably slowly, slipping and sliding in Bryant's vision, unclear. It raised its hands before its face, fingers writhing.

Bryant screamed, doubled his volume with the Lord's Prayer. The creature reached out long arms, grasping for the priest's face.

"Where's Nadia?" Bryant's voice cracked.

Icy cold scratches lightly raked his cheeks.

"No Nadia." Its voice was a dry, resonant echo.

The priest groaned, squeezed his eyelids shut and started again with the prayer, tried to picture nothing in his mind but the holy love of a God who had never seemed more distant.

Cold, clammy palms pressed against his face and he felt the creature lean in. Its breath was dry and putrid. "I watched as you built your walls, never facing me." Its lips, like frozen sandpaper, swept and nibbled across his mouth and nose.

Bryant yelled aloud, "Please don't forsake me, God!"

The creature pulled back but kept its flat-palmed grip tight on Bryant's face. "There's no god to help you."

Bryant swallowed bile, forced his eyes open to stare into the eternal onyx gaze of the thing that held him. The Gangle Man, she had called it. It had called itself. "If you're real, God is real!"

The thing laughed again. "Oh, I have always been real. Isn't it gods that man made up? I am eternal. And I am patient."

The priest tried to thrash away from the grasp, but his body was paralysed, his head held fast. "I renounce you! In the name of the Father, Son and Holy Ghost, I cast you out! Begone, Devil!"

The creature's disparaging chuckle rumbled on for several seconds. "Devil?"

Bryant sobbed, his faith crumbling as the thing's laughter faded. Snot and spittle covered his lips. "Why me?"

The Gangle Man stuttered its dry laugh. "Why not? Does the tree ask the lightning why it burns?"

Like a striking snake, the creature slammed its mouth over Bryant's right eye. He howled as its icicle tongue pried apart his eyelids and it began to suck, long, deep, slurping pulls. Bryant shrieked as his eyeball stretched and compressed. It pulled against his skull, pressed down and shifted. Pain lanced into his head as his eye detached with a sharp snap of nerves and muscle.

The Gangle Man leaned back its head, mouth open, a deep sigh of satisfaction audible even over Bryant's cries as it chewed and swallowed. Through his remaining eye, streaming with tears of pain and fear, Bryant saw that pale, smiling face briefly as it revelled. His vision filled with iciness again, then darkness as the Gangle Man latched over his left eye.

The pain was even greater, the roughness of its lips grating his skin, its frozen tongue piercing in. It sucked and Bryant's eyeball popped out faster, more agonising than before. He cried aloud for God, for mercy, as he turned blind eyes up, seeking any kind of Heaven, seeing only blackness. He wished for oblivion, but all he had was cold and dark and agony.

The weight against him lifted, his limbs freed. He staggered to his feet, hands flying up to cover empty, bleeding sockets.

The Gangle Man's dry laughter reverberated through the room. Its voice, suddenly loud though soft, spoken directly into Bryant's ear, "Have you learned a lesson, man-child? There are none so blind as those who will not see!"

Bryant stumbled for the door, arms outstretched. He hit the wall, the shelf of horses, swept them clattering to the floor as he groped for the way out. His fingers found the doorframe and he fell through. He bumped into something large and warm and solid.

"Mind your step, Father," Stephen Clarke said. "Don't fall down the stairs and break your neck!"

Carol Clarke burst out a laugh. "Oh, Stephen!" She blocked the way beside her husband.

Bryant pushed against them and they vanished into nothingness. He stumbled forwards, found the bannister, half-ran, half-fell down the stairs. He lurched to the front door and pulled it open, ran out into the street. He tripped over something and immediately the familiar stench of the blind hobo he had spoken to outside his church rose in his nostrils. The man's voice was still as rough as ever. "See you around, Father James Anthony Bryant."

THE
GOODBYE
MESSAGE

SIMON STARED AT THE ANSWERING MACHINE ON HIS STUDY DESK, the small red triangle beating like an electronic heart. He pressed the button. "You have one new message," said the mechanical female voice. There was a pause and a click, then:

"Goodbye."

This voice was also female, but altogether more human, filled with loss and longing. The sound of someone saying the last thing they ever wanted to say.

"Are you all right, love?"

Simon jumped, turning to his wife. "Sorry, didn't hear you come in."

"What's the matter?"

"Listen," he said, pressing the play button again.

"Goodbye."

Jen frowned. "Strange. Who is it?"

"Dunno."

"Bizarre." She turned to leave.

"Every day this week," Simon said.

"What?"

"Every day this week I've got that same message."

He watched his wife's face to see if his concern was mirrored there. He didn't know why it disturbed him so much, but something about the message scratched deep into his bones.

"Bloody weird." Jen gave a small laugh. "Cuppa?"

"Sure, thanks." He stood motionless for several moments after she left, the desperate, pain-filled voice from the answering machine echoing through his mind.

* * *

Simon shifted things around on his desk, sipped from the steaming mug of tea, adjusted the height of his chair. Anything to keep his eyes from falling on the accusatory white screen of his laptop. Empty, like his mind. He sighed, stretched, cracked his neck. He attacked the keyboard, typed PROCRASTINATION five times.

He deleted the words and pulled his notebook over. If ever a thing was misnamed; the book contained no notes. He remembered a bookstore signing, months ago, someone asking the *author du jour*, "How do you cope with writer's block?"

The man had smiled and winked. "I write."

"But then you don't have writer's block," the punter said, confused.

"I write anything, describe the room around me, or think of any random situation and write about that until inspiration hits."

Remembering the guy's easy confidence, Simon started in at the keyboard again.

I'm sitting in a beautiful house, drinking tea made by my beautiful wife and I'm a fucking loser. Maybe one book was all I had in me. Maybe I should give it all up and go back to the university, beg for my job back.

He was fairly certain it wasn't the kind of thing the writer at the signing had meant, smug behind a table creaking under the weight of bestsellers, signing with a smile and a snappy answer for all the bullshit questions.

"The wind will change and that frown will never go away," Jen said from the doorway.

Simon looked up, smiling in spite of himself. "I've got nothing."

She walked in, eyes smoldering. "You're such a cliché." She stood in front of his desk and slowly unbuttoned her blouse.

"Cliché, am I?" He leaned back to watch.

She let the blouse fall open, put her hands on the desk. "Yes. You need to take your mind off it for a while."

Simon lost himself in her smooth cleavage. "You should be encouraging me to work. I need to produce something if I'm going to get another big advance."

Jen stood with a half-smile, reaching for her buttons again. "Well, if that's the way you feel."

He stepped around the desk, grabbed her before the blouse closed. "Screw that."

* * *

Simon rested on the pillows, awash in afterglow. He watched Jen dress, check herself in the mirror.

"I have to go into the office this afternoon," she said. "The big Seattle deal's coming to a head."

"You think it's gonna happen?"

"Hope so. I might have to go over there and make it work though."

Simon swung his legs off the bed, looked out at pine trees and distant mountain peaks. "How long will you be away?"

"Only overnight, if I even have to go. You'll survive."

"Hope so."

She kissed him, turned away to continue dressing. "Don't give yourself such a hard time, okay? Take your notebook out to the Three Cups. Drink coffee, have a change of scene, see what happens."

"Yeah, maybe." He watched an eagle drift by, riding thermals. He envied it.

"I'll see you at dinner time."

"Seeya."

Clouds floated past a thousand miles away as he sat on the bed. The front door clicked shut and the old Ford kicked up gravel on the driveway. *I really am a cliché*, he thought. *In every way.*

With a sigh he dragged himself up and trudged back to the study.

He would go out. It was a twenty-minute walk to the village; the fresh air and exercise would do him good. He'd take the notebook and write down anything he saw, maybe copy snippets of conversations overheard. Anything to get the juices flowing.

Something looked different.

He stood in the centre of the study and turned a slow circle. What had he seen? His eyes fell on the old Remington typewriter, sitting on its shelf like a trophy. A gift to the teenaged Simon so many years ago, a never-give-up reminder. And now a mockery, a fuck-you-failure testament. It always sat there, with a blank sheet of paper in it symbolising a new story to be told. But the page wasn't blank any more.

He strained up on tiptoes to read the page without having to touch it.

IF NOT

Two tiny words, stark on the plain white paper.

IF NOT

What the hell did that mean? And who had typed it? Some silly joke of Jen's?

IF NOT

If not what?

He'd ask her about it later. Grabbing his notebook and pen, he left the house, suddenly desperate for fresh air and sunlight.

* * *

They sat with Chinese take away cartons, chopsticks clicking into noodles and a BBQ pork special. The television garbled away about falling stock prices.

"Why would I type something there?" Jen asked around a mouthful.

"I dunno. I didn't do it, and you're the only other one here."

"True," she conceded. "But it wasn't me."

Simon stopped eating to look at her. She chewed on, reaching for another container, then paused when she realised he was staring at her. "What?"

"Don't you think it's a bit strange?"

She put down the container. "Yeah, I do. But it wasn't me."

"So it must have been me?"

She shrugged.

"I know it wasn't me either," he said, anger tinging his voice.

She picked up the container again, breaking eye contact. "I'm sorry. I don't know what to suggest."

"You think I'm going mad?" he asked. "You think I did it and don't remember?"

"No one's going mad, sweetie."

He resumed eating, staring at the television. She'd always been the strong and steady one. He was the flaky one. Maybe he *was* going crazy.

* * *

Jen busied herself in the bathroom getting ready for bed and Simon stood in his study. Nervously he approached the typewriter.

IF NOT

It was still there. He pulled the paper from the carriage and screwed it up, sending it arcing over his desk to the wastepaper basket. It rattled on the rim and dropped in. *Not a complete loser yet then*, he thought with grim humour.

He really didn't remember typing the words.

With a sigh he went to the desk and got a fresh sheet of paper, wound it carefully onto the carriage.

At the door he flicked off the light and stopped, distracted by a soft red glow. The answering machine.

He crossed the room in darkness and pressed the button with a trembling finger. "You have one new message," the electronic woman said.

"Goodbye."

Tears hung on the edges of the voice, ghostly soft, sadness like he'd never heard before.

"What the *fuck*?" he hissed, and hit delete.

* * *

Simon nursed a mug of hot coffee between his palms, waiting for toast to spring up from the toaster. "I forgot to ask yesterday," he said. "How did the meeting go?"

Jen sniffed, annoyed. "Looks like I have to go to Seattle. It's a royal pain, but I need to nail down the details."

"You can't do it over the phone?"

"Doesn't look like it. You know how these people are, always got to be wined and dined."

Simon nodded, sipping his coffee. "I guess so. And you are good at it."

"That's why I get the big bucks," she said with a grin.

"So when are you going?"

"Sheila's sorting things out this morning. Probably tomorrow." She giggled at his crestfallen expression. "I'll only be gone overnight, sweetie. You'll cope."

He laughed at himself. "Yeah, I guess so."

"Did you get anything down yesterday?" she asked.

"Actually, I did. Went to the Three Cups and kinda observed stuff. Made some notes."

"Well done, you!"

He smiled, hating himself. He'd barely scribbled half a page and even that was bullshit.

Fat lady likes blueberry pie. Weird old guy probably has a secret.

He had a secret too.

* * *

"I'm going to Sally's for coffee and a catch up," Jen called from the hallway. "Then to the office."

"Okay, hon," he yelled over the sound of running water as he rinsed the dishes. "Have fun."

"Don't beat yourself up, okay?"

"I won't." He would.

"Okay, sweetie. Love you."

"Love you too!" That wasn't a lie. That was never a lie.

He wouldn't torture himself in front of the laptop today. Getting out into the world was a good idea. Jen's ideas always were. He'd had a false start yesterday, but today would be different. If nothing else, the walk had been worthwhile. He'd do it again, only this time he'd look more closely, make more notes.

As he entered his study, the phone rang. For a moment he was too scared to pick it up, then cursed himself and grabbed it. "Hello?"

"Simon Taylor?"

"Yep. Who's this?"

"I'm Claire Foley, calling from the *New York Times*. We're doing a piece on rising stars, new big things in fiction, that kind of thing. We'd love to interview you, maybe talk a bit about what you're working on right now."

Panic flooded his veins. "Er, right. Yeah. That's very good of you." *The New York freaking Times?* "I'm actually just heading overseas for a short trip. Can you maybe call me back in a week?"

"Of course, Mr. Taylor. I'm sorry, your agent didn't mention a trip when I rang her for your number."

Why had he lied? "Oh, no problem." His laugh sounded nervous. "Just crossed wires."

"Not a problem." She sounded so chirpy. "I'll call back a week from Monday?"

"Sure. And thanks."

"Until then."

The phone clicked dead and Simon sat, stunned. What the hell was wrong with him?

The page in the typewriter had moved again.

"You are kidding me," he whispered, walking cautiously around his desk.

IF NOT

Shivers wracked his body, dread soaked through his gut like a stain. "I didn't type that!" he yelled. He dragged the paper out and put a fresh, blank sheet in its place.

The light on the answering machine blinked. Had it been blinking a moment ago during the call?

"Goodbye."

The voice made him want to cry.

"What the fuck is happening?"

The laptop was on, pictures of their trip to the Grand Canyon and Death Valley drifting over each other as the screensaver. He would get the phone company to trace the calls or something. There must be a way for them to figure out why he kept getting this message.

He moved the mouse and the empty word processor page still sat there. Except it wasn't empty.

STOP ME

Two words in neat Arial font at the top of the page, the cursor blinking relentlessly right next to them.

Simon stared. "I didn't type that either!" He grabbed his notebook and pen and ran.

* * *

Simon smiled apologetically at the Three Cups staff. They'd mopped and tidied everything except his table. An empty cup and the notebook sat in front of him. On the up side he'd covered several pages. Observations, snatches of conversation, ideas and scenarios. On the downside he was still too scared to go home. *Goodbye. If not. Stop me.*

He gathered up his things, realising he'd pushed the hospitality of the cafe staff as far as he could.

"Thank you," one waitress said as he headed for the door.

He nodded back at her, too embarrassed to say anything.

"Hey, are you okay?" She sounded genuinely concerned.

He paused, hand on the door handle, reluctant to turn around. "Sure, I'm fine."

"Really?" She came over, eyes troubled.

Jesus, did he look that bad? "Yeah, really. Thanks."

Outside in the fading light he pulled his cell phone from his pocket and hit the quick dial for Jen's cell.

"Hey, sweetie, what's up?"

It felt so good to hear her voice. "You still at the office?"

"Yeah, things are coming to a head. Still a lot of work to do."

He sighed. "And you're still going to Seattle?"

"'Fraid so. I've got an 11:00 a.m. flight tomorrow, 3:00 p.m. meeting and overnight in some shitty hotel. I fly back the next day."

He didn't know what to say. He felt empty.

"You okay?" Jen asked.

He sucked in a quick breath, drawing himself up. *Pull yourself together.* "Yes, yeah. Fine. Sorry, just a bit lost in everything right now."

"Don't let it get to you, sweetie," Jen said softly. "You're not a production line. You had a massive hit, you're really good at what you do. You can do it again."

"I know, Jen. I just feel so useless."

"You're used to a strict schedule, all those years of university lecturing. We made a big move, *you've* made a big change, giving up work. Give yourself time."

Goodbye.

stop me.

"Sure, hun."

"Hey," she said sharply, but he could hear the smile in her voice. "What am I always?"

He laughed. God, he loved her. "Right," he finished sarcastically.

"That's correct, husband. I'm always right. There's some Bolognese sauce in the freezer. Get some spaghetti on. I'll be home by seven, okay?"

"Okay."

"Love you."

"Love you too."

* * *

Simon knew the Bolognese sauce would be burning on the stove top, but he was frozen. His legs like thousand-year-old oak trunks, unmoved and unmovable. He'd put the block of frozen meat sauce into a pan, filled another with water and put it on to boil. He'd ducked into his study to put the notebook on the desk and the typewriter paper was no longer clean and white.

IF NOT

He'd moved his mouse, a floating photograph of Jen laughing outside a light-polluting Vegas casino fading away to reveal the bright white page of the word processor.

STOP ME

He hadn't been in more than a few minutes and had only just entered the study. He hadn't typed either pair of words. He was sure of it. Certain. But he'd almost expected them. And the red flashing light on the answering machine. But something else iced his limbs into immobility. A Post-it note pad, always beside the laptop. There were two words on it, in scratchy, shaking biro, as if written by someone aged and infirm.

SIMON PLEASE

Cold waves rippled through his body. Was he *really* writing these things? Was it someone else?

He snapped his head back and yelled at the heavens. "What the fuck is going on?"

He turned to the answering machine and stabbed the delete button with an angry index finger, not prepared to hear that heartrending voice again.

He screwed the Post-it note and the page from the typewriter together and threw them into the wastepaper basket with ten times the necessary force. He deleted the words from the word processor and closed the program.

"Simon? You here? What's happening?"

He strode from the study, face twisted in fury, taking deep, ragged breaths. Sounds of frantic activity came from the kitchen.

"Simon?" Jen called again. "You okay?"

The smell of burning meat sauce filled his nostrils as he turned into the kitchen, along with something else, metallic and harsh.

Jen looked up. "Jesus, Simon, what the fuck? The water boiled away and burned the pan to shit. The sauce is ruined!"

He looked at the floor, all his anger dissipating in the face of her disapproval. "I got kind of caught up, forgot all about it."

She ran water into the blackened pan and it hissed its hatred of him, steam flooding the kitchen. It helped clear the acrid smell of burnt meat and metal. Spatters of meat sauce, like drops of blood from a gunshot to the head, covered the stove top and granite counter. Jen began mopping up.

"Seriously, Simon, you're worrying me," she said.

He didn't know how to reply. He was worrying himself.

Jen stopped cleaning. Her eyes softened when they met his. "Oh, Simon, it's okay."

She reached for him and he fell into her arms, sobbing quietly into the sweet-smelling soft fabric of her sweater.

* * *

They cooked a frozen pizza and ate in front of old favourite DVDs. He told her about the message and she said that first thing tomorrow he had to ring the phone company and get it sorted out. Clearly some kind of fault on the line. He didn't feel convinced but agreed he would.

He told her about the typewriter and the word processor and the Post-it note. Something in her eyes disturbed him, a level of doubt he'd never seen there before.

"Stress can be a funny thing, Si." She gently stroked his hair.

"Stress?" Could it really be something as simple as that? He wanted her to be right. But even then, only more concerns arose.

"Sure, sweetie. Perhaps you're *really* stressed about this and your subconscious is playing tricks on you."

"I don't like that idea," he said.

"I don't either," she confessed. "I don't like it at all. But maybe that's what it is. Since the last book tour you've been so hard on yourself."

"The advance will only last so long," he told her, desperation in his voice. "And who knows about royalties in this business."

She shrugged and pulled him close. "The advance is going to last a while yet and I'm earning good money. There's no rush. You need to take a break."

"Maybe you're right."

She laughed and kissed him. "What am I always?"

He smiled.

"I have to go to Seattle tomorrow," she said. "But I get back the next day. Why don't you look online, find us a cosy cabin in the upper mountains and we'll have a long weekend of it. We can drive up when I get back Friday and stay 'til Monday. I'll tell Carl I won't be back, home or office, 'til Tuesday."

That did sound pretty fantastic. "Really?"

"Sure. Three days in the mountains, no phone, no internet, no nothing but us."

"Okay. I'll book it."

"But not tonight," she told him. "Tonight you stay out of the study and forget about everything except me and this big old couch we love."

* * *

They had a lazy morning of love-making and an indulgent breakfast. She kissed him when her cab for the airport arrived and he chased her down the driveway for an encore. The cab driver smiled good-naturedly at their teenage antics. He waved as the cab drove away, her face a portrait in the rear screen as she waved back.

The air was fresh and the sky blue, the smell of pines intoxicating. It made a kind of twisted sense, his stress manifesting in little sabotages of his writing implements. The phone message was still something frightening. Perhaps it was simply a line fault and another contributor to his stress, the thing that had driven him over the edge.

He went back inside and tidied the breakfast things, washed up, made the bed. He refused to even think about the fact that he should be writing, let alone struggle to actually write anything. Domesticity became a security blanket of mundane activity. He put on laundry, organised his underwear drawer while he put away already laundered clothes.

It was hours before he finally drew a deep breath and headed for the study to book them a cabin. Part of him braced in anticipation. Fuck it. If they were there again, he wouldn't let it upset him. They had a plan, they were going to deal with it.

White paper stood stark against the dark wood of the shelving, sticking out of the typewriter like an abusive tongue.

IF NOT

He ground his teeth. What did it mean? He hadn't even replaced the paper last night.

He ignored it and walked around his desk, studiously not paying attention to the blinking red light on his answering machine. The Post-it note pad had spidery scrawl on it again.

SIMON PLEASE

He turned it face down on the desktop. He moved the mouse plugged into his laptop and the photos slipped away to reveal the reopened word processor program, two words and a blinking cursor.

STOP ME

Simon bit down his frustration and opened a browser, clicked a bookmark for a cabin rental company they'd used before. Book the cabin, take the break, don't think about anything else. He looked up to the calendar hanging beside the window to check Saturday's date and his stomach froze solid.

Not Seattle

Scrawled right across the week in the thin black felt tip pen he used to mark important dates.

Bolts of dread cut into him. He looked at his watch, blurry on his shaking wrist. Two-thirty in the afternoon. He ran from the study to the living room, fumbling the remote control with numb hands. He flicked channel after channel, not wanting to see anything but desperate to find...something.

He landed on a news channel and images of burning wreckage. The picture blurred with his tears as the announcer's voice threaded through his mind.

"...authorities say it will be some time before any cause is determined. What is certain, however, is that there are no survivors. Crews will be working for some time to get the inferno under control here at Seattle's Tacoma airport..."

Simon fell backwards onto the couch, short, shallow breaths rattling in his throat.

Not Seattle

He sobbed aloud, his heart shattering, hands clawing at his face, slipping on tears. Minutes, hours, years later, he found himself back in the study. The typewriter, the laptop, the post-it note, the calendar.

IF NOT

STOP ME

SIMON PLEASE

Not Seattle

All backwards.

NOT Seattle, Simon, please. Stop me. If not...

He walked on numb legs to the answering machine and pressed the button with an ice-cold finger.

"Goodbye."

How had he never recognised her voice before? Perhaps because he'd never heard her so sad.

THE OCEAN HUSHED THE STONES

THE FIRST TIME A DOOR APPEARED IN JOSEPH'S BEDROOM WALL he was too scared to open it. He stared at it all night, in case someone—or something—opened it from the other side. Some time close to dawn sleep stole him despite his reluctance. When he woke mid-morning, the door was gone. He'd slept through his alarm, late for work. Sandra *tut-tutted* but winked as he hurried in, dishevelled and contrite.

The next night Joseph tossed and turned, refusing to look. Then finally gave in and there it was again. Eventually, he became braver. After staring for a couple of hours, he moved closer and listened. Pressed his ear tight to the hard wood. He heard an ocean sucking rhythmically at pebbles. It reminded him of childhood holidays, the beach of his youth always hard and rocky, never the white sand of television advertisements. The holidays themselves were hard and rocky too, a family grimacing through fake smiles, desperately pretending everything was okay. But that was before. In England. Now, in Australia, the sand *was* white, and childhood far away, in distance and time.

Joseph sank to his knees, comfortable in the warmth of the early autumn night, and listened to that impossible sea ebb and flow. Nostalgic pain curled his gut. He woke in the cool dimness of dawn, his ear pressed against a hard, plain wall, neck cricked. He crawled back to bed and slept again, fitfully, until his seven-thirty alarm roused him.

"You looked tired, Joe." Sandra's eyes were kind, her head tilted to one side with concern.

Joseph followed a tumble of wavy blonde hair, over one tanned shoulder, down towards the enticing swell of equally golden cleavage, snapped his gaze back up again. If she had noticed, she made no sign of it. "Not been sleeping well." He forced a smile, like the ones from those old holidays. "I'm fine."

"Are you? Really?"

She seemed to care, but was it simple human kindness or did she actually like him? In the three years he'd been working this dull job, she had been the receptionist and they'd always got on well. They chatted easily, she smiled often. She'd been with some sporty guy for a long time, but that had ended badly more than a year ago. And for a year, Joseph had been too nervous to ask her out.

"Joe?" She laughed softly. "You in there?"

He started. "Somewhere, yeah. I'll be fine if I can get a good night's sleep."

She leaned back in her swivel chair, elbows on the hard, black plastic arms. There was something impossibly sexual about the position. Or was that his wishful thinking? "What are you, Joe? Not thirty yet, right?"

"Twenty-nine."

She laughed again. It suited her. "Same as me. You should be out partying, living it up."

"That what you do?"

She glanced down, slight smile. "Not really. But I like to go out."

An awkward silence yawned open between them. Was this where he was supposed to suggest they do something together? Something other than the regular, interminable work functions Beek insisted on. She looked up without raising her head, eyes sultry under shining curls. That slight smile widened a fraction more.

"Sandy, need these by ten!"

They both startled. Sandra sat her chair back up and reached to take the manila folders from Mr. Beek. "Yes, sir."

Beek slapped Joseph on the shoulder, rocked him forward. "You well, Joe?"

"Yes, thanks, sir."

"Attaboy. Get to it then, those orders won't fulfil themselves."

"Yes, sir." He glanced at Sandra and she winked, then rolled her eyes subtly.

Joseph smiled, headed to his desk in the cubicle farm. He ground his teeth as he heard Beek cracking on to Sandra, making inappropriate comments about beach bodies and a job well done or something. It wasn't only the sexual harassment that made him angry. There was jealousy too.

* * *

At home that night he couldn't stop thinking about the interaction. If Beek hadn't interrupted them, he would have asked her out. He was sure of it. Of course, it was easy to be sure when it was impossible to prove. He seethed, knowing deep inside that most likely the painful silence would have stretched out until he'd mumbled something inarticulate and hurried away. To the ordinary routine of his life, pushing papers, making calls, drinking with the same small group of friends, superficial as old paint. No aspect of his life had any depth. Never had since Charlie... How was he supposed to know if Sandra was attracted to him or simply friendly? How did any of this stuff work?

There had been those work-related social events and he always spent a lot of time with Sandra at those. Weekend barbeques or evening drinks, all the employees *en masse*, that ridiculous thing where people tried to pretend they wanted to spend time with folks they wouldn't think twice about socialising with otherwise. But Joseph and Sandra genuinely enjoyed each other's company, he was certain she reciprocated that much at least. She was funny, and smart. They talked about life and philosophy, she knew all about ancient history and had a passion for archaeology. He'd tried several times to convince her to follow it through, go back to school, and he thought maybe she would one day.

Two days ago there had been one of those awkward social nights out. Beek insisting everyone go to the pub after work to celebrate the news that Anaya Gupta was pregnant. Joseph was happy for Anaya, she was a lovely woman, but even she groaned at the suggestion of drinks.

"I'm pregnant, I can't drink!"

"Have a lemonade," Beek insisted. "Just to celebrate!"

No one ever denied him, and the uncomfortable gathering occurred just as Beek wanted it to. He drank more than anyone else, became increasingly loud and offensive. And Joseph had found himself in a corner of the pub with Sandra, away from all the others.

"Beek gets too handsy," she said. "Better to keep a distance and let him notice someone else."

"He shouldn't get away with it," Joseph said. "I'll help. I'll... I don't know, testify for you or something."

Her smile had been liquid gold. "You're kind. But I need this job for now."

And that had led to them discussing her going back to university again. They laughed, made dumb jokes, she put a hand over his. And he'd allowed himself to think that maybe there was more than friendship there. He had longed to lean forward and kiss her, felt certain she would have allowed it, returned it. But he lacked the courage. That was the night the impossible door appeared the first time.

He gazed listlessly through the TV, the flickering program forgotten. How could she be attracted to him? "Fucking worthless," his father had called him so many times. But what did his father really know anyway, drinking too much, hitting his wife, hitting his children. Dead at forty-seven from a heart attack was the best thing that ever happened to Joseph's father and his family. A shame it couldn't have been before Charlotte died two years earlier. How their mother screamed that day, how she thrashed her fists against his father's chest in fury until Dad had cuffed her to the ground. Then drank himself into a stupor again. Joseph had been numb for months, then moved as far from it all as possible.

Why was he wallowing in all this again, more than a decade later? His father had been dead eight years, he hadn't spoken to his mother in nearly as long. He'd done a good job of burying it all. Was he looking for someone to blame for his lack of ability in asking out Sandra? That wasn't so bad. His traumas were real. But there was plenty of blame to go around. He wasn't free of it. He wished every day for a chance to change things. Wished every day that he could go back, or that he had been stronger in the face of the tyrant who called himself Dad. But the past was the past and all that remained was pain. And the memory of Charlie's love, even if nothing but hurt hung from the memories.

The TV show ended, credits rolled, and he blinked. His eyelids hung like empty sails, his head ached with fatigue. Only 9:30, but he was spent. Nothing to stay up for anyway. He trudged upstairs, washed, changed, pissed, fell into bed. He vaguely thought about the impossible door but was so tired darkness swept over him and he was asleep in moments.

He dreamed of the family holidays. Always Brighton, the pebbled beach, the inevitable rain, long days on the pier that drove out into the water like an elongated city with a funfair at the end. He'd made proper friends back then, he and Charlie both laughing and running, happy to have freedom from the cramped, terraced south London house they endured as home. Only a year apart in age, they had always been mates, never warring like so many siblings did. They got up to mischief, rode the rides, smoked cigarettes, ate hot, salty chips and too many sweets. Sometimes at night, after their father had drunk himself unconscious, they would sneak out again. Sit on the beach and look at the stars as the ocean hushed the stones. He loved those nights more than anything else. That one week every summer at Uncle Adam's holiday flat on England's south coast was all Joseph took from childhood that had any real joy in it. That and the constant love of his sister.

In the dream he walked the pier with Charlie, watching the ocean strobe by underneath through the wooden deck. Then those two square towers, one either side, flags snapping atop each one. Five round windows in a row high above, between the towers, gates beneath. Entrance to wonderland in his child's mind, more magical than any forest or castle in the stories he escaped into at home. This was real, touchable. The smell of popcorn and candy floss, ocean salt and seaweed, gulls screeching, people laughing, hectic calliope music and ringing machines. People *everywhere* and none of them his parents. There was genuine magic in the place.

Dream Charlie squeezed his hand, dragged him forward and the portals warped and stretched. Every atom of pleasure corrupted with them and dread flooded in. He tried to pull Charlie back but she was too strong, hauled him through, and the other side was empty and dark. Not night-time dark, but the sun occluded. Or like the sun was going out, shrunken and reduced to a glimmering haze, struggling to live on. They were the only living things anywhere nearby, shivering in the icy coldness of death.

Joseph pulled again but she dragged him. Tears froze on his cheeks as he tried to call her name, tell her this was wrong, but no sound escaped his constricted throat. She laughed and whooped, teeth bright in her smiling face, freckles wrinkling over her nose as her auburn hair danced in the icy wind.

The ocean crashed below, sucked against the stones far behind on the beach. How could he hear that? Gulls moaned, plaintive cries in the leaden sky. When he looked up they were featherless and fleshless, bird skeletons etched black against the haze, wheeling and calling, mournful and lost.

Charlie's hand wasn't in his any longer and he stopped, spun around. She was nowhere to be seen. He stood alone on the bleached and weathered abandoned pier.

"Charlie!" he cried, but it came out the same desolate caw as the gulls.

He stumbled forward, hugged his arms to his chest for warmth, his feet numb in the tattered black Converse High Tops he always wore. He ran alongside the Palace of Fun, silent and still, as waves crashed against the pylons below. Sideshows and gift shops and cafés slid by as he forced himself on, trying to call for Charlie but croaking like a seabird. He found his way into the funfair, turned right, slipped and staggered across the ice-rimed wooden planks, heading for the helter skelter. Their favourite, white and red and blue in wiggling vertical stripes. The blue, red and yellow wooden steps leading up to the door, the winding staircase inside. In the death's realm parody the paint peeled, the slide spiralling down the outside hung broken and ragged, wood rotted through. Skeletal gulls flocked in, landed on every available perch, cried and whined. Joseph climbed the broken blue steps, ran into the darkness and found himself in the cool white tiles of a bathroom.

He fell to his knees and howled. The top of the helter skelter high above broken open like a boiled egg, the dying sun weakly staring down at him. Why couldn't he ever save her? He would do anything to save her, give anything.

He sobbed, fell forward, his head hit the cold side of the bathtub, and he jerked awake. Shivering in his bed, eyes wet from dream tears, hands shaking in rage and grief, he lay staring at the ceiling of his one-bedroom flat. Sydney autumn warm, but the place was damp, mould speckling the edges near the old, cracked coving.

And it wasn't warm. He was still cold, freezing in a soft icy breeze. A wan light spread out from the far wall. New fear crept in as he sat up. The door was back. This time it stood ajar, two or three inches of cold blue light, like his dream of the end of the world, seeped into the room. And that frozen breeze came with it. Tiny ice crystals glistened on the carpet, on the wooden corner of his bed nearest the portal.

Joseph sat with the duvet pulled up tight under his chin, staring. Would something come through? Was he expected to go in? Was he still dreaming? Under the covers he gathered a pinch of flesh on his thigh between forefinger and thumb, squeezed and twisted viciously. He grunted in pain, let go. Nothing had changed. His leg throbbed, he sensed the bruise forming immediately. Could a person dream pain?

Tears of frustration, of renewed grief for Charlie, of fear, tickled over his cheeks. Was this a chance? Or a trap? He watched the door, barely daring to blink, until sleep dragged him back to his pillow and he slipped into darkness again, then the alarm bleated at 7:30 a.m. In the warmer light of day, the chill and the door were gone.

* * *

"Hey, Joe, you okay?"

He forced on a smile, turned to Sandra behind her desk. "Yeah. Still tired, that's all."

"You wanna get a drink tonight?"

Heat flooded his face. "What? Oh. Er…"

She laughed, as deep as her tan. "You are *so* English, god. If I kept waiting for you, you'd never ask, would you?"

He managed a weak laugh in return. "I would have. Was thinking about it last night, how to…you know…"

"You wanna get a drink tonight? That's how. Simple."

He nodded, cheeks still burning. "Yeah. That simple. And yes, I'd love to."

"Great. See you at five-thirty." She grimaced, gestured to encompass her desk, the entire office, the horrors of the working life.

"See you then. Better get going, these orders won't fulfil themselves."

She smiled, waved him away with one hand as she tapped a button on her console and took a call. He walked to his desk feeling ten feet tall. She really did like him, they were going to get a drink. All his agonising, all his uncertainty. What a fool. The image of her perfect face, tumbling hair, wonderful curves, stuck to the back of his eyes like sun glare. He realised his mouth was stretched in a grin and he didn't care.

* * *

"So why aren't you sleeping?"

Joseph sipped beer and wondered what to tell her. That a mysterious door kept appearing in his bedroom wall at night? That it was frozen on the other side and he could hear an ocean sucking at pebbles? That he never saw it actually appear or go away, it was just there and then it wasn't? "Bad dreams. Not sure why now, but I've had a run of them."

"You stressed about something?"

"Maybe. Not directly. I mean, the job pays well enough and keeps me entertained, but it's not any great drain on me. I've got nothing to stress about, I guess."

She did that thing where she tipped her head to one side to look at him. It inflamed something in his gut. "You said maybe, then that there was nothing to stress about." She sipped, waved a forefinger at him. "You're talking in circles."

He smiled, looked away. Drank more beer. He knew he was heading from social drink to drunk somewhere between this one and the next, but he didn't mind. Sandra drank with casual abandon, already a little giggly, though she had become serious. "I've got stuff coming up. Memories. I guess maybe it's stressing me out."

"What kind of memories."

"Sort of teenage stuff." A trembling rippled through his gut, emotion he wasn't prepared to release in conversation yet. Not with anyone, but especially not like this. He looked at Sandra and her eyes were soft and genuinely concerned. She waited patiently. Maybe he could talk to her about it one day. Not now, but she could be someone special. He swallowed hard, then downed the rest of his schooner. "It's messy, complicated stuff. I'll tell you one day."

She nodded, sat back and drained her own glass. "Fair enough. Get me another drink. Let's see if we can push those memories aside for tonight, at least."

Relief filled him and he took the glass. She let her fingers trail over his, smiled, eyes hooded. More emotions stirred in his gut, and lower down. Entirely more acceptable ones.

After two more drinks, she said, "You're not entirely here, are you?"

"What do you mean?"

"You keep drifting off. Is it really just tiredness? Am I boring you?" A genuine concern in her eyes.

He couldn't let her think that, and alcohol had softened his resolve to privacy. "It's not you, really. I'm so happy to be hanging out with you."

"Me too." She blushed slightly. "We fit well together, you and I. You know that, right?"

"All those awful work dos."

"But not awful, because we always hang out."

He smiled, warmed inside. "That's true."

"So what is it? You can tell me."

He took a deep breath. "Just lately, the last few days, I've been struggling with memories of my sister." He wasn't prepared to mention the door yet, lest she think him mad, but he knew the door and his sister were connected somehow.

"Memories? She…died?"

He nodded. "Suicide."

Her fingers covered her mouth as she uttered a breathy, "Oh!"

They were quiet a moment, sipping beer.

"I'm so sorry, Joseph. Recently?"

"No, a long time ago. She was only sixteen. I found her." The image flooded his mind. A deep tub, filled crimson, Charlie's face twisted in agony laid back against the ceramic. Not at peace. Still in pain, he would never forget that. One arm lost in the still, red water, the other hung over the side scattering a ruby flood down the whiteness. A razor blade glittered in the life-soaked, thick pile rug. "Cut her wrists in the bath."

"Oh, Joe."

"Our family life was bad. Our father was a violent drunk. He died of a heart attack two years later. Maybe Charlie would have hung on to life if the old man had left sooner, but life is full of maybe and what if."

She moved around the table, pulled a chair close to his and sat to hug him tightly. "No wonder you're not sleeping if all this is coming up for you. Why now, do you think?"

He shrugged, pushed away thoughts of the cold door, enjoying the warmth of the embrace. Remembered the drinks a couple of nights before and how they'd enjoyed each other's company then. The night the door first appeared. "Thinking about the future, maybe. It can dredge up the past."

She nodded against his shoulder. "There always is a future." She looked up, caught his eye. "I'd like to be part of yours."

"Me too."

Her lips met his, soft and hot.

* * *

Joseph was no virgin, but his experience of intimacy had been fractured and inconsistent. He rolled up onto one elbow to look at Sandra in the wan moonlight through the open curtains. Sandra, sleeping beside him. In his bed. He shook his head in wonder. Regardless of his less than stellar track record, he had a hard time believing any sex could be better than what he had experienced this night. Twice. And she'd stayed, no intention of running out. She'd said so many little things that convinced him this was the start of something wonderful.

A cold gust tickled his skin. He gasped, the moonlight shifting to something weaker. He sat up, knowing what he would see. The door stood wider than before, open about halfway. Icy wooden planks stretched away, a peeling once-white fence to the left, restless ocean beyond. The waves sucked at the pylons, shushed against a pebbly beach somewhere impossibly behind him.

He remembered Charlie, so many years ago. *This is our place, Joe. Brighton Pier. Let's always come, every year, until we're old!*

His face folded in on itself in grief. Sandra slept on, oblivious. He stepped from the bed and the thin carpet crunched with a dusting of ice, his feet instantly throbbing with the cold. He crept to the door, leaned to look through. All the familiar sights, but dead and rotting, abandoned. The dying sun he had dreamed gazed weakly above. Skeletal gulls cawed.

And he remembered his own resolve. That he would do anything to save her, give anything. Give *up* anything.

He looked back over his shoulder at Sandra. She breathed deep and even, tugged the duvet up and rolled onto her side. He stood on a threshold, Sandra on one side, Charlie on the other. He knew it as well as he knew his own name. He finally had something of enough value to give up. Impossible, but nevertheless a fact, unfair choices forced upon him. He could be happy, maybe, if he stayed. But it would be with the old grief and guilt built in. The other, the cold way, possible redemption. And more? The selfish choice was obvious, sleeping soundly in his bed.

It was no choice at all.

"Charlie," he whispered, his breath a curling cloud in the dimness.

He pulled on jeans and jumper, socks and shoes. Cons, like he'd always worn as a kid and had never quit the habit. For several minutes he stood by the bed staring down at Sandra, the lines of her under the covers. The fall of hair across the pillow. The warmth of her. The certainty of her. His chest was hollow, an echo chamber of loss. He hoped she could forgive him, one day.

The cold wind bit into him as he stepped through the door. He stopped, looked back. Sandra slept on, his crappy flat an oasis of warmth and wonder. He swallowed, turned and walked along the pier. When he looked back again, the door was gone. The cold was absolute.

He shivered violently by the time he reached the helter skelter at the end, and the white tiled bathroom inside. Charlie lay in the scarlet bath just like his dream. Just like his memory. But that had been at home, not in Brighton. She had been nearly seventeen the night of The Bath, but she looked younger here, maybe fifteen. Perhaps that was the chance he had. He didn't pause. He lifted her from the water, his arms stained red, and staggered down the stairs, out of the helter skelter. Gulls swooped and snapped, screeched and screamed. Joseph ran, head down, weathering the stabs and cuts of those dead beaks.

His limbs ached, his joints swollen and tight from the cold. He cried, sobbing for great gasps of air as he forced himself on. The entrance that had warped into death in his dream drew nearer and he simply had to get to it, get through it. The bony gulls flocked and harangued him, dragged at his clothes and hair, tore his skin. He stumbled to his knees, the impact a dull agony that made his jaw slam shut.

"Noooo!" he roared, and forced himself back to his feet, tasting blood. Stumbled on.

The weight of Charlie threatened to drag him back to the frozen wood and part of him wanted to go. Lie down with her, let everything freeze over and be done. Then the heat of Sandra's touch came back to him, everything he had given up. He couldn't let it end, couldn't lose it all. He pushed on, like trying to walk through deep snow. His arms burned with the effort but he would never let Charlie go again. He would not let her down.

Eyes squeezed shut, teeth gritted till they creaked, he drove forward. It felt as though his skin peeled from his bones then sudden light and warmth and the chattering of hundreds of voices. Laughing and shouting, gulls and ocean. A bus blared its horn on the seafront road. Joseph gasped and Charlie laughed, slapped at his shoulder.

"Put me down, you goof!"

He almost dropped her, stared into her green eyes as her feet hit the deck. Tears poured over his cheeks.

She put one hand under his chin, looking up at him. "What's wrong?"

"Nothing. I just… Nothing."

The sun's warmth was like hot water pouring over him, every colour too bright, too real, the edges of everything too sharp. This was reality as he hadn't known it for years.

"Come on, Joe, let's head back. Dad'll get angry if we're late."

Joseph swallowed, trembling weakened his knees. The fucker was still alive, of course. That was the point. He remembered those nights under the stars. "Maybe we can come back out later?"

She nodded. "If he drinks enough. But let's go."

"Yeah, okay."

Charlie's face fell and she nodded again, turned towards land.

"*You* okay?" Joseph asked.

"Of course." She smiled at him, kissed his cheek. "Come on."

And he saw it. The fear in her eyes that he had never noticed before but saw so clearly as twenty-nine-year-old Joseph in sixteen-year-old Joseph's body. A fear that should never live in fifteen-year-old eyes. Almost two years before The Bath. They were both scared of their dad, both hated him for his violence, his disdain. Both hated their mother for her weakness. But the terror Joseph saw now was something else. Something worse. How could he have never known? Did he know? Was he as bad as his mother?

No more.

Back at Uncle Adam's flat, Dad was already drunk. He barely acknowledged their return. Mum asked flatly about their day, going through the routine. In the bathroom, Joseph looked at his youthful face, astonished and appalled.

He struggled with his parents' orders, forced to be a child again. Ate his mother's dry dinner, ignored his father's angry asides. He needed space to think and gladly accepted the nine o'clock bedtime. He lay in his small room, Charlie next door in hers. They always had separate rooms, since they were little more than school age. He ground his teeth, listening, knowing he was right, hoping his father kept drinking.

Then his father's voice, low and mumbling, from Charlie's room. Her small noises of upset that he recognised as a specific pain. How could he have been so stupid? So blind, and ignorant? Or maybe scared? He slipped from bed, padded towards the kitchen. His mother dozed on the sofa, an empty bottle of cheap German white wine beside her, the glass overturned in her lap. She knew. She did nothing.

Shudders wracked every inch of Joseph as he returned carrying a long carving knife. His father's face whipped up, his back arched under the covers. Charlie lay beneath him, eyes squeezed shut, bottom lip pressed white by her top teeth. Joseph strode in as his father's face turned to fury, but he gave the man no chance. The knife rose and slammed down, again and again. His dad bucked and howled. Charlie screamed, scrambled out from under him. Their father wailed, high-pitched like an animal, then wet and gurgling, bubbles of shining red. Charlie tried to haul Joseph back but he ignored her, driven by the strength of years of anger. The knife plunged, the wet sound of flesh parting, of bones scoring, until the bed was a ragged mess of bright red shredded sheets.

Joseph staggered back, gasping and crying. Charlie grabbed him, climbed up him, arms around his neck, legs over his hips. She sobbed uncontrollably into his neck.

A slurred voice at the door. "Oh, Joe..."

He held Charlie in place with one arm, held the knife out with the other.

His mother looked from Joseph to the knife and back again. Her mouth fell open.

"Take it," Joseph said. "This is where you finally protect us."

His mother took a step forward. Then another. Face crumpling into tears, she reached for the knife.

CRYING
DEMON

CLAUDE STOOD WITH HIS BACK TO THE ROUGH BRICK WALL, trapped. Would it be another beating, or just a merciless verbal barrage? Big Tim was there, a giant among year 10s with a brain inversely proportional to his mass, so fairly safe to assume fists would fly. Claude had nearly made it home, only one block away, but the bicycles skidded up, cut him off, encircled him. Now the old drama would play out again.

"What's up, Claauuude?" Tim drew the name out as an insult.

"Just want to go home." Claude's voice was barely above a whisper.

"What's that, gayboy?" A heavy slap whipped Claude's face to one side and he tasted blood inside his cheek. "You made me look like a fool in chemistry."

"It's not my fault you're too dumb to know—" Another slap prevented him finishing the sentence.

Pointless to even engage, he raised his arms to cover his head and braced for the onslaught.

"Not gonna talk any more, fag?" Tim asked.

"Just slap him," another one said, but Claude had his eyes closed and didn't know who. It didn't matter, they were all basically the same person who thought being gay was the worst insult, even though Claude wasn't gay. Who needed to assert themselves physically because they were so insecure, because they were beaten at home and abusers learned to pass that horror on. They were the broken ones and Claude needed to just walk away, tell an adult, rise above it. It had been repeatedly explained and was fucking worthless. He couldn't walk away when they surrounded him. He had told adults, so many times, and they had repeatedly punished the bastards, but that just made them come back harder, meaner, more carefully out of sight. All such bullshit.

Claude even tried being the bully himself once, passing it on to another kid, but that only triggered a week of physical sickness and shame. Guilt still burned his cheeks at the thought of it.

And then the fists started to fall. Claude cried out, tears fell, his face and body flinched and throbbed with the assault. He fell and they started kicking, gravel scraped his cheek, a tuft of dry grass poked his cornea, his elbow whined as it struck the wall, and then silence. Fading laughter and the whirr of bicycle tyres. He opened his eyes, one swollen almost shut already from well-placed knuckles, and he was alone on the quiet street, bruised, bleeding, among the dirt and grass and tattered chip wrappers. Reduced to nothing once more.

Wincing against a dozen or more hurts, he picked himself up and limped home.

He called out a hello to his mum as he entered the house but hurried upstairs before she could emerge to greet him.

"Good day, love?" she sang after him.

"Yeah, fine." What was the point in telling her any different? "I've got homework."

"Okay, love."

He went into the bathroom to clean up. It didn't look as bad as it felt. After he'd washed and pressed a flannel soaked in cold water to his bruises, the attack was almost unnoticeable. Except for the swollen eye, already darkening. He'd have to think of a way to explain that.

Buzzing in his pocket distracted him and he pulled out his phone. A message from Aaron.

u ok?

At least he had one true friend who cared. He tapped a reply.

Who told u?...

...big tim boasted to camille and she told my sister

Bloody fast. i only just got home...

...so you ok?

Yeah i'll be fine...

...get online want to show you something

Claude went into his room and pulled his laptop from his bag, plugged it in. He booted up an app so they could chat by voice and Aaron answered right away.

"Sure you're okay?"

"Yeah, it's just pain. Who cares, right?"

"I do. Your mum and dad do."

"But no one can do anything. Tim's had his fill for a while. Might leave me alone for a few days. He'll drop out at the end of the year anyway, be selling us fries by Christmas. What do you want to show me?"

"Check it out."

A JPG file popped into the window and Claude opened it. He sat back in shock at the sight of a boy, no older than himself, lying on a concrete floor, naked. His chest flayed open, ribs on display like a white cage smeared with blood. "The fuck, man?"

"You think it's real?" Aaron asked.

"How the fuck do I know? Why are you sending me this?"

"It's from a game."

A kind of relief leaked through Claude's shock. "So it's not real then."

"Well, that's the thing. Apparently it is. It's a game on the Dark Web, but you have to finish it."

"What do you mean?" Claude leaned closer to the screen, half-turning his face away even as he did so, trying to decide how authentic the image was.

"If you don't finish, you become part of the game. Like this kid."

Claude laughed softly. "That's some real urban myth bullshit, man."

"Remember Clare Bailey? Went missing a couple of months ago, we had school counselling and everything?"

"Yeah."

"Apparently she played. That's how I know about it. My sister heard the rumour but didn't follow it up. I did."

A chill tickled through Claude's bruised stomach. "So don't play, I guess. Why would you anyway?"

"If you complete it there's a serious reward."

"Like what?"

"Dunno. Still trying to find out. But I need to dive the Dark Web deeper to learn more."

"Isn't that dangerous?"

"Nah, I use Tor to route through to some message boards. There's no risk. People are paranoid. I use a fake email, of course. And VPN as well as Tor. Here's another."

A second file popped into the feed, an animated GIF.

"I don't want to see more!" Claude said.

"This one's different."

Grimacing, Claude opened the image. It was a young girl, maybe seven or eight, standing in a dark corridor, shifting rapidly, uncannily, like she stood on undulating ground but everything was sped up. She wore a stained and tattered nightdress, her long, black hair greasy and hanging over her shoulders. Her face was a blur, the features somehow smudged as she vibrated, the GIF repeating over and over. Her head quivered side to side, the dark smear of her mouth stretching and closing, stretching and closing.

"Shit." Claude clicked the image away. "That's disturbing."

"Right?"

"You should be careful."

Aaron laughed. "I will. But I have an idea. We find the game and send it anonymously to Tim."

Claude paused, thoughts tumbling together for a moment. Then he smiled slightly, winced as his split lip stung with the movement. "Just to fuck with him?"

"Sure."

The sick feeling leeched back into Claude's stomach, a visceral clenching. "Nah. I don't want to be like them. I want to be better."

"We're *not* like them. This is revenge. You know a turd like Tim would never be able to finish a game like that. It's a kind of puzzler RPG apparently."

"Yeah, but it's not real. How can it be?"

"Who knows, man?"

Claude's mum called up the stairs, time for him to walk the dog and feed the chickens before dinner.

"I heard that," Aaron said. "Go do your chores. I'll let you know what happens."

"Be careful."

Claude signed out and headed down, deciding a wayward cricket ball during sports that afternoon would be his explanation for the black eye.

* * *

At school the following day Tim was suitably mellow. He grinned crookedly at Claude once or twice, clearly admiring his handiwork in Claude's swollen eye, deep black now and already yellowing around the edges.

Claude wished just once someone would beat the shit out of the big idiot, but he was smart enough to know it would be short-term enjoyment and ultimately unsatisfying. He'd rather just be left alone to his science fiction and role-playing games and love of physics without being attacked and called gay because of it. It really didn't seem like too much to ask.

At lunch, Aaron caught up with him. "You gotta come over after school. I was up half the night, you won't believe what I found."

"Really?"

"Yeah, I have to go to the library and do the homework I ignored last night. But come over later! You can have dinner at mine. I okayed it with Mum."

"All right." Claude sent his mother a message and she replied that he call her to pick him up no later than nine o'clock. A fair deal for a school night.

* * *

They sat in Aaron's room with the door shut, huddled close together at his desk. The laptop screen was solid black, but for a single white pentacle upside down in the centre. They'd been staring at it for several seconds.

"I'm gonna click it," Aaron said eventually.

Claude frowned. "I dunno, man. The forum said you have to finish the puzzle or the code will wipe your drive."

"It also said the puzzle was easy. You can have as many tries as you like. And it would give up the link for Crying Demon."

It had taken Aaron most of the previous night to find his way through the mire of data, but only a few minutes to explain the results. Crying Demon was, apparently, a game created by someone possessed by the Devil. At least, that was the most common story. Others had it that it was made by a victim of child abuse, or created by an abuser. Others still that it wasn't actually made by anyone, but existed of its own volition. It seemed largely irrelevant. The game allegedly contained a maze and puzzles, and if you got lost or stuck you became physically trapped inside. If you beat it, you got access codes to a stash of digital currency, easy to use on the Deep or Dark Web for all kinds of nefarious transactions. Or perfectly legal ones, simply remaining anonymous.

"It's all bullshit," Claude said. "Has to be. How can you be actually trapped in a game?"

Aaron clicked the pentacle. A hissing erupted from the speakers and slowly turned into a distant scream, a voice from a closed basement, a cry of agonising pain. The pentacle broke apart into pixels and drifted away to nothing. A white spot appeared in the centre of the screen and expanded into a monochromatic corridor. Whether it was poor-resolution graphics or heavily filtered video they couldn't tell. The screaming continued and another voice rose under it, repeating a phrase in reversed speech, staccato and echoing.

The boys glanced at each other, half-smiling. Claude's stomach rippled with nerves.

"W, A, S, D?" Aaron asked.

Claude shrugged.

Aaron put his fingers on the keyboard and pressed W. The vision moved forward along the corridor and the screaming faded to near-silence, but the backwards speech continued.

Aaron stopped and the scream surged back. He hit W again and the vision moved on, wailing fading. He used the mouse to look around, but the flickering, poorly resolved environment was unchanging. "Keep going?" he asked.

"What else is there to do?"

After several minutes of walking the corridor, they came to a solid wall. Dead end.

"What the hell?" Aaron said quietly.

He pressed D to rotate the view one-eighty and the vibrating, smudge-faced girl from the GIF of the night before stood right behind them. She launched forward with a screech that made their ears sing, and both boys leapt back from the desk. Aaron's chair went over and he went with it, but Claude saw the girl's mouth stretch impossibly wide as she lunged and the screen went black. After a few seconds, the white pentacle returned.

"Jesus fuck and shit," Aaron said, picking up his chair.

Claude's heart slammed against his ribs. He took a few deep breaths, shook his head. They both broke into nervous laughter.

"How was that a puzzle?" Aaron asked. "One corridor and a jump scare."

"It's all a myth," Claude said. "Crying Demon doesn't exist. It's trolls fucking with people."

"Nah, the stuff I read last night, the screengrabs I saw. There's more than just that." Aaron clicked the pentacle and began walking the passage again. This time he scanned around more as he went, checking above as well as to either side. The passage was open to a night sky, as poorly resolved as the rest, pixelated birds or bats flitting by periodically. Then a kind of awning appeared, a white inverted pentacle flickering beneath it.

"Mouse click for jump?" Claude said.

Aaron left-clicked and nothing happened. He right-clicked and their point of view sprang upwards. The scream returned, intensified, became an ululating wail and the screen spread into bright white. The boys sat back squinting. The white resolved into a room with three doors, old banded wood like a medieval castle. Each door had a set of Roman numerals above it, VII, XIX and VI VI VI.

"Seven, nineteen and six-six-six," Claude said.

Aaron grinned. "Six-six-six is the number of the beast. My dad loves Iron Maiden, that old metal band. Plays that shit all the time."

"Guess that's the one then."

Aaron clicked at the door and the screen went to black with a single line of white text, a URL, across the centre. As Aaron hovered the mouse it became a hand to activate the link. He clicked.

Blood poured down the screen, catching on unseen areas to spell out the words "Crying Demon" in a broken, crabbed variety of fonts, each letter a different typeface, some capitals, some lower case. Laughter bubbled up again, the strange, backwards speech babbled beneath it, repeating a single phrase over and over and over. A glittering START button resolved at the centre of the screen.

"Don't!" Claude said.

Aaron grinned. He hit the back button on the browser and the screen returned to nothing but the link. He highlighted and copied it.

"What are you doing?" Claude asked.

"I set this up earlier, fake profile." He opened another chat app. His profile pic showed a pretty blonde leaning forward to display a deep cleavage. The username read: *iSwallo451*.

"Who's that?" Claude asked.

"Some random off an image search. I friended Tim with it last night, the dick accepted right away." He connected to a username, *LordTim69*, and typed "Amazing!" then pasted the Crying Demon link.

"Wait!" Claude said, but Aaron hit SEND.

"Fuck that guy. You seen your eye lately? Let's give him a scare."

A response from Tim popped up.

...whats this?

Aaron grinned at Claude, then wrote.

youll love it…

They sat waiting for a response, but nothing happened. After a few minutes Aaron shrugged. "Oh well. Guess we'll see."

Claude swallowed rising nausea. "Hopefully he'll ignore it."

"You're too forgiving. Let's finish those character sheets for Friday's game session. Kate and Mohammed have said they're in."

"Okay."

* * *

The following morning at assembly the mood was sombre. The teachers sat on stage, faces serious, downcast. Once everyone had filed in, the headmaster stepped up to the lectern and cleared his throat.

"Ladies and gentlemen, we have some concerning news. One of our students, Tim Howell, has gone missing."

White heat flooded Claude. Aaron's gasp beside him seemed to come from far away.

"If any of you spoke to Tim yesterday after school," the headmaster continued, "in person or online or anything else, please come directly to my office. Even the most insignificant detail could be helpful. That's all for this morning. Off to your classes, please."

The hall erupted into hundreds of hushed conversations.

"What the fuck?" Claude said, eyes wide.

Aaron was pale, his lips trembled. "Is it really possible?"

"Should we go to the Head?"

"And tell him what? That a fucking Dark Web game ate Tim? That's insane, right?"

The rest of the day was a trial of guilt and fear for Claude. He and Aaron walked home from school together and not much conversation passed between them at first.

Eventually, Claude said, "Did we kill him?"

Aaron shook his head. "It can't be real."

"I didn't think so, but is there another explanation?"

"I've been thinking about it," Aaron said. "I reckon this whole thing is set up by some child molesters or some shit. Right? Like a trap. They scare kids into going somewhere, sneaking off, then they come and collect them. Maybe Tim ended up in a white van last night, you know?"

Claude nodded slowly, turning the idea over in his mind. "Yeah, maybe," he conceded eventually. He looked up. "In which case, we have to do something! Tell someone. We could play the game, find out what the trap is, and tell the police."

Aaron shook his head, staring at his shoes. "No way. I'm not chancing it. Tim was a prick, I fucking hate him. So should you. Look what he did to you just recently, let alone all the times before. Too bad for him, it's done."

Aaron strode away.

"Wait!" Claude called. "How does that make us any better than him? Now we're worse!"

Aaron yelled back without turning around. "No! Fuck him! I'll see you tomorrow, Claude."

* * *

Claude sat at his desk, the message app open in front of him, *iSwallo451* typed into the username box, but the password field was blank. He'd tried quite a few, but no luck. His phone buzzed and a message came through from Aaron. He opened it, hoping his friend had changed his mind.

…Mohammed can't make Friday after all. You ok to play Saturday?

Claude sighed, replied *yeah*, and turned back to his laptop. His eyes narrowed. The message gave him a clue. He typed the name of Aaron's dark elf assassin into the password field and the app opened up. The last two messages were right there.

…whats this?

You'll love it…

And above those, the link for Crying Demon. *Amazing!*

Claude's hands were trembling as he stared at the lines of text.

He'd meant what he said to Aaron, couldn't allow himself to be like Tim. And he couldn't condemn even a dick like Tim to child molesters. He had to be better than that. Should never have let this happen.

He clicked the link. The page poured down, the START button emerged, and Claude clicked before he could think more about it.

His screen crumbled into a swirling mass of pixels that slowly resolved into a corridor. It appeared to be video, gloomy like the place was lit with low-wattage bulbs. Or maybe he was trapped in some perpetual dusk, right before a night that would never fall. His fingers found the keyboard and he began to move forwards. The corridor moved under him, monochromatic, jagged in resolution. There were many turns this time, lefts and rights that made little sense. But Claude was a role-player. He dragged over a pad and pencil and sketched as he went, mapping as accurately as he could. Backwards gibberish and distant moans and screams leaked thickly from the speakers and he wanted to turn them off, but feared he would miss some essential sound component of the game if he did. Though it wasn't much of a game, just seemingly endless corridors. A pointless maze.

He emerged into a room, geometric patterns on the walls, fuzzy in low res. Across the space was a young child, standing with her arms hanging limply at her sides, rocking back and forth on her feet. Her head rose to observe Claude, but her swaying didn't cease. The only exit was a door directly behind her.

Claude moved to the wall and slid along it, never letting her out of his sight, then turned quickly through the door. He hurried down the next corridor, this time the dusky sky purpled with approaching night, a few stars starting to come out. He jumped as a still image flashed onto the screen along with an echoing gun shot. A naked man, clearly resolved in a high-definition photo, erection in hand, grinning widely. A small, naked boy lay curled on the ground behind him.

"Fucking hell," Claude moaned.

Another gunshot and the image was gone. The corridor continued.

The screaming rose as his movement ceased, so he carried on, mapping as he went, another room, two slowly swaying kids this time, a boy and a girl, heads down. Two exits and he chose the one on the left for no particular reason, marking the other door on his map.

The corridor devolved into stark black-and-white, badly rendered, the white blowing out occasionally. Another flash frame photograph, a woman in a hooded white robe atop a cliff, leaning forward arms outstretched, well beyond tipping point. The corridor returned and Claude kept going. More turns, more rooms, more ghostly undulating children with black eyes staring or heads hung. He checked corners and walls, looking for anything a bit different to the endless wandering. More flash frames of the gross and the grotesque. The backwards phrase repeated again and again, drilling into his brain.

Another figure stood in front of Claude, blocking the way. A stocky young man this time, swaying and staring at the ground. The figure was like the others: low res, blocky, too bright in the highlights, almost black in the shadows. As Claude approached, his breath caught. It was Tim, toes pointing slightly in towards each other, knees a little bent, head hanging, arms limp at his sides. He wavered like seaweed in a lazy current.

Then Tim looked up sharply, raised one arm. At first, Claude thought the bully was reaching for him, then realised he was pointing back the way Claude had come.

Heart racing, Claude turned and the girl with smudged features rushed up behind him, hands clawing forward. Her mouth stretched open and she began to wail, but not a human sound. Electronic, an old modem scream trying to reach a dial-up connection it would never find. It grew louder and louder, pinging and screeching, and Claude pressed hands over his ears, but the wail became a squeal and it was inside his head, forcing out against his ears, pressing into the backs of his eyes, and he sobbed. This was it. The end and it was going to hurt. He realised he wasn't in his chair any more, but in the pixelated corridor, standing in the cold air, the dusky sky high above, the concrete hard beneath his feet. The backwards speech rose in volume, began repeating more rapidly until it warped into words he could understand.

"Never leave, eternal dusk, crying demon. Never leave, eternal dusk, crying demon."

Claude screamed as the girl's icy cold fingers wrapped over his shoulders, hard like bone.

"Never leave, eternal dusk, crying demon."

Then another noise. "Claude!"

A different weight on his shoulder. A slap. "You right, buddy?"

* * *

Claude fluttered his eyes open, in his chair, at his desk. His computer screen was blank, the laptop gone to sleep. Aaron stood looking down at him, eyes concerned.

"Dude," Aaron said, almost a whisper. "When I came in, for a moment I thought I could see right through you."

"Through me?"

"Like you were a ghost. Had to touch you to make sure I wasn't tripping out."

Claude blew out a slow breath. "Thank fuck you did."

"What do you mean?"

Claude paused, wondering how much he should let on. Deciding to share nothing for the moment, he forced a laugh. "Wouldn't want to be a ghost!"

That swaying, flaccid figure of Tim, pixelated and monochrome... He fought back the urge to vomit.

"I wanted to say sorry," Aaron said. "Then you weren't answering texts for so long, so I came over. I lost my temper, but it's not your fault. You're right. We fucked up. *I* fucked up."

Claude checked the time. He'd been home over two hours, though it felt like less than thirty minutes. How long had he been in the game? *Had* he been *in* the game?

"I fucked up," Aaron said again. "What are we going to do?"

A sense of finality settled over Claude. He pointed to the map sketched on his pad. "This is the game," he said. He told Aaron everything.

"Are you serious? You were in there?"

Claude shrugged. "You said you could see through me. Another few seconds and I'd be done. She had me."

"Far out…"

"I have to go back."

Aaron looked up sharply. "What?"

"I've got a map to Tim. I've got to go back for him."

"And do what?"

"Bring him out. Save him. You have to watch me play. Don't watch the game, have your back to the screen and watch *me*. I'll go in and go to Tim. I reckon maybe it's timed. You don't find the way out before a certain amount of time passes and she gets you. I'll go to Tim. When I start to feel like the game's got me, I'll grab him. When you see me fading, slap me like before, bring me out. Maybe I can bring him with me."

Aaron stared silently for a moment. Then, "You think that'll work?"

"Fuck knows, but I have to try. We have to do something."

"Do we?"

"If we don't, we're worse than he ever was. I can't live with that. If it doesn't work we go to the Head tomorrow and tell him everything."

Aaron took a shuddering breath. "Okay."

A few minutes later they were set up. Aaron sat beside the desk, where he couldn't see the screen, watching Claude. Claude wore headphones and flexed his fingers a couple of times, then reached for the mouse. "Let me start to fade," he said. "But you hit me hard before I go too far, right?"

Aaron nodded, fear stretched white across his face.

Claude clicked the link. The sounds were a hundred times worse in headphones, the screams and reversed speech worming directly into his brain. He tried to ignore everything as he navigated the corridors following his map. He avoided the rippling ghost children, ignored the flash screens as best he could. They were all different this time, randomly generated, scenes of child molestation, gore, surgical procedures, suicide. He pushed on along the final corridor to where he had last found Tim.

The unfortunate bully stood there like before, eyes downcast, swaying. Claude moved around him, looked back and forth along the corridor. Nothing. He was still in his chair, still in his room. Aaron sat wide-eyed in his peripheral vision, staring. Claude clicked for action against Tim but nothing happened. He moved forward, tried to walk through him, but was prevented until he manoeuvred around.

"Not enough time," he muttered to himself, realisation dawning. Previously he had been cautious, moving slowly, looking everywhere. This time he had followed his map directly. He estimated he had several minutes before the clock began to run down. Maybe he could find a way out, finish the game. Would that still give him a chance to save Tim? Could he maybe save Tim and score the digital currency reward?

He moved away from Tim, further along the corridor than he'd been before. A T-junction at the end offered him left and right. He chose left, moved along as the screaming and backwards talking increased in volume.

-flash- A young man holding a dog over the flames of a bonfire.

More corridor, another junction up ahead.

-flash- A naked man crouched over the corpse of a woman, reaching into her eviscerated mid-section, eating her organs. His head snapped around and blood poured from his mouth.

Claude cried out as the image blinked away and he was back in the corridor. Mist drifted from his mouth as he yelled, the air so cold. Hard concrete pressed against his feet. He looked around frantically, his room gone, Aaron gone. He was in the game.

The grating whine and pings of an old modem pushed through the background noise. Spinning around, he saw the smudge-faced girl bearing down on him. He screamed and ran, hammering back along the passage. He tasted blood on the icy air, smelled vomit and shit and stale piss. The corridor seemed endless. He'd only made one turn, he needed a corridor on the right, that's where Tim was.

Hard, frozen fingers raked his back and Claude wailed and tried to double his pace. His lungs burned with the effort even as they sucked in so much frozen, fetid air. A dark gap appeared on his right and he turned, skidded and stumbled. The cold hands grabbed at him again and the backwards speech rolled forward.

"Never leave, eternal dusk, crying demon. Never leave, eternal dusk, crying demon."

Claude yelled incoherently, tears streamed his cheeks, his stomach felt like water, his legs like seaweed. He drove himself on, saw Tim's back up ahead. The modem scream intensified, battling with the chant in volume.

"Never leave, eternal dusk, crying demon."

Claude leaped forward and wrapped his arms around Tim as the girl's frigid hands closed over his shoulders like metal clamps. They squeezed, blackness swam at the edges of his vision and then repeated strikes around his back and neck, Aaron yelling his name.

The world cracked and fractured. Pixels and video streaked and swarmed through his eyes and he was falling, a massive weight in his arms, then an impact took the wind out of him.

He heard Aaron first, sobbing loudly and repeating, "Fuck me, fuck me, fuck me."

Claude rolled over on the floor of his room and pressed into something hard and cold. He leapt up, head swimming. Aaron was backed against the door, hands over his mouth.

On the floor at Claude's feet was Tim, face down, motionless. Claude crouched and tipped him over. Tim flopped onto his back. He was cold like he'd been in the fridge, his skin grey blue and dull, his eyes wide, staring, pupils dilated so far only a tiny band of colour remained. He was long dead.

Claude's scream joined Aaron's as he heard the pounding of feet on the stairs, and then his father yelling his name and rattling the door.

IN
VAULTED HALLS
ENTOMBED

THE HIGH, DIM CAVES CONTINUED ON INTO BLACKNESS.

Sergeant Coulthard paused, shook his heavy, grizzled head. "We're going to lose comms soon. Have you mapped this far?" he asked Dillman.

"Yes, Sarge."

Coulthard looked back the way they had come, where daylight still leaked through to weakly illuminate the squad. "Radio it in, Spencer. See what they say."

"Yes, Sarge." Corporal Spencer shucked his pack and set an antenna, pointing back towards the cave entrance. "Base, this is Team Epsilon. Base, Team Epsilon."

The radio crackled and hissed, then, "Go ahead, Epsilon."

"We've followed the insurgents across open ground to foothills about eighty klicks north north-east of Kandahar, to a cave system at... Hang on." Spencer pulled out a map and read aloud a set of coordinates. "They've gone to ground, about eighty minutes ahead of us. We'll lose comms if we head deeper in. Orders?"

"Stand by."

The radio crackled again.

"They'll tell us to go in," Sergeant Coulthard said.

Lance Corporal Paul Brown watched from one side, nerves tickling the back of his neck. They were working by the book, but this showed every sign of a trap, perfect for an ambush. It would be dark soon, and was already cold. It would only get colder. Though perhaps the temperature further in remained pretty constant.

He stepped forward. "Sarge, maybe we should set camp here and wait 'til morning."

"Always night in a fucking cave, Brown," Coulthard said without looking at him.

"You tired, possum?" Private Sam Gladstone asked with a sneer. The new boy, Beaumont, grinned.

"You always a dick?" Brown said.

"Can it!" Coulthard barked. "We wait for orders."

"I just think everyone's tired," Brown said. He shifted one shoulder to flash the red cross on the side of his pack. "Your welfare is my job after all."

"Noted," Coulthard said.

Silence descended on the six of them. They'd followed this band of extremists for three days, picking up and losing their trail half a dozen times. He was tired even if the others were too hardass to admit it. Young Beaumont was like a puppy, on his first tour and desperate for a fight, but the others should know better. They'd all seen action to some degree. Coulthard more than most, the kind of guy who seemed like he'd been born in the middle of a firefight and had come out carrying a weapon.

"Epsilon, this is Base. You're sure this is where the insurgents went?"

"Affirmative. Dillman had them on long-range scope. Trying to shake us off, I guess, going to ground."

"Received. Proceed on your own initiative. Take 'em if you can. They've got a lot of our blood on their hands. Can you confirm their numbers?"

"Eight of them, Base."

"Received. Good luck."

Spencer winked at the squad. "Received, Base. Over and out." He unhooked his antenna and slung his pack.

"Okay, then," Dillman said. He shifted grip on his rifle and dug around in his webbing, came up with a night sight and fitted it.

Brown sighed. No one was as good a shot as Dillman, even when he was tired and in the dark. But it didn't give much comfort. "We're not going to wait, are we?" he said.

Coulthard ignored him. "Pick it up, children. As there are no tracks in here," he kicked at the hard, stone floor, "we move slow and silent. Spencer, you're mapping. I want markers deployed along the way."

"Sarge."

"Let's go. Beaumont, you're on point."

"Yes, Sarge!"

"Slow and steady, Beaumont. And lower that weapon. No firing until I say so unless you're fired on first."

"Yes, Sarge."

The kid sounded a little deflated and Brown was glad. Youth needed deflating. They fell into order and moved forward. Spencer placed an electronic marker and tapped the tablet he carried. It began to ping a location to help them find their way back.

It became cooler and the darkness almost absolute. The light that leaked through from outside couldn't reach and blackness wrapped them up like an over-zealous lover.

"Night vision will be useless down here," Coulthard said. "We're going to have to risk torchlight. One beam, from point. Dillman, go infrared."

"Way ahead of you," Dillman said, and tapped his goggles. He moved up to stand almost beside Beaumont.

The young private clicked on his helmet lamp and light swept the space as he looked around. The passage was about five metres in an irregular diameter and as dry and cold as everything else they'd seen over the last few days. Dust motes danced in the torch beam, the scuff and crunch of their boots strangely loud in the confined space.

"All quiet from here on," Coulthard said and waved Beaumont forward.

They fell into practised unison, moved with determined caution.

"I'm a glowing target up here," Beaumont whispered nervously.

"That's why the new boy takes point," Coulthard said. A soft wave of giggles passed through the squad before the sergeant hushed them.

Dillman patted Beaumont on one shoulder. "I got your back, Donkey."

Beaumont's torch beam shot back into the group as he looked around. "Don't call me that!"

Laughter rippled again. Brown grinned. Poor sap. Caught petting a donkey back in Kandahar, just a lonely kid far from home, taking some comfort by hugging the soft, furry creature's neck. Of course, he'd been spotted, photographed and by the time he got back to barracks the story had him balls deep in the poor animal.

"Enough!" Coulthard snapped. "Are we fucking professionals or not?"

Their mirth stilled and they crept forward again. The ground sloped downwards and Spencer paused every fifty yards or so to place a marker. After about three hundred yards the passage opened out into a wider cavern. Something lay rucked up and definitely man-made on the far side.

Weapons instantly trained on it and Beaumont moved cautiously forward. "False alarm," he called back after a moment, his voice relaxed and light. Relieved. "Someone's been here. There are blankets, signs of a fire, an empty canteen. But it looks months old, at least."

The squad relaxed slightly as Beaumont shone his torch in a wide arc, illuminating the cave. Nothing but rough, curved rock. A few small fissures striated the walls on one side, black gaps into the unknown, but nothing big enough for even a child to get through. On the far side, a larger gap yawned darkly, a tunnel leading away and down. Large rocks lay scattered around the opening.

Coulthard nodded the squad forward.

"Looks like these have recently been moved," Gladstone said.

Brown moved in to see better. "Looks like this passage was blocked up and those fuckers cleared the way."

Dillman kicked at a couple of broken stones. "I guess they weren't so keen to ambush us here and are looking for a better option."

Brown shook his head. "Why would this passage have been blocked? And by who?"

"Emergency bolt hole they knew about?" Coulthard mused. "Move on."

The tunnel beyond was around three metres in diameter, sloping down again. Beaumont's was the only light, but in the otherwise total blackness it made the tunnel bright, shadows flickered off the irregular surface.

Beaumont took his flashlight from his helmet and held it at arm's length to one side. "If they do ambush and shoot at the light…"

After a couple of hundred metres, Brown, bringing up the rear, paused and looked back. "Hold up," he said quietly.

Coulthard glanced over his shoulder. "What's up, Doc?"

"Kill the light, Beaumont."

"Gladly!"

There was a soft click and the tunnel sank into blackness. Within seconds, their eyes began to adjust to something other than the dark. In crevices on the walls and ceiling of the passage, even here and there on the floor, a soft blue glow emanated. Almost imperceptible, easier to see from their peripheral vision, a pale luminescence. No, Brown thought. Phosphorescence. He crouched and looked closely into one crack. He pulled out a pocket knife, flicked open the blade and dug inside the crevice. The blade came out with a sickly blue smudge on it.

"Some kind of lichen," he said. "I've heard of this kind of stuff but always thought it was green."

Gladstone pulled his goggles down and flicked the adjustment. "Doesn't matter what colour it is, it's giving enough light for night vision."

"Lucky us," Coulthard said. "Goggles on, people. Keep that light off, Beaumont."

"Thank fuck, Sarge."

Brown pulled his own goggles down and watched the squad move forward in green monochrome. He was glad they didn't need harsh torchlight any more, but the glowing blue lichen gave him the creeps. He stood up and followed before they got too far ahead, shifting his heavy medical pack as he moved.

They continued silently for several minutes, Spencer periodically dropping markers. At a fork they tried the left-hand way and quickly met a dead end. Backtracking to the main passage, they travelled further and found a small cave off to one side, too low to stand upright. No passages led from it.

"Looks like this one tunnel is gonna keep heading down," Beaumont said. His voice had lost some of its excitement.

Coulthard raised a fist bringing them to a halt. "How far?" he asked.

Spencer checked the tablet that shone in their night vision even though its brightness was down to minimum. "Seven hundred and eighty-three metres."

"Three quarters of a K in, really?" Dillman whispered.

He sounded as nervous as Brown felt. The strange lichen continued, scattered randomly in cracks and fissures. Occasionally a larger patch would glow like a bright light, but for the most part it was soft streaks like veins in the rocks.

"Move on," Coulthard said.

After another couple of minutes, Spencer whispered, "That's one kilometre."

Before any discussion could be had about that fact, Beaumont hissed and cursed. "Sarge, got something here."

The squad sank into fighting readiness and crept apart to cover the width of the tunnel.

"Bones," Beaumont said. "Just a skeleton."

Coulthard turned. "Doc, go check."

Brown went to Beaumont and looked down on the bones lying at the curve of the tunnel wall. Streaks of the blue lichen wrapped the skeleton here and there, like snail trails. He crouched for a closer look. "Male, adult. No discerning marks of trauma that I can see at first glance."

He took a penlight torch from his pocket and lifted his goggles. "Mind your eyes."

The squad looked away as he clicked on the light and had a closer look. The bones lay scattered, no flesh or connecting tissue remained to hold them together. "There's a kind of residue," Brown said quietly. "Like a gel or something." He took a pen from his pocket and dragged the tip along one femur. It gathered a small wave of clear, viscous ichor. It was odourless.

He put one index finger to the same bone and gently touched the stuff. It seemed inert. As he brought it close to his face to inspect he frowned, then pressed his finger to the bone again. "This is warm."

Tension tightened the squad behind him.

"What's that?" Coulthard asked.

Brown swallowed, heart hammering. He looked at his fingertip then gripped the bone, felt the heat in his palm. "This skeleton is warm. And too clean to have rotted here."

"What the hell?" Beaumont demanded, his voice quavering.

"You shitting us?" Gladstone asked. His voice was stronger than Beaumont's but with fear still evident.

Brown held one palm over the skeleton, only an inch or so away from touching, moved it back and forth. "It's warm all over," he said weakly. His mind tried to process the information but kept hitting dead ends. The cold rock under his knee seemed to mock him.

"Warm?" Coulthard asked.

Brown's heart skipped and doubled-timed again as he spotted something beneath the bony corpse. "Hey, Dillman."

"What?"

"When you scoped those fucks we were following, what did you see that you thought was funny?"

A tense silence filled the space for a moment. Then Dillman said, "One of them had a big fucking gold dollar sign on a chain around his neck. Fancied himself a rapper or some shit."

Brown used his pocket knife to hook up a chain from where it hung inside the stark white ribcage. With a toothy clicking, he hauled it up link by link. Eventually a metal dollar sign emerged from between the bones, its surface no longer gold but a tarnished, blackened alloy.

"What the actual fuck?" Beaumont asked in a high voice. He shifted from foot to foot, looked wildly around himself.

"These bones are too clean and white to have decayed to this state," Brown said. He shone his penlight among the bones to reveal coins, a cigarette lighter, the half-melted remains of a cell phone, belt buckles. Two automatic pistols, both with traces of the gel-like slime, were wedged under the pelvis.

Coulthard stepped forward, leaned down to stare at the corpse like it was a personal insult. "You trying to tell me this is one of the guys we're chasing."

Brown shrugged, hefted the pen to make the dollar sign swing.

"Fuck this," Spencer said. "What the hell can do that to a person?"

Brown shook his head. "Who knows?" He played his torchlight around the walls and ceiling of the tunnel.

"And where did it go?" Gladstone asked weakly.

"Go?" Coulthard asked.

"I think it's pretty clear someone or something did that to him and is no longer here, right?" he said.

"Some kind of weapon?" Beaumont asked, still agitated.

"What kind of weapon does this?" Brown countered.

Coulthard stood up straight. "Can it, all of you. We have a mission and we'll keep to it. We'll find answers on the way."

"It's still warm," Brown reminded him. "This happened very recently, I think."

"Then we move extra fucking carefully," Coulthard said.

A burst of gunfire and distant shouting echoed up the tunnel. Epsilon squad froze and listened. A scream, another burst of gunfire then a deep, concussive boom.

"Grenade?" Dillman asked quietly.

Silence descended again.

"Lights off, mouths shut," Coulthard said. "Brown, up front with me in case we come across any more bodies. Beaumont, rear guard. Move out."

Brown nodded as he pocketed his knife. He wasn't happy about it, but that was a smart move by the sergeant. Beaumont had sounded very spooked by this encounter and understandably so. His nerves were like an electric current through the squad. Best he go to the back and have a chance to calm down. Reluctantly the squad fell into place. Brown glanced once more at the skeleton on the tunnel floor, and shivered as they moved almost silently away.

They travelled in silence for another ten minutes before Spencer whispered, "Two klicks."

A distant scream rang out, cut off equally fast. Several bursts of gunfire. They froze and listened but heard nothing more.

"Move on," Coulthard said tightly.

"Are you sure, Sarge?" Brown asked, but the sergeant's only answer was a shove in the back.

Several minutes later, Spencer said, "Three klicks."

Brown pointed and Coulthard nodded. Two more skeletons lay on the tunnel floor. Brown crouched and felt the warmth rising off them, stark against the cold rock all around. Two AK-47s and a variety of other metallic objects littered the ground.

"What the fuck, man?" Beaumont said, his voice still high and stretched. "What can do that?"

"Should we go back?" Brown asked.

"There's still five more of them somewhere ahead," Coulthard said. "And whatever is doing this is ahead as well. We'll go a bit further."

"We gotta go, Sarge!" Beaumont said. "Seriously, how can we fight this fucking—"

"Pull it together, soldier!" Coulthard barked. "Get your shit in order. We go forward for another little while and see. This tunnel has to change at some point, branch off or open out or something. I want to see what happens. If nothing happens by five Ks in, we turn around."

"Five Ks?" Beaumont sounded like a child. "Fuck man, five Ks?"

"Move out," Coulthard said softly, his voice and demeanour a perfect example of calm.

Brown wondered if the sergeant felt anything like as calm as he acted. It seemed Beaumont was the one having a far more sensible reaction to all this. He bit his teeth together to stem his own trembling and walked on.

The way was still lit by the strange veins of lichen, the tunnel remained a three metre or so diameter throat down into the foothills of the mountain range beyond. They heard nothing more for several minutes.

"Stay alert," Coulthard said. "How you doing, Donkey? Feeling okay?"

Beaumont didn't answer.

The sergeant laughed softly. "Sorry, Josh, I'm only ragging ya. Seriously, you feeling okay? You were a little rattled back there."

No answer.

Sam Gladstone said, "There's no one behind me, Sarge."

"What?"

"He was bringing up the rear, but he's not there."

Coulthard spat a curse. "Beaumont!" he called out in a harsh whisper. "Fuck, surely he hasn't panicked and run back."

"Wouldn't I have heard, Sarge?" Gladstone asked.

"I don't know. Would you? Spencer, leave your tablet here and double time back up the tunnel. If you don't catch up to him in a few hundred yards, we'll have to let him go and I'll kick his fucking ass when we get back."

"Righto, Sarge."

Spencer put down his gear and jogged away. They stood in uncomfortable silence for a few minutes.

"Nervous kid," Brown said eventually. "First tour."

"Don't make excuses for him," Coulthard said. "He's a fucking soldier."

Spencer walked back towards them, holding something out. "We need to get the fuck out of here," he said. Hanging from his fingers was a chain with two dog tags.

"The fuck?" Dillman whispered.

"Beaumont's?" Coulthard asked in a tight voice.

"He's a fucking skeleton just like the insurgent fuckers we found. Nothing left but buckles and weapons and shit. He's just fucking bones, Sarge!"

Dillman began muttering and shone his helmet lamp frantically in every direction. The mood of the squad began to fracture.

Coulthard swatted Dillman's lamp off. "Stow that shit! Everyone stay calm."

"Calm, Sarge?" Gladstone asked. "Seriously, we're in deep shit here."

"Stay. Calm. Spencer, did you recover Beaumont's weapon."

Spencer shook his head. "Left it there. The strap is gone, too hard to carry. But I took his clips."

"Fair enough. Now, we need to reassess what we're doing here."

"I think we should leave, Sarge," Brown said. He tried to keep his voice calm but heard and felt the quaver in it.

"It ain't that simple."

"It must be," Dillman said. "Fuck those guys, if they're even still alive down there. Whatever got Beaumont can get them. We'll wait outside the caves and pick off any who come out."

Coulthard held up a hand, a pale green wave in their night vision goggles. "Chill, everyone. It ain't as simple as leaving. I'm with you, in any other circumstances I would absolutely call an abort. But whatever took Beaumont, it took him from the back."

"Which means it's behind us," Brown said, realisation like an icy wave through his gut. "Or there's more than one, ahead and behind."

"Exactly."

"Does that mean we should carry on though?" Gladstone asked. "Maybe it's only gonna get worse."

"Maybe. Or maybe there's another way out." Coulthard picked up Spencer's tablet, checked the display. "We've still got a bunch of sensors, yeah?"

Spencer dropped Beaumont's tags into a pocket. "Yeah, plenty."

"Okay. We carry on for another kilometre and see if it leads to any branches in the tunnel, any other way out. If it does, we can maybe go around whatever's in here. If not, we turn around and risk facing it. Spencer, it's unlikely, but do we have any signal down here?"

The corporal pulled out his gear and spent a moment trying to get a response from Base. Then he went wide-band, looking for any transmissions. He found none and no one responded to open hails. "Nothing, Sarge."

"I didn't think so. Okay, Brown, you stay in the middle. Me and Spencer will take point. I want Gladstone and Dillman on rear guard, but you two walk backwards. We move slow and you don't take your eyes off the tunnel behind us. Let's go."

They moved slowly on again. Brown felt more than a little useless in the middle of the group, but he knew what Coulthard was doing. Protect the guy with the best chance of helping any wounded. Except it looked like whatever was in these caves didn't leave any wounded. He heard a gasp from Gladstone and turned to look.

"See that?" Gladstone whispered to Dillman.

"Yeah. There!"

Brown saw it too. He lifted his goggles to see with unfiltered eyes. A movement, more a shift of light across the darkness, like a ripple of wan blue luminescence. He caught part of a smooth, glassy sphere, a glimpse of something globular, but it pressed into the wall and vanished.

The others had stopped to watch. All five of them stared hard, but the tunnel was black as death and still.

"Keep moving," Coulthard said.

Brown walked backwards as well, eyes trying to scan every inch of the tunnel behind them.

"There!" Gladstone said sharply.

He'd seen it too. A glassy flex of movement on the ceiling about thirty metres back, closer than before. Almost as if a giant water droplet had begun to swell and hang, only to be quickly sucked back up.

"It's fucking following us," Dillman hissed and snapped on his helmet light again.

"But what is it?" Spencer demanded. "Is it even alive? Doc?"

Brown jumped as he was directly addressed. "I'm no expert here," he said. "Whatever it is—"

His words were drowned out by Gladstone's screams and Dillman's shouts of fright as the torchlight reflected back off a huge slithering mass across the ceiling right above them. It ran and undulated like an upside-down river across the rock then expanded, long and pendulous, extruding from the tunnel roof like a clear jelly waterfall. The huge, gelatinous blob unfurled itself and dropped.

Dillman leapt to one side, the deafening bark and muzzle flash of his weapon filling the tunnel as Gladstone tried to run backwards, but skidded and fell. He knocked Brown back, who dropped onto his rump in surprise and scrambled away, scrabbling for his weapon as Coulthard and Spencer aimed theirs above his head and let rip.

Gladstone's screams were bloodcurdling as the thing landed across his legs. Brown tried to see through the bursts of muzzle fire and caught staccato images like through a strobe light. Gladstone's legs, clothing and flesh alike melted away inside the transparent blob in an instant, leaving only bones. He tried to batter it off with his hands only to raise fleshless, stark white fingerbones in horror that fell and scattered across his lap. The meat of his arms was gone to his elbows in a second. Tenticular appendages lashed forward from the globular mass and retracted like a frantic sea anemone as it filled the tunnel with its bulk. Hails of bullets from Dillman, Spencer and Coulthard slapped and sputtered into the thing with little effect. It seemed to flinch and flex away from the bullets, then surge forward again, relentless. Only Dillman's torch beam seemed to really hold it up. Gladstone's screams cut abruptly short as it reached his torso and then Brown was up and running.

He pounded down the tunnel and realised the others were with him. At least, Spencer and Coulthard were. They panted as they ran, intent only on putting distance between themselves and that fetid horror. He didn't dare look back for fear the thing was bulging along behind them, for fear he'd see Gladstone finished off or Dillman caught. He stumbled and nearly fell sprawling at one point as the tunnel floor became broken rock and one wall half-fallen, almost blocking the way. The result of the grenade they had heard earlier. Bones scattered as he kicked unwittingly through another skeleton.

A brighter glow began to fill the tunnel ahead and he pounded for it, heedless to any danger before them compared to the certain death behind.

They burst out into a dizzyingly huge cavern, skidding to a halt on a rock ledge that protruded into space hundreds of metres above the cave floor. The ceiling was lost in swirling mists far above, but a soft blue glow leaked through. The walls of the gigantic space were streaked with the strange lichen and the entire place swam in a surreal glow, almost like wan daylight leaking through tropical waters, incongruous several kilometres underground. Filling the floor and rising high into the wisps of mist was a structure clearly constructed by intelligent design, a huge spiralling tower, hundreds of metres high, with a base at least a kilometre across. Curving buttresses met smaller towers in a circle around it. Monumental, the organic-looking structure appeared to have been painstakingly carved from the rock itself. From their ledge, a mammoth stairway led down to the building's lowest levels and the cave floor. Each stair was around two metres high and a similar width, hundreds of the giant steps leading down into haze. The air was colder and damp, smelled metallic and ancient. Everything about the sight emanated age, beyond any span of history. Geological age.

"Fuck me," Spencer said, lifting his goggles. His voice held the taint of madness.

They jumped and spun at a scuffing, puffing sound from behind. Dillman staggered from the tunnel mouth, moaning in agony. His left arm was nothing but useless, dangling bone, his hand gone. Half his face was missing, teeth grinning from the exposed skull where the bubbling, bleeding skin still retracted. "Saaarrrge," he slurred, reaching out with his good hand as he fell to one knee.

Spencer staggered backwards and turned, vomited noisily. Brown hurried forward, his medical training taking over, pushing shock and horror aside for the moment. But he didn't dare touch the poor bastard. He looked closely, trying to ascertain where the damage ended. Dillman's shoulder was eaten away and still melting. The cartilage holding the whole joint together disintegrated as Brown watched, and Dillman's arm bones fell to the rock with a clatter. The flesh of his neck liquefied and blood pulsed from the exposed carotid artery.

Dillman scrabbled at Brown one-handed as the medic gaped, at a total loss, even as the creep of disintegration slowed to a stop. But the damage was irreversibly done and Dillman's lifeblood pumped out. Coulthard's barrel slid into Brown's vision, pressed up against Dillman's forehead, and barked. The poor bastard flew backwards as the back of his head exploded out across the cave wall.

Spencer continued to empty the contents of his stomach as Brown sank to his knees and shook, mind flatlining. Coulthard moved to the mouth of the tunnel they'd emerged from and stared into the darkness. He flicked on his helmet torch and the beam pierced the black. He played it over the walls and ceiling.

As Spencer finally stopped puking, gasping short, shuddering breaths, Coulthard said, "Doesn't seem to be following us. Maybe it just guards the tunnels."

"Guards?" Brown managed.

Coulthard gestured at the impossible subterranean structure. "I don't think anyone is supposed to find that, do you?"

"But what is it?" Brown asked. "What manner of creature…?"

"Best not try to figure it out," Coulthard said. "Ours are soldier minds. That kind of question is for scientists."

"I can't believe it didn't get all of us," Spencer said.

"Out of practice maybe," Brown wondered. "It's not that quick, for all its deadliness. We only saw four insurgent bodies too. So four more got past it. It didn't like our lights, though they only slowed it."

"The flashlights were more use than the gunfire," Spencer said.

"Maybe too bright out here," Coulthard said, staring out into the wan blue glow of the cavern.

"Look."

Coulthard and Brown turned to see where Spencer pointed. Several giant staircases like the one in front of them led from the cavern floor up to various ledges around the walls. Their ledge covered a hundred metres with another staircase leading down from the far end. On that stairway, four tiny figures were clambering resolutely down. They moved as if exhausted, sitting on the edge of each high step before slipping onto the one below. One of them was being helped by the others, clearly wounded.

"Fuckers," Coulthard said. He went to Dillman's corpse, unslung the man's sniper rifle and fitted a telescopic sight. Moving to the edge of their own top stair he dropped onto his belly and unfolded the supports beneath the rifle's barrel to aim across and down.

"Seriously, Sarge?" Brown asked, incredulous.

"We have a fucking job to do, gentlemen. I'll see that done properly, at least."

He squeezed the trigger and one insurgent's head burst with a spray of blood they could see from afar, even with the naked eye. The others became frantic, scrambling like frightened ants. Coulthard fired again and a second man went down as his chest burst open. Another shot and the wounded insurgent was hit in the shoulder and spun around to drop to the rock and crawl into the lee of a huge step out of sight. They had finally realised where the fire was coming from and the other man scrambled into cover as well.

"Fuckers," Coulthard said again. He kept his eye to the sight and lay still, breathing gently.

Spencer sank to curl up against the wall at the back of the rock shelf. His arms wrapped around his head and he rocked gently.

"Spencer's lost it," Brown whispered to Coulthard.

"I know," the sergeant said without taking his eye away from the telescopic sight. "Give him some time and see if he comes around."

"How much time do we have?"

"Who knows? Right now, that fucking thing isn't coming out of the tunnel and I'm certainly not going back in. There's one unhurt insurgent bastard down there and one with a shoulder wound of unknown severity. For now, I plan to wait them out and give Spencer a chance to get his shit together. I suggest you have a rest."

His tone brooked no further discussion. Brown moved well away from the tunnel mouth and sat down against the stone. It was cold on his back. Clearly Coulthard had lost it too, only he was dealing with it in a typically old-school military way. The big, musclebound sergeant had seen more action than the rest of them put together and he let all that training take over. Maybe it was a good strategy. If the man could divorce himself from his emotions and let his experience run him like a robot, perhaps that would actually see him out of this alive.

Time ticked by. Brown began to worry about more mundane matters like where they might sleep, how much they had left in the way of rations and water, whether there was any way out other than the way they had come in. And he certainly wasn't keen to go back up the tunnel either.

He jumped as Coulthard's rifle boomed.

"I knew I could outwait him," the sergeant said with a smile in his voice.

"Did you get him?"

"Yep. He didn't think I'd wait on a scope all that time. I've sat for longer than ten minutes, you murderous insurgent motherfucker. You're a fucking amateur, you had to peek. A dead fucking amateur now." He stood and slung the rifle over his shoulder. "All dead except the shoulder wound, and I reckon he'll bleed out if nothing else. Let's go and see."

Brown stood, brow knitted in confusion. "Go and see?"

"Yep. What else is there to do?"

Brown thought hard but came up empty. The sergeant had a point. They at least needed to look around if they didn't plan to go back up the tunnel they had entered by, so they might as well finish the job while they searched. It was pragmatism taken to the max, but it made a cold sense.

Coulthard went and crouched beside Spencer. "How you doing, soldier?"

"Not good, Sarge."

"Me either. But we gotta move, okay?"

Spencer looked up, his narrow face white as bone under his brown crewcut. "I got a little boy at home, Sarge. He's gonna be two next month. I'm due home in time for his birthday. I missed his first."

Coulthard patted Spencer's shoulder. "We'll get out and get you on a transport home just when you're supposed to be."

"We won't, Sarge. None of us are getting out." He pointed at the spires and tower filling the cavern. "What the fuck even is that, Sarge? We're gonna die here." He sounded perfectly calm about it.

"We're getting out," Coulthard said firmly.

"My wife always worried I'd come home with no legs from an IED. 'You won't get killed,' she said one night when we'd been drinking. 'I can feel that.' She was always what she called spiritual. Thought she was fucking psychic, you know? But it was harmless. 'You won't get killed,' she said, 'but I have a terrible feeling you're going to be maimed by a mine.' Great fucking prophecy, eh, Sarge? For all her spirituality, she certainly didn't foresee this shit!"

Coulthard laughed. "I don't think anyone foresaw this shit."

"I was supposed to go home in two weeks, Sarge." Spencer's eyes brimmed with tears.

Brown gaped as Coulthard did something he would never have anticipated. The sergeant gathered Spencer into a tight hug and held the man against his chest.

"Let it out, solider," Coulthard said, and Spencer sobbed.

Brown stood uncomfortably off to one side for a good minute while Spencer bawled. The medic wondered why he felt so calm, so cold inside, and realised he had his terror, his panic, locked up in his chest. His true self and all the emotions it harboured was in a sealed box inside him, and at some point he would have to unlock that box. It frightened him to think what might happen when he did, but for now, it stopped him falling to pieces. Did that make him a better soldier than Spencer? A worse human being? For all the atrocities he'd seen, all the wounds and trauma he'd become accustomed to, surely this day's experiences should break him. He had no wife or kids like Spencer to yearn for. But the sergeant did and he was holding it together too. Maybe Spencer had just lost control of his locked box for now.

Coulthard pushed the man away. "Right, now on your feet, son. Feel better."

"Sorry, Sarge, I just…"

"Fuck sorry, Spencer, it's all done. You ready to move out?"

"Yes, Sarge." Spencer's voice still quavered, but there was some confidence back in it.

"Brown?"

The medic nodded, shook himself. "Yes, Sarge." *At least*, he thought, *as ready as I possibly can be.*

Coulthard sniffed and settled his pack. "Well, I am certainly not going back the way we came. That thing in the tunnel, whatever it is, seems to want to stay there, so we'll leave it well alone. There must be another way out. Nothing that size," he pointed at the monumental structure filling the cave, "can possibly only have one tiny tunnel leading in. Let's go."

"Sarge," Brown said, finally ready to give voice to a nagging worry that had tickled his hindbrain since they had emerged onto the rocky ledge.

"What?"

"The thing in the tunnel hasn't followed us out. Maybe you're right and it's too bright in here."

"Yeah. And?"

"Well, if it's meant to guard this place but hasn't followed us out, that must mean something."

The Sergeant narrowed his eyes. "Like maybe there's something else in here to do the same job and that thing only worries about its tunnel?"

"Something like that."

"You have a point. Better keep your weapon ready. Let's go."

They moved along the ledge, heading for the giant stairway leading down that the insurgents had used. Brown whistled softly as they came abreast of a massive bronze plate pressed into the wall, ten metres high and five wide, inscribed with strange cursive symbols and patterns that made him dizzy to look upon. His eyes kept sliding away as he tried to make sense of them and nausea began to stir his guts.

"Over there," Spencer said. "And there."

They followed his pointing finger and saw other plaques on other ledges dotted around the cave. Small tunnel openings here and there accompanied them just like the one they had entered through.

"Any of those tunnels could have a fucking monster like the one that attacked us," Brown said.

"We have to assume each one does," Coulthard said. "We have to keep looking for something else. Move on."

Another twenty metres along their ledge gave them a vantage point past the monumental structure and they all saw it at once. On the far side of the vast cave, at the top of another giant staircase that went even higher than where they currently stood, a huge tunnel mouth yawned open.

"That must be fifty metres wide," Coulthard said. "We have a fighting chance in a space like that."

"Probably where the insurgents were heading too," Brown said. "Means going through that structure though."

"Or around it on ground level."

A scream ripped through the air. High pitched and horrified, it was the voice of a man staring into hideous death and it cut suddenly short.

"Came from down there." Spencer pointed down the stairway they had nearly reached, where the insurgents had died under Coulthard's fire.

"Seems like old Shoulder Wound survived after all," the sergeant said.

"Until just then." Brown felt the lock on the box in his chest loosening.

"All right. Silence." Coulthard raised his weapon and headed for the stairs. "We have no choice but to go through, so let's *fight* our way through."

He moved to the first stair and jumped down. The riser was a few inches above his head, but he walked forward and jumped down the next. Brown and Spencer followed.

Brown's knees jarred with every drop and he wondered how long they would hold out. How long could any of them last with this kind of exertion? The insurgents were about two thirds of the way down and had looked spent, sliding off each step, staggering around.

And assuming they made it down, they would have to climb up even more stairs to get to the wide tunnel they had seen. And all the while fighting past whatever had triggered that scream? Basic training or advanced combatives, nothing prepared a soldier for this. Ready for anything? No one had ever listed this place under the heading of "anything".

His lock loosened a little more, so Brown stopped thinking and kept moving.

He stopped counting the drops at fifty, but after a few more Coulthard paused and raised one fist. They froze, crouched in readiness. Coulthard tapped his ear. Straining to listen, Brown heard a scratching, scrabbling noise. Distant, but getting quickly nearer. Coulthard crept to the edge of the step they were on to look down and immediately burst into action. He raked his assault rifle left to right, the reports of his short bursts shattering the quiet and bouncing back from the distant walls all around. Brown and Spencer joined him at the edge. Spencer added his ordnance to Coulthard's straight away, but Brown paused momentarily, stunned.

A flood of creatures flowed up the steps towards them like roiling black water. Only twenty or so steps below and fast getting closer, they scrambled on too many legs, black bodies like scorpions, but where the stinger should be on the end of the waving tails was a leering face, almost human though twisted somehow into something hideously uncanny, eyes too wide, mouths too deep. Those mouths stretched silently open or gaped like fish as the creatures chittered over the stone edges. Each was a metre or more long, two vicious mandibles at the front of the thorax snapping at the air as they came.

Brown brought his weapon up and added his fire to the fray. Their bullets tore into the things, shattering hard shells and causing gouts of glowing blue blood. As one fell, its fellows swarmed over it. Some staggered from shots striking their many limbs and fell from the sides of the staircase. Brown realised the things were screaming, in fear or pain or triumph he didn't know, but they had no voice and just hissed thick streams of air from those stretched and awful faces that wavered atop their segmented tails as they ran.

There was no way Brown and his colleagues would be able to scramble up the stairs ahead of these horrors, so here they had to make their stand. Coulthard plucked a grenade from his belt and lobbed it past the first wave. It detonated in a cloud of shining black carapace and stone chunks. Spencer emptied his clip and expertly switched in a new one. He resumed firing as Brown switched in new ammo. Coulthard threw two more grenades and switched clips to resume firing. Brown threw a grenade of his own and switched in his last clip. Their automatic fire stuttered and roared, controlled bursts as training took over.

The creatures were only five steps away, then four, and ammo was running out. Brown, Spencer and Coulthard yelled incoherent defiance and raked fire across their advance. Spencer lobbed a grenade, then the things were too close for any more explosives.

Three steps and their numbers finally began to thin, two steps, almost close enough to touch.

Suddenly the men were stumbling left and right, firing in short bursts as the last of the things breached their step and tried to clamber onto them, heavy, sharp mandibles snapping rapidly for limbs. Spencer screamed as one drew close, his weapon clicking absurdly loudly, empty. Brown fired three short bursts and then there were no more creatures coming. Coulthard blew two away right at his feet, turned and killed the last one right before it leapt onto Spencer.

Everything was suddenly still, their ears rang.

Dave Spencer looked up at his sergeant with a smile of relief just as Brown raised one hand and shouted, "Stop!"

But Spencer finished taking a step away from the corpse at his feet and his foot vanished over the edge of the stairway. As his face opened into an O of utter surprise, he dropped from sight.

Brown and Coulthard rushed to the edge, but Spencer was lost in shadow. He found his voice a second later, his howl drifting up before cutting off with a wet thud. Silence descended heavily throughout the enormous cavern.

Brown, on his hands and knees, began to tremble uncontrollably. "So much for his psychic fucking wife," he muttered.

Coulthard was beside him, breathing heavily from exertion, as Brown was, but there was anger in the sergeant's demeanour too. "Took the fucking radio with him," Coulthard said eventually.

He stood and yelled and screamed, kicked at the corpses of the horrible scorpion monsters all around. Brown turned to sit and watch, glad in a way that the man was finally letting some emotion out. Like a pressure cooker, he had surely been close to blowing for a long time.

Eventually the sergeant slumped back against the step above and slid down to sit. "So all we have is what we're carrying and no comms."

Brown nodded. "I've got what's left in here," he hefted his weapon, "and that's it. You?"

"Same."

"I still have two grenades."

"I got none. But we each have pistols," Coulthard said.

"Might save that for myself," Brown said quietly, and he meant it. At some point, sticking the barrel of the .45 against his temple and pulling the trigger seemed like a good option. He looked at the chitinous corpses all around. "Think we got them all?"

"Hope so. These ancient fuckers were no match for the tools of modern warfare."

"Tools which will be empty very soon if we need to use them again."

Coulthard just nodded, staring at the ground between his feet. Eventually he sniffed decisively, stood. "Right, let's go."

Brown looked up at him, stark against the backdrop of shadowy mist and the wan blue glow of the lichen. "Yeah. Okay."

They began to drop down the steps again, picking their way through the broken bodies, blue blood and shattered rock of their battle. In places, their grenades had sheered the steps into gravel slides they carefully surfed on their butts. Here and there some of the creatures still twitched, but they avoided them and preserved their ammo. After a dozen or so stairs the corpses ended. Another couple and they came across red smears on the stones and a few lumps of flesh and ragged clothing.

"A lot of blood," Brown noted. "Those things clearly enjoyed the dead as well as the one who survived. I sure hope that was all of them."

Coulthard nodded and continued down in silence. Eventually, gasping, with legs like jelly and bruised feet, they reached the bottom to stand in swirls of mist.

A low moan rose, vibrating the air all around them. The stone floor thrummed. Then it faded away. As Brown and Coulthard turned to look at each other, it rose again, louder, stronger. Then again. And again. Each time, it vibrated more deeply, sounding more strained and desperate, accompanied by a heavy metallic clattering. Then silence fell and pressed in on them for a long time.

Eventually Brown said, "What the fuck was that?"

Coulthard looked towards the tall structure in the centre of the cave. From ground level it punched up high above them, wreathed in tendrils of blue-tinged mist. Brown began to get dizzy as he stared up at it. The smaller towers surrounding the base, connected with curving buttresses, were each some thirty metres high. In the base of each smaller tower was a hollowed out circular space, and in that space sat a statue. From the few he could see, Brown realised that each statue was turned to face the centre tower. They were almost human-like in form, seated cross-legged, but each had four arms with eight-fingered hands, held out to either side as though awaiting an embrace. Their bellies were distended and rolled with fat, their faces wide with four eyes, two above two. Brown moved to better examine the nearest one and the level of detail was phenomenal, disturbing. Not so much carved, as real living things turned instantly to stone. He wondered if in fact that's exactly what they were. Each was at least three metres tall and corpulent.

Coulthard's gaze was still fixed on the main tower. Brown moved to stand beside him and realised he was looking at a doorway, a dark opening in the rock wall several metres high and a couple wide. "The moaning came from inside, don't you think?" the sergeant asked.

"Who cares?" Brown said, stunned.

"I have to know." Coulthard walked towards the door.

"Sarge? Seriously, let's just go. What if more of those…" Brown's voice trailed off as Coulthard approached the opening.

Soft blue light pulsed from inside as the sergeant drew near. The moan rose again, shaking everything. Brown put a hand to his chest as the deep moan sounded a second time and made his heart stutter. His feet were frozen to the spot as he watched Coulthard step through the high entrance.

The sergeant stopped just inside and his gaze rose slowly upwards. He was framed in the blue light, that pulsed more and more rapidly. The groaning became a wail and Coulthard's weapon dropped from lax fingers to hang by its shoulder strap.

"Chains," Coulthard stammered. He looked left and right, up and down, his sight exploring a vast area. "Giant chains right through its flesh. Through all those eyes!" He dropped to his knees, head tilted back as he looked far above himself. "This is a prison. An eternal prison!" He began to laugh, a high, broken sound that came from the root of no sound mind.

The moan stirred into a deep, encompassing voice that reverberated through the cavern. "*Release me!*"

Chains rang as they were snapped taut and relaxed again. Whatever slumbering monstrosity that filled the tower and split the edges of Coulthard's mind thrashed and its voice boomed again. "*RELEASE ME!*"

"Sarge!" Brown yelled, his stomach curdled with terror. "We have to go!"

He wanted to drag his sergeant away, but had no desire to risk seeing what the man saw. "*Sarge!*" he screamed.

Coulthard's face tipped slightly towards him and Brown took in the sagging cheeks, drooling mouth, wild, glassy eyes, and knew that Coulthard was lost. No humanity remained in that shell of a body. With a sob, Brown ran.

He raced around the tower and leaped for the first step of the stairway on the far side. He hauled himself up as the voice burst out, over and over, "*Release me! Release me! Release me!*"

Brown scrambled up stair after stair, rubbing his hands raw on the rough surface. He sobbed and gasped, his shoulder and back muscles burned, but he hauled on and on. He couldn't shake the image of all those swarming scorpion things from his mind and imagined them racing up behind him but didn't dare to look. The voice of whatever was imprisoned below cried out again and again.

At some point, more than fifty steps up, Brown collapsed, exhausted, and blackness took over. He assumed he was dying and let himself go.

He had no idea how much time had passed when he woke again, unmolested. The massive cavern was still.

Brown dragged himself to his feet and began the shattering climb once more, step after step after step. Time blurred, his mind was an empty darkness, until he pulled himself over the top of one more step and saw a flat expanse of rock stretching out before him. On the far side, some hundred metres away, the huge yawning tunnel stood, threatening to suck him in.

Brown laughed, dangerously close to hysterical, and gained his feet, stumbled forward into the gloom. He didn't care what might be there, he just needed to leave the hideous monument and its prisoner behind.

More of the softly glowing lichen striated the walls and he dropped his night vision goggles into place. The sight before him stopped him dead, confused. A grid, some kind of lattice. He looked up and down as realisation dawned. A giant portcullis-like gate filled the tunnel, thirty metres high, fifty metres across, fixed deeply into the rock. He walked up to it and found it made of cast metal like the huge plaques they had seen, the criss-crossed straps of bronze at least twenty centimetres thick. Each square hole of the lattice was perhaps half a metre or a little more across. If he stripped off his gear, he might be able to squeeze through. Or he might very well get stuck halfway.

But it didn't matter. Beyond the gate, beyond the weak glow of the cavern behind him, uncountable numbers of clear, globular shapes moved and writhed, tentacles gently questing out and retracting again, waiting, hungry. Hundreds of them.

Brown fell to his butt and sat laughing softly. He checked his rations and canteen, tried to estimate how long he might survive, and gave up when his brain refused to cooperate. He looked back across towards the tunnel they had emerged from. Compared to the swarm waiting beyond the gate, the one or two in that tunnel seemed like far better odds. Assuming it was only one or two. And assuming he had the strength to get back down and up again. And that there were no more guardians waiting for him in the cavern. And that whatever was imprisoned below didn't thrash free in its rage.

Lance Corporal Paul Brown, experienced medic and decorated soldier, lay down and pulled his knees up to his chest. His brain couldn't work out what to do, so perhaps he would just have a sleep and, refreshed, maybe then decide which suicidal option for escape might be the best one to try.

* * *

SPECIAL COMMUNIQUE.
ATTN: COLONEL ADAM LEONARD – DIRECTOR,
UNEXPLAINED OCCURRENCE DIVISION.

YOUR EYES ONLY

SUBJECT – DISAPPEARANCE OF EPSILON TEAM, NORTH OF KANDAHAR, AFTER TRACKING ENEMY INSURGENTS TO UNDERGROUND HIDEOUT.
SURVIVORS – 1: LANCE CORPORAL PAUL BROWN, MEDIC.

REPORT: After non-response from Epsilon Team for thirty-six (36) hours after their last communique, a second squad was sent to investigate. They found Lance Corporal Paul Brown of Epsilon stumbling through foothills some seven (7) kilometres south of Epsilon Team's last known whereabouts. Brown was wearing nothing but ragged underwear and his helmet, raving and largely incoherent, his left arm below the elbow was just bone, no hand, the flesh stripped away presumably by acid or a similar agent. His body was covered in various other wounds, some similar to his arm (though none as severe) and others clearly made from impacts, falls, scrapes, etc. He carried no gear except a flashlight, which he pointedly refused to relinquish. He made almost no sense except one phrase, repeated over and over: "Never let it out! Never let it out!" Current assessment by psychologists suggests Brown may never recover his faculties, but therapy has been started. His extensive injuries are being treated and are responding satisfactorily.

We're still trying to establish further facts but are preparing an incursion squad to Epsilon's last known whereabouts. Due to your standing request to be informed of any unusual occurrences, I am sending this wire. Our squad will be entering the cave at the last known location of Epsilon Team at 0800 tomorrow, the 14th, should you wish to accompany them.

Please advise.

HER GRIEF
IN MY HALLS

THIS OLD TWO-STOREY QUEENSLANDER CREAKS AND MOANS, but I never mistake its sounds for *hers*. Its voice is as aged and distinct as the sugar cane industry in the tropical north, but *hers* is different. The house complains of generations, but *she* cries for grief. For loss. Maybe for justice.

Of course, I didn't expect her when I moved here after my wife died, looking for solitude and financial relief. High on the ridge, far from any town, this place was cheap and I could buy it outright. With no debt, I need very little to survive. Selling my paintings once a month at the markets an hour away and the interest on my savings, together, earn me enough.

Hide, paint and mourn my Sarah, that's all I wanted to do. But I'm not alone. I bought a house with an occupant, though I've never seen her. I wonder how long ago she lived. I *must* see her, as much to prove I'm not going mad as to satisfy my curiosity.

Her footsteps beat a melancholy cadence as she walks the rooms and landings above, her silky wail of despair strangely melodic. Each time I've leapt from my chair and run for the stairs, I've been overwhelmed by the knowledge that she's gone before I've taken two steps. I used to be afraid, until I realised that she ran from me, and perhaps it was her fear that should bother me more.

So I've resolved to be more subtle.

My home's entrance is grand. An arched door surmounted by stained glass opens onto a black and white tiled floor. The staircase rises up one side and the landing passes across two walls like a Western saloon, leading to four bedrooms and two bathrooms. The ground level has a library to one side, a large living room to the other, kitchen and dining room directly ahead of the front door. A simple but effective arrangement and far more space than I need.

The ridge the house sits upon is one of many, knifing down to the muddy sea. Beyond the acres and acres of sugar cane fields I'm letting go wild, rainforest surrounds me, abundant with verdant life and myriad creatures that forage and hoot and howl and whistle. Mercifully few people, though. The monthly market crowds are more than enough. So I take care of the too-big house with my echoes and *her* shrieks, and I don't need anything but for humanity to leave me to my grief.

I use the large living room as my studio and spend evenings in the library, surrounded by thousands upon thousands of pages. I do love books. That's the only time I hear her, she only ever walks and moans as I read. When I'm still. Never at night when I'm in bed. Never during the day as I paint or cook or cry. Just of an evening as I sit lost in novels.

After some thought, I've moved the drinks cabinet into the library and brought down the mirror from the dresser in the smallest bedroom, which I've set atop the shiny wooden surface. It's angled to the library door, and in the hall by the entrance is the wardrobe where I store my boots and coats. One of its doors is open just so. Its mirror sees the one in the library, and sitting in my leather chair, I can see the reflection of a stretch of second-storey landing and two doors. Not mine or the smallest room, but the other two which I keep made up as rooms for guests I know I'll never entertain.

I sip rich, sweet port, and the novel is forgotten on my lap as I observe my cunning arrangement. The footsteps began some minutes ago, pacing overhead, around my bedroom. It's never bothered me that she starts there, at least not since I understood she was more afraid of me than I of her. It is the master bedroom, after all. I can only assume she was once the lady of this house.

Sometimes she treads the balcony that skirts the upper storey, a match for the veranda below with its intricately-wrought iron curlicues and rails rubbed smooth by who knows how many hands in the last century. But this evening she doesn't go outside and I hear my bedroom door click open. Her sad step moves onto the landing.

It's always hot and humid. The fan turns lazily, but the sweat that beads my brow and soaks my palms cannot really be blamed on the climate. My heart begins to race. Her cry sounds, that desperate *oooooh* of longing. It carries a pain that echoes my own.

The night outside buzzes with life. A gecko somewhere high on the wall *tick-tick-ticks* as it hunts. I'm rigid, barely breathing as I watch the dim reflections. A movement makes me stifle a gasp. Pale, floating lace tickles the edge of my view and she wails again. My hands tremble as the fluttering white resolves into a dress and I can see her plainly. After all I've heard these months, I still find it hard to believe the sight before me.

Her hair is long and dark, falling in soft waves over slim shoulders. Her hands are raised as if to accept a parcel, her skin ivory pale. I can't quite see a face and lean forward to get a better look. She notices the movement in the mirror and startles. Her head snaps around and for a moment our eyes are locked. She's beautiful and terrified and mortified, and her full mouth widens in shock as she cries out and dissipates like mist in a sudden breeze.

And I am bereft.

I saw to the very heart of her anguish, observed her pain laid bare, felt so briefly that her anguish matches mine, and I am ashamed. My cheeks are awash with tears. For her, for my Sarah, and for myself. Loss is a black hole that sucks light and happiness away. That poor woman. Her pain is lodged alongside my own now, transferred in that tormented look.

The rational part of me thinks she looked Victorian. Her dress with its full skirts, its intricate sleeves and high lace collar. Perhaps she came to this home when it was new. Perhaps it was built for her by some adoring husband, or hopeful suitor.

I cannot know for certain. I only know I desperately want to see her again, if for nothing else than to apologise, but I wonder if I ever will. With shaking hands I pour more port and drink. And pour and drink again until a stupor stills me in my wing-backed chair.

* * *

Weeks have passed and finally I hear her again, having all but given her up as gone for good. The familiar shuffling across my bedroom floor makes my heart skip. I haven't been able to paint since our encounter. Since I looked into her eyes. I've simply moped, venturing out only a handful of times for supplies. Mostly booze.

Dear Sarah, what would you make of me now?

But I hear her, pacing above. The furniture and mirrors have been returned to their former locations. My cunning merely feels cruel. A clever trick that hurt us both. She paces and I rise quietly, stand slightly uncertain of foot from a fine Shiraz, and walk silently to the library door. There I wait, gaze resting on the landing.

My bedroom door drifts open and she steps out, looks directly at me and her lips part to release that desperate sound. She lifts her hands as though she wants me to place something there, expression twisting. In confusion, I raise my own hands. I don't understand. She cries, her voice a distant howl, then she wafts apart and away. As she goes, she reaches forward one hand, grasping towards the door at the end of the landing. The door to the smallest room.

Then I'm alone with only our combined despair. I finish the Shiraz.

* * *

Over the following days I find the will to paint again, but the woman is my only subject now. She inhabits my waking mind and my dreams. I can't shake the sensation that I've interrupted her in the middle of something important, some eternal, unresolved nightly mission, and if I want to learn more I must let her finish her wandering. But how to let her do so, and observe it, without spoiling her progress? I'm drawn to the smallest bedroom, the way she reached for it. Does she travel there when she roams unimpeded?

I fill canvas after canvas with her image, and by night I eschew the library, sitting instead in that smallest room, in a threadbare armchair by the bed, reading by a bedside lamp. The lampshade is of glass panels and beads, dragonflies dancing around its border. Its multi-coloured light is poor. There's no fan up here and the air is close and sticky, but I endure the discomfort for over a week before I hear her again.

I don't notice her footsteps at first as I read, but jump when her moan drifts along the landing. I put my book aside, stare at the closed door. She wails again, nearer this time, and her footfalls seem solid. The door yawns open.

I sit perfectly still as she glides in and her face changes as she sees me. She turns, points urgently to the corner with the small single bed, then reaches for me, supplicating as she tatters, swirls and fades.

Once more I feel her sorrow, and I weep. I can't help but remember Sarah and imagine her berating me for hiding, for taking on the ancient grief of others as if my own is not enough. She would tell me to get on with my life, but what is my life without her?

What was the woman pointing to? There's nothing in the corner, under the bed or mattress, except polished floorboards, inscribed here and there by long dead boring insects. The walls are pressed horsehair boards inside and painted weatherboard without, a deep burgundy that appealed to me greatly when I inspected the place, but it does draw in the heat terribly.

In a frenzy of confusion I retrieve tools and tear up the flooring and pry off wall panels to expose the bones of the house but discover only wooden trusses and dust and cobwebs and nothing else.

Returning to the library, I sit beneath the fan and think. The smallest room is often reserved for the smallest person. If I can aid my guest will it salve my own misery?

* * *

Steeling myself against the scrutiny of others, I travel to the nearest town. The records office is tiny and combined with the local library. There is no microfiche. Everything is kept in carefully maintained registers, defended daily against the march of dust and mites. A woman with large-framed glasses, Hi, I'm Joan on her name badge, judges my request with tight lips and seems to decide

I'm harmless. She sets me up in a back room with a tower of ledgers, replenishing each as I finish it with another one bigger than the last.

Joan is happy to know someone is living in the old house again. It seems the place has a history. It was built by a very rich man who intended to continue the growth of his fortune with sugar. He and his young wife moved into the newly built abode, and everything was fine until the birth of their child. The baby was born hale and well, a boy, Nigel Anthony, only offspring of Cecil and Madeleine Wilmer, for the birth killed the mother.

Madeleine. My ghost has a name at last.

Cecil collapsed into inconsolable despair, his family destroyed the moment it was made, and eventually he left, taking his son with him, leaving the house and his grief behind. But Madeleine had no such luxury.

Does she mourn the loss of the boy? Or the loss of a chance to know him, to hold him? Does she know he lived or fear he died too, wondering why his ghost isn't there for her to care for?

Joan brings me new tomes and I learn that Nigel Anthony Wilmer grew into a successful young man. He eventually become a magistrate well respected throughout the state of Queensland. His professional life is documented in several newspapers of the time. He was a good man, it seems, one of whom his mother could be proud.

I make copies of all the articles I can find and take them home.

* * *

Her footsteps have been slow along the landing, almost as though she anticipates something. Anticipates me, perhaps. I stand in the smallest room, two particular articles held before me. One of her son's birth, another lauding his reception of an Order of Australia. Surely enough to make a mother relent in her despair.

The door opens and I smile as she slides in, but her lips are turning down in pain the moment she lays eyes on me. I brace against the wash of shared desolation and raise the papers higher. "Can you see—?" I begin, but she yowls and swirls away.

* * *

I was foolish before, I know full well that my presence disturbs her. Perhaps I was being selfish. I wanted to see her receive the news I had found. This is not about mending my heart, but hers.

I have spread several articles celebrating Nigel's life on the bed in the smallest room. Had they chosen a name before he was born? Will poor Madeleine be able to read these scraps of news, see her son's name and know he had the thing that was denied to her, a life fulfilled? He lived to eighty-one years old.

It's another week before I hear her again, and I remain in the library with wine and book, the door closed, her privacy assured. She makes her way through the house, her voice a miserable song of loss. The door to the smallest room clicks open and I hold my breath. The entire house holds its breath, it seems, silence descends like a shadow.

But there is no cessation in her cries and tears are dampening my cheeks again. She walks and laments, clearly unmoved by the messages I have left her. Does the strange distance between here and where she truly is blur her vision? I pour more wine and lift my book and try to close my ears to her weeping.

* * *

Another week has passed and I have a final plan. The library door has been shut every night while I wait and now she walks again. I hold onto my patience until I'm sure she's out of my bedroom, treading the landing towards the smallest room.

"April 14th, 1881, Nigel Anthony was born to Cecil and Madeleine Wilmer," I say in a firm but calm voice. I speak loudly enough to ensure I'm heard through the closed door, but not so much that I might seem to be shouting and scare her. "Poor Madeleine died," I continue, "but Nigel did not."

There's a moment of stillness and I'm sure she's there, stopped to listen. I have to assume so and I press on, reading aloud clearly and slowly, mentions of Nigel's schooling, graduation, his career and commendations. I mention Cecil too, where I can, and his successes after he moved away with his son. It takes several minutes of oration to snapshot long and celebrated lives to the wife and mother lost in my halls.

I finish and wait, sipping dark Merlot across dry lips and tongue.

Relief floods me as I hear her again, and it's a different sound. Tears, but of relief more than grief. Her wail is replaced by a sigh of something hard to define, but I desperately hope it's closure. Then, like air escaping a previously sealed vessel, she goes. Her presence slips away, not like the disintegration I've witnessed, but an utter removal. Without understanding how I know, I am convinced she's truly gone this time.

My own grief surges back as I find myself absolutely alone at last and it's almost too much to bear. Only the knowledge of Madeleine's escape keeps me from falling to pieces, but I let myself wallow, and drink, and bask in solitude.

* * *

Almost a month after Madeleine left, I realised that a ghost remained within the walls of my house. Me. Perhaps, I thought, it was time to move, though I've come to wear this home like a favourite old bathrobe. I'm reluctant to leave.

But a journey begins with a single step and so I've decided to attempt to rise from my despair *in situ*. A gathering of artists will arrive tonight and we'll discuss things and eat canapés and drink fine wine. I'm frightened of the possibilities, but excited too. And more than a little guilty. I'm sorry, Sarah, it's time. I know you would have told me that before I even came here, but I was ever the obtuse one.

THEY ALL COME THROUGH LONDON IN THE END

On a late train home, Bruno was tired, pissed off. The rocking of the carriage, the staccato percussion of the wheels on the Underground tracks, lulled him, but his disgust kept him mildly alert. He put in the hours, he worked diligently, he sucked up to all the right people. But yet again, he'd been passed over for promotion. Yet again, he'd been taken for granted, left in his rut, while someone else rose to greater heights.

Well, fuck them all. His savings account grew at a snail's pace, but it grew. Another few years and he'd have enough. The resort on the Thai island of Ko Pah Ngan lived in his dreams like a jewel, shining out of reach. For now. He would soon be able to buy one of those small wooden houses and move there. The cost of living on the island was a joke, but a good one, that he'd learned about on holiday some twelve years before. He'd done the maths. Now forty-four, he figured he had another forty years of life in him, give or take a bit. In Thailand he could live for a year on what he could live on here in London for a month. Forty months' salary, a little under four years of full-time income, would see him set for life out there. And he nearly had it. Idiots toiled away in the giant, rain-soaked corporate entities of the west. Idiots gave everything for a tiny house and a giant television. He did nothing but work, eat and save. Two or three more years and he'd give everything up for paradise. Beaches, cocktails, good books and laid-back people forever more. He'd never work another day in his life.

The train slowed, still in the darkness of the tunnel. He sucked in a breath, sat up, ready to alight at Clapham North, his dingy, dreary south-of-the-river home suburb. The train slowed to a complete stop, still in darkness. Bruno grimaced. *Come on. I just want to go home.* His wristwatch read 11:22 p.m. He needed to be up again at 6:30 to make the same journey back, staying late like a fool for nothing.

But not for nothing. For the money.

For the savings.

For Ko Pah Ngan.

He squeezed his eyes shut. *Two or three more years.* It had been his mantra for a while, but he really believed it this time. He almost had enough. So close.

The driver's voice sounded out, tinny over the PA. "Bear with us, ladies and gentleman, we've been requested to wait just short of Clapham North. There's been a bomb scare and they're not letting any trains through." Fatigue coated the man's words like dirt.

There's another one utterly resigned in his life, Bruno thought.

"We may have to back up to Stockwell," the driver went on. "Extra night buses are being arranged."

Mutters and groans rippled through the carriage, the few passengers looking at each other with despair and resignation. Bruno slumped. So close to home he could almost smell it. He'd get out and walk along the tracks if they'd let him. Fucking terrorists and the state of fear the media whipped up. He leaned back against the seat, stared at the advertisement above the window. Charles Leventer MP, new Leader of the Opposition, and his vision for Britain's future. Bruno sneered. Politicians were all the same, narcissists and crooks. Looking away, he pressed his forehead against the window, stared through his reflection into the blackness of the tunnel. The glass was cool on his brow, his breath made a cloud that faded and was replaced by the next exhalation.

Something moved in the darkness.

An extra beat pulsed in Bruno's heart. He sat back, squinted. Movement again, black on black, like tar rippling in the night. He glanced around the carriage but no one else paid attention, lost to phone screens and books.

He tried to use peripheral vision. The reflection from the lights inside made it hard to see anything, but he was sure he hadn't imagined it. Then again, a ripple in the pitch. He cupped his hands around his eyes, pressed the edges of his palms to the glass. The tunnel wall, a metre or two away, resolved into view, some miscellaneous pipes and wiring, a steel box padlocked shut. And a small black hand, splayed against the old brick like a gecko's. Bruno blinked rapidly, refocussed. He let his gaze follow the tiny fingers up an arm no thicker than a broom handle, past a lump of elbow. It strained his eyes to keep focus, like the thing was hardly even there, made of something blacker than night. The arm led to a knobbed shoulder, then the curve of a narrow jaw below an unusually long, thin head. Huge eyes blinked open, sudden and purple in the darkness, like whiteness under ultraviolet light in a nightclub. Bruno gasped.

The thing clung to the wall about two metres off the tunnel floor, legs as thin as its arms, feet higher than its head, less than half a metre long. Its body no thicker than Bruno's wrist, filament ribs like a fish, flexing with each breath. Soft, aqueous-looking thing, its small mouth with tiny teeth split in a sharp grin before it skittered away, faster than Bruno's eye could follow. Heart hammering, he shifted left and right, hands to the window, trying to see it again. He breathed hard, short and sharp.

"You okay, mate?" A large man opposite, brow creased, Aston Villa football shirt stretched across a rotund gut, garishly colourful in the fluorescent lights of the carriage.

Bruno licked his lips, took a shuddering breath. "You didn't see that?"

The Villa fan opened his mouth to speak when the driver's voice crackled over the PA again. "Brace yourselves for a late night, folks, we're going back to Stockwell. Sorry about that." Bruno caught a muffled, "Fucking los—" as the mic was clicked off.

Complaints and altogether too British laughter at the ridiculousness of it all filled the carriage as it rattled and started back the way it had come.

Bruno cupped his hands back to the window as the train moved and caught a slice of pale light. A door half open in the brickwork, a door *made* of the bricks. Wedged in the light from behind, a tall man in silhouette. The slender black creature scuttled around the door frame and inside. As the train gained speed, the flash-frame image moving away, the tall man briefly caught Bruno's eye as the thing squirmed around and sat on his shoulder like a pet. Then they were gone into the darkness.

* * *

Bruno slept fitfully and dreamed of dim corridors and rooms lit pale and endless, filled with impossible, slick black, skittering creatures. It seemed like only five minutes later that he was back on the platform at Clapham North, waiting for his early train to work again. Could he really have seen that thing? Perhaps it was a fever-dream from fatigue. But he was not an imaginative man. He read voraciously and loved the stories of others, but knew he could never come up with the wonders he enjoyed in fiction. He recognised in himself a bland and lifeless inner world. Perhaps that's why he read so much. And perhaps that's why he yearned for a simple life of beaches and sunshine. His parents were dead, mother years ago when he was only in his twenties, father three years and counting, chewed to the bone by cancer. He'd had no meaningful relationship in, well, ever, if he was honest. His friends were work colleagues, superficial at best. Maybe he should consider upping his roots and taking the Thailand option early, especially if he was starting to hallucinate on his commute.

But it had all been so real.

He stared hard down the tunnel, the light quickly fading into darkness as the tracks, grimy silver edges, shining on top, vanished into the black. A strong curiosity, an urge to investigate, gripped him. There were those small alcoves in the tunnel walls for maintenance workers to step into as trains whipped past. He could easily avoid the rails and just move along that wall, look for the strange brick door.

"Pull your head in, dickwad."

Bruno jumped as a station employee dragged at his shoulder.

"Train's coming. You'll lose your bleeding head leaning into the tunnel like that."

Bruno muttered apologies, felt his cheeks redden. What was he even thinking, he was no adventurer. Was his life so dull that he really entertained ideas like that? First hour this morning he would put off work and go through his finances again in detail. It would be disastrous to pack it all in before he had enough money, but maybe he *did* have enough. Especially if he sold all his stuff. Warm, metallic air drove into the station ahead of the train and he boarded with slumped shoulders.

* * *

The train ride home was as depressing as the day had been, and late as usual. After spending altogether too long confirming what he already knew—that he was far from solvent enough for the "Thailand Gambit"—he had to work extra hours into the night to make up the time. If anything, he'd need another four or five years to save enough, given the crash in interest rates on his savings.

Good god, his life was a treadmill of shit.

He stepped from the train at Clapham North and paused. The platform was empty. The train pulled away, heading for Clapham Common, and he was left in a strangely quiet limbo. He stood on the central walkway of grey tiles, yellow lines and MIND THE GAP painted before each edge. The walls on the other side of both tracks curved up to the rounded ceiling, billboards for movies and videogames, holidays and mortgages. Nobody stood or sat waiting for the next train, no one on the stairs leading up to street level. Bruno strolled towards the tunnel mouth from which he'd just emerged. It was just up there, not far at all.

He shrugged his coat on more snugly, pulled his messenger bag from his shoulder and slung it across his chest, bandolier-style. There were cameras everywhere, surely he'd get in trouble the moment he left the platform. But he couldn't help himself, his curiosity burned. He jumped down onto the gravel between the tracks and the platform and hurried into the gloom. He paused in darkness, heart racing, expecting to hear an angry voice from the station PA. None came.

He was in the right place, station side of the tunnel. The brick door he'd seen would be on this side, some unspecified distance along. He squeezed his eyes shut, thinking about what he'd seen. The steel locker! That would be a good marker. It had been on the wall, padlocked shut. The padlock was a burnished bronze. The locker itself, probably an electrical box of some kind, had a dent in the upper right corner, like it had been hit with a hammer. Bruno smiled to himself, pulled his phone out and used its flashlight to begin the search.

After five minutes he began to worry that perhaps he hadn't been as near to the station as he thought. Would he end up walking all the way back to Stockwell? A rush of hot, metalled air drove at him and panic washed his gut. There had been a maintenance arch maybe fifty metres back and he couldn't see another one immediately ahead. He turned and ran, visions of being smashed to paste by the rushing train made him whimper. The hiss of the tracks became a hum that became a roar. Light flooded around the bend he was racing through and he howled out loud, convinced he was finished. Then the alcove appeared and he threw himself in seconds before the train buffeted past, a flicker-play of bright square windows, bored faces, gusting hot wind, and dust and detritus.

Then it was past and Bruno leaned his hands on his knees, coughing and gagging against the fine black dust that coated everything. He spat, and it was like tar.

"Fucking idiot." His voice was hoarse. His hands and clothes, no doubt his face and hair too, were covered in a layer of shadowy grime. The idiocy of it all only strengthened his resolve.

He had to know.

Pushing off from the alcove, he ran back towards Stockwell, shining his light along the wall. He passed another arch, then a regular doorway in the brick that was definitely not the one he'd seen the strange tall man in.

Then there was the dented steel box. He slowed his pace, heart fluttering, stomach swimming with nerves and excitement. In sudden concern, he shone his light over the wide brick tunnel, wondering if any of those slick, skinny creatures were around, watching him with their large purple eyes. Nothing.

The brick door had been marked with a symbol, scratched white paint in the shape of a crescent curved to the right, with a horizontal line through it. It only took another thirty seconds and Bruno stood before it. The steel box, this mark, it was all real. So that creature had to be real too. And the tall man in the tunnel—did he live down here?

He had to be real as well.

Bruno shined his light close, ran his fingers along the mortar lines. He soon picked out the edges of the door. Without knowing about it, it was unlikely anyone would ever spot it. Now how to get it open?

The tracks hissed, the warm air pushed against him again. Did he have time to run back to the alcove twenty metres back? But if he could just get in here… He pushed hard against the door and nothing happened. No marks of entry, no handles. Could it only be opened from the inside?

The sound increased, the air blew stronger, black grit and dust swirling at his ankles. Frustrated, Bruno hammered against the brick and was about to turn and run for the alcove when something shifted under his hand. He paused, pressed his weight against the spot, and a brick slid in, easily as though it were on oiled tracks. The door clicked and popped and swung inwards.

Bruno jumped through as the train thundered past.

The same wan light he'd seen the night before leaked along a corridor of old red brick, the ground beneath his feet a patchwork of smooth grey flagstones. The passageway bent slowly to the right, the source of the light unseen. Bruno left the brick door slightly ajar and crept forward, trying not to think about what he was doing. Along with the nerves, he thrilled with excitement.

He deserved something interesting in his drudgery of a life.

The passage sloped down as he rounded the bend and then opened into a larger room. The ceiling was vaulted brickwork, arches rising to meet in a central cross. Three other doors led from the room, one centred on each wall. The one to his left revealed a passage that went only ten metres or so before ending in collapsed bricks and dry earth, some calamity in the distant past. The other two doors led away, one into darkness, the other into light, the source of the weak illumination in the tunnel.

Bruno headed into the light.

Voices rose in the distance, echoing against the brick. Low male tones, then a sudden outburst.

"No, no, no! This can't be happening!"

Bruno frowned, vaguely recognising the voice. Sounds of scuffling, a metallic clang.

"You can't do this! I will be missed!"

"Oh, no you won't. That's the beauty of it."

The second voice was soft, sibilant. It put Bruno's nerves on edge.

He crept along, thankful for the soft-soled Hush Puppy shoes he paid extra for. Something his mother always taught him, the importance of a good shoe over a fancy one. He took a deep breath, appalled at the inanity of his train of thought.

He froze. In the bright room before him an overweight, naked man was being strapped to a metal table with tight leather belts at ankle and wrist. Three other men were doing the strapping, each one tall and thin, with pasty white skin and eyes slightly too large. *Humans who had never seen the light of day*, Bruno surmised, *lurking in these catacombs between the tracks.*

They wore long-tailed black suits, like Victorian funeral directors, surreal in their anachronism.

Bruno stifled a gasp when he saw the captive's face as the man thrashed against his bonds. Charles Leventer, Leader of the Opposition, and almost certainly the new Prime Minister when the election rolled around. The chance of the incumbent party remaining in office, according to most pundits, was close to zero.

Along the far wall of the room, glass and steel cabinets stood floor to ceiling. Things writhed and twisted behind the tinted panes.

"Stop fighting," one of the pale men said. "It'll be over soon."

Leventer bucked and thrashed again, surprising strength from a man so portly and seemingly docile, if his public appearances were any indication. The back of his head cracked into the metal table and he grunted, fell still.

"Now you've hurt yourself, you see."

One of the other pale men chuckled. "Savour that pain. It will be as nothing compared to what's coming."

The third pale man spoke. "The other one, the Russian, isn't here yet."

"No matter. We'll use this one to invite him in. They all come through London in the end. We have time, and patience."

While they spoke, one went to a glass-fronted cabinet and opened the door. The slick, sinuous creature Bruno had seen in the tunnel, or one just like it, whipped out and hopped to the man's shoulder, curling one rubbery arm around his neck. The man returned to Leventer and the future Prime Minister began gasping and whimpering.

"What's that? What the *fuck* is that?"

"It's you, Mr. Leventer." The pale man leaned over the table and the creature hopped down onto Leventer's chest. He began bucking again and one of the pale men beside him cuffed a narrow, white-knuckled fist across the point of his chin, stunning him into stillness once more.

The creature looked up at its master and the master nodded. "This is the one you've been studying. In you go."

The creature's tiny shadow face twisted into glee and it grabbed Leventer's face and chin, forced his mouth open wide. Leventer moaned and squirmed as it put first one tiny sharp foot, then the other into his mouth. Leventer's throat bulged as the foul thing forced its way in and down. His legs drummed the tabletop, his fists clenching and relaxing spasmodically. He began to shudder, then violently vibrate.

The creature was half-in and half-out, its eyes rolled back, when

Leventer's flesh started to pulse and ripple. Then the thing slipped all the way in and was gone. Leventer's chest flexed wide, then collapsed slowly in on itself, his eyes bulged in agony, but no sound could escape his occluded throat. Then his shuddering increased rapidly and a stream of viscous, dark red fluid burst from his anus, sprayed across the table. His penis stood up and gouted the same stuff, two streams jetted from distended nostrils, two more from his ears. His eyes bulged, then fell into their sockets only to make way for two more torrents of thick red liquefied innards to shoot upwards. Leventer's body emptied like a rubber sack, not even bones standing through the pallid flesh. His mouth flopped, stretched and empty.

Bruno shook, swallowing down bile, frozen to the spot in terror and disgust. Leventer's insides coated the table, pooled beneath it, sluggishly running into a drain and slipping from view.

The politician's body began to slowly re-inflate, gradually regain its previous shape. The eyes snapped open and had become the glowing purple of the invading creature. Then he blinked rapidly and looked human once more.

But Bruno knew the man was anything but.

The pale men undid the straps and Leventer—what *had been* Leventer—sat up and smiled broadly. Something inside Bruno snapped and he turned and ran.

"Someone's there!" a voice behind him barked. "Trigger the defences."

Bruno had no idea what that meant and put his head down as he bolted. This was surely the worst decision of his life. He pounded along the passage, into the square room and headed for the brick door and the normality of the dark train tunnel. A twanging sound rang against the brick walls, like a hundred guitar strings pulling taut. Before Bruno could consider what it might be, he screamed in pain as the stump of his left shin slammed into grey tiles and he skidded on the bone end and fell. White agony lanced through him as he looked back and saw his foot still in its sensible Hush Puppy, spinning on its own a metre behind him. The weak light reflected on a tight, sharp wire across the passage at ankle height. *Trigger the defences.* Blood pooled where he lay, his desecrated leg pounding in pain. The brick door was only twenty metres away, and he spotted another glittering line of death, this time stretched across at knee height between the door and where he lay.

The image of Leventer bursting from inside himself flashed across Bruno's mind, and despite the horrendous injury, sheer panic drove him up. He hopped to the next trap wire as skittering sounds of pursuit hurried along the passage behind him. He gritted his teeth and stood on his severed bone stump to swing his good leg over the trap. New, unbelievable pain streaked through every nerve. His vision narrowed, bile burst from his throat, but he refused to fall. Over the last wire, spitting bitter vomit, one hand against the wall to steady himself, he hopped furiously for the brick door. Then he was through, stumbling and staggering in the darkness, thoughts of Clapham North platform the only thing in his mind.

Time and again he lurched, ground his severed leg into the filthy gravel and screamed. Refusing to give in to anything, distantly marvelling at his own tenacity, he pushed on. Perhaps he was good for something, after all. Perhaps he was greater than he'd imagined. But those men, those creatures, his foot left behind in a catacomb, how could all that have really happened? How long had those freaks been taking people over? Who was really real in the world any more?

Bruno's mind pulled as taut as the wire that had amputated his foot and threatened to snap, to send his consciousness spiralling into an abyss of black despair. And part of him welcomed it, wished it would happen so all he had witnessed could be erased. The tracks sang as a train approached and Bruno was tempted to throw himself across the rails and let it take him, end everything.

Maybe there was a heaven and it would be even better than Thailand.

The light of the platform glowed ahead and Bruno whimpered, redoubled his efforts, hopping and stumbling along. The hot Underground air drove against his back, the light of the train filled the darkness between him and the platform. Then he was grabbing the tiled edge, hauling himself up as the train whistled past and slowed to a stop. He rolled on the cold tiles, vision swimming, images of liquefied red and shining, tight silver flashing over and over and over.

Voices carried, echoing in the rounded platform confines.

"That bloke was on the tracks!"

"Lost his bloody foot to the train, look!"

"Call an ambulance!"

Hands scrabbled at Bruno's coat and messenger bag, pulled him from the edge deeper into light and safety.

"It's pissing blood!"

"Who's wearing a belt? We need a tourniquet!"

Merciful blackness slammed shut across Bruno's mind.

* * *

The doctors told him he had remained in an induced coma for the first four days after his accident. What was he doing down on the track anyway? Did he fall? He raved, swimming in a sea of morphine and disbelief, demanded to talk to the police. The police came and listened to his story, exchanging glances of thinly veiled contempt. Overheard snippets from staff eventually led Bruno to realise they'd written him off as insane, that he'd attempted suicide. The police had been through his records, found that three times in fourteen months he'd been passed over for promotion, every time to someone younger who had been at the company less time.

The last one only a week ago.

"No wonder the poor bastard was suicidal," one nurse whispered to another while Bruno feigned sleep.

Well, fuck them all. He was past caring, and couldn't let himself remember too much for fear his mind would snap. Close a door on that experience and throw away the key. They'd had to take off the rest of his lower leg, left around six inches below the knee. They talked about prosthetics and rehab, compensation, disability allowance. Fine, he'd jump through all the hoops. Hop through the fucking hoops. And once it was all done, he'd sell up, pack up and buy that little house on Ko Pah Ngan. One thing was certain, no creepy inhuman creatures were body-swapping powerful figures on that tiny island. Nothing there was important enough to warrant their attention.

A couple of newspaper reports mentioned the things he'd said, all with the caveat of "lunatic ravings" or "confused ramblings." A couple of reporters from edge-of-society papers and websites came to see him, but he recognised them for what they were and told them to fuck off. He focussed tightly on recovery and the dream of Thailand, assisted by compensation.

The night before he was to be moved from intensive care into the main ward, a tall doctor came to visit. The man was thin and pale, gently shaking Bruno's shoulder to wake him. The clock read 3:15 a.m.

Bruno blinked, smacked dry lips. "What's happening?" he asked groggily.

The doctor smiled, leaned forward. His skin was more than pale, it was fish belly-white, his eyes too large for his face. "Took us a while to find you." The voice was a whisper, sibilant.

Bruno drew breath to scream but shadows behind the head of his bed writhed and shifted. Something thin and shining black dropped and landed on his chest. His scream began, but was quickly muffled as the creature grabbed his face and thrust first one, then the other tiny sharp foot down his throat.

WATERS STRANGELY CLEAR

UNDER GREY SKIES THREATENING RAIN, Howard Bloch drove east. Behind the wheel for hours already and still Skye's voice echoed through his mind, biting, mocking him.

"So you're really going?"

"I have to!" Infuriated at her refusal to understand.

"A Halloween party? You're a grown man!"

"It's our conference. It's my *job*."

"The *conference*," disdain drooled from the word, "is a lame excuse for grown adults to act like children."

"I'm a regional sales manager. The year's targets and strategies are laid out over three days."

"As an excuse to then have the lame-ass party."

So much more hung off that phrase. Lame-ass job, lame-ass husband, lame-ass man. He had shrugged, no idea how to respond.

"You're really going? To talk about tacky Halloween decorations instead of staying to save us."

"Is there us any more?" he'd asked.

"I guess not."

Her eyes were wet with hurt and anger as she'd turned away. Without another word, he'd wheeled his suitcase out to the car and driven off.

On I-95 somewhere north of Boston, Howard's eyes were wet too. He loved Skye... Had loved her more than life itself. His breezy, beautiful songstress. She'd loved his stability after a childhood with commune-living parents who spent their days stoned, talking about permaculture farming and the spirits of the wind. But her spirit had been like the wind too and perhaps it was inevitable she would grow bored of him. But was that all it was? Boredom? Their life lacked adventure, that was one constant complaint from Skye. *You're so pragmatic, there's not an esoteric bone in your body!* Isn't that why she married him? Maybe they should have had kids, but that was something she resisted. Their slight misalignment on so many things seemed to have widened through the years until now all the gaps appeared insurmountable.

He took the Yankee Division Highway off I-95, squinted at his phone's GPS as it directed him towards Essex Bay. The leaden skies broke, rain bucketing over the windshield as he finally spotted the sign directing him north: INNSMOUTH, 6 MILES.

"Backwater place for the conference," Howard muttered as the day grew unseasonably dark, even for the end of October.

Head Office had sung the virtues of the location, old-world charm and a powerful sense of the macabre, like a town that time forgot. "This year is an auspicious one for the company," the memo had said. "And we're returning to the source for a very special conference." Perfect for the best Halloween party yet devised, apparently. Always in place of a Christmas celebration, Day & Gohn Inc. made its fortune from Halloween merchandise, so that holiday was its central focus. Until now the annual conference had always been in Pittsburgh, much nearer to Howard. Why the CEO, Geoffrey Day, had insisted on the change was a mystery.

Howard drove past Essex Bay, out of sight in the darkness somewhere east of him, and entered Innsmouth. He was exhausted, eyes red and gritty from the long journey, strained from staring through the downpour. All he wanted was a hot bath and a soft bed, tomorrow would be better. He missed Skye already.

The rain fell, hard and heavy, and he slowed, staring past the swiftly whipping wipers at a town of wide extent and dense construction. Everywhere seemed dark and still, though it was only just before seven o'clock. Few lights shone in the windows, chimney pots stood inert on sagging gambrel roofs. As the road descended towards the harbour, the sense of broken-down decay became stronger, some roofs fallen in entirely, some walls missing windows like skulls with black, empty eye sockets. Other buildings were in better condition, Georgian houses with cupolas and widow's walks guarded by curlicued iron railings. Three tall steeples stood out against the ocean horizon, black against the dark of night. Howard drove past a factory built of brick, sturdier looking than most buildings he had seen, though the majority of the rest of the waterfront bore structures seemingly uninhabitable due to decay.

Not so much old-world charm but a derelict, forgotten ghost town. Where was everyone? He passed the sand-clogged harbour surrounded by stone breaker walls and there, on a slight rise above the small port, was the Deepwater Hotel. That, at least, was well-lit, an air of vibrancy about it. He turned onto Maron Road to access the lot and parked, the hammer of rain the only sound after he killed the engine. Cold permeated the car, as though the turning of the key had swung wide some unseen refrigerator door behind him.

With a shiver, he got out, hunched against the rain, to smell a sharp, briny tang of saltwater and old seaweed on the icy breeze. He dragged his case from the trunk and ran to the hotel lobby. No one greeted him at the door, the reception desk unmanned. From somewhere distant he heard the quiet murmur of voices and the chink of glasses. He realised a stiff drink before his bath and bed would be most welcome, assuming it didn't involve too much socialising. He wasn't yet ready for people, Skye's disappointment still raw and smarting. Had she really finished with him right there by the front door? The chasm between them finally whole? Surely there was a way to find common ground again if they tried.

"Help you? Conference is it?"

Howard jumped, the disembodied voice sudden and sibilant. He turned, no one to be seen. When he returned his gaze to the desk he jumped again, a man waiting as if he had been there all along, looking with one eyebrow raised. Had he been there all along? Surely Howard would have noticed. The man's face was pale, almost grey, his mouth flat and wide, eyes too large as he stared.

"Yes, conference," Howard managed, unsettled by the cold perusal. "Howard Bloch," he added, and spelled out his surname. People always assumed a CK.

"Three-fifteen, third floor. No lift, broken. Stairs are that way." The pointing finger was greyer than the man's face, long and trembling slightly as it indicated dark wooden stairs, highly polished, with a thick bannister and intricate balusters like kelp weed twisting upwards.

Howard glanced down at his heavy case, fatigue sinking deeper into his bones. He opened his mouth to speak and the clerk said, "No bellboy. Finished for the day."

"Right." Howard took the offered key, careful not to touch the pale hand, and turned away.

"Dagon's eyes see you."

Howard turned back. "Pardon me?"

"I said have a nice stay." The man's expression was unchanged, without any apparent emotion.

"Right," Howard said again. "Thanks."

He wheeled his case towards the stairs but was intercepted by someone emerging from a pair of heavy wooden double doors to one side. "Howie Bloch!"

Howard winced but couldn't help smiling. At last, some normalcy. Something familiar. "Dean Stringer. How many times do I have to tell you not to call me Howie?" His mother had called him that, her soft voice plaintive as she mollified him after another of his father's alcoholic outbursts. His mother's own breath sour with bourbon and cigarettes and surrender. He'd always promised himself any marriage of his would never be like theirs. Instead he'd managed to make one so dull it had withered on the vine and died.

Dean Stringer smiled. "Howard, sorry. Good to see you, man!"

"You too."

They shook hands, Dean's grip firm and vigorous. "You believe this place? Like something from…I don't even know!"

"It's pretty weird."

"The boss man says it's important to be here this particular Halloween. Reckons it's a perfect time for company growth."

"Perfect time?"

"Alignment of stars or some shit." Stringer laughed, shrugged.

"Great location for us, though, right? Try selling these people Halloween décor. That'd be like selling snow to the Eskimoes, am I right? Really test your skills, Mr. Regional Sales Manager of the Year."

Howard laughed. "That was last year."

"Maybe this year too! You'll find out in three days."

"We'll see." Honestly, Howard doubted he would qualify. He worked well, always had, but the slow dissolution of life with Skye, particularly over the last few months as the breakdown gained momentum, had certainly affected his performance. It must have affected his sales, even though he had met all his targets. Someone else would surely have exceeded theirs by more.

"Drink!" Dean exclaimed. "Come on."

"My bag," Howard said weakly. "I've only just driven in, I feel… rumpled."

"A drink first!"

The hotel bar was busy with Day & Gohn Inc. staff and the buzz of life and activity was like a bath in itself. Howard drank his first beer reluctantly but soon relaxed and met others he knew well, new employees he hadn't met before. He felt isolated among the crowd, but bourbon followed beer and in an hour he was warm and laughing, not sparing a thought for life beyond the job.

Dizzy and staggering, he fumbled the key into the lock of 315, left his clothes on the floor as he fell into bed a little after midnight. The sheets were so cold they felt damp, the high ceiling with pressed metal edges spotted with blackened mould and rippled with water stains, but he didn't think much about it before sleep closed over him like a wave.

* * *

Howard woke from dreams of rolling seas and curdled stomachs. Of leaning over the sides of creaking boats with peeling paint, staring into gloomy depths where things unrecognisable looped and flew. His mouth was dry and furry, his head thick.

He staggered from bed, went into the small bathroom to piss, and winced at the yellow-stained toilet bowl, the rust-streaked tub with its dripping shower head, lumpy with lime scale. But relieved, and revitalised with a long drink, though the water was bitter and hard, he returned to the room and its small window. His view looked south over the harbour. He smiled. The rain had eased, though the skies were still slate, and people milled in the street. Some buildings seemed to be shops with their doors open. Everything appeared more alive, more intact, than it had in the rain-soaked night before. Howard was glad of that. After a breakfast in the bustling hotel dining room—bustling only due to his fellow company staff—he headed into the main conference rooms and was soon lost in the business of sales districts, new products, electronic gadgets to hide around the house to turn it into a terrifying haunted experience. These were things he understood.

During lunch he was slapped hard on the back by Geoffrey Day, CEO. The man was tall and broad with a wide face and protuberant eyes. Not so pale as the desk clerk of the night before, Howard was nonetheless struck by their similarity.

"Good to see you, Bloch!" Day exclaimed. "All well?"

"Absolutely!" Howard lied, thoughts of Skye slipping back into the cracks between his thoughts, and hurried away.

By evening he was back in the bar, sampling the food and more of the booze. One day down, two to go, then the party. He began to relax. Dinner was ordinary, an uninspiring fish stew with hard, tasteless bread, but he and Dean had decided to go further afield the next day and explore the town, find restaurants to try. Thankful though he was to have Dean nearby, he had trouble connecting with anyone else, the faces all blurring into one seething mass. He shouldn't be here, not really. He was made remote by thoughts of home and Skye. And that made him tense and bitter, hurt by the thought their marriage was done. They should have had kids. He should have insisted. He smarted that now they never would. But it wasn't too late.

Avoiding conversation, Howard found himself on a weathered leather bench seat when a slim, dark-haired woman sat beside him. He estimated she might be five or six years younger than his grizzled thirty-nine, and she retained an attractiveness that spoke of a youth turning eyes wherever she went. As general conversation lulled she smiled at him, held out a long-fingered, slim hand.

"Darya."

"Howard. Darya is a lovely name." He took her hand, glanced down at its icy coolness.

"I never could get used to New England winters. It's why I went away. I'm always cold!"

"It's barely autumn yet."

She gave a shrug. "Yet already freezing."

"And so damp here too," Howard said.

"Always. It means 'sea', by the way."

"What does?"

"Darya. It's Iranian."

"Oh, right. You're Iranian?"

"No, my parents just liked it. I'm New England born and bred."

Howard laughed. "Yet you never got used to the winters."

"No, that's why I went away."

A silence fell, a moment of awkward strangeness following the awkward conversation. Darya flickered another smile and Howard sucked in a quick breath, tried to rein in sudden disorientation. "Drink?" he said.

Darya visibly relaxed, eyes crinkling. "Yes! Vodka and soda?"

"You got it."

Dean stood at the bar, half a smile pulling up one side of his mouth like he'd been caught by a fisherman.

"What are you grinning about?"

Dean nodded back towards the table in the corner. "Chatting up the new girl, eh?"

"New is she?"

"I haven't seen her before. No one I spoke to has. Must be new."

Howard grunted. "And I'm not chatting her up."

"What, because you're married? What happens on tour, stays on tour, buddy. I won't tell your wife."

"Gee, thanks! How's your wife?"

Dean grimaced. "Honestly, I don't think we'll be together much longer. I'm feeling a bit lost, truth be told. Long story. I'll tell you later."

Howard nodded, unsure what to say. He was certainly the last person to offer advice. Dean gathered up four glasses in a tenuous two-handed grip and returned to his table where several employees sat laughing and talking over one another drunkenly.

Howard waited at the bar and eventually the woman serving turned her attention to him. He startled slightly, convinced for a moment it was the desk clerk from the night before wearing a straggly ash-blonde wig. Their resemblance was uncanny, but the woman had a kind of fatty lump just below her bottom lip and eyes a pale grey where the man's had been sickly green. They must surely be related, though. Family business, Howard presumed. He ordered the drinks, bourbon and coke for himself, and returned to Darya.

Their conversation was messy, continued to be awkward, but they drank more and cared less. Darya moved closer, put a hand on his arm, his knee, his thigh. In her presence he felt dizzy and weirdly dislocated. He repeatedly pushed away thoughts of Skye, playing over and over in the back of his mind those last words.

Is there us any more?

I guess not.

The evening rolled on and the bar became ever less occupied, then Darya leaned forward, whispering. Her lips were cold against his ear, but the words heated him. "Shall we go upstairs?"

"My room?" he asked, trembling like a teenager.

She nodded, slipped her fingers around his, gently pulled him up and away. They climbed the stairs quickly, stumbling drunkenly and giggling. In his room they didn't speak again, plucked and fumbled with each other's clothes, kissing every newly revealed bit of skin. Her tongue was cold and brackish in his mouth, as though she had drunk vodka and seawater all night not vodka and soda, but the taste wasn't unpleasant. As they kissed he became dizzier still, lost in lust and booze.

She was cold all over, the poor thing not lying about never getting warm. He gasped as she took his cock in her mouth, his shock as much from the icy chill of her tongue as the sharp sexual pleasure. They rolled onto the bed, he atop her, and inside she was as cold as out, and though the fact discomforted him, he was too drunk and too rampant to care. The booze made him clumsy but gave him time and the sex was good. She bucked beneath him, staring up with wide eyes as though she couldn't believe her own orgasm, and that inflamed him and he was spent, explosively and totally. Still without words they rolled over and entwined. As sleep stole over him, he realised she was still cold.

* * *

Howard dreamed of a city underwater. It's twisting spires stretched up through waters strangely clear, the surface of the ocean unseen far above. This was no earthly sea, that he knew without doubt, intrinsically. This place existed everywhere, just below the surface of real life. It could be entered from anywhere, go from it to anywhere else, like it flowed intertwined with the threads of the tapestry of reality.

Howard walked its streets, marvelling at serpentine architecture, rounded byways, the smoothness of every feature. Straps of kelp rose in clumps, undulating in soft currents. He came to a temple in the city's centre, a tower of intertwined columns winding upwards, surrounded by smaller spiralling towers buttressed to the middle with arcs of dark stone. Giant double doors, forty feet high, thirty feet wide, inscribed with disturbing symbols, swung silently open and he realised everywhere was silent. Inside the temple, rows of pews rose from the ground as if carved. Or as though they had been grown like intricately managed coral. Hundreds of people occupied them, rocking gently as if moved like the kelp by deep, gentle waves. All had hoods or long hair shadowing their faces, not a visage visible in the dimness. An altar at the end of the temple stood on a raised dais, impossibly tall figures stalking slowly around it. Whip-thin and angular in their movements, they reached long, stick-like arms towards the congregation. Those arms bent once about one-third along, the forearm too short. Then they bent again further up, double-elbows uncannily placed as they gestured complicated patterns, a silent sign-language Howard could not understand but yearned to know. He realised he was holding his breath, had been all along. For how long? Hours? He knew if he breathed in he would drown, but suddenly felt like he was drowning anyway. And part of him longed for that watery suffocation. Panicking, he gasped, ice cold salt water flooding his mouth and lungs.

He jerked awake, bounced on the cold bed, heart pounding, breath short. He tasted salt water, but realised that would be from kissing Darya, not from the dream. Wouldn't it? He rolled over and saw she was gone. Disappointment carved a hole in him. His brain was foggy with sleep, with drink, with the remains of the powerfully clear dream. He lurched from bed to piss, the air cold against his damp skin. His feet squidged against the hard, worn carpet as he walked, leaving a trail of wet footprints. Still drunk, confused, bereft, he ignored it, pissed, and fell back into bed and a restless, dreamless sleep.

* * *

"You're not the only one who got lucky last night!" Dean was enthusiastic over breakfast in the hotel dining room of dark wood and sallow serving staff. They looked a lot like each other. Just how big was the family running this business?

"What do you mean?" Howard had a headache from ruptured sleep and too much bourbon, his mood sullied by that and by guilt over what he had done. He and Skye weren't finished yet, and Darya hadn't even stayed the night, creeping out like it was nothing but a booty call. There had been a text message from Skye when he awoke:

Sweetheart, we really need to talk. When you get back, let's take a break somewhere. We need time together.

She was prepared to attempt reconciliation. And so was he, desperate for it, in fact. But would he have to tell her about last night? Could he live with the guilt either way? He found himself questioning what the fuck he was doing about anything in his life but knew one thing. He wanted Skye.

Dean was saying something.

"Sorry, what?"

"Man, you are out of it. Too much to drink, eh? I was saying that a few of us scored last night. That girl you took upstairs, she's not with the conference. She's local."

Howard frowned. Nodded dumbly. "She said something about that. But she moved away."

"There's a few of them, they came to hang out knowing we were in town." Dean leaned forward, conspiratorial. "You look at most people here and who can blame them? It's ugly central in this town, right?"

Howard tried to remember what he and Darya had talked about all evening but it was hazy. He couldn't remember much at all. "You scored too then?"

Dean beamed. "And it was good, man!"

"Was she…" Howard swallowed, shook his head. He had been about to say *Was she cold*, but that just seemed absurd.

"Was she what?"

"Doesn't matter. Good for you, man." He pushed his plate aside, appetite gone. "I gotta call my wife."

"Guilty conscience!" Dean grinned around a mouthful of toast, wagged a butter knife like an accusatory finger.

Howard walked around the harbour, talking to Skye about the future, and he felt encouraged. The conversation was uncomfortable, but she reiterated her desire for a break. He said he would like that. She told him to enjoy his conference and his party, and it sounded as though she meant it. He hung up wracked with guilt.

He looked around, wondering if he might see more of Innsmouth before day two of the conference, but though the town wasn't nearly as dilapidated as he had thought that first night, it was still run down, dirty, uninviting. Pale, wide faces stared around door frames, as if wishing him away, hoping he wouldn't stray into their shop. One large building had a peeling sign, MARON SHIPPING AND FREIGHT. He'd seen that name in several places around town. For some reason that unsettled him. With a shiver he returned to the hotel.

* * *

During lunch, after eating floury apples and damp sandwiches of fish paste, Howard went upstairs to nap, to catch up from his disturbed sleep of the night before. He dreamed again of the underwater city, walked to the high, wide doors but paused, nervous. He thought of Darya, of Skye, and cried out in frustration. Ice water flooded his mouth and he startled awake. His clothes were wet, like the mother of all cold sweats. He changed and went back downstairs for the afternoon session. What he would give to be warm and dry.

* * *

Rather than brave the unwelcoming streets with Dean, he ate the hotel stew again. The same lumpy casserole as before. The meat was tough for fish, odd lumps in places, the gravy waxy and thick. He would kill for a good old burger and fries, but didn't really care. He thought only of seeing the conference out, enjoying the party, then getting home to Skye. Even the party now seemed like a chore. Skye had been right, it was grown adults trying to recapture lost childhood and it was sad. The hotel had used the company's products to decorate in preparation and it all struck him as garish and tacky.

He promised himself he wouldn't drink again, but Dean returned and bought the first round and anything seemed better than sobriety at that point. By around ten o'clock he was warmly inebriated, relaxing, when Darya appeared beside him.

"I'm sorry I left without saying goodbye. You were sleeping. You were…very deep."

Howard licked suddenly dry lips. "I didn't expect…"

"You didn't expect me back? I had to work, but I came as soon as I finished." She raised a glass, clinked it against his. He opened his mouth to speak, to say something about Skye, about his life, but she silenced him with cold lips over his. Her briny tongue caressed his and dizziness swept through him. Over her shoulder he saw Dean entwined with another woman, similar looking to Darya. Dean gave a thumbs up, then returned all his attention to his new friend.

Howard tried to glance around the bar. So many other people there, but they were so many blank faces in a sea of weirdness. Only Darya appeared solid. Only she showed any detail for his eye to lock onto. He swallowed hard, wondered if he was more drunk than he had realised. Darya kissed him again, cold and salty, and it inflamed every fibre of him. She pulled back, handed him another drink. Where had that come from? It tasted strong, at least a double measure. With an internal sob of frustration, he swallowed it down and let his mind swim.

Darya pulled him by the hand, led him to his room, where they repeated the night before, faster, harder, better than ever. As he frantically kissed along her neck, thrusting powerfully, his lips passed over a row of thin striations. He leaned back to look and saw three almost imperceptible slits in the skin at the side of her throat that quickly closed together as though they had never been. Darya pulled his face down between her breasts, bucking up into him desperately.

* * *

Howard dreamed again of the serpentine temple, the tall, rangy priests exhorting the congregation with complicated signs. As he stared, he began to somehow understand the gestures. *He is ready to rise* and *He has slept for long enough.*

Something in the broken, truncated messages caused rills of terror to flood through Howard and he felt the intense pressure of his held breath. He wanted to breathe deeply and join the huddled masses and simultaneously wanted to run far away, to Skye, and feel the genuine warmth of her embrace.

The urge to run won out and he stumbled from the temple, along the softly winding streets. He remembered this ocean was not earthly, but a place in between, a place that flowed within all things. He kicked hard from the street and swam up, keeping only Skye in his mind, and found himself swimming over their shared bedroom, so far away. She slept there, alone in the bed, one arm thrown across where he should have been. Across her pillow was the shirt he had been wearing the day before he left, looking rumpled and unwashed. She must have it there for the scent of him. His heart ached.

He gasped, ice water rushed through him, and he woke.

Darya was gone.

* * *

The mood in the dining room was sombre, faces dark. It took a moment to find out why, but Howard soon discovered there had been a tragedy. Dean Stringer was dead.

"What happened?" Howard asked of Sarah Cheeseman, taking a spare seat at the table she shared with two others.

"Drowned," Sarah told him.

"What?"

"But found in his bed!" Gary Clarke said, shaking his head.

"Drowned in his bed?"

Gary barked a laugh. "According to the authorities I overheard talking to the boss, he fell in the harbour and drowned late last night. A local carried him to bed, not realising he was dead, thinking he was just drunk."

Howard frowned. "Who does that?"

Gary shrugged. "No idea. But you can't actually drown in your bed, can you!"

"Geoff Day was here a moment before you arrived," Sarah said.

"Despite the horrible event, we're to see through the conference and party."

"It's what Dean would have wanted, according to Day," Gary said, his face bleak.

Howard mechanically forked wet, thin scrambled eggs into his mouth, not really tasting them.

* * *

Howard wanted to go home, but it was October 31st, last day of the conference and Halloween. It was a long drive. He was prepared to make his excuses and leave, but Geoff Day opened proceedings with a request that everyone honour Dean Stringer by sticking together, considering the Day & Gohn Inc. family had meant so much to Dean. *Had it really?* Howard wondered. Haunted faces filled the auditorium, all wearing a mask of determination. He would look like a dick if he ran out now.

"Call me superstitious if you will," Day said in a strong voice, "but this Halloween sees a planetary conjunction that occurs only once every few hundred years. And it's happening on *our* day, on Halloween! That's why we're here, in this place, at this time. We'll see our numbers grow!"

Day went on to announce the year's best performers, and Howard gasped when he was named again as Regional Sales Manager of the Year. Confused by the applause and faces that still bore shock under a veneer of celebration, he went to the stage, accepted his plaque and bonus cheque. How could he have outperformed everyone despite his crumbling life? Was his competition here that weak? He needed more from life than everything represented by this award. And he knew there was so much more to be experienced.

During lunch he called Skye and said how much he missed her, and he wasn't lying. But something else had occurred to him and he knew it would appeal to her esoteric mindset.

"I'm going to swim the sea of dreams tonight and come to you," he said, huddled for privacy in a corner under the polished stairs.

She laughed. "That right?"

"I'm serious. This place has been giving me crazy dreams. Last night I swam to you and watched you sleeping."

"That's a little creepy, love."

"No, it was beautiful."

"It sounds like a nice dream," she said, amending her opinion.

He took a deep breath, ready to test his theory. "You're sleeping with my blue shirt on your pillow."

Her gasp at the other end was quickly suppressed, then a moment of silence.

"Skye?"

"How could you know that?"

"I think it's wonderful."

"But how could you know?"

"I told you, I've been dreaming, deeper than you could imagine. I'll come tonight, in your dreams, and we'll swim together."

Skye laughed again, but there was an edge of nervousness to it. "You're kinda freaking me out, but okay. I'll look forward to that."

* * *

The conference wrapped and when they emerged from the meeting rooms back into the bar, it was dressed up like a funfair haunted house. Cobwebs everywhere, bats and pumpkins and witches on broomsticks swung from every available point. Among the regular Halloween décor were bizarre chitinous creatures, like plastic parodies of lobsters and crabs with uncannily articulated limbs, set as if they crept across every surface, hunting for something.

Music blared from the rig of a DJ in one corner, rotating lights with blue and green filters turned, casting flickering underwater shades across the walls and ceiling. Food and drinks were laid out on tables. Howard ignored it all, keen to be on his own. Darya came to him, her hips swaying like a soft tide, eyes hooded. He saw her now as cold and dangerous, the image of Dean with another woman disturbingly similar to Darya leapt through his mind and made his stomach churn.

She held out a drink, began to say something. Howard pushed the drink aside, shook his head. "Not tonight! No more, okay?"

Her face flashed fury and, for a startling moment, sharp teeth bristled behind her full lips, three slits either side of her throat gaped angrily, then flattened shut again. Howard's mouth fell open, fear trickled through his limbs. Darya's expression softened as she glanced past Howard's shoulder. He turned to see what she was looking at and saw Geoff Day gesture to the woman, his fingers mimicking the silent sermons he had witnessed in his dreams. *Enough*. Howard's eyes widened and he turned back to see Darya's reaction, but she had already turned away, offering his drink to another employee. Gary Clarke, he realised absently, who he had spoken to over breakfast.

Howard looked back to Geoff Day, but the boss was already deep in conversation with others, his face wide with laughter.

Howard hurried to this room. He locked the door and sighed with relief. All he wanted was to hold Skye. And he wanted to show her the wonders of the world he had discovered under reality. The peculiarity of people notwithstanding, that place called to him, cajoled him to fly in its endless depths, and he had to take Skye there. He would show her adventure. He could ignore the dark city. These people be damned, he and Skye had journeys to enjoy.

He watched the hours crawl by until he was sure Skye would be in bed, then fell into his cold, damp sheets and closed his eyes. He relaxed and breathed deeply, thinking only of sleep and the deeps of the ocean below the world. He smiled as he gently walked the streets of the serpentine city, supported by the salt waters of infinity. But not to be tempted, he kicked away and swam up, distancing himself from the temple, thinking only of Skye.

He saw the floral designs of the bed linen in the shadows beneath him and swam down to her. His held breath began to burn his lungs, but he knew he had held it for impossibly long periods before this dream, on previous nights. He could hold it longer still. Long enough to show her wonders.

He put a hand on Skye's shoulder and she startled awake, looked around herself with wide eyes. Then she looked up at Howard, her expression both impressed and full of disbelief. He nodded, pointed at the pillow below her, his shirt. *You're dreaming*, he said with complicated patterns of his fingers that suddenly came as naturally as blinking. *We're dreaming together in the oceans of infinity.*

He pushed aside his guilt at thoughts of what he had done with Darya, took Skye's hand. She let herself be lifted and they swam together. Unsure where to go, they drifted, and then there was the city below them. He was shocked to see the entire congregation in the streets outside the temple, looking up with wide, sad faces. The tall priests stalked among them, more than a dozen of them, then as one they turned their thin faces upwards too. Their wrongly jointed arms raised and together they spoke in sign, telling Howard and Skye to breathe, to let infinity in and feel the sacred blessing of the eternal Dagon.

Of course.

Howard laughed, knew that any resistance was pointless. The ocean was already in him, had been since his lips had first touched Darya's. This was inevitable. He turned Skye to him and her face was twisted in terror, eyes wide. She shook her head side to side, hair floating behind like a halo in the currents. She opened her mouth to scream, tried to pull away from him, but he held her tight, his hands around her upper arms. He opened his mouth and drew in a great breath of salty ice water and nodded at her to do the same. As her scream came to an end she had no choice but to do so and he refused to let her go. This was them together at last. Always together.

* * *

Geoff Day, CEO of Day & Gohn Inc., stood with Cecil Maron, the Innsmouth Chief of Police, Geoff's cousin on his mother's side. Beside them stood Stanley Maron, Cecil's brother, the town's forensic examiner. They surrounded Howard Bloch's hotel bed, where Howard lay cold and wet. His blackened eyes stared unseeing at the mould-stained ceiling.

"You've filled in the paperwork?" Geoff Day asked his cousins.

Cecil nodded. "Drowned in the harbour. Hell of a thing."

Stanley signed off the sheets of paper on the battered clipboard, returned it to his cousin.

"The next of kin?" Day asked.

Cecil laughed, a clotted, wet sound. "Wife. Spoke to the local PD this morning. Says it's the damndest thing, they found her dead in her bed at home. All signs point to drowning."

Day joined in the laughter as they left the room, allowing hotel staff in to tidy up. "Dagon's eyes see you," Day said to his cousins as they parted in the hotel lobby.

"And find you pious," they both replied in unison as they stepped out into the rain.

DREAM
SHADOW

THE BLONDE LAUGHED, A SOFT TINKLING SOUND. Tall and beautiful, Craig knew her from somewhere. A famous model perhaps. He slouched on a banana lounge, sipping a cocktail, admiring the lights and architecture of the city skyline.

"Craig Thomson," he said as she passed. "Wanna join me? You really should try...whatever this is I'm drinking."

The blonde smiled. Her smile grew wider. And wider. Her teeth shifted, elongating as her eyes became black. Her mouth opened, revealing row upon row of razor points. With a spasm, her spine curved up, rolling her shoulders forward, her hands extending into long, thin talons. With a cry Craig dropped his drink and staggered to his feet. This wasn't supposed to be happening. He knew he was dreaming. He always knew. He struggled to change her back but nothing happened. Laughter stuttered out of her like gunshots into thick tar. She lumbered forward, reaching for him.

"Not happening!" he yelled, desperate to wipe her away completely, but she kept coming.

Craig brought all his will to bear and ordered the dream to finish, determined to wake up. The hideous parody of the blonde began to fade and he felt something sucking away from him. Some presence drew back, slipping out of his dreamscape. A thing that should not be there. He refused to let it go, tried to pull it back into his dream, the better to see what it was, but it was strong. Like a riptide it pulled him with it as it tore from his dream. His mind stretched, images and sounds fracturing, spinning away. With a gasp he awoke. He sat up and saw a dark shadow scurry from the open window of his room.

Craig scrambled from the bed. Falling to hands and knees he lunged forward, leaning out into the warm summer night. His brand new patch of lawn, a dark square of neatly trimmed green, was bathed in wan moonlight. His eyes scanned to the shrubbery at the back fence, newly planted, tags still on the trunks of some, and he saw the shadow again. Vaguely man shaped, bent and scrawny, arms too long, legs too short, it pressed up against the unblemished new wood of the fence and vanished, melting through the planks.

Craig panted, staring, heart hammering. Wide awake, he pulled on shorts and an old T-shirt and clambered out the window. He went to the fence, looked over into the bushland beyond. With a thump in his chest he saw the scrawny, bent shadow standing in the trees not twenty metres away, watching him. "Who are you?"

As he scrambled over the fence the thing vanished. Wincing at the dry sharpness of gum leaves and twigs against his bare feet, he ran to where it had stood. Nothing was there.

* * *

"Sure it wasn't a roo or something?"

Craig hitched an eyebrow, elbows propping him against the bar, his glass condensing on a stained beer mat. "Really, Kate? You think I couldn't tell if it was a roo?"

Kate looked at her drink, her dark bob of hair swinging down to veil her eyes. "You said yourself you were dreaming."

"It was right at the window. When I saw it, it bolted and went through the fence. Not over it, *through* it."

Kate shrugged. "You're not trying to give me a hard time for selling you the place are you?" She looked up, green eyes playful, a tiny smile tugging one side of her mouth.

Craig couldn't help smiling back. "Of course not. It reconnected us after all these years. Even if the house was crap, I still wouldn't change that."

Kate's smile escaped the side of her mouth. She looked away, eyes scanning the fridges of premium beers behind the bar. "So what was it then?"

"Dunno. When I looked over the fence it was standing there watching me. Then it just vanished."

Rather than offer any explanation Kate sipped her pink alcopop straight from the bottle. Craig watched her, drank his beer, lost in thought. The bustle of the pub faded, the deranged electronic songs of the poker machines muffled, as he admired her. Two months ago he had been second guessing his decision to move back to his home town, wondering if it really was the change he needed or a step backwards. Then he went to look at a house in a new development on the suburb's edge, and who should arrive to show him around but gawky little Katie Pearce. Only she wasn't so gawky any more. The girl he had teased at school had become a very beautiful woman, radiant smile replacing chunky braces, inviting curves supplanting boyish straight lines. The local girl made good. The idea of moving back near where he had grown up had a whole new appeal. He had come to look at the house a second time as much to see her again as the house. The third time they were together in the house it was to sign contracts, and they had sealed the deal passionately right there on the brand new kitchen counter. Now he wondered how much he could really tell her about last night. Would she think he was mad? He guessed most people would. He tried to picture the thing again. All he could see was the silhouette of it. Even though it had stood for a moment in moonlight, it was nothing but an inky shadow.

Kate stood from her barstool. "I have to get back to work."

"Sure. You got more haunted houses to shift?"

She pushed Craig in the chest, then caught his shirt and pulled him back to her, planting a kiss on him. "I'll come over later? Maybe it'll come back and you can show me."

"I'm not sure I want it to come back or for you to see it."

Kate ran a hand through Craig's sandy hair, down onto his freckled cheek. "We'll talk about it later. Enjoy your day off."

Craig watched her go, counting his lucky stars. Thankful that he had met her again right after she had told her previous loser boyfriend to take a running jump. He had needed to shake things up, force a change from his stuck-in-a-rut life. Now he had a house of his own, he had Katie. All certainly change for the better. Still staring at the door long after she had disappeared into the sunshine, he swallowed the last of his beer.

* * *

He stood at the rickety gate and smiled. Even now, grown as he was, this place was comfort. Peeling weatherboard, cobweb-covered sash windows, rusting tin roof, all just like it had ever been.

The front door stood open behind a tattered screen, the house cool and dark. "Hello? Aunt Betty?"

A short, fat floral dress appeared at the end of the hallway. "Craig?"

"Hi. How are you?"

"Not dead yet. Too stubborn to die. It's good to see you. You need something?"

Craig opened the screen and stepped inside. "It's a bit embarrassing really."

The old woman disappeared back into the depths of her house, voice floating back to him through the gloom. "Nothing can embarrass me, love."

Craig took a deep breath, tasting lavender and over-boiled greens, nostalgia on the air. He turned into the dark lounge room as his aunt slumped into a worn armchair and muted the TV. She flapped a hand at him. "Come in."

Craig smiled. "I hope I'm not disturbing you."

"No. Just sitting in the cool, waiting for something interesting to come on the telly."

Craig sat on the edge of an old sofa covered with a faded floral design like his great aunt's dress, feeling like a fool. "Sorry it's been a while since I visited."

"You're a grown man with a life. I don't mind."

Craig took a deep breath. "I remember when I lived here after mum and dad died you used to tell me the best bedtime stories."

Aunt Betty shook her head, her eyes wet. "Too young, Craigey. You lost them too young."

"But you were here."

"I'm your dad's aunt. Family. What about my stories?"

Craig rubbed a hand over his face. "When I was little this place was a bit scary for me. Suddenly living here, not really understanding where mum and dad had gone, why I couldn't go home. But your stories used to make me feel better. You'd tell me a story and then you'd turn out the light and I'd lie there, scared again. To get to sleep I used to shut my eyes and pretend the story was real, that I was the hero. It got to the point where I could fall asleep and dream your stories, controlling what happened. I've been able to do it ever since. It's called lucid dreaming."

Aunt Betty's eyebrows raised. "You never told me this before."

Craig shrugged. "It seemed kinda private."

"So why tell me now?"

"Something really weird happened last night and I need to talk to someone about it. You know I moved into my new place last week?"

Betty made a wry face. "You told me you were going to be moving in sometime around now." She shook her head. "Like a cancer these new land releases, eating away the bush. Everything's changing." She held up a hand. "Not that I hold it against ya, everyone needs a place to live. I remember when this house was surrounded by paddocks instead of neighbours, that's all. Now there's a thousand houses between me and the trees."

Craig nodded. "Trouble is, ever since I moved in there my dreams have been out of whack. Last night I had a terrible nightmare and saw some kind of weird creature outside my window when I woke up."

"Weird creature? You were probably still dreaming." Betty looked uncomfortable.

Craig shook his head, staring at the threadbare carpet. "No. Definitely not. Do you know any legends about weird creatures in this area?"

Betty laughed. "The only weird creatures I know are all these Asians moving in and taking over the shops." She laughed again at

Craig's shocked expression. "Don't worry, you know I'm not a racist. I'm only pulling yer leg."

Craig chuckled, not entirely sure just how racist the old lady may or may not be. She had grown up in a very different country to the one he knew. "I mean…well, actual creatures, like…" He slumped. "I have no idea what I mean."

"You talking about a bunyip or something?"

"Maybe. But not really a feral beast. This thing was more intelligent, I think. Like it was after me."

"You were making a new life, with your job and all that. Why'd you come back here?"

"I told you before, I wanted to own my own home, my own piece of the country. No way I can afford to in the city. I had to look in the suburbs. I guess I thought it would be cool to come back near where I grew up. Near you. And where I could get a new house, bush right over the back fence. I'm still making a new life."

"And you found little Katie Pearce too, didn't ya. Not so little any more!"

"Aunt Betty!"

Betty cackled, hauled herself up and disappeared through a clicking bead curtain, colourful drops of plastic over a faded linoleum floor. Craig sat and stared at family photos on the mantelpiece, shots of him growing up interspersed here and there. Old watercolours of the Australian countryside hung on the walls, horse-drawn carts and men with pitchforks, images of a world long gone.

His mind tumbled with memories, not all of them welcome. This was the very couch he had sat on when he was nine years old and the police had told him that his parents were never coming back. The same couch he had sat on numerous times after that as the police told his great aunt what mischief they had picked him up for that time. The old oak dining table and chairs still stood in the corner where he had sat and scowled and ignored the counsellor the school had arranged. The counsellor who told him he had every right to be angry but that he had no right to take it out on others.

Was he seeking some kind of catharsis moving back here? Would he have really gone through with it if he hadn't met Kate again?

His aunt came back carrying a tray with two tall glasses and a jug of cordial, ice cubes chiming around the top. The glasses had scuffed, swirling designs in green and red, the very same glasses he had drunk from as a child. "When I was a kid there was nothing out here," Betty said as she poured. "Just a few houses, this one included, dotted around on sheep stations. Slowly the farmers sold the fields and the developers built the houses and thousands of people moved in." She handed him a cool glass. "But back in the day we used to have a lot of aboriginal folk around. They used to tell all kinds of tales about strange creatures."

Craig took a long gulp, feeling ten years old again. "You remember any of them?"

Betty nodded, her thin, blue-rinse hair like a halo of tiny clouds. "Bits and pieces. One thing I remember is that none of them would go anywhere near the bush out west of here for any length of time. And they would never stay out there overnight."

"Where my house is now?"

"They said the land there had some evil spirit. Something was trapped out there and it would haunt your dreams if you tried to sleep there. Drive you mad, they said, feeding off your nightmares."

Craig laughed. "You're making this up."

Betty's eyes were sad. "I wish I was. They called it a dream shadow."

* * *

Craig stood in the doorway, waving languidly. Kate backed her small Japanese hatchback off his faux red brick driveway, waving back and pulling faces. He laughed, exhausted, feeling the fatigue that could only come from fucking the way new lovers do.

Kate leaned out the window as she reached the road. "Call me tomorrow?"

He blew a kiss. "Sure."

"Whatever it was last night, I'm sure it was just…you know…a random event."

"You probably scared it off!"

Kate's mouth opened in mock outrage. "Fuck you!"

"Tomorrow. I'm tired."

With a laugh and a rev of the engine Kate pulled away, pausing at the mouth of the cul-de-sac before disappearing towards the main road.

Craig's eyes traced the half-moon of houses and neat front lawns. Newly rolled turf made geometric ladders of the nature strips, some of the two-storey houses on the south side still unfinished, blue tarpaulin covering wooden frames. He closed the front door and wandered into the lounge room, slumped onto the sofa, staring through glass doors into his garden. The night was silvery with moonlight, the lawn standing out while the borders sank in black shadows as the heat slipped out of the day. Was it a dream shadow he had seen the night before? Was it anything? Maybe he *had* still been dreaming. Regardless, he was a talented dreamer and he could choose not to dream. *Drive you mad, feeding off your nightmares.* Well, maybe he wouldn't dream for a while. If it was real he would starve it out. Let it go somewhere else.

A pulse of shock washed ice through his groin as he stared at the shadow on his lawn. Lost in thought he had been staring at nothing and there it was. Staring back at him, jet black and featureless in the moonlight. Heart hammering, trembling from head to toe, he refused to look away. The thing had no eyes, no face, no detail. Just solid blackness in a caricature of human form. Yet he knew it was staring right at him.

He sucked a long, slow breath in through his nose, swallowed the rising lump in his throat. The shadow stood and stared.

Craig's shock and fear became a molten anger. He strode to the sliding doors, slamming one aside. "Fuck off!"

The shadow stared.

With a snarl of rage he walked out into his garden, hands

raised as if to slam two fists down onto the thing. "This is my place now!"

As he drew within a metre of the shadow, close enough to feel a chill from it, it melted away into the grass. He stood, face twisted, his breath coming in short, furious gasps.

* * *

The night was dark and warm, barely a breeze stirring the curtains at the open window. Craig lay on his bed, covers thrown aside, exhausted. He knew the thing was waiting out there. He was tempted to call Kate back, but that just made him feel stupid. She had to work tomorrow. So did he, for that matter. He relaxed, concentrating on nothing but his breath, letting sleep come. Black, quiet, dreamless sleep. Stick to the plan. He would starve this thing out of his life, whatever it was. That was the simple solution.

He stood in a wide-open paddock, lush grass swaying in a soft breeze. Bright sunshine bathed him. Something large and dark approached across the field. His heart began racing. This couldn't be happening. He could choose not to dream. He had *always* been able to choose not to dream. He tried to blank out the thing approaching. It resolved into a huge creature, some cross between a bear and a dinosaur, all fur, scales, claws and teeth.

He cried out, bringing his entire will to bear, trying to delete the thing from his dream. The creature grabbed him and lifted him high into the air. With a roar it slammed him down. Pain lanced through his body. He could see into the creature's glowing eyes and he knew that it would come for him every night. He knew he couldn't stop it, couldn't change it. It was beyond his control. As a giant hand with black, ragged claws swept through the air towards him he screamed himself awake.

Hours later, as dawn began to smudge the horizon with orange and grey, he sat on his bed, sobbing, exhausted after waking time and again, nightmare after nightmare. Whatever this was, it was in this place and now he was in this place too.

* * *

"Oh, Craigey, you look awful!"

Craig smiled weakly. "I had a bad night, Aunt Betty. I just need to sleep."

"What about work? Have you eaten? Let me make you some eggs, then you can sleep."

"I called in sick." Craig followed his aunt into the kitchen, sat heavily at the red and white Formica-covered table. Betty busied herself, taking crockery and ingredients from glass panelled cupboards and an old fridge. Craig leaned on the table and laid his head on his arms.

"What kind of bad night?" Betty asked as she whisked.

His voice was muffled. "This thing, whatever it is. It attacks me in my dreams. Gives me nightmares. All I can do is wake up."

Betty was still for a moment. "Maybe that's what drives people mad, the lack of sleep."

He looked up, his eyes dark, desperate. "What am I going to do?"

His aunt turned from the counter. "Go somewhere else." The ancient toaster behind her skipped with a metallic twang, toast popping up. She turned and began buttering.

"This was supposed to be my dream. Owning my own home."

Betty scrambled eggs in a battered pan. "Maybe some places aren't meant to be a home."

Craig ate the eggs and drank some strong, sweet tea, feeling better immediately, looked after and safe. This was the way home was supposed to feel. However many difficult, painful memories this house held there were at least as many good memories. His aunt had been good to him, taken care of him, rebuilt his life here. No house was a home until memories had been made there. He went to the spare room, his old room, and collapsed onto a creaking metal-framed bed, familiar swirls of black ironwork standing over each end. He curled his fingers in a multi-coloured crocheted bedspread and closed his eyes. Sleep fell over him like a heavy cloak. Quiet, dreamless sleep.

* * *

Late afternoon sunlight washed pale through the net curtains over Betty's ancient stainless steel sink. A colourful knitted tea cosy covered a tea pot between them on the table, tea leaves telling unknown fortunes in the empty cups.

"Oh, love, please don't."

"Aunt Betty, people have been making the land their own for hundreds of years now."

Betty's eyes were wide, her brow creased. "Craig, if this thing's real you have to be careful. The way you were this morning..."

He shook his head. "I refuse to give up my land. I've slept, I feel refreshed, ready. This...ghost or whatever it is lives on my property."

Betty looked down at her hands folded in her lap. "Your property? Lines drawn on a map by some local council cashing in doesn't really make it yours. A huge debt with the bank doesn't really make it yours. People these days don't understand the land. We always used to live with the land. Nowadays people just live off it. You can't keep changing the land and not expect it to fight back."

"This morning I was exhausted, terrified. I can't change this thing in my dreams, I can't cast it out of my dreams. But they're still *my* dreams. Didn't you always teach me to fight for what's right?"

"Sometimes it's more like that old country song, love. You gotta know when to fold 'em."

Craig stood, bent to kiss his aunt. "If I can't beat this thing, then maybe I will have to move. But not without a fight. Tonight, I'll face it in a dream and take it on."

* * *

Kate stood outside Craig's house, gently chewing at her lower lip in thought. Things had moved fast between them, too fast if her dad was to be listened to. But she was smitten. And that was okay. Craig was a good guy. Only recently, this thing with the dreams and the monster, it had all come out of nowhere. While she didn't want to outright disbelieve him, was he a little crazy? Maybe it was an anxiety thing, and she could probably help him through that.

But he hadn't answered calls or texts all day and that was unusual. It went against all protocol, but she still had a key for his house, a spare the real estate had held while trying to sell the place. She should have given it to Craig when he bought but had honestly forgotten all about it. And she was worried for him. He hadn't gone to work, apparently, wasn't answering her. Surely that was grounds enough to check inside, just to be sure.

She nodded, assuring herself it was the right thing, and turned the key in his door. "Craig!" Her voice echoed a little in the still sparsely furnished home. He'd said he was planning to slowly fill it with furniture but was in no rush. He wanted to "feel out his style". She grinned, called out his name again. No reply.

The kitchen and lounge room were empty, still. Kate stood, conflicted. A person's bedroom was their private sanctuary. Could she really go in there uninvited? She'd been invited often enough, and that filled her with good memories. She smiled, then stilled as a soft sound came to her. A shallow, fast breath, almost panting. Like a hot dog, broad smile splitting its snout. But there was something a little more desperate about this sound. And it was coming from Craig's bedroom.

Frowning, she moved cautiously forward, gently pushed the door wide. Craig sat on his bed, head up against the wall. His eyes were wide and bloodshot, staring a million miles away at nothing as tears poured over his cheeks. A rivulet of bright scarlet trickled from each nostril. His mouth hung open, drool stringing from one side, as his chest rapidly pulsed with terrified gasps.

"Craig?" Kate said, and her boyfriend started screaming.

WAYS TO LIVE AND DIE

THE OLD HOUSE ON THE CORNER WASN'T HAUNTED, but the dead could be summoned there. So the local legends said. Salman stood on the pavement outside, staring at broken shutters hanging off the windows, the crooked siding, paint peeling, off-white like old sunburned skin. The roof had holes in it, more joists showing than tile remaining, the entire property sagged in the middle as if exhausted. Ready to give up but unable, just yet, to fall.

The yard inside the low, rusting chain-link fence ran wild with tall grass gone to seed. Why the place wasn't condemned was a mystery. Salman turned a slow circle, taking in the middle class suburb. Not affluent but not poor. A nice neighbourhood full of families, low crime, clean and pleasant. Except for this one squalid sore in the flesh of an otherwise healthy body.

"Dump, ain't it."

Salman jumped, turned to seek the voice. A teenager sat astride an old Chopper bicycle, arrived as if by magic, unheard and unnoticed. Salman hadn't seen a bike like that since the 70s, couldn't believe they still existed, but the kid's was shiny and new. A wry smile pulled up one side of the lad's mouth.

"You like my wheels?"

"I had one. When I was your age."

"Oh yeah? And what's my age?"

Salman lifted and dropped a small shrug. "Thirteen? Fourteen?"

The kid laughed, a strangely guttural sound. "Sure, okay." He gestured with a side-nod to the broken-down old house. "You thinking about talking to someone dead?"

"You don't believe the stories, do you?"

"Doesn't matter what I believe. You're the one standing here looking sad as hell. Do you believe it?"

A bolt of pain through Salman's chest, a swish of Charlotte's shiny black hair in his mind's eye. "Nah," he said, though his voice had a weak edge. "Just urban legend, right?"

"You askin' or tellin'?"

Salman sniffed, annoyed this kid wrong-footed him at every turn. "You local?" he asked instead of answering.

"Been here a long time, yeah."

"This place been here all along? Run down like this, I mean."

The kid looked towards the house at last, nodding softly. "Been here since before most of the rest of the neighbourhood. Dilapidated for nearly as long as I've known it. Some things are kinda trapped in time."

"Why hasn't it been bulldozed? Or renovated? Why does no one live here?"

The kid shrugged and stood up on his pedals. "Dunno," he called over his shoulder as he powered away and turned into a lean to make the corner past the east side of the property. Then he was gone and Salman stood alone, staring at degradation, smelling Charlotte's perfume. Trying not to cry.

* * *

"I walk past it every day on the way to and from work." Salman drank his beer, watched the condensation pattern the glass rather than catch Steve's eye.

"That doesn't mean you have to buy into the stories."

"I know. Yeah, of course. But I just…wonder, you know?"

"How can it be true, Sal? You're not a superstitious man as far as I know."

Salman laughed softly. "Much to my mother and father's chagrin. Non-practicing is as bad as apostate in their opinion."

"Right. But that's because you're a…what do they call it? A critical thinker?"

"I guess so."

Steve took a long pull of beer, then leaned forward, elbows on the table. The bar was raucous around them but not so much they needed to shout. "So be critical about this. You take something personal of the dead person into the house, squeeze a drop of your blood onto the floor, and they appear and you get three questions, right?"

Salman nodded without looking up. He didn't want to see the scepticism in Steve's eyes, but more than that, he didn't want to see the pity.

"How does that make any kind of sense to a critically thinking man, Sal?"

Salman ran a tongue over his teeth, unsure what to say. Of course it was rubbish. But he needed something. They sat in silence for a few moments, the low roar of conversation all around like the tide going in and out. Glasses rattled, someone laughed too loud.

Steve put a hand on Salman's forearm. "She died hard, dude. She died *horribly*. But it's been six months. If they don't have any more answers for you by now, maybe you need to accept they never will."

Salman sucked in a quick breath, couldn't trust himself to speak without bawling.

Steve squeezed his arm. "I'm so sorry."

Salman nodded. He put his other hand over Steve's, squeezed back. The man was a damn good friend, always there for him. Tears breached despite his willing them not to, dropped onto the table like shining medallions on the dark wood, reflecting neon lights above.

"I'll get us another round," Steve said, and slipped away.

* * *

"Mr. Abeyan?" the police officer had said, standing at the front door. Light from the porch illuminated him like a saint against the dark rainy night, gave his whole body a halo. Beside him stood a female police officer, her face a picture of practiced sympathy, and the bottom fell out of Salman's world.

"You found her?" he managed.

"Can we come in?"

"Yes, of course."

"We should sit down, sir."

"This way."

"I'm so very sorry to tell you, Mr. Abeyan, that your wife Charlotte has died."

The next few days were a blur, rain and darkness and tears and anger and denial. The car was broken almost in two by the trunk of a large oak tree, the conflagration started from the ruptured fuel tank. Her body could only be officially identified by dental records. Speed in excess of one hundred and twenty kilometres an hour, according to the experts, to cause that level of damage. But the road was straight as a fence post. No evidence of any other vehicle, no skid marks. The limit was eighty. Why was she going so fast? Why did she leave the road?

"Was your wife suicidal, Mr. Abeyan?"

"No!"

"She hadn't been acting strangely in the days leading up to the accident?"

"No."

"No arguments with anyone? No enemies?"

"Enemies? Of course not!"

They wanted the same answers he did, albeit for different reasons. Would those answers do either of them any good?

* * *

He stood outside the broken-down old house again, feeling like an idiot. A desperate, pathetic, lost soul. Because that's what he was. But he had to try. The night was dark, no moon, no clouds, any stars not obscured by light pollution weakly spackled the indigo sky. He looked around, then hurried up the path. As he reached the front door a soft whirring sounded behind him. He froze, deep in the shadows of the leaning porch, looked back.

The kid on the Chopper shot past, tires on the cement making the only noise, then he leaned into the corner, whipped out of sight. He hadn't even glanced at the house as he sped by.

Salman swallowed, took a deep breath, pushed against the door. The wood had swelled with damp and rot, but it was clear from the sidewalk it wasn't closed. A bar of darkness an inch wide ran top to bottom. It flexed slightly under his palm, but shifted in, pushing a drift of dirt and leaves with it. A musty smell wafted into the cool night, hints of fungus and something animal, wild. Salman slipped inside and gently pushed the door to again behind him. Under his Hush Puppies, the floorboards creaked, one loud enough that he feared it would give way. So he stood still, let his eyes adjust until shapes drifted up out of the blackness. Edges of door frames, forgotten furniture, deeper darkness where the floor had indeed fallen in. The legend said nothing about going far, so he figured this was enough.

He carried a small glass statuette of an otter he had given Charlotte on their fifth anniversary. She loved the thing. It was as personal an item to her as he could imagine, always on the table beside her as she slept. Now it stood guard over an empty space. He gripped it tightly, felt its crystal edges pushing into his flesh, then took a quick breath, relaxed before he crushed it and lacerated his hand. Only one drop of blood required. He took out a folding pocket knife Charlotte had given him as a gift, smooth mahogany, two silver studs through the body, a three-inch, gleaming steel blade. He pressed it gently to the edge of his left thumb where it wrapped over the glass otter's neck, felt the electric sting of his skin parting. He refolded the knife, held it in the other hand, and squeezed his cut thumb against his forefinger. He watched a bead of blood, black as tar in the dimness, rise and bulge, then drop to hit the floorboards between his feet.

He held the glass otter, thinking only of Charlotte, her black hair, her smooth cheek, the touch of her fine fingers as they trailed along his spine. He begged her forgiveness for his foolishness, but willed her to come to him. Let her tell him she had been speeding just for the fun of it, that she had swerved to avoid a deer, that she had died instantly, not screaming in an inferno. Would those simple, mundane things give him any closure? Was that better than agony? Or suicide? Did any of it matter now?

"Haven't seen that for more'n forty years." The voice was low, distant like it came over a weak phone line. Male.

Salman snapped his eyes up, stared right into the face of a stubbled, thin and ugly face not three feet from this own. He cried out and staggered back, hit the door and banged it hard against the frame it was too swollen to fit into any longer.

The man laughed, thumbs hooked into the straps of grubby denim overalls. His body was sticks and angles, barely any meat or muscle on him, and the shapes of the room behind him were clear through his gossamer presence.

"Surpriiiise!" he said, a long drawl.

"What?"

The thin man pointed to Salman's right hand, still holding the small folding knife. "That's mine. Well, *was* mine. How did a guy like you end up with it?"

A gift from Charlotte, bought in some antique store. Salman lifted the glass otter stupidly, looked from it to the knife and back again. "But this. I'm here for this. For Charlotte."

"Shoulda only brought the possession of one dead person." The man's laughter was like nails on a blackboard. "Man, the things I did with that little knife." He stretched, looked around. "Where are we anyway? Is this that old house that's always been falling down? Man, I lived my whole life in Rotorua and never came in here. Until now, I guess."

"Who are you?" Salman asked.

"Who am I? Reginald T. Peabody, at your service. Murdered thirteen women between 1968 and 1976, all along the Coromandel Peninsula, never too close to home. Skinned some of 'em with that very blade you're holding. I lost it from my pocket sometime in '75, two years before they put me in jail. Three years before I got shivved and died in my cell. That's two."

"Two what?"

"Questions. And that's three. You just used up all the power you had here, ya useless idiot." Peabody leaned his translucent head back and laughed again, screechy and drilling.

Salman stood immobile but for trembling through every muscle. His mouth grew dry, his eyes wet. Eventually, he managed to draw breath to speak again. "You mean it worked and I got you?"

"Yes, dumbass. Try catching up and playing along."

Salman shook his head, turned to leave. It was all a nightmare. He'd wake alone on his cold sheets any moment.

"The hell are you going?"

Salman ignored the ghost, dragged the damp and swollen door open again.

"Oh, man, that was some crash, huh?"

He turned back, trembling redoubled. "What?"

"Your wife. What a wreck that was."

"You know about it?"

Peabody smirked, shrugged. "Seems I can kinda access things if I concentrate."

Salman swallowed. "Can you see what happened?"

"Ah, is that it? You don't know anything but the end result? You came to ask her if she suffered? Tell her that you *looove* her?"

"Can you tell me?"

"Yep."

Salman stared, waiting.

Peabody's smirk deepened. "But I won't. You used up your questions, remember?"

The fact that he could have known despite calling up the wrong shade, but that he'd blown it, made icy knives turn in Salman's gut. "Why don't you tell me anyway? What's it cost you?"

"What's in it for me?"

"I have no idea. What do you want?"

"Now finally you ask a smart question. Took you long enough."

Salman knew this would be nothing good, whatever happened. But he *could* know, and that's what he wanted. Even if he'd lost the opportunity to talk to Charlotte one last time, to tell her how much he loved her, how he missed her, he could still know. Closure, to stop the open wound of her loss from continual bleeding. Then he thought of something else, and managed to suppress a smile. He'd just come back another time, bring the glass otter but throw the evil knife away. Buy a new blade to drop his blood. It had worked once, he'd just do it again. He *could* talk to Charlotte.

"Don't work that way."

Salman started, looked up. The shade could read his thoughts? "What?"

"Ya get three questions. Ya asked 'em. You're done."

Hope and happiness folded in on themselves and fell away into a black pit somewhere deep inside him.

"But I can tell ya what ya wanna know. If ya do somethin' for me first."

Salman nodded, resigned. "What do you want?"

"See, I got away with my crimes, up to a point. I was random, just picked any pretty girl I saw. They couldn't catch me. Until my dumb wife started to think too hard. She turned me in."

"You had a wife?"

Peabody frowned. "That so hard to believe?"

Salman shrugged, didn't trust his melancholy tongue to speak.

"So I want you to get her. She's over eighty now anyhow, nearly dead already. But ya go and hurt her, kill her, make sure she knows it's me making it happen. She lives right here in Rotorua still."

"Revenge?"

"Yup. Then I'll tell ya anything ya wanna know. Ask thirty questions if ya like."

* * *

Two days later Salman returned to the old house. He walked like a man heading for the gallows. His shoulders sagged, his feet dragged, three-day growth darkened his jaw. He shifted side to side under the weight of the five-gallon can he carried.

Peabody flickered into life as Salman shouldered the swollen door open. Chopper tires whirred by on the pavement behind, but Salman didn't bother to look.

"Ya did it?" Peabody's face bore expectation like pain.

"You can't see? You can't *access things*?"

Peabody frowned, concentrated. Then his face sagged. "Ya didn't do it. She's still alive."

"I thought about it. Hard. But some answers are not worth it. Besides, I had a look on Google."

"The hell is that?"

"The sum of human knowledge. You've been gone a while, things change. I can know anything by looking it up on a computer. You're not a serial killer. Maybe you wish you were, but you're just a lousy wife abuser. *She* killed you, back in '77, after you got drunk and beat her once too often. Your ninety-pound wife stabbed you fourteen times, and didn't go down for it."

Salman began splashing gas all over the floorboards and walls as Peabody spat and cursed, swung insubstantial punches, useless kicks.

"Your wife is a hero, Reginald T. Peabody. She's lived nearly fifty years of happy, fulfilled life since she ended you. Lovely lady, makes great lemonade. Her husband is a decent guy too. He was in real estate. They made good money and retired happy. Wouldn't surprise me if she lived another decade, she barely looks or acts sixty-five let alone eighty-five."

"You son of a…!" Peabody danced a jig of impotent rage.

Salman smiled. "I should thank you though. You made me realise something."

Peabody stilled, tipped his head to one side.

"There are many ways to live," Salman said. "And having unanswered questions is okay. There are many ways to die too. Charlotte knows I loved her. I know she loved me. Maybe I'll see her again one day and we can talk, or maybe not. It doesn't matter. You know what your wife said to me? She told me to make sure I didn't let Charlotte's death kill me too." He flicked a match. It flared bright in the dim house and Peabody mutely shook his head. "She's very wise," Salman said, and dropped the match. He walked out as a blossom of heat and flame unfolded behind him.

A young man on a shiny Chopper bicycle headed down the road, away from the old house, into the sunset. Salman stood and watched the place burn for a while, then turned and strolled away as the sound of sirens rose in the distance.

YELLOWHEART

Anya filled the car with unleaded and looked back over her shoulder to the service station's small shop. Olivier and Sara moved around inside, laughing together over something. She tried not to let envy bite deep again, glad her friends were happy. She only wished her relationship with Gavin was still like that. It had been, not so long ago.

She clicked off the petrol and hung up the pump. Leaning forward to see Gavin, sitting alone in the car, scowling from the passenger seat, she mouthed, *You want anything?* and pointed to the shop. He shook his head, gave only the weakest of smiles. Maybe this whole trip was a mistake.

"You okay?" Sara asked in the shop.

Anya forced a smile, realising her concerns must show on her face. "Sure."

"He's not going to make an effort, is he?"

Anya let the smile fall. "I don't know." She glanced back to the car, but Gavin stared straight ahead, his curly dark hair a cloud in the shadows, reflecting his mood. "I'm sorry, you guys. I don't think this was such a good idea after all."

"It's okay," Olivier said. "We love you, Anya. We're here for you."

His hint of a French accent charmed her, always had. He'd been in Australia for fifteen years, since his mid-teens, but it persisted. In high school, she had been seduced by it, but after a couple of years they had settled into a tight friendship that lasted ever since. Olivier hooked up with Sara in their early twenties, around the same time she had got together with Gavin. Their trajectories remained similar for a long time, but the last couple of years, things had significantly diverged. A long weekend away in the middle of nowhere, the four of them hanging out and drinking and laughing and enjoying the outdoors like the old days, had seemed like such a good idea before they left.

"It'll be okay," Sara said. "I know Gavin's moody, but we'll have fun. He'll loosen up when we get there."

"It's more than moody." Anya gently chewed inside her cheek. "Whatever, we're here now, right? Nearly, at least. Let's see how it goes. I'm sorry if I've brought you on a horrible holiday!"

"It will be fine!" Olivier said, putting one arm around her shoulders and squeezing. "He'll get into it, you'll see."

Anya nodded, but didn't catch Olivier's eye. She didn't want him to see her doubt. She worked hard, she was motivated, she exercised, she ate well, all the good stuff a person was supposed to do. Gavin just wallowed. Everything was someone else's fault. Like his art career, failed because the industry had gatekeepers and no one would give him a chance.

"I'm too fat, but fuck it, this is a holiday!"

Anya startled at Sara's sudden outburst. "You are not fat! You're a real woman, with curves." Anya had always tended towards tall and skinny. She liked her body but sometimes wondered what it would be like to have a butt and boobs like Sara. She knew Gavin resented Olivier's height and broad shoulders, and thought that was just dumb.

Sara grinned, holding up a packet of Extreme Cheese corn chips. "I just love these things, they're like crunchy crack. I don't care if they'll go straight to my arse."

Olivier hugged her from behind. "I don't blame them, it's a gorgeous arse."

"Get offa me!"

They devolved into laughter and Anya was drawn with them, all three giggling as they went to the counter to pay for the snacks and petrol. She caught Gavin looking over from the front passenger seat. He gave her another weak smile. He was trying.

She winked at him, then paid for the fuel.

"Should we stock up on more food?" Olivier asked.

"No, not now." Anya checked her phone for the time. "It's getting late, it'll be dark quickly this time of year. We can head back into town tomorrow or Sunday if we need to stock up. We've got plenty of grog, plenty of snacks, and essentials like bread and milk. And the Airbnb thing said they'd leave a stock of local produce on the table for our arrival. Pretty sweet deal." She glanced back to the car. "I'm sorry we didn't arrive earlier like we planned."

Sara patted her arm. "Gavin's little hissy fit delayed us but hasn't spoiled anything."

"I should have left him behind, and the three of us would have a better time." She noticed both Olivier and Sara pause, clearly at a loss for a reply. She thought maybe it was because they agreed with her, but they all knew she was being harsh. "I'm kidding!" Was she? "Come on," she said quickly to dispel the moment of discomfort. "I can't wait to see the place."

Anya pulled back out onto the single lane highway, the mountains of Tasmania's north-west a magnificent vista in the late afternoon light. Leaving the small service station behind, and then a scattering of houses, they passed through farm country and into trees. She kept the music up loud enough that talking was difficult, Olivier and Sara happily canoodling in the back seat. Gavin didn't seem to care about the beauty of the landscape, staring forward without reaction. He gently twisted the dark grey titanium thumb ring he wore, a habit of nerves she found increasingly more annoying.

Fuck this, Anya thought, and turned the music down again. "Isn't this amazing," she said, loud enough that it was clear she was addressing her friends in the back. Even so, she glanced over at Gavin.

"I've always loved this part of the country," Sara said, leaning to look out through the front. "It's only three hours from home, why don't we come more often?"

"We forget," Olivier said. "It's too easy to get caught up with work and whatever. We need to remember to switch that shit off." He leaned forward too, slapped Gavin on the shoulder. "Gotta be glad to get away from that shop for a while, eh?"

Gavin jumped at the contact, looked back in surprise. "Wish I could get away from it forever."

He speaks! Anya thought to herself.

"You should," Olivier said. "Look out for somewhere different, have a change. It must get old, selling guitars and amps to other people all the time."

Gavin made a noise like the grunt of an animal. "Look out for what? What else can I do?"

"You should get back to why you started there in the first place," Sara said. "You know, start playing again, get a band back up and running."

Another creative endeavour that turned out to be too hard because some actual effort was required, Anya thought.

"There's no point," Gavin said, sounding genuinely chagrined. "You can never rely on other people to keep to practice times, gigs are always half-empty. The labels only want manufactured pop anyway, not real music."

All of that was demonstrably untrue, Anya thought, but there was no point in trying to tell him so.

"But you have to have a go," Sara persisted. "You'll never get anything you don't go after."

Gavin shrugged. "Maybe."

Anya loved her friends for trying, but she was embarrassed on Gavin's behalf. She caught Olivier's eye in the rear-view mirror and he gave a small smile, but it was pained. A roadside sign gave her a chance to change the course of conversation to something less uncomfortable.

"Mole Creek up ahead! We turn off here, so that means we're nearly there."

The road became narrower until Anya was watching carefully ahead for oncoming vehicles. She'd need to move onto the gravel and grass off the tarmac if they had to share the road with anyone else. Then the tarmac ran out and the hiss of tyres became a subtle roar as the whole vehicle vibrated and jounced on an unsealed surface.

"Not the best maintained road," Sara said, holding onto the passenger strap above her head. "I hate this!"

Anya smiled. "Don't worry. According to the posting when I booked, it said once the asphalt runs out, you follow the road for three more Ks, then turn left up a track marked with a sign that says Yellowheart Cabin."

"And then we're there?"

"Well, almost. Then it's another four Ks up that road."

"Ah, fuck. Be ready to stop if I get sick."

Anya glanced in the mirror, but Sara wasn't joking, her face drawn, and a little pale. Olivier held her tightly against him like he could absorb the vibrations for her. Anya did some quick mental arithmetic. Seven Ks of this, at a safe forty kilometres an hour, that was less than twelve minutes. "Only ten minutes," she said, rounding down for Sara's sake. "I didn't know you got car sick."

"Only on rough roads like this. And only since I lost the baby. Before I got pregnant it was never a thing."

Anya winced, remembering Sara and Olivier's distress at the late miscarriage, the still birth. Such a terrible time for them and they hadn't tried again since, nearly two years later. She wondered if they ever would. "That's so weird," she said. They had all talked so much about it before, she was at a loss for anything else to say.

"I know, right? Pregnancy does fucked up things to a body."

"It's really unfair how much of the burden the woman has to take in procreation," Gavin said. "Nature is stupid."

Sara laughed. "You're not wrong."

There's the old Gav, Anya thought. Dryly funny and genuinely kind-hearted. Sara groaned, looked down at her lap.

"Remember the pictures we looked at," Anya said, keen to change the subject. "Think about the destination. That bright white weatherboard cabin on the rolling grassy hillside. Wide verandas all around, open fireplace, the mountain rising up behind."

"It looks like a classic hunting lodge inside," Olivier said, catching on. "All polished dark wood furniture and exposed beams."

Anya glanced at Gavin. He caught her look, held her eye for second then said, "All that booze we have in the back!"

She sighed, but gave a wry grin. Was that really him trying to join in? They went on in silence for a moment, then Olivier was the first to spot the sign as Anya was too busy avoiding the worst of the pot holes.

"There! Yellowheart Cabin."

"Almost there." Anya made the turn, looked into the mirror and gave Sara a grin.

Sara's face twisted in alarm, almost fear. As Anya opened her mouth to ask what it was, Gavin yelled, "Look out!" and slapped his hands forward onto the dash.

Anya snapped her eyes forward, saw the screen filled with the figure of a person, a tall, thin man in dark blue mechanic's overalls and heavy black work boots that looked comically too large for his feet, right in the middle of the road. He stopped, looked at them and grinned. Anya hit brakes, skidded on the gravel as she swerved and the car listed quickly to the left as one front wheel dipped into a rain channel down the side of the rough track. With a shudder, she brought the car to a stop less than a metre from a thick-trunked gum tree, everyone rocking forward and back with cries of alarm. The car stalled and jerked, then everything fell silent and still. Their gasps filled the empty air. Anya sat up, hands shaking, gut roiling with adrenalised shock. She looked back to the road, hoping she hadn't clipped the man. There was no one there.

She jumped out, checked the other side of the road in case she'd knocked him down, looked into the thick bush, gum trees and scrub, saw no one. The others got slowly out, pale, concerned. Sara leaned on her knees, breathing deeply.

"You all saw him, right?" Anya asked.

They nodded, looked around, brows cinched.

"Must have run off," Gavin said. "Gave him a scare, I suppose."

"Chilly," Olivier said randomly. "Autumn is further along up here than down in Hobart."

"High country," Sara said, forcing a smile.

The banality of shock, Anya thought. She turned back to the car, crooked and angled into the rain channel. "I'll back it out. You guys stay out here so you can lean on one corner or another if it needs grip."

Within minutes they were on the move again, the sky beginning to darken in the gap between trees above the road, gloom settling beneath. Anya drove more slowly, paranoid for sudden pedestrians. There was nothing here, bush for miles around. Who was that guy? She saw another sign, YELLOWHEART CABIN, pointing up to the left. "This is it!"

She turned into a long driveway that curved around to the right, rising towards the top of a large, rounded hill. They emerged from trees into open grass and Gavin said, "You are fucking kidding me."

Anya came to a slow halt, staring in disbelief. The cabin stood some fifty metres ahead, exactly as the Airbnb app had shown in the pictures, assuming the pictures had been taken thirty years ago and no maintenance had been done since. The bright white siding was peeling and rotten in places, the tin roof rusted and bent. The all-around veranda was there, but the railing broken and hanging in places, missing in others. She could see at least two spots where the floorboards of the veranda had fallen in completely. The windows were grimed and curtained by cobwebs, and the smooth rolling grassy hill all around marred by tussocks and scrubby bush. A rusty, broken old truck stood crooked on three wheels right next to the cabin and beyond that a large garage lay fallen in, slumped in the middle like it had decided life was too hard and had given up.

"This isn't right," Olivier said.

"It's the right place," Sara said.

"I know, but it's not what was advertised. This is not acceptable. Look at these pictures." He pulled his phone out, went to tap up something, then grunted in annoyance. "No reception up here, of course. You?"

Sara looked at her phone, shook her head. "Nope. But we've all seen the pictures. We know this is taking the piss. Nothing we can do about it now though."

Anya gripped the wheel in frustration. What a complete mess. She should have known better. For a moment she imagined an alternative weekend, where she told Gavin to go fuck himself, she was done with him, then went to Olivier and Sara's place to get wasted on good wine while Gavin packed his things. Right now she'd be warm and drunk in Hobart, and that would be infinitely preferable. None of the others were speaking. She glanced around at them, then at the louring sky outside. Night and rain clouds racing each other to arrive first. Glancing at her phone in the centre console, she tapped the button and confirmed she had no reception either. Really no surprise. But who would she call anyway? This is the situation they were in, and that was that.

"Let's go," Gavin said. "This is fucked."

"Go where?" Sara asked.

"Fucking anywhere! Back to a town nearby, Deloraine or something, and get a hotel or a motel. We can't stay here."

Soft rage heated Anya's spine. "Hell, no." She would not give Gavin the satisfaction, not after all the fuss he'd made about them going in the first place. "The owners are clearly taking the piss, like Sara said, but we're here now. It's going to be night soon, and maybe inside it's all good. Either way, I'm not driving back down that horrible road in the dark, so we stay." She looked back to Sara and Olivier. "Yeah?"

They grinned at her, shrugged. "Sure," Olivier said. "It's an adventure, right? We used to crave adventure when we were younger. We've gone soft."

"I'll drive back then," Gavin said.

Anya rounded on him. "We stay!" She drove the last bit of driveway, parked right beside the abandoned truck, and got out. Sara and Olivier joined her.

Olivier went to the big, rusty wreck and looked in the tray. He pulled aside a filthy canvas tarp and lifted out a heavy crowbar. He threw it back in and moved more tarp. "Couple of old shovels in here too."

"You expecting treasure?" Sara asked with a smirk.

"I'm expecting a body. I'm glad it's just old junk.

"Come on."

The three of them grabbed their packs from the boot and each took a shopping bag of food or booze. Gavin stayed in the car, face a rock carving of anger and frustration. Anya swallowed down her own anger. This was the last chance for them, whether he realised it or not, so she had to treat it that way. Try to meet him halfway and give him the opportunity to come around.

She went to the passenger side and pulled open the door, smiled like when she still loved him. "Come on, Gav. It'll be fun. Let's eat something and get drunk."

He looked up at her for a moment, then sighed. Even managed a smile. She saw the decision in his eyes, as he told himself, *Try harder, for her.* He obviously remembered the conversations they'd had. She softened to him then, allowed herself to think it might be okay. "Really fucking drunk!" he said.

"Sure!" She turned to Sara, who was stepping gingerly up the crooked steps to the veranda. "It said there'll be a key in an old Weetbix tin beside the door."

"Got it!"

Inside the cabin wasn't as bad as Anya had anticipated. It wasn't great, but after the outside she had been bracing herself for an absolute disaster. The furniture was just like the photos, but not polished to a shine any more, the upholstery threadbare, the rugs thin and grubby, but it was mostly sound. Weird pictures and a few stuffed heads adorned the walls, a couple of deer and a wombat.

"Who the fuck hunts and mounts a fucking wombat?" Gavin asked, pointing at the thing like they couldn't see it.

Olivier snorted a laugh, Sara joined in, then even Gavin started to guffaw. Anya felt the tension break like a cut wire and let out a breath of relief. Their laughter rippled around several times, slowing almost to a stop before starting up again afresh.

They put the supplies on a slightly rickety dining table and Anya pointed to two doors off to the right. "Those are the bedrooms, side by side." She turned, pointed opposite. "That's the bathroom. Tank water, but given the time of year and the rain lately, we shouldn't run out."

"Which room do you want?" Sara asked.

"No preference."

They went and opened both doors, looked in. Each room had a double bed, chest of drawers, old-fashioned wardrobe. All a bit tatty but sound enough. They were a mirror image of each other. Anya went into the one on the left, threw her bag on the bed. As Sara and Olivier took their stuff into the other one, Gavin joined her. He put his bag down, turned on the spot to inspect the place, then put an arm around her. "Right proper shithole you've brought us to," he said.

"Only the best for you and my closest friends."

He kissed her and she hoped things might turn around yet.

"Nice spread they've left us!" Sara called out.

The main room of the cabin had a big brick fireplace on one wall, sofas and armchairs scattered around, the dining table and six chairs to one side, and a large kitchen at the back. Sara stood at the kitchen counter sorting through produce.

"A dozen eggs, some carrots and potatoes, a loaf of homemade bread. And some kind of mushrooms."

Olivier was on his knees at the fireplace, stacking wood into the grate ready to get a blaze going. The house had the close coldness of damp, though everything appeared dry. "Some kind?"

"There's a note. It says, 'Local produce, everything here came from no more than three kilometres away. The mushrooms are only found in this part of Tassie.'"

"Seems bloody unlikely," Gavin said. He went to look, then shrugged. "They look like normal mushrooms to me, just a bit smaller."

"I can cook up a great vegie omelette with all this," Sara said. "No need to even open our stuff yet."

Anya smiled. "Good idea. You do that, I'll pack our things in the fridge, and Olivier can get the place warmed up."

"What shall I do?" Gavin asked.

Sara glanced back over her shoulder. "Dance for us, bitch!"

Even Gavin laughed, then said, "I think I might do the most important job of all and open the booze." He started rummaging in cupboards for wine glasses, then pulled out a bottle of red and handed everyone a generous share. Within ten minutes the crackle of the fire made the place warmer, its orange glow softening every edge as the night outside darkened all the windows. Sara's cooking filled the cabin with savoury aromas. Anya draped an arm over Gavin's shoulders, kissed him, then went around drawing the curtains.

As she pulled the last ones together, movement caught her eye. She stopped, opened them again, wondering if it was a wombat she'd seen. Out near the rusted truck, low to the ground. Darkness was coming on quickly and she peered into the gloom, then saw movement again. A head turned, with bright eyes and white teeth, the dark blue overalls almost lost in the shadows, the man's back strangely arched as he crawled on hands and feet, grinning, out of sight under the broken vehicle. Ice water swirled into her gut and Anya let out a nonsensical cry.

"What is it?" Olivier came quickly to her side, Gavin following.

"Out there, under the truck!"

"What?"

Anya looked at the two men, then back out into the night, unsure she could even believe her own eyes. "That fucking guy we nearly ran down on the way in. He just crawled under the truck."

"What?" Olivier leaned forward, looked out.

"What do you mean, crawled?" Gavin asked.

"Exactly that, fucking crawled!"

"Come on," Olivier said. He pulled out his phone and fired up the flashlight. "Gavin! Come on!"

Gavin copied him and the two went through the front door. Anya watched intently from the window, trembling. Sara had stopped cooking and watched from the other side of the kitchen bench. "Creepy fucker," she said, as the men shined their lights around outside.

Anya moved to the door. "Seriously." She leaned out. "Underneath."

"I know," Olivier called back. "Nothing but grass and dirt." He stood up, raised his voice. "Anyone here? Is there anyone out there? We booked with Airbnb."

The men came back inside, closing the door against the dark and the chill. "Nothing," Gavin said.

It had been almost dark out there already, and Anya was spooked by the close call on the road. The guy's appearance was burned into her memory. Maybe she was seeing things. "Probably a wombat or something and I just freaked out."

"It's the wombat who should be freaked out," Gavin said, pointing to the ridiculous stuffed head on the wall.

"Maybe that's his dad or something," Olivier said.

"My name is Inigo Mon-wombat," Sara said from the kitchen. "You killed my father, prepare to die!"

Laughter filled the cabin again and everyone returned to their wine, Sara to her cooking. Anya decided to let it slide, but she would make sure the place was well locked up before they went to sleep.

Sara's omelette was delicious, the local mushrooms meaty in texture and peppery in taste. They had it with hunks of the homemade bread, thickly buttered, then retired to the sofas. Anya and Gavin curled up together on one, Sara and Olivier on another, but within reach to pass a second bottle of wine back and forth to refill glasses. Warm relaxation washed over them as the fire crackled and shadows danced. The alcohol seeped slowly through Anya's stress.

As they chatted, Anya blinked, everything suddenly a little blurry. Maybe the wine and tiredness, plus the shock of the near accident, was getting to her. She looked up and saw Olivier moving one hand back and forth in front of his eyes, watching it intensely. Sara stared at Olivier with fascination, a smile tugging her lips. As Olivier's hand moved, visual echoes of his fingers dragged through the air. "The hell?" Anya breathed.

Gavin sat up, moved away from her, and stared at the fire, then the walls of the cabin. "It's all moving," he said, voice tight with concern.

"What's moving?" Anya asked, following his gaze.

"The fucking walls are breathing!" Gavin's voice had risen an octave.

"Chill out, guys," Olivier said. "I think they've played a nasty trick on us. We're tripping."

Anya turned her attention back to him, saw Sara grinning broadly, like a fake circus clown. "Tripping?"

"I think maybe there was something psychoactive in those local fucking mushrooms," Olivier said. "Fuckers if they think it's funny, but you know, it's okay. Don't let it bother you, yeah? If you get upset about it, you'll have a bad trip. I've done acid and mushrooms before, it'll all be okay. It'll pass in a few hours, we just have to ride it out. Yeah?" He looked around at the others.

"Jesus," Anya said, then couldn't suppress a laugh. She felt disembodied and elated at the same time. The walls did indeed seem to flex back and forth ever so subtly if she watched them, the curtains rippled gently. The fire was amazing, bright and dancing, mesmerising in its complexity. "This weekend is just getting weirder by the minute."

Olivier and Sara giggled, but Gavin was quiet. She turned to him and saw his face crumpled like he was about to cry. He looked around, movements erratic, jerky. "The shadows are coming," he said. "They're closing in."

Anya put a hand to his head, brushed back his hair. "It's okay, it's a drug. Don't panic. It'll be okay."

He pushed her hand away and moved to the other end of the sofa. "Everything's going dark!"

"Don't stress it, bro," Olivier said in a singsong voice, his French accent more pronounced than it had been in years. "It's a trip, man. Relax and smile, it'll all pass. It's all fake, just your brain doing backflips."

"Everything's turning black!" Gavin said, genuine panic tinging his voice. "Where are you guys?"

Anya moved closer again. "We're right here. I'm right beside you."

"Where are you all?" Gavin shouted, looking right through her and frantically scanning the room.

Anya looked to Olivier for guidance, scared for Gavin's well-being. Olivier stood and pulled a heavy blanket from the back of the couch. He moved to Gavin and gently wrapped him, tucking it in.

"It's okay, Gav. Yeah? Everything's okay. Just relax, mate. Deep breaths."

Gavin looked left and right, not seeing Olivier or anyone else, but he gathered the blanket around himself and curled into a tight ball on the end of the couch, pressed up against the threadbare arm. One hand worried at the other, twisting and twisting the dark metal of the titanium ring on his thumb.

Olivier went back to Sara. "Poor bastard," he said. "He's having a bad one. That came on so fast."

Anya frowned, wanting to comfort Gavin but scared to freak him out further. She tried to suppress the effects of her own trip, the bright colours, sense of euphoria. Despite her concern, her lips stretched into a rictus grin as she ground her teeth together. She needed to calm herself too, or she'd sink into a downward spiral like his. "Will he be okay?"

"Yeah. He'll have a rough time now, but it'll pass. We'll watch him."

Anya saw the look in Olivier's eyes that made her think he wasn't so sure, but she chose to accept his words on face value.

A rapid ticking echoed through the cabin, a thousand tiny feet skittering across the floorboards. Anya imagined that skinny bogan in the dark blue overalls and heavy boots, reduced to only a few inches high, replicated by the dozen, hundreds of him shooting across the floor towards her on his tiny hands and feet. She bolted up on the sofa, hauled her legs up under her and looked frantically around.

"Rain!" Sara said, unable to contain laughter. "It's just raining."

Olivier laughed too. "She's right. It's the metal roof. Don't panic.

Our biggest concern is leaks, but there's no sign of water damage in here. We have no choice, so let's just enjoy this ride. It'll end soon enough."

"I'm giving this place one fucking star on Trip Advisor," Sara said, and exploded into more laughter.

Anya relaxed, let giggles of relief bubble out of her. "Maybe two stars, seeing as the omelette was so nice."

"That was me, not those bastards!" Sara said, then frowned. "That fucking wombat on the wall is breathing. Look at his little mouth moving up and down!"

"He's stuffed!" Anya said, even though she could see the thing shifting unnaturally too. Just the trip, she told herself. Just the trip.

"He's definitely stuffed now," Olivier said. "Someone cut his head off and glued it on the fucking wall."

It wasn't funny, but they all three devolved into hiccupping giggles nonetheless. Olivier got up and locked the door, then sat back with Sara as the laughter reduced. Anya checked Gavin, still tightly curled up, eyes darting left and right from under the edge of the blanket that cocooned him. He reached out, as if grabbing for something in the air, then looked at his palm in distress. He buried himself deeper in the blanket. Anya gently stroked his hair. "It'll be okay," she said softly. He didn't seem to notice her.

* * *

The shadows that had begun to close around Gavin after everyone had eaten finally became total. He sat curled under a large bush in some earthy corner of this new world. The leaves were thick, spongy, more like meat than plant, each longer than he was tall, a cathedral of giant shadowed foliage. He pulled two tightly around himself, offering only a slight comfort, a vague protection. Everything was monotone, varying shades of black and dark grey. The ground outside the shelter of the plants undulated, rocky for the most part. The sky roiled almost black, but shot through with deep purples, blues, occasional striations of crimson. Millions of motes drifted in the air like ash. When he reached out to try to catch them, they vanished on his palm, insubstantial as smoke.

Time seemed rubber, inconsistent. He closed his eyes and then jerked awake, feeling as though he had been unconsciousness for minutes or even hours. Then he would stare at the black and barren landscape and seconds would leak past like tar, the gaps between one breath and the next punctuated with extended stillness. There was no sound.

Had he always been here? He remembered people, a slim woman with blonde hair and blue eyes, the memory of her stirring an ache inside him. He recalled another woman, shorter, curvier, with black hair, and a man, balding, tall. Who were they? Why were they important?

He needed to find a way…somewhere. He did not belong here. He shouldn't be here. But the thought of striking out into that black and shadowy wasteland terrified him. He blinked again and sensed hours passing.

* * *

Dawn smudged the world outside the windows a pinkish grey. Anya blinked heavily, finally feeling the effect of the psychoactive fungus drifting from her. "I think I can finally sleep," she said, mildly concerned at the slur in her voice.

Olivier nodded. "Yeah, I think we're through this. A good sleep is the best thing for us now." He glanced down at Sara lying against his chest, already dozing.

"What about Gav?" Anya asked. He had been fitful all night, sometimes closing his eyes and quietly moaning for an hour or more at a time. Now his eyes were open again, looking furtively out from the edge of the blanket, but he showed no signs of moving, nor any recognition of his friends. "It doesn't look like he's coming out of it."

Olivier came to crouch beside Gavin. "He must be more sensitive. And, you know, his depression and stuff. Maybe that's part of why it's hit him really hard. Or he got more mushrooms in his serve? He just needs time for his body to process it." He looked up, must have seen the concern in Anya's eyes. "I've seen bad trips before, he'll be okay. I promise."

"Will he though? The term 'acid casualty' exists for a reason."

Olivier smiled. "This isn't some potent chemical made in a home lab. It's natural. Let's leave him to rest, I'm sure he'll be fine."

Anya wasn't entirely sure she believed him, but none of them were in any shape to drive Gavin to a hospital, and what other choice did they have beyond that? As far as she knew, a hospital couldn't do anything anyway. She put an arm around him, started to tell him it would all be okay, but he cried out, shook her off. Olivier shrugged, offered a soft smile.

She felt awful leaving him, but he was safe enough on the couch. And she was so tired. She smiled back at Olivier as he guided Sara into their room, then she retired to the one she was supposed to be sharing with Gav.

This is quite the metaphor for our relationship, buddy, she thought ruefully as she left the bedroom door ajar and went to collapse on the bed. It was cold, but the mattress soft and comfortable. Without bothering to change out of her clothes, she dragged the duvet up around herself and tumbled into a dark and dreamless sleep.

It seemed only moments later that Olivier gently shook her shoulder. She immediately smelled toast and bacon and coffee, and her stomach rumbled. She rolled over, surprised at how rested she felt.

"Sara's cooking breakfast, even though it's nearly noon," Olivier said.

"Wow. Hell of a start to our little break. How's Gav?"

Olivier winced. "Still out of it."

"Really?" She climbed out of bed and hurried into the front room. Sure enough, Gavin remained tightly wrapped in his blanket, peeking over the edge of it. He didn't acknowledge her as she crouched beside him. "Gav? You okay?"

He looked around, quick, darting movements of eyes and head. "Who's there?" His voice was weak, like thin paper. See-through.

"Gav, it's me. It's Anya. Are you okay?"

"I hear voices," Gavin said, so quietly she almost missed it. "Voices from somewhere."

She looked over at Olivier. "He's talking to himself."

"Yeah. Still not really back on board, but he's coming around, I think. More responsive than last night."

"Really? I dunno, Olivier. Maybe we should get him to a doctor."

"What can a doctor do? They'd just tell us to keep him safe."

"Would they?" Anya frowned, recognising echoes of her own thoughts. "Is there no antidote for this?"

"I tried to look that up," Sara called from the stove. "But still no reception, inside or out."

"But there's not," Olivier said. "Only time."

"And if he's permanently affected?"

Olivier shrugged, face pained. "I don't think he will be."

Anya watched Gavin, mixed emotions swirling in her. On the one hand, she still remembered the man he had been, the one she loved. She cared for that guy. But that guy hadn't been around much recently. And, if she was honest, she could see shadows of the man he was now in her memories of the good times. Had there always been a veneer? Was the real Gavin the surly, moody, bitter person who blamed everyone else for his own shortcomings. This whole weekend was a mistake, she shouldn't have tried to save anything. Perhaps she had needed to make that mistake to recognise it. "You really think he'll come around? And be okay?"

Olivier nodded. "I really do. Look at this." He showed her a photocopy of a hand-drawn map. "I found it on that little table by the door. There's a marked trail that goes up the mountain behind us. Hard going, it says, but at the top the view is magnificent. It says a three-hour round trip, and these things always over-estimate hike times. And I bet we can get phone reception at the top. We can ask advice from the hospital."

Anya frowned. "Maybe. That might be quicker than trying to manhandle him into the car and drive anywhere, given how he reacted just now."

Olivier nodded. "Exactly. And I bet they'll tell us there's nothing to do but wait. Let's do it. If it doesn't work and Gavin is still in bad shape when we get back, we'll drive him down to Deloraine or something before dark."

"Breakfast is ready," Sara said, putting three plates on the table.

Anya looked from Gavin to the breakfast, which smelled amazing, to Olivier. "Okay. Yeah, okay."

"You think the owners knew the stuff they left was trippy?" Sara asked as they sat down to eat.

"Must have," Olivier said. "They wouldn't just leave random fungus, surely?"

"Well, it looked like regular mushrooms, only smaller. I'm not well-read on drugs, but I've never heard of magic mushrooms that look like that."

"Might have been a mistake," Anya conceded.

"Mistake or a really shitty trick," Olivier said. "Either way, combined with the false advertising about this shithole location, I can't wait to get reception back again. I've been mentally composing my reviews and emails all morning."

They gorged themselves, Sara's unspoken self-appointment as chef most welcome. The food and coffee helped push the remnants of the previous night's effects from her body and Anya decided she was energised and ready to go. They got dressed and packed sandwiches and water, put on their boots.

Anya crouched in front of Gavin, squeezed his hand. "We'll be back soon. I'm going to call someone, yeah? Find out how to help you. Stay here, okay."

Gavin whimpered, looked down at her hand holding his and shook it off.

Anya sighed and left, stepping out into a cool but clear, blue day.

* * *

Gavin had no idea how long he had hidden in the thick, fleshy leaves of the strange plant, but his body ached and his mind whirled.

Weird, distant voices kept coming to him through the disturbingly still air, the ashy motes drifting endlessly. Nothing was familiar. The rocks and gravel around him were both dark and glassy, yet strangely matte. The sky roiled and blurred, even the colours in it muted and dark.

A distant voice again, muffled not only by miles but as though it were coming through walls or water. Words that stretched like hot wax, incoherent.

"I hear voices," he whispered to himself, as much to test his own ears as anything. "Voices from somewhere." His words were clear, his breath puffed with condensation as though it were freezing. But he wasn't cold. He felt something on his hand and looked, shook it away. But nothing was there. He should move, go somewhere.

Trembling, he crawled out from the safety of the large plant and shakily stood. The desolate expanse stretched away in every direction, but behind him a huge mountain rose up, stabbing into the churning sky with ragged edges of black stone. Perhaps if he got high enough to see around, he might be able to decide where to go. To find help. Bent half over, wincing with the vulnerability of exposure, he scuttled for the slope at the foot of the mountain.

* * *

Anya, Olivier and Sara made their way up the gently sloping ground behind the dilapidated cabin. After a short way, Sara paused. "Look at this."

Hanging from a small tree were strange constructions of twigs and broken, weathered wood. Pyramids and diamonds, from a few inches tall to a couple of feet, tied together with dried grasses and dark strips of leather. Something about the designs was strangely disquieting.

"Creepy," Anya said. Some had small animal bones or feathers suspended inside. She curled a lip, turned away. "I don't like them much."

"Some kind of bogan art installation?" Sara asked.

Anya had no answer. They headed for a wooden sign that said simply, TRAIL, and pointed to a gap in the bush. The three entered the trees across a slippery, wobbling wooden bridge over a stony creek and followed the metre or so wide track as the ground became steeper. The air was cold but the sun warm, so the sudden damp and chilly confines of the forest was a slight shock to the skin, a mild stun to the breath. Anya's arms stippled with goosebumps and she pulled down the sleeves of her jumper. She had a raincoat, tied by its sleeves around her waist, but decided to save that. If the going was as tough as the photocopied flyer suggested, she'd be warm enough from exertion soon. It was labelled as being steep. She looked forward to the exercise, the chance to work frustrations from her muscles.

Tall gums interspersed with pines loomed over them, with ferns twice as tall as Olivier and doubly broad underneath, like multi-limbed umbrellas. Dozens of dying, brown fronds hung like skirts below their dark green caps. The ferns' fine leaves cast strange, tooth-like shadows in the small patches of sunlight that speared through the dense canopy. Last night's rain dripped and glistened, but the ground, while wet, wasn't muddy.

"So we're looking for red markers pointing the way up," Olivier said. "On the way back there should be yellow ones."

Sara pointed. "Like that."

On a gnarled, dark tree ahead of them, a triangle of red-painted metal had been punched into the trunk with a single nail. The long sides of the shape made an arrow pointing up and to their right. Olivier moved nearer, looked past the tree, and nodded. "Another up there, see?" He moved around the tree. "And a yellow one here pointing back down. Pretty cool."

"Simple but effective," Anya agreed.

They moved on, the trail often clear to the eye, but sometimes as good as indistinguishable from the general bush. On several occasions they stood shoulder to shoulder with trees and rocks, bunched together, looking for the next red arrow. It became a game to see who could spot it first, then scramble, sometimes on hands and feet for purchase up steep inclines, to get there before the others. In places, the trail became so steep and the forest so thick that they used crooked and ancient tree roots like ladders through the wet, almost black earth. Slick moss, dark and dense, sometimes made footing treacherous. Tiny toadstools, patches of greasy white fungus, and spiky lichens were ubiquitous. Water ran in small waterfalls between clefts in the rocks, and pooled at the base of trees. More than once, fluffy white strands sat like hair atop toadstools of various shades.

"You know it's fucking damp when the fungus goes mouldy," Sara said with a laugh, and a mildly disgusted twist of the lips.

Despite the cool, Anya had a sheen of sweat on her face and arms, now with her sleeves pushed back up, and it trickled occasionally down her back. "This is great," she said as they paused to catch their breath. "This place is fucking primeval. And it's quite an effort to get up!"

"More like a bloody mountain climb." Sara grinned. "I'm glad we brought lunch with us. How far do you think we've come?"

Olivier checked the time on his phone. "We've been going just under an hour, so I guess that makes us about halfway up or a bit more?"

"Holy shit," Anya said. "I hoped we were further than that."

"The view from the top will be great. We'll be so high." Sara pulled herself up from the rotting fallen trunk she had been leaning against. She pulled out her own phone and held it up and they all mugged for a selfie. Then she looked at the screen. "Still no signal. Come on, let's keep going. We can eat and enjoy the view when we get there, and rest up for the return journey."

"I reckon coming back will be a lot quicker than going up," Olivier said, wincing at the seemingly endless steep slopes ahead of them.

They moved on, Sara in front, then Olivier, then Anya happy to bring up the rear. Occasionally they got to walk side by side, but every time the path narrowed again to precarious trails little more than wombat tracks they fell back into single file. When Sara pulled up short with a yelp of surprise, Anya thought her friend had caught herself on a branch or rock. Then Anya's stomach lurched at the sight of a tall, thin man up ahead of them. His dark blue overalls were grubby and stained, oversized black leather work boots scuffed and muddy. He had scrawny bare arms poking out from under loose shoulder straps and his face was stubbled, narrow, big eyes too wide apart and almost no chin that slipped into a wattled neck. He could have been thirty or sixty, she honestly couldn't tell. But he was familiar. He held three large, dead possums by their tails in his left hand and a broad-bladed hunting knife in his right. The silver of the knife edge glittered in a ray of sunlight through the canopy. Olivier quickly stepped up next to Sara, pressed together with her on the narrow path.

"G'day!" the man said, and grinned. He had half his natural allotment of teeth and what remained were tobacco-stained where they weren't blackened.

"We saw you on the road!" Anya said, nerves tightening her throat. She was shocked to see him, but another part of her felt pleased he was most definitely not some kind of hallucination after all.

"What road?" he asked.

"The dirt road, leading up to Yellowheart Cabin. Yesterday."

He twisted his face in thought, then shook his head. "Yeah nah, not me. Maybe you saw my brother? I got a few brothers around here, and a dad. Though Dad's too old, so he don't walk about outside any more."

"Is your brother your twin?" Sara asked.

"Nah. But some people think we look alike. Maybe ya saw Glen. But I ain't Glen, I'm Dylan." He gestured with the bunch of possums. "Youse want one o'these? Good bush tucker."

"No! Thanks." Olivier's face was twisted in horror at the thought and Dylan laughed, wet and guttural.

"Youse staying at the Yellowheart, ey?"

"You know the owner?" Anya asked.

"Everyone knows everyone around here." He leaned forward, looking down at Sara with sudden intensity. "You're really pretty."

"Hey!" Olivier pushed a little further forward.

"Hey what? You don't think she's pretty?" Dylan jabbed towards Olivier with his knife, a casual yet menacing gesture. "You shouldn't hang out with someone who can't tell ya how pretty ya are," he said to Sara.

"Let's go," Sara said. "Can you step aside, please. Let us pass."

Dylan didn't move but leaned to one side to appraise Anya. "You're pretty too, but I like my women to have some meat on their bones. So I prefer this one." He grinned broadly at Sara.

"You're a gross asshole!" Sara said, as Olivier stepped forward again.

"Please move aside," Olivier said. "I won't have you terrorising these women."

"Or what?" Dylan took one swift step forward and down the slope, made Olivier jerk back in surprise. Then Dylan's knife was right in front of Olivier's throat, almost touching the skin. "I don't take kindly to rudeness."

Anya swallowed, forced herself not to point out who was the rude one. No way would this guy accept any argument like that. She'd met her share of hateful bullies in her life, and recognised one when she saw him. She watched Olivier's fists clench tight and liquid fear swirled in her gut. Was he about to hit the bogan fool? He'd get his throat slit for sure. For a moment everything was a frozen tableau, tension tight like the skin of a drum, but about to split wide open.

Then Dylan leaned back and laughed that wet sound again. "Youse have a good walk."

He strode off between the trees so fast it was almost as if he flew. Branches whipped and snapped back from his passage and Anya saw a flash or two of dark blue before he was swallowed up by the gloom.

"Jesus fucking Christ." Sara's breath was short, her voice small.

"That was singularly unpleasant," Olivier said.

Anya moved forward, put a hand on his shoulder. "You okay? I thought you were about to hit him!"

"I was, but the knife…"

"Yeah."

They fell into silence, the trail suddenly colder than it had been. Or was that simply the lack of exertion? "Let's keep going," Anya said.

"You sure?" Olivier asked.

"Yeah. Fuck that guy. We're nearly at the top, aren't we?"

"We must be."

After another fifteen minutes or so, the trees began to thin, the incline reduce, and the muddy, rocky trail became a boulder field. Broken trees lay crisscrossed, in various stages of decay, between the healthier surviving trunks. The friends slowed, stepping carefully so as not to twist an ankle or fall.

"The flyer said you have to follow the markers across the top to the lookout," Olivier said, looking for the next one.

"There," Sara said, pointing off to their right.

A whip of darkness snaked out of scrubby brush beside Olivier and whacked into his leg. He cried out in pain and went down.

"The fuck?" Anya said, staggering back, as Olivier howled and held his shin just below the knee.

Sara ran towards him and something blurry hit her and sent her sideways with a tight scream. Anya blinked, trying to understand what she saw. It had no form, like a moving heavy shadow that rose up from the stones and melted away again.

Olivier, still whimpering in pain, used his free arm to crab-crawl away from the thick bushes, his eyes wide as he watched for another attack. Sara picked herself up, face grazed and red along her left cheek.

"What hit me?"

Anya shook her head. "I didn't see." She rushed forward, met Olivier on the other side from Sara and between them they hauled him to his feet. He howled in pain and she let out a horrified, "Oh!" when she saw blood on his leg.

Olivier's face was scrunched in agony and he yowled as he tried to put weight on the injured leg and went down again, nearly taking the two women with him. They braced and pulled him back up. His leg, a few inches below the knee, wasn't the right shape at all, like he had a second joint there, going ever so slightly sideways.

"Is it that fucking redneck asshole?" Sara asked, dragging at Olivier.

Anya shook her head. "No. I don't think so. Let's get over there, into the light." All she could see in her mind's eye was the darkness whipping and moving. Sometimes shaped vaguely human, other times low, like an animal. But it seemed to be gone for now and she wanted only to be in bright sunshine.

The sun was warm as they lowered Olivier onto a large, smooth boulder. He gasped short, shallow breaths, both hands gripping his leg just above the knee like he could choke the pain out of the wound lower down. His face was grey, sheened in sweat.

"It's fucking broken," he said from between clenched teeth.

"Yes, I think so." Anya crouched for a closer look. She tried to move the pants leg and Olivier cried out. She watched the red stain on the material, but it didn't seem to be spreading fast. "The bone must have split the skin, but it's not bleeding too badly."

Sara looked around, one hand pressed to her injured cheek, the other absently rubbing at her ribs on the same side. Anya wondered how hurt her friend was.

"What the fuck hit me? What broke his leg?"

"I don't know."

"What was it?" Sara said, leaning down to grip Anya's shoulder. "You saw it? What *was* it?"

"I don't know! I didn't see... It was just darkness. Like shadow."

Olivier shook his head. "Something in the shadows, you mean?"

"No! It's... I don't know." Anya felt like she was losing her mind. Had her eyes refused to see what it was? Did her brain protect her from something unspeakable? How could shadow strike anyone?

Olivier leaned his head back and roared in pain and frustration. "How the fuck am I supposed to get back down like this? I can't stand, let alone scramble over all those roots and rocks."

Sara crouched, pulled her phone out and stabbed the button with a finger. Then again, harder. "Fuck! Still no fucking signal." Wait here. She stood and hurried away across the boulders towards the red marker. Anya and Olivier waited anxiously as she disappeared between trees towards the lookout. After a few minutes, Sara reappeared. Tears were visible on her cheeks long before she reached them. "Nothing," she called out. "The view is amazing, but there's no signal at all."

"Fuuuck." Olivier's voice was tight with pain.

Sara crouched by him again. "We'll get help. Send someone."

"What, and I wait here?"

"I guess so? We'll go back down, drive until we get a phone signal, then send someone in. They can get a helicopter to you, maybe?"

Olivier's face crumpled. "Before dark?"

"If we go now, sure. Maybe."

He shook his head. "I don't want to be here alone."

"I'll wait with you," Sara said. "Anya can go for help."

"No. I don't want any of us here, especially if it gets dark. And Anya shouldn't go alone. Something is wrong with this place."

Sara frowned. "What do you mean?"

He stared at her, pale and sweating. "Seriously? Find me a sturdy branch. For a crutch. You two can help me down, yeah? I don't want to stay here."

Anya exchanged a glance with Sara. She couldn't blame the man for wanting to get moving. Apart from the dark and the cold and the wet, whatever hit him was still out there. She wouldn't want to be on her own either, or sitting still, waiting with someone else. "Sure. We'll get you down between us. We can, sure."

"Here, try this." Sara held up a branch about as thick around as Anya's upper arm, and nearly as tall as she was. One end was ragged where it had broken off, the other forked making the whole thing into a knobbly Y. Sara snapped off the longer ends of the fork and offered it over. Olivier stood on his good leg and sank the crook of it into his armpit. Sara took his other arm across her shoulders and they began to hobble forward. Olivier whimpered with pain, but grit his teeth and pushed on. Anya watched in dismay. This rough terrain was bad enough, but the steep, muddy trail, especially where it was virtually vertical with only tree roots to hold onto, would be another matter. But what choice did they have?

She felt superfluous, useless, as she watched Sara lead a limping and softly crying Olivier back towards the last marker they had passed. The yellow arrow pointing the way seemed almost to mock them, indicating the narrow, steep trail traversing between the trees. But the gloom disturbed her more.

* * *

Gavin huddled in the questionable shelter of a small rocky outcrop. Whatever those things were, shadowy, limned by the strange ambient non-light of this darkened world, obscured in part by the swirling flakes of ash, they had come too close for his liking. Striking out with the rock had felled one, then another had come right at him. With courage born of terror, he had launched himself at it and shoved it away, then retreated once more. Thankfully, whatever the things were, they appeared to be moving on, back the way they had come. They yawned and moaned, made stuttering, chittering noises, and occasionally yowled. Gavin feared them.

When he was sure he had been alone for a long time, he cautiously emerged from cover. He had learned nothing, the only change in his surroundings being the gradient of the stark, dark landscape. And he couldn't help thinking he was heading in the wrong direction. A high vantage afforded him no real view, all distance occluded by darkness and swirling ashy clouds. If anything, he would likely find succour on the flat, not the peak. He needed to go back. Picking up a large, heavy rock, as round as his head, he carefully picked his way down the gritty, shadowed slope.

* * *

Olivier's face remained a grimace of pain, white and waxy as he struggled down the twisting, uneven trail. Sara sweated and gasped with the exertion of half-carrying him, but clearly had no intention of stopping. Her muttered words of encouragement had become a mantra. The woman was strong, and determined as hell. Anya helped where she could, often moving down ahead of them to offer a hand for Olivier to lean against in the steeper sections. In places he sat and agonisingly bumped down over roots on his butt, or slid on his belly over wet rocks. Every time his injured leg even tapped an outcrop he yelped in pain and new tears squeezed from his eyes. They moved from one yellow marker to the next, the descent seemingly endless.

"Are you bleeding much?" Anya asked. "Should we try to dress it?"

"No, don't touch it! Please. Just let's get me to a fucking hospital."

"Okay, easy now. Keep moving."

There was a sudden bang, like a gunshot but muffled, more concussive. The three friends froze, Anya scanning every overhanging fern or tree limb for shadows, watching the darkness under every rock in case it moved.

"What was that?" Sara asked.

"No idea." Anya pointed down over a rocky outcrop to a tree with a yellow arrow. "Keep moving."

As Olivier whimpered in pain, despairingly slow over the rocks, there was another soft thwack from further down and to their left.

"Ignore it," Anya said.

They made another hundred yards down and across the slope, then another whack echoed dully through the trees. Anya caught sight of movement and froze. Wordlessly, she pointed. Between gnarled, silvery trunks, they watched Dylan, the tall, skinny bogan, slip effortlessly along a narrow trail. He paused and pressed something up against the trunk of a half-fallen gum, and gave it one solid hit with a dirty hammer. As his hand came away, they saw a bright yellow arrow.

"He's moving the fucking markers," Sara said, her voice barely above a whisper. It was almost empty with exhaustion, with despondency.

"Fuck!" Anya spat, more loudly than she'd intended, and Dylan spun around, stared straight up the steep incline at them.

His mouth split in raucous laughter. "You caught me!" he called in a singsong voice.

"You fucker!" Sara yelled.

Dylan seemed to lean sideways strangely, crookedly, then he was off through the trees and gone from sight.

"We've been following those for ages," Anya said. "How far off course are we?"

"Straight down," Olivier said, gasping between words. His eyes rolled, sweat stood out on his forehead, the skin of his face ash grey. His lips were purpled.

"What?"

He pointed. "We go straight down. The cabin is at the foot of this mountain. Get out of this fucking bush, then find our way along the flat back to the cabin."

"But what if we're already so far off course that we miss it?" Sara asked. "We came a long way up along the roads to get to the cabin."

"Chance it." Olivier bit off a sob, whether of pain or frustration or both Anya couldn't tell. "Just get down."

"Yeah. Okay."

They looked left and right, then Anya said, "There's not a better way. It's all fucking rock and scrub. Let's just go."

For another fifteen minutes they forged their own route off the mountain. Where they could, they traversed using trails, whether the original path or animal tracks they couldn't tell, and didn't much care. Where necessary, they simply scrambled over the least steep sections, using rocks and tree limbs to support their descent. Anya's legs were like jelly, regularly threatening to collapse under her as she stood downslope of Sara and Olivier, helping the injured man by providing her body as a stake to lean on. Olivier's pain-wracked face and Sara's obvious exhaustion forced her to ignore her own discomforts. She would not be a weak link in the face of their strength.

They came onto a more level section, slightly less thick with trees.

"I don't remember this," Sara said.

Neither did Anya. "We can't be back at the bottom yet. I wonder how far that fucker led us?"

"Look."

They turned to see what Olivier was staring at. A small wooden shack, blackened and mossy with damp, stood to one side of the slightly open space. A soft curl of smoke wound up from a tin chimney. Anya drew breath to celebrate, thinking they had finally discovered help, when the sight of strange stick arrangements made her pause. Dozens of them. Some on the ground, twigs and branches arranged into tall pyramids, like teepees without skins covering them. Like the ones on the small tree behind the cabin. Inside each, suspended from the pointed top, were weird, meaty pieces of…something. Animals? Hanging by strings, some dripped gently. Others were fuzzed with mould. More, smaller, constructions hung from trees, triangular arrangements woven together, gently twisting in unfelt breezes. Some of the hanging ones had adornments of feathers and small animal bones, plus the dripping, fleshy things that might have been animal parts far fresher than the bones. Then Anya glimpsed one suspended object that had a distinct dirty fingernail. Another looked like a flaccid penis, still bristling hair at the base. Her voice froze in her throat.

"The fuck is this?" Sara asked.

Someone stepped out of the hut and each of the friends made a strangled noise of shock. The man was about five feet tall, broad but not fat, with stumpy-fingered hands hanging limply at his sides. His face was all wrong. Wide, the nose at an almost forty-five-degree angle to normal and squashed flat, one eye low on the cheekbone, the other halfway up his forehead instead of in line with the first. His mouth hung open on one side, the lips thick and wet. Dark, broken teeth stuck out from the open side, a string of drool trailing off his square, stubbled chin.

"G,day," he said, and twisted his face in what might have been a smile. "Long way from civilisation, huh?" His voice was slushy and slow.

"We need help," Anya said, as if that need might ward him off. She didn't think for a moment that this broken man might be anything but trouble.

"Youse got turned around, ey?" said a voice from behind them, and Anya's stomach fell.

With a swish of wet brush, Dylan strode around an outcrop of rock and came to stand beside the other man.

"You moved the fucking markers!" Sara yelled at him.

"Why would I do that?"

Anya felt tears prickle at her eyes, but refused to let them fall. She focussed on her anger instead. Dylan didn't have his knife in hand right now and she thought she could beat his ass if need be. And Sara was tough and went to kickboxing twice a week. They could beat these two lunatics to a pulp and feel a lot better for it.

"Your friend get hurt?" Dylan asked, but he grinned like it was a huge joke.

"Let's just go," Olivier said, his voice thin.

"You're hurt, mate," Dylan said. "Can you stop me and Clive here having our way with these two beauties?"

Clive grunted a *huh-huh-huh* of laughter, his short fingers suddenly grasping at the air beside his legs. Dylan did a kind of lascivious, swaying walk towards them, grinning. His hand came up and he had the knife, the blade impossibly silver. Anya had no idea where he'd drawn it from. Her hands shook uncontrollably.

"Just go," Olivier said, pulling at Sara.

They turned and stumbled away, down the slope again, slipping on the wet mud and tripping over some rocks. Olivier yelled out in pain, but didn't stop, Sara straining to support him. Anya ran to help, her back itching at the thought of Dylan's knife plunging into her at any moment.

"Youse be careful now," the bogan called, and Clive let out his *huh-huh-huh* again.

The trees swallowed them, Anya's ears alert for any sound of pursuit, but she detected none. They came along a high ridge, where thick tree roots seemed to be all that held the dirt together.

"Along there," Olivier said, gesturing with his chin to the left. "Then down the slope."

A blur of darkness shifted beside rocks some twenty or thirty feet downslope. Anya gasped, opened her mouth to shout, but a streak of black shadow came shooting up at them. It looked like someone had simply rubbed out reality with a broad eraser and all that existed beyond it was endless night, some infinite void of space. Then the darkness hit Sara in her left shoulder and blinked out. She yelped in pain and spun around from the force of it. Olivier's arm slipped from her shoulders and he stood up tall, teetering for balance, arms pin-wheeling. He let out a roar of pain as he stood down on his broken leg in an effort not to fall, but it folded beneath him and he pitched headfirst down the steep slope. Anya screamed, incoherent and impotent, too far away to grab for him. Sara came scrambling up onto her knees, face twisted in pain, one hand pressed to her shoulder. They watched as Olivierhung for a moment in freefall, then struck the twisted roots face first and flipped over. A sickening snap echoed up and his body ragdolled over and sideways, then slid and bumped across rocks and roots to finally lay still not far from where the streak of dark had originated. His limbs were splayed, his broken leg further crooked, and his head looked entirely the wrong way for his torso, glassy eyes staring emptily back up to them.

Sara screamed.

Darkness burst from the rocks near Olivier's inert form and Anya braced for its attack, but it swept over rock and a fallen tree, down the slope away from them.

* * *

Gavin had worked his way back down the steep hill, slipping on scree here and there, feeling terribly exposed every time there was open ground between outcrops of black rock. And then he had seen movement. Another group of those creatures, shadowy and indistinct, heading straight towards him.

Without waiting to risk an encounter he had stood from cover and thrown the large rock he carried with all his might. It sailed faster and straighter than he could have hoped, striking directly into one of the monsters. They scattered for a moment, in surprise or pain he couldn't know. And then one began racing down the slope at him, its multiple limbs thrashing the air, stirring the ash clouds into swirling vortices. As it came within a few feet of him, he panicked and ran, staggering blindly away and down, desperate to outrun it.

Without even looking back, crying tears of terror and loneliness, he fled.

* * *

Sara slid down next to Olivier, wailing and crying with abandon. Anya gasped as she caught up with her friend, desperately trying to get air into a chest that felt as though it would never breathe properly again.

"No, no, no," Sara said, dropping to her knees beside her partner. She picked up his head, and pressed her face to his, crying uncontrollably. There was no question the man was dead.

Anya crouched beside her friend, arms around her, squeezing. "I'm so sorry," she said, thinking there had never been such inadequate words.

Sounds from above came to her, branches whipping and a rattle of falling stones. She imagined Dylan and Clive moving preternaturally easily through the bush, coming down the steep trails with shining knives in their hands.

"We have to go, Sara."

"We can't leave him! Not here. Not like this."

"We have to! I'm sorry, but we can't carry him. We'll get down then send for help, someone will come up and…and collect him."

Sara turned haunted eyes to her friend. "What the fuck is happening here?"

"I don't know. I…I just don't know. Let's go."

"How will they find him?" Sara pulled her phone out and took photo after photo, of Olivier's inert body, of the surrounding bush, then upslope and down. Still sobbing, she pressed her face to Olivier's again, kissed him wetly, then laid his head gently back against the damp, loamy earth. She closed his eyes, hiccupping suppressed sobs. Then she stood, pocketed the phone, and they started down again. Sara kept one hand pressed to the shoulder that had been hit, that arm hanging down, swinging limp. Her face was pale.

"How hurt are you?" Anya asked.

"Don't know. My hand is just pins and needles, my shoulder hurts like hell."

"Is something broken?"

"I don't know, but it's not my legs, so let's keep moving."

Unburdened from helping Olivier, their descent was swift. They almost ran, jumping over fallen trees, ducking between scrub and over rocky outcrops. They found trails that zigzagged, traversing the steepest parts, and only occasionally had to clamber or slide where no path was apparent. The ground began to level, the incline more a gentle slope than a steep hill. The bush thickened, more giant fern trees grew from the wet mud.

They emerged suddenly into open space. A grassy hill curved gently away from them, the sky blue and sunny, though some thin cloud had begun to gather. They gasped, looked left and right.

"There!" Sara said.

Over the rise of grass Anya could just make out an edge of rusted tin. More than a kilometre away, but it looked like their cabin. If not, it was some kind of habitation at least. They turned and ran for it, Anya's lungs burning with the effort, but she had new-found energy in her muscles at the thought of getting away.

"We just get Gavin and get in the car and drive the fuck out," she said as they ran. "Leave anything else behind."

"Amen," Sara said. "We need to get the police."

They came over the rise and saw the cabin down below them, the rusted-out truck and Anya's car right beside. Anya let out a sob of relief as they stumbled towards it.

* * *

Gavin had found his way almost to level ground. The strange, black landscape extended endlessly in every direction, but he recognised some of the rocky formations. A sense of relief flooded him, only to be replaced by new despair. So what if he had found his way back to where he started? What did that even mean? He had no idea how he'd got to this dark and frightening place and even less idea of how to get out. Where would he go? Where did he belong? He simply knew it wasn't here. Had he died? Was this Hell? The thought struck him like a hammer blow, a sudden and concrete conviction. He gasped, lungs tight, legs trembling.

He saw the large, thick, spongy plant he had first been hiding beneath. Where and what had he been before that? He couldn't remember. But there was security in the familiar. He needed to rest, let this panic attack pass, if it ever would. Out in the open he was too vulnerable.

He turned towards the welcoming, broad, meaty leaves, then spotted two of the monsters, shadowy, multi-limbed and sinuous, appear between him and safety. Their form flexed and shifted, he couldn't hold a solid image in his mind. "No!" he yelled, desperate to get back into his safe place. He ran for them, determined to simply barge his way through.

* * *

"What the fuck is that?" Sara screamed as a dark blur of shadow billowed up from the ground and rolled towards them.

Anya refused to be beaten now. They were almost back to the cabin, back to Gavin, to her car keys inside. Whatever this dark, blurry presence was, it was in their way. She couldn't focus on it, like trying to see something through murky water. But she saw enough as it flailed towards them. The long crowbar still stuck up from the bed of the rusty truck where Olivier had dropped it a lifetime ago. She snatched it up and brought it around her head in an arc like the mother of all home-run swings.

The shadow creature whipped up some appendage, a strange and sinuous arm, and shock rippled through Anya as the crowbar met resistance. The black limb flexed around the crowbar and fell away, the shadow dropping lower with it. Anya didn't waste time wondering if it she'd done enough. She hauled the crowbar back over her head and brought it down, two-handed, with all her might, directly on top of the blurry, black shape. It collapsed heavily and sank away, leaving a dark stain on the grass that seeped swiftly from sight, leaking away back towards the cabin.

"The fuck was it?" Sara asked, staring.

"I don't care. Let's just go."

Still holding the crowbar in case she needed to fight again, Anya ran for the cabin, Sara on her heels. Anya hit the door, but it didn't budge, locked closed. The women exchanged a horrified glance, both remembering the key in Olivier's pocket.

"Gavin!" Anya yelled. "It's us. It's Anya! Open up!"

"Can he unlock it from inside?"

"I don't know."

There was no reply from Gavin.

"Fuck it," Anya said, and swung the crowbar to smash out the window beside the door. She swept the metal bar around the frame, clearing out shards of glass, then clambered through.

Her eyes fell on the sofa and she let out a constricted wail of horror. Gavin sat on top of the blankets, soaked in blood. One arm lay out to his side, clearly broken, twisted almost back on itself between the wrist and elbow. And his head had been stoved in from the top, a broad split cleaving the skull, revealing white bone and pink brain, all running with bright, red blood. It dripped from his nose, poured over his eyes, as if whatever blow had caused such destruction had only just been struck.

Sara clambered in beside Anya and they stared in shocked silence.

Anya felt strangely detached from everything. That Gavin was brutally murdered seemed like something somebody else was feeling, a sensation she was being told about rather than experiencing. Part of her wanted to drop to the wooden floor and curl up and cry, but another part, a stronger part, refused.

Her keys were on the table and she snatched them up. "We have to go."

She climbed back out the window and Sara followed, still

clutching her injured shoulder. As they walked to the car, movement under the old truck caused them to dance backwards. Anya whipped the crowbar up and set her feet like a batsman awaiting a pitch.

Dylan emerged from under the rusty chassis, rising like a snake, to stand some feet in front of them. He grinned, broken and yellow teeth glistening wet in the wan sunlight. "Youse guys have a good stay at Yellowheart Cabin?" he asked.

"What?"

"You enjoyed my mushrooms? I hope you'll give us a good review on the line there." He tipped his head back and roared with guttural laughter. Then he snapped his face back to them. They jumped again. "Youse come back now, yeah? And tell your friends about my place."

Anya roared in hate and anger, and ran at him with the crowbar raised. Dylan, laughing horribly, twisted to one side in a way no human spine would allow, and landed on his hands, then scuttled away on hands and feet faster than any person should be able to crawl. He vanished past the cabin, laughter trailing.

With a sob, Anya dropped the crowbar and unlocked the car. They fell in and she started the engine. As she backed up to turn around, they saw movement at the front door of the battered house. Dylan and Clive carried Gavin's body out. Anya paused, staring in disbelief. The men set Gavin down on the broken veranda and Clive crouched to sniff at the smashed skull. A tongue, far too long, flickered out and tasted the blood. Dylan stared hard, not taking his eyes from Anya's, and drew his shining knife down Gavin's torso, from chest to groin. As his free hand began to fish inside, his gaze still fixed on Anya's, she let out a sob and peeled away, fishtailing wildly along the dirt road away from Yellowheart Cabin, back down the hills towards civilisation.

* * *

Anya shook her head, refusing to believe what she was being told. "How can it be over? Nothing is over!"

Detective Bowen gave a weak smile, looked away. At least he had the decency not to try to hold her eye. "Officially over. Of course, it's far from finished for you, probably never will be."

"Don't patronise me!" Anya snapped.

"You have to at least find their bodies!" Sara's voice had an edge of steel, of raw defiance. Though she knew as well as Anya the bodies would likely never be found, not even their bones. But that didn't mean they would stop insisting. Sara sat up straighter, wincing as her arm, tight against her chest in a sling, shifted. Doctors said her dislocated shoulder would heal, she had told Anya, if she kept it in the sling now and did the required rehab exercises later. "You have to find that fucker Dylan. Interrogate him!"

Bowen winced. "We told you, there's no trace of them."

"But you found Yellowheart Cabin," Anya said.

"Yes, Yellowheart Cabin has been checked thoroughly, but you must be mistaken. You can't have stayed there." He held up a hand to forestall both women's outrage. "The place is derelict, most of the roof fallen in, everything broken and weathered, soaked from the rain. Decades abandoned. Look!"

He pulled over an iPad and flicked up some images, handed it over. Anya and Sara put their heads together, looking at exactly what the detective had described. It was in a poor state when they had been there, but nothing like this. In these photos, it was definitely Yellowheart Cabin, but it was totally ruined.

"And no trace of Gavin's body?" Anya asked, handing the tablet back.

"We have him listed as a missing person."

Anya knew he would remain so. She sighed, looked at Sara.

"It's been less than two weeks," Sarah said, almost a whisper.

"We have to list him as missing, as we have no other evidence of his presence with you," Bowen said. "Olivier is filed as deceased, given the photos, despite the lack of a body. There's paperwork, waiting periods, but…" He trailed off.

Sara suppressed a sob. Anya put a hand on her friend's knee. The selfie halfway up the mountain, the numerous shots after he fell, all evidence enough with the metadata from Sara's phone. Olivier's corpse could be anywhere in such dense bush, they had said, or even taken by animals by now. Anya knew that to be true, but the nature of those animals was something she tried not to think on too deeply. Her description of the experience, and Sara's, had been put down to extreme post-traumatic stress after Olivier's accidental death while bushwalking. Coroners had looked in detail at the injuries he had sustained and agreed they were consistent with a bad fall. The police psychologist had been the most infuriating, obsequious asshole Anya had met in a long time.

"We should go home," Anya said.

Sara had moved into Anya's flat because her own reminded her too much of Olivier. That was the main reason anyway, but Anya knew it was fear too, and she didn't blame her friend. She was glad to have Sara around, the only other one who really knew what had happened. Who believed her. Sara sat stubbornly, staring at the detective.

"What the hell were you thinking, trying to walk in such steep terrain?" Bowen said into the heavy silence. "Why even go up there?"

Anya, in furious frustration during the first days, had opened the app on her phone to show Bowen the post for Yellowheart Cabin, but no such listing existed. "Did you follow up with Airbnb?" she asked now. "How else would I have known to go there?"

Bowen nodded, letting out a frustrated sigh. "We did, to humour you."

"Fuck you! What did they say?"

"We officially requested the information from the business, but they assured us there had never been a listing like the one you described. Our IT people went through their records and there was nothing for Yellowheart Cabin. Never had been. Their record-keeping is good."

"What?" Anya looked at her hands, gripping each other in her lap, knuckles white.

"But we all saw it," Sara said. "All four of us. We chose it together."

"Did you push him?" Bowen asked suddenly.

Anya had no energy left to even be angry. "No," she said, barely more than a breath.

"Fuck you," Sara said, though she sounded equally deflated.

Bowen had rigorously grilled both of them, together and separately. His scepticism unrestrained, he'd said directly to Anya and Sara there was clearly something weird going on, but he didn't know what. As he wouldn't believe the truth, Anya had no idea what else to tell him. He couldn't prove Olivier's death was anything but a terrible accident, even though it most certainly wasn't. But there was nothing else to say if he wouldn't accept the story, if he couldn't find the evidence, the real perpetrators. By now there was no real conviction in the question, as both women's distress continued, real and unrelenting.

Anya had had to admit to Bowen that Gavin had been depressed, and their relationship rocky. Other friends and family the police questioned also confirmed Gavin's state of mind. His mother even consoled Anya at her son's disappearance, and Anya couldn't bring herself to dissuade the woman of the mundane assumption. Whether it was better to think him missing than dead, she didn't know. Given the certainty of his death, the violence of it, and the subsequent desecration, and her guilt in association with how it had impossibly happened, she thought it best to consider him missing herself.

"I'm sorry, really I am," Bowen said, and he seemed sincere. "The files will remain open, but the search in the region you described is over. We can't look any harder, we can't commit any more resources. I promise you, our efforts were thorough. There's nothing there, except the dilapidated wreck I just showed you."

Anya stood. "Come on." She helped Sara up and they both walked to the office door.

As Anya pulled it open, Bowen said, "For what it's worth, I believe you."

They both turned back. "What?" Anya didn't trust him.

"I believe you had a terrible time up there. I believe there may well have been awful men who did awful things. This job has taught me that much. I'm sorry there's not more we can do."

Anya nodded, unsure how to respond.

"They weren't awful men," Sara said quietly. "They were something worse than that."

ACKNOWLEDGEMENTS

FIRSTLY, THANKS TO ANTHONY RIVERA and Grey Matter Press for their belief in this book. Thank you to all the editors and anthologists who originally put their faith and money behind the previously published stories in this collection.

A body of work in short fiction is a strange and amorphous thing as it grows, and it's gratifying to see those disparate parts, from so many different homes, coming together here. But it wouldn't happen without those original publications.

So, on that front, huge thanks to everyone who works in the field of publishing short fiction. It's an artform with an illustrious past and, hopefully, a robust future. Thanks to my early readers, who help to polish these stories into something better.

Thanks to all my fellow writers, especially in the horror community. It really is a community and your support and friendship gives me strength. Especial thanks to Paul Tremblay, Chris Golden, and Jo Anderton for their early reads of this collection and the wonderful things they said about it, and to John F.D. Taff for his frankly humbling Introduction.

Lastly, and always, all my love and thanks to Halinka and Arlo. In a world of darkness, you both are my light.

This book is for my best boy, Penry. I miss you.

ABOUT THE AUTHOR

ALAN BAXTER is a British-Australian multi-award-winning author who writes horror, supernatural thrillers, and dark fantasy. He's also a martial arts expert, a whisky-soaked swear monkey, and dog lover.

He creates dark, weird stories among dairy paddocks on the beautiful south coast of NSW, Australia, where he lives with his wife, son, and hound.

The author of nearly twenty books including novels, novellas, and two short story collections, so far, you can find him online at www.warriorscribe.com or find him on Twitter @AlanBaxter and Facebook.

Feel free to tell him what you think. About anything.

COPYRIGHT INFORMATION

MORE DARK FICTION FROM
GREY MATTER PRESS

"Grey Matter Press has managed to establish itself as one of the premiere purveyors of horror fiction currently in existence via both a series of killer anthologies — *SPLATTERLANDS, OMINOUS REALITIES, EQUILIBRIUM OVERTURNED* — and John F.D. Taff's harrowing novella collection *THE END IN ALL BEGINNINGS.*"

- *FANGORIA Magazine*

GREY MATTER
P R E S S

MANIFEST RECALL
BY ALAN BAXTER

Following a psychotic break, Eli Carver finds himself on the run, behind the wheel of a car that's not his own, and in the company of a terrified woman he doesn't know. As layers of ugly truth are peeled back and dark secrets are revealed, the duo find themselves in a struggle for survival when they unravel a mystery that pits them against the most dangerous forces in their lives.

A contemporary southern gothic thriller with frightening supernatural overtones, Alan Baxter's *Manifest Recall* explores the tragic life of a hitman who finds

himself on the wrong side of his criminal syndicate. Baxter's adrenaline-fueled approach to storytelling draws readers into Eli Carver's downward spiral of psychosis and through the darkest realms of lost memories, human guilt and the insurmountable quest for personal redemption.

"If you like crime/noir horror hybrids, check out Alan Baxter's *Manifest Recall*. It's a fast, gritty, mind-f*ck." — Paul Tremblay, Bram Stoker Award-winning author of *A Head Full of Ghosts*

GREY MATTER
P R E S S

greymatterpress.com

DEVOURING DARK
BY ALAN BAXTER

Matt McLeod is a man plagued since childhood by a malevolent darkness that threatens to consume him. Following a lifetime spent wrestling for control over this lethal onslaught, he's learned to wield his mysterious paranormal skill to achieve an odious goal: retribution as a supernatural vigilante.

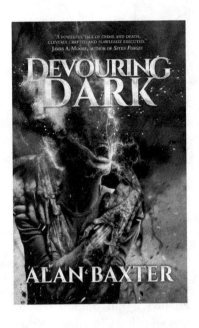

When one such hit goes bad, McLeod finds himself ensnared in a multi-tentacled criminal enterprise caught between a corrupt cop and a brutal mobster. His only promise of salvation may be a bewitching young woman who shares his dark talent but has murderous designs of her own.

Devouring Dark is a genre-smashing supernatural thriller that masterfully blends elements of crime and horror in an adrenaline-fueled, life-or-death rollercoaster ride that's emblematic of the fiction from award-winning author Alan Baxter.

"*Devouring Dark* is a powerful tale of crime and death, cleverly crafted and flawlessly executed. I'm a fan of Alan Baxter and *Devouring Dark* is a perfect example of why." — James A. Moore, author of *Seven Forges* and the *Serenity Falls* Trilogy

GREY MATTER
P R E S S

greymatterpress.com

BEFORE
BY PAUL KANE

In 1970s Germany, a mental patient at the end of his life suddenly speaks for the first time in years. A year later in Vietnam, a mission to rescue a group of American POWs becomes a military disaster.

In present day England, the birthday of college lecturer Alex Webber sends his life spiralling out of control as a series of disturbing hallucinations lead him to the office of Dr. Ellen Hayward. And things will never be the same again for either of them. Hunted by an immortal being known only as The Infinity, their capture could mean the end of humanity itself...

Part horror story, part thrilling road adventure, part historical drama, Before is a novel like no other. Described as "the dark fantasy version of Cloud Atlas," Kane's Before is as wide in scope as it is in imagination as it tackles the greatest questions haunting mankind—Who are we? Why are we here? And where are we going?

"Paul Kane is a first-rate storyteller, never failing to marry his insights into the world and its anguish with the pleasures of phrases eloquently turned."
— Clive Barker, author of *The Hellbound Heart* and *The Scarlet Gospels*

GREY MATTER
P R E S S

greymatterpress.com

LITTLE BLACK SPOTS
BY JOHN F.D. TAFF

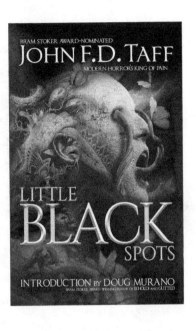

Bram Stoker Award-nominated author John F.D. Taff – modern horror's King of Pain – returns with *Little Black Spots*. Fifteen stories of dark horror fiction that expose the delicate blemishes and sinister blots that tarnish the human soul.

From a man who stumbles on a cult that glorifies spontaneous human combustion, to a disgraced nature photographer who applies his skills for a vile outcome.

Where a darkened city parking structure is malevolently alive, and a Halloween costume has a husband seeing his wife in a disturbing new light.

When a ruined man sees far too much of himself in his broken family, and a mysterious bottle of liquid c omes with a deadly secret inside.

Little Black Spots is a beacon shining its light into some of life's most shadowy corners, revealing the dark stains that spatter all mankind.

"Taff's horror is grounded in our day-to-day lives, in our families, our work, our most private thoughts. His stories vibrate with emotion and his prose is deeply satisfying. And just as addictive."
— Ray Garton, author of *Live Girls* and *Ravenous*

GREY MATTER
P R E S S

greymatterpress.com

AVAILABLE NOW
FROM GREY MATTER PRESS

Before — Paul Kane

The Bell Witch — John F.D. Taff

The Devil's Trill: The Ladies Bristol Occult Adventures #1 — Rhoads Brazos

Dark Visions I — eds. Anthony Rivera & Sharon Lawson

Dark Visions II — eds. Anthony Rivera & Sharon Lawson

Death's Realm — eds. Anthony Rivera & Sharon Lawson

Devouring Dark — Alan Baxter

Dread — eds. Anthony Rivera & Sharon Lawson

The End in All Beginnings — John F.D. Taff

Equilibrium Overturned — eds. Anthony Rivera & Sharon Lawson

The Fearing Series: Books I - IV — John F.D. Taff

I Can Taste the Blood — eds. John F.D. Taff & Anthony Rivera

The Isle — John C. Foster

Kill-Off — John F.D. Taff

Little Black Spots — John F.D. Taff

Little Deaths: 5th Anniversary Edition — John F.D. Taff

Manifest Recall — Alan Baxter

Mister White: The Novel — John C. Foster

The Night Marchers and Other Strange Tales — Daniel Braum

Ominous Realities — eds. Anthony Rivera & Sharon Lawson

Peel Back the Skin — eds. Anthony Rivera & Sharon Lawson

Savage Beasts — eds. Anthony Rivera & Sharon Lawson

Secrets of the Weird — Chad Stroup

Seeing Double — Karen Runge

Served Cold — Alan Baxter

Splatterlands — eds. Anthony Rivera & Sharon Lawson

Suspended in Dusk II: Anthology of Horror — ed. Simon Dewar

CPSIA information can be obtained
at www.ICGtesting.com
Printed in the USA
LVHW101250070622
720689LV00016B/34